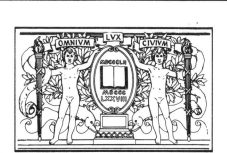

WARRIOR IN BRONZE

WARRIOR IN BRONZE

George Shipway

Walker and Company
New York

Oz Edition

First published in the United States of America
in 1985 by the Walker Publishing Company, Inc.

Published simultaneously in Canada by John Wiley & Sons
Canada, Limited, Rexdale, Ontario.

Library of Congress Cataloging in Publication Data

Shipway, George
    Warrior in bronze.

    Reprint. Originally published: London : Davies, 1977.
    1. Agamemnon (Greek mythology)--Fiction. I. Title.
[PR6069.H5W37   1985]   823'.914   85-5402
ISBN 0-8027-0849-8

Printed in the United States of America

10 9 8 7 6 5 4 3 2 1

To
Lorna

. . . γυναικὶ
καλῇ τε μεγάλῃ τε καὶ ἀγλαὰ ἔργα ἰδυίῃ

ACHAEA c. 1300 B.C.

DORIS

LOCRIS

EUBOIA

Parnassos Mt.

AITOLIA

Delphi

Orchomenos

L. Copais

BOEOTIA

Helicon Mt.

THEBES

R. Asopos

Aphidna

Corinth Gulf

Cithaeron Mt.

Dyme

Pellene

Eleusis

Sicyon

Megara

ATHENS

Corinth

ISTHMUS

Hymettos Mts.

ELIS

Stymphalos

ELIS

Nemea

Salamis

ARCADIA

Rhipe

MYCENAE

Pisa

Mantinea

ARGOS

Midea

Epidauros

Tiryns

Lasion

Lerna

Nauplia

Asine

Troezen

Tegea

Hermione

Aigion

Messene

SPARTA

PYLOS

Therapne

LACONIA

N

Cythera

0 Miles   20   40

THE AEGEAN SEA
c. 1300 B.C.

N

THRACE

Hellespont

MYSIA

Troy
R. Scamander

Ida
Mountain

Dodona

EPIROS

THESPROTIA

Iolcos

LESBOS

LYDIA

EUBOIA

SCYROS

L. Copais

ITHACA

Thebes

CHIOS

Elis

Corinth

Athens

ANDROS

SAMOS

Mycenae

Argos   Tiryns

CYTHNOS

Pylos   Sparta

NAXOS

Miletos

MELOS

CYTHERA

THERA

0 Miles   50   100

CRETE

Amnisos

Knossos   Malia

Gortys

Phaestos

Dikte Mountain

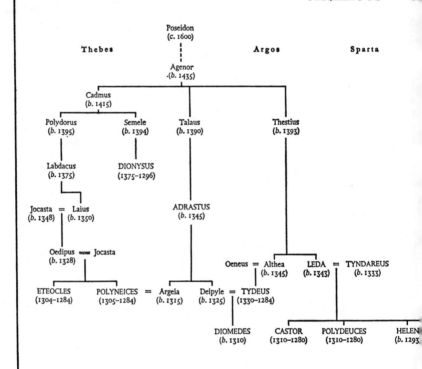

Poseidon
(c. 1600)

Thebes

Argos

Sparta

Agenor
·(b. 1435)

Cadmus
(b. 1415)

Polydorus   Semele   Talaus   Thestius
(b. 1395)   (b. 1394)   (b. 1390)   (b. 1393)

Labdacus   DIONYSUS
(b. 1375)   (1375–1296)

Jocasta = Laius   ADRASTUS
(b. 1348) | (b. 1350) (b. 1345)

Oedipus ~~~ Jocasta   Oeneus = Althea   LEDA = TYNDAREUS
(b. 1328)   (b. 1345)   (b. 1343)   (b. 1333)

ETEOCLES   POLYNEICES = Argeia   Deipyle = TYDEUS
(1304–1284) (1305–1284) (b. 1315) (b. 1325) | (1330–1284)

DIOMEDES   CASTOR   POLYDEUCES   HELEN
(b. 1310)   (1310–1280) (1310–1280)   (b. 1293)

Notes: 1. All dates are B.C. and are conjectural.
   2. The names in capital letters are of those who play
   leading parts in the story.
   3. Wavy lines indicate irregular relationships.

THE HEROES

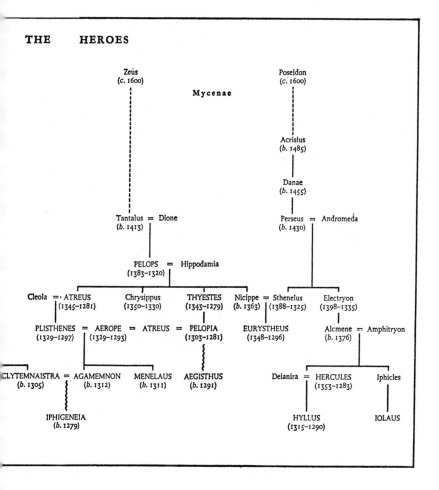

Mycenae

Zeùs
(c. 1600)

Poseidon
(c. 1600)

Acrisius
(b. 1485)

Danae
(b. 1455)

Tantalus = Dione
(b. 1413)

Perseus = Andromeda
(b. 1430)

PELOPS = Hippodamia
(1383-1320)

Cleola =⸱ ATREUS   Chrysippus   THYESTES   Nicippe = Sthenelus   Electryon
       (1345-1281)   (1350-1330)   (1343-1279)   (b. 1363) (1388-1325)   (1398-1335)

PLISTHENES = AEROPE = ATREUS = PELOPIA   EURYSTHEUS   Alcmene = Amphitryon
(1329-1297) (1329-1293)   (1303-1281)   (1348-1296)   (b. 1376)

CLYTEMNAISTRA = AGAMEMNON   MENELAUS   AEGISTHUS   Deianira = HERCULES   Iphicles
(b. 1305)   (b. 1312)   (b. 1311) (b. 1291)   (1353-1283)

IPHIGENEIA   HYLLUS   IOLAUS
(b. 1279)   (1315-1290)

Chronological Note

SCHOLARS still dispute the chronology of the Greek Heroic Age; hence it would be a rash scribbler who ventured on definite dates. However, a distinguished archaeologist who recently excavated Troy estimated the city's destruction by the Achaeans at *c.* 1270 B.C., by which time their leader Agamemnon may have been in his early forties. I have therefore placed his lifetime in the years 1312–1270 B.C. The Greek legends from Homer onwards, on which my tale is based, and in particular the detailed genealogies they contain, do not in general contradict this time-scale.

Chapter 1

THE palace's summer bedrooms gave on to a balustraded balcony shaded by a sloping terrace roof which overlooked the town. The balustrade's veined marble pillars supported an alabaster parapet soft enough to be cut by the small toy daggers we wore at our belts. The rail therefore was scratched and notched throughout its length; and all our nursemaids' scolding failed to stop an enchanting game. Nobody who mattered ever noticed; the bedrooms were always deserted during the day; except for servants we had the balcony to ourselves from dawn till dusk.

This was our playground; here my earliest memories begin.

From our eyrie the palace walls fell down like sheer white cliffs. The road which climbed the hilltop from the Northern Gate – not the Gate of the Lions, of course, which was only a postern then – curved between tiers of flat-topped houses and ended at a flight of steep stone steps leading to the Great Court's entrance directly below. On the citadel's guardian wall sentries looking small as flies paced the rampart walk. Broken, stony ground sloped from the base of the wall to a shallow valley thronged with houses painted yellow and red, white and blue and green like jewels spilled from a lady's casket.

From the balcony's height the buildings looked tiny as those small baked-clay cottages which slaves gave my sister to house her dolls. It seemed possible to lob a stone on to the farthest roofs – an illusion, as it proved. Our most strenuous throws just cleared the road beneath; although Menelaus, taking a run which bruised his chest on the parapet, once hit the guard-house roof at the top of the steps. Unluckily a sentinel observed the whole performance; and a stern message from our mother forbade a repetition. So I never had a chance to beat my brother's record, an improbable feat in any event, for Menelaus was always stronger than I.

Cultivated land surrounded the villages; olives and vines terraced the hillsides; sheep grazed wiry grass which bordered the forests of oak and cypress. In the crystalline sunlight of spring and early autumn you could sometimes catch a glimpse of the sea near Nauplia, a shining blade on the horizon's farthest rim. The whole mightiness of Mycenae, we thought in childish ignorance, was spread like a gaudy tapestry before our eyes.

We were very young then – Menelaus seven, myself a year older – and could not conceive of the vast foundations supporting our family's dominion.

The patterned floors of the summer bedrooms extended to the balcony and offered a smooth surface for games we played with ivory discs: the patterns made convenient aiming marks and goals. The object was to throw or slide your counters within the chosen goal and knock your opponent's out. Our throws were erratic; we lost many counters which bounced between the balustrade pillars and dropped the height of eight tall men to the road below.

The disaster which struck one bright spring day had nothing to do with accident. We had tired of the game, and were leaning side by side over the balustrade, chins just topping the parapet, trying to distinguish the warriors' evolutions on the Field of War in the distance. A chariot crunched slowly up the road from the gate, the occupants, judging from their armour, a Hero and his Companion returned early from parade. The Hero dismounted, spoke briefly to his driver and began to climb the steps. He came directly below our interested faces. I juggled in my hand an ivory disc – a finger's-breadth thick, a palm's-width across.

The temptation was overpowering. I reached out and dropped it.

The counter struck his helmet; ivory clicked on the boar's-tusk crest and spun away in the dust. The man jumped, lifted hand to helmet, raised his face and stared at the heads which peered at him from far above. In horror I recognized my target, and recoiled from the railing.

'Thyestes!'

'You fool!' Menelaus whispered.

Neither of us dared look out again. We heard the chariot's bronze-tyred wheels descending the path, and the guard commander's voice calling a salute. Then silence. We stared dumbly into each other's eyes and awaited the doom which must fall on our heads surely as leaf-fall follows harvest. In a futile attempt to hide the evidence I feverishly told our attendant slaves to gather the counters littering the floor and conceal them under a bed.

Menelaus said in a strained voice, 'He's a long time, Agamemnon. Do you think he didn't see us?'

'No. Nothing escapes Thyestes.'

We were deadly afraid of Thyestes. Everyone was. I cannot think of him, even now, without a shudder of loathing.

Footsteps clumped the wooden stairway. We backed from the bedroom in panic like a pair of frightened mice, shuffled to the balcony and pressed our spines against the balustrade. Two formidable figures crossed the floor. One, as we expected, was Thyestes; the second his brother Atreus, Marshal of Mycenae.

A gold-studded belt, drawn tightly at the waist, secured a short leather kilt and emphasized Atreus' slim hips and powerful wide shoulders. Muscles rippled like lazy snakes beneath a skin burned oaken brown by the suns of forty summers. He was immensely tall, the biggest man I have known, taller than myself when I reached my prime. His face was sharply cut and lean, flat-cheeked and eagle nosed; yellow hair unflecked by grey curled behind his ears and caressed a beard trimmed short to a tilted point, the upper lip clean shaven in a fashion then prevailing. His mouth was thin and mobile, curving easily to a smile and as easily to a cruel knife-edged gash; deep furrows joined the corners to his nostrils. Before all else you noticed his eyes, a blazing blue beneath shaggy brows the sun had bleached near white.

He dismissed the servants, and rocked silently on his heels. I glanced once at his face, and looked quickly away, and examined miserably the deerskin boots which encased his legs to the knee. They were laced with silver wire; golden-corded tassels dangled from the tops. He carried a chariot whip, the long oxhide thong looped between finger and thumb, and idly tapped the butt against his thigh.

The tapping ceased. 'A stone struck Lord Thyestes. Which of you threw it?'

I flicked a glance at Menelaus, who was staring, fascinated, at

3

the whip. 'Not a stone, father. A counter we use for our games. It ... slipped.'

'From whose hand?'

I licked my lips, and swallowed. Thyestes stirred impatiently. 'What does it matter? Impertinent little rats! Flog them both, brother, and have done with it!'

The growling voice recalled the man, though I did not dare look at him. He had discarded helmet and cuirass and wore an armour undershirt: a sleeveless woollen garment descending to the kilt. A handspan shorter than Atreus, his bull-necked head crouched on his shoulders like a brooding bird of prey. Heavy, thickset shoulders, and muscles cording arms and legs like hawsers intertwined. Thyestes moved clumsily, lacking his brother's sinuous grace but – as many a foeman found to his cost – he was quick on his feet as a cat. A bushy brown beard framed features harsh as wind-eroded rock. Only the eyes were sentient, deeply sunken, pale green like the offshore sea. When he was angry the pupils darkened, turned stone-grey flecked with white, twin ice-pools frozen hard.

He was angry now. My knees quivered; I was glad of the sun-warmed parapet which supported my shoulder-blades.

Atreus repeated, 'From whose hand?'

'I can't remember,' I muttered. 'It was mischance. We never intended ...'

Menelaus pushed himself from the balustrade and stood shakily upright, hands clenched tight at his sides. 'I dropped the disc, father,' he said in a tiny voice.

I raised my head to see Atreus' response. He might not have heard. His gaze was fixed on me; the long searching look a man gives a horse whose quality he doubts. I saw contempt in his eyes and, strangely, a flash of admiration. You could say I was overly young to read the thoughts of a man four times my age. True – but this percipience, an ability to probe men's minds and motives is a gift The Lady bestowed on me at birth. Without it I could not, today, be where I am.

'Insolent little swine!' Thyestes snapped.

Atreus roused himself. 'You aimed deliberately, Menelaus?'

My brother bowed his head. Atreus coiled his whip-thong round the handle, tightly ridging the shaft, and said briskly,

4

'Right. You shall be taught to respect your elders. Turn round. Fold your arms on the balustrade, and don't move!'

Menelaus obeyed. He sank brow on forearms, his hands gripped the parapet's edge. Atreus moved behind him, raised the whip and slashed it down. A weal scarred the boy's thin back. The second cut slammed a finger's width from the first, the third and fourth criss-crossed it. Red droplets beaded the skin. Menelaus squirmed a little, and bit his wrist.

Atreus ended the thrashing, unwound thong from shaft and dropped the lash distastefully. It trailed a scarlet smear on the painted plaster. Menelaus sank to his knees, scraping his forehead on the balustrade pillars. He had not uttered a sound, but now he moaned very softly. Thyestes stepped forward and lifted a foot. Atreus moved sharply to block the brutal kick.

'Enough, brother! The child has learned his lesson.' He added sternly, 'He is of our blood. Would you treat him like a slave?'

Thyestes scowled. Atreus gestured him to the stairway. As they went he said across his shoulder, 'Call the servants, Agamemnon. See his cuts are washed and anointed.' He paused at the head of the stairs and tugged his beard. 'You are both growing up,' he mused aloud, 'too old to idle here in charge of slaves and nursemaids and tumble into trouble. Time you began your training. I shall see to it.'

His teeth flashed white in a sudden smile, and he clattered down the stairs.

I did as I was told, and sent a man for the palace physician. Then I went to my brother. He lay curled up on the floor, eyes screwed tightly shut. Tears trickled down his cheeks.

'Thank you, Menelaus,' I whispered.

(Several years later Atreus recalled this episode. 'I knew perfectly well you were guilty,' he said, 'and you proved yourself a liar and a crook. I decided then you should follow me on Mycenae's throne. You see, Agamemnon, a king must be entirely unscrupulous, ready at need to betray his dearest friend – even his beloved brother. I think you meet the measure very fairly – just the kind of ruler our treacherous Heroes need.')

* * *

The transition was abrupt. Menelaus and I shifted quarters to the squires' wing: long gloomy chambers, dormitories and

5

living rooms combined, on the first floor facing the mountains. The squires under training – about twenty sons of noblemen from Tiryns and Mycenae – quickly put us in our place. All were equal here, royal offspring like ourselves no more favoured than the rest. A young Companion named Diores had charge of this turbulent gang, a stocky dark-haired man with a scathing tongue and ready whip, who stood no nonsense from cocky children.

I shall not detail the training we endured for the next four years: a rigorous routine painfully familiar to every man of noble blood. We were routed from bed in the dark and running the fields before sunrise, Diores loping in rear, his lash drawing blood from the laggards. We paused to draw breath on reaching the Field of War: an extensive stretch of level ground six hundred paces from the citadel's gate where Mycenae's warriors paraded. Two narrow watercourses, dry in the summer moons, meandered across the surface: a test for aspirant Companions, who had to carry them at a gallop. Here we wrestled and boxed, jumped ditches and walls and performed strange muscle-racking exercises. Later we progressed to more exciting work: weapon training, spears and swords and bows; the care of arms and armour; battle drill and archery.

One day I objected sulkily to Diores that fighting on foot like common spearmen was hardly gentlemen's work. He forbore, for a change, to bite my head off, and said, 'Squad – down shields. Rest. Listen, and get this into your stupid skulls. You hope one day to be Heroes – The Lady save us! What *are* Heroes? They're men of noble blood, and the best fighters in the world. A Hero leads spearmen and bowmen, slingers, horsemen and charioteers: whatever they do he must do better. So he learns to fight on foot like a spearman, shoot like an archer, ride like a scout and drive like a Companion. Which will take you years, and you've hardly started. At the end, if you survive, you'll be fit to ride a chariot in the forefront of the battle where Heroes always fight. Until then you work. On your feet, scum! Take up shields!'

In the afternoons Diores herded us to the palace wine stores and taught us vintages and serving: essential knowledge for budding squires – servants handed food at meals, but wine was a gentleman's business. Finally we observed the lords at dinner

6

for three successive days, watching from the gallery above the Hall and listening with half an ear to Diores' running commentary. Then he loosed us on a banquet which King Eurystheus gave to a visiting lord. I was told to attend on Atreus, Menelaus on Thyestes. We were timorous as kittens; and the brilliant scene, the noise and pageantry and splendour were no anodyne for nerves.

The Great Hall of Mycenae is sixteen paces long by fourteen wide, the floor laid out in patterned squares, red and yellow, blue and white. A charcoal fire burns day and night throughout the year on a circular hearth in the centre where food is cooked. Four fluted wooden columns frame the hearth and support an opening in the ceiling which a gallery surrounds, all roofed by a clerestory whose windows admitted light and air and allowed the smoke to escape. A single massive portal closed by brazen-plated doors led to the vestibule and portico beyond.

Brilliant painted patterns blazed from every handsbreadth of the ceiling; lions hunted stags along one wall, the figures large as life, colours flaring from the plaster. On another men in chariots drove to war, armour yellow-gold, horses paired in white and black. Winged dog-headed monsters flanked a red-veined marble throne and headed twin processions of birds and beasts and butterflies: an iridescent riot which seemed to live and move.

Torchlight shivered stars from crystal and silver and gold; the air was scented with charcoal smoke, roasting meat and wine. Squires filled silver flagons from a wine store adjoining the vestibule and threaded a way through tables and gesticulating men: two hundred bare brown bodies gleaming with perfumed oil, bedizened with golden bracelets and necklaces and gems – a job that required a dancer's poise and a steady hand. You also had to dodge the foraging dogs: fast, heavy Molossians which Heroes kept for hunting, willing to tackle anything from a stag to a charging lion. Meanwhile Diores, from a seat near the door, watched like a falcon and counted each drop we spilled.

Nobody noticed the squires except when he wanted a drink. I kept – my primary duty – the Marshal's goblet abrim; but any lord, as I passed, could demand I filled his cup. Edging between outer tables on a journey from the wine store I felt fingers

7

pluck my kilt and paused to do the bidding of the owner: a man whose body was white as a woman's. I saw his face in profile, hollow-cheeked and thin, features finely cut, a short fair beard. A Hero or Companion – no lesser mortals dined in the Hall. A resemblance to someone I knew flitted across my memory and escaped in the general din.

He tapped his empty cup, and smiled.

I stooped to obey his order, and glimpsed the opposite side of his face. From jawbone to temple the cheek was smashed and sunken, the skin grey-white and crumpled. His right eye, fixed and glazed, stared blindly from deep in the socket. The beard straggled limply across this frightful scar, like grass struggling to survive on barren ground.

I averted my gaze and filled his cup, a crystal goblet engraved with running hounds. He said, 'A paler wine than I last was served. What is the vintage?' He spoke softly and slowly, and hesitated between words as though he had to drag them from deep recesses in his mind.

'From Attica, my lord, and ten years old.'

He sipped, and rolled the liquid on his tongue. 'Full and mellow, perhaps a trifle sweet.' I waited, flagon in hand – according to Diores' lessons I could not go till he gave me leave – and wondered who he was. I knew by sight the household nobles and nearly all who lived outside the citadel: they constantly came and went within the palace. Not this one; and I could hardly have failed to notice his ghastly appearance.

He said, 'What is your name, lad?'

'Agamemnon, my lord.'

The good eye widened, a spasm twitched the unmarred side of his face. 'Indeed? An uncommon name. Surely I know it ... you must be ...' His fingers stroked the pitted scar; furrows creased the forehead above the eye that searched my face, the other brow stayed smooth, unwrinkled – a most disturbing phenomenon. 'Impossible,' he muttered. 'You're too old. Or too young. So hard to remember. The years run together like streams in spate, the waters flow so fast I see no more than a blur. You should have a brother, boy, a brother. Tell me ...'

'Yes, my lord: Menelaus.'

'That's the name, that's it! All is coming back!' He spoke feverishly, stuttering, groping for words. His hand reached out

8

and gripped my knee. Diores had warned me that amorous gentlemen heated by wine often tried to fondle personable squires waiting beside the tables; unless I was bent that way I had best leave swiftly on urgent errands. I did not draw away. No lewdness existed here, only an urgent excitement betrayed by the working face, by sweat drops beading his cheeks. None the less I felt embarrassed. The man was decidedly odd, and I wished he would give me permission to go.

'Your mother,' he said hoarsely. 'No, don't tell me! Let me think ...' He ran fingers through his hair, golden and streaked with grey despite the comparative youthfulness his unscarred features attested. 'Anaxibia? No, that's another. Who was Anaxibia ...?'

I opened my mouth to tell him and caught, across the boisterous Hall, Atreus' eyes on mine. He looked both anxious and angry, and beckoned imperatively. Welcoming the pretext I said gently, 'I am summoned elsewhere, my lord. Have I your leave?'

Like the flame of a torch plunged quickly in water his face went blank, expressionless; the tenseness left his limbs and his body went lax in the chair. 'Leave?' he asked vacantly. 'Certainly. Why are you here? Ah, yes, the wine. Very passable, perhaps not fully mature; a thought too sweet for my taste. Where did you say it came from? No matter – off you go.'

I hastened between the tables to the Marshal's side. 'Pour wine,' he snapped. 'My throat is dry as a virgin's crotch. Where the blazes have you been? Your job is to keep my goblet filled – haven't you been told?'

'Yes, my lord,' I answered submissively. 'I was delayed in serving a gentleman yonder' – I pointed my chin to the outer tables – 'who asked me —'

'I saw you.' Cold blue eyes bored into my brain. 'His name is Plisthenes. You will never, Agamemnon, speak to him again. Is that understood?'

I nodded mutely, and tilted the flagon.

*　　*　　*

The strenuous existence which a squire suffered under training often made me yearn for my former life – a pampered child in the mighty Marshal's household. At the end of the day I

9

dropped into bed and slept like a corpse; and seldom found the energy to cross the palace courtyard to Atreus' apartments or the quarters where my mother lived.

But I cannot honestly say I missed my mother.

A delicate subject.

Aerope was then about twenty-five years old, small and dark, vivacious and voluptuous and fatally attractive. Lively hazel eyes in an oval face the colour of old ivory, a flawless skin, short tip-tilted nose and wide red mouth. Her open bodice revealed imperious breasts, nipples painted scarlet, inviting the clasp of a lustful masculine hand.

Lest sunlight darken delicate complexions many of the palace's noble ladies lounged all day indoors gossiping and prinking, only venturing out at evening to take the air in litters or to lie on rooftop couches watching the world go by. Not Aerope. She handled the reins as cleverly as any Companion, and followed boar hunts dressed like a man in kilt and deerskin boots, galloping her chariot over the roughest going. Amid all her entertainments she found time, in successive years, to bear me and Menelaus and our sister Anaxibia: a harmless little creature who lived in her mother's apartments and hardly enters my story.

Aerope had forbidden us unannounced visits to her rooms since a day when Menelaus and I, both very young, trotted in unexpectedly and found Atreus caressing her in a most familiar way. We were neither surprised nor shocked; to small children the relationships of adults are both esoteric and uninteresting; but Atreus, flushed and annoyed, ordered us sharply away. We ran out, hurt and chastened.

On the occasions, nowadays infrequent, when I visited my mother I expected to find Atreus there – and usually did. She inquired sweetly after my health, hoped I was not overworked, and exclaimed at my physique – I was growing fast and developing hard muscles. Atreus amiably ruffled my hair and tweaked an incipient beard. I answered as manners dictated and left when politeness permitted. These were duty visits, which did not altogether account for the awkwardness I felt when talking to them together, an embarrassment never sensed when I met them individually.

Which was strange, for where else should my father be except at my mother's side?

*   *   *

A messenger driving lathered horses arrived from Tiryns with news that flung the palace into confusion. That remote, majestic figure King Eurystheus of Mycenae hastily called his Councillors to the Throne Room and, behind closed doors, debated an intelligence which was obviously disturbing. With a fourteen-year-old's avid curiosity aroused I loitered in the vestibule until the Councillors, looking serious, spilled into the Court. Atreus came out last, walking slowly, chin in hand. His eyes lighted on my face and the absent expression cleared.

'Anxious to discover what it's all about? Well, there's no harm and' – he spoke half to himself – 'it's time you began to learn the intricacies of government. Word has come to Tiryns that Hercules sacked Pylos and killed all King Neleus' sons save only Nestor.'

Everyone knew of Hercules, Warden of Tiryns, who years before had left his native Thebes under a cloud, fled to Mycenae and taken service under King Eurystheus. He was a mighty warrior whose deeds resounded throughout the land and far beyond the seas.

I said so.

'Maybe,' said Atreus sourly. 'The king at first employed him as a huntsman, and Hercules – by nature a rover – roamed all over Achaea destroying beasts of prey. If you judged by his bragging you'd conclude that no one else had killed lions and boars before. Over the years he developed into a sort of hatchet man and troubleshooter – Eurystheus allotted him all kinds of unpleasant labours. He's collected during his travels a ruffianly gang, scum of every description, commanded – so far as they *can* be commanded – by his son Hyllus.'

'How did it happen,' I asked, 'that Hercules became Warden of Tiryns?'

Atreus sighed. 'The man is a robber, a freebooter, and more than a little mad. He lifted cattle and horses; and angry rulers, knowing him Eurystheus' man, sent embassies to complain. The king recalled Hercules and, to keep him quiet, gave him charge of Tiryns.'

II

'Yet he has managed to sack Pylos.'

'He led a warband into Arcadia in pursuit of cattle raiders.' Atreus gritted his teeth. 'Fair enough – but he lost the rustlers' track and instead marched clean across Achaea to attack a realm with which we have no quarrel! This is the kind of anarchy we had in olden times before Perseus branded order on the land!'

'So,' I said, 'what now?'

'The king has summoned Hercules to Mycenae to account for his invasion. Eurystheus *must* control the lunatic, or he'll have a dozen rulers reaching for our throats! I wish I could devise a way of getting rid of him once for all. The trouble is,' said Atreus sombrely, 'the blaggard has become a legend in his lifetime, and attracts worshipping supporters – Heroes who should know better – besides his riffraff rabble.'

A visitor three days later gave Atreus the chance he wanted. Journeying with a small retinue a seaman from Iolcos arrived on a rainswept winter's day. He announced himself as Jason, a son of Iolcos' ruling House, and Eurystheus made him welcome. He had come with a proposal which he explained to the king in Council on the morning after a banquet in his honour. I was present in the Hall as Atreus' squire: the Marshal insisted nowadays I attend him on formal occasions, often at the expense of my training on the Field.

The Council consisted of older, wiser Heroes on whom Eurystheus relied. They assembled in chairs in front of the king, while Atreus and two senior Scribes – Curator and Procurator* – stood either side of the throne, ready to tender expert advice on war or economics. Eurystheus invited the visitor to state his case.

Jason was a stocky man with a neat brown beard, a broken nose and harsh storm-beaten features. His eyes were black and piercing; he had a mariner's rolling gait and spoke in jerky sentences, wasting never a word. He brought information, he declared, about a land called Colchis, far beyond the Hellespont on the shores of the Euxine Sea. Had anyone heard of it? No one had. Very well: he wanted to mount a seaborne expedition and sail to faraway Colchis. Therefore he had come to mighty

---

* Linear B ko-re-te and po-ro-ko-re-te.

Mycenae, Achaea's wealthiest realm, to seek silver to pay his shipwrights, supplies to stock the ship and men of courage and purpose to form the crew. Iolcos, a penurious kingdom, rent by dynastic dissension, could provide neither one nor the other.

'What,' asked Eurystheus benignly, 'is the object of so hazardous a voyage?'

Jason said tersely, 'Gold.'

The Council stirred in their seats. Nothing makes men jump like the mention of gold, second only to iron in rarity and preciousness. Atreus said sharply, 'How do you know? How can you be certain there's gold in Colchis?'

'Had it from a Thracian who went there overland. Terrible journey. Took him three whole years. Lost an arm on the way, but brought back this.' Jason fumbled beneath his cloak and produced a sheepskin pouch. He loosened the string and poured in his palm a yellow glittering sand.

'There you are. River gold.'

Eurystheus stirred a fingertip in the little heap. 'It looks genuine enough. Atreus, send your squire to fetch a goldsmith. We'll have this assayed.'

When the man arrived Eurystheus tossed him the pouch. 'Examine this thoroughly, and ascertain the worth in sheep and oxen.' The smith squatted beneath the clerestory where the light was strongest, unfolded his scales and juggled weights, gritted the gleaming grains between his teeth and muttered to himself.

Atreus said, 'There may be gold in Colchis, Jason, but have you any proof there's enough to make a voyage worth while?'

'The Thracian's word, no more. A river flows through Colchis to the sea; the bottom's awash with gold. The locals peg fleeces to the bed. Wool filters the silt and traps the gold. After a time you haul up a golden fleece.'

The Curator stooped and whispered at length in Eurystheus' ear. The king meditatively examined his fingernails, and said, 'I am reminded of a factor which may bear on our discussion. Achaea contains no indigenous sources of gold; we import all we have. The bulk comes from Egypt: a supply which over the last few years has been drying up because their campaigns against the Hittites absorb Egyptian resources. The situation is becoming serious: we need gold to pay for imports. So we must find alternative sources, or trade will quickly decline.'

The audience nodded gravely. I suspect, with after-knowledge, the king's exposition passed well above most Councillors' heads. While Heroes cannot be faulted in questions of war and weaponry their mastery of economics is sometimes frail. But Atreus grasped the point, and said, 'I agree. We should at least examine the Colchis deposits.'

The goldsmith returned from the hearth, bowed to the king and mumbled, 'My lord, the sample is pure high-quality gold, and worth ten oxen or fifteen sheep.'

Eurystheus lobbed the pouch to Jason. 'We will support your venture. I shall let you have warriors from Tiryns and Mycenae. Silver will be given you, and ten cartloads of corn and oil. How many ships are you taking?'

'One. A fifty-oared galley. I call her *Argo*.'

'You know your business best.' Eurystheus looked doubtful. 'I'd suppose you needed more. However. Have you recruited crewmen from the lands you traversed while journeying here?'

'Not many. They believe it a fool's errand.'

'When people realize I'm supporting the expedition you'll have a flood of volunteers. One condition, Jason. Half the gold you find will be delivered to Mycenae. Agreed?'

'Agreed, sire.'

Eurystheus rose creakily – winter's dampness stiffened his joints. 'The Council is ended.'

I followed Atreus into the vestibule. He leaned against a pillar and scrutinized, eyes remote, the accoutrements of a sentinel who paced outside the portico. 'Fellow's helmet plume needs combing,' the Marshal murmured. Then he clapped my shoulder. 'I've had an idea for getting Hercules out. The moves will have to be subtle, but I believe the plan will work.'

*   *   *

Jason concluded his arrangements and interviewed Heroes who volunteered for Colchis. Meanwhile an outrider from Tiryns announced Hercules was coming.

I was engaged on the Field of War and missed his arrival. On returning to the citadel I met an entourage gathered outside the Northern Gate – and a villainous lot they looked. Diores identified some characters as we passed: Iolaus, Hercules' nephew, a bitter-faced young man, trap-mouthed and restless-eyed; and Hercules' son Hyllus, not much older than I, a surly youth with a brooding air. A seasoned bunch, their armour grimed and dented – not the sort of men you would care to meet in a narrow pass in the dark.

Hercules, Eurystheus and the Marshal were closeted in conference. I learned later they questioned him closely about the Pylos escapade. Hercules, surprised and hurt, explained that his cattle-thieving quarry had crossed into Pylian territory; and during a night pursuit – typical of Hercules to go on fighting after sundown – gave him the slip and he found himself at dawn below the rock of Pylos. A quick reconnaissance disclosed a yawning gate and sentries half asleep. Cheated of his prey, irritable and frustrated, Hercules pounced on a heaven-sent gift, caught the garrison literally napping, killed everyone in sight, collected all the booty his warriors could carry and marched away, satisfied with a job well done.

Atreus listened incredulously, met the king's despairing look and rolled his eyes to the ceiling. They made no attempt to expound the enormity of an unprovoked attack on a friendly city: Hercules' brain was not of the kind to unravel political niceties. Eurystheus, instead, casually mentioned Jason's mission and suggested the dangers involved would daunt the bravest paladin: men of proven valour flinched from a venture so hazardous. Of the few that offered to serve, Jason chose only the most renowned.

Hercules swallowed the bait like a hungry shark. 'Why hasn't the idiot come straight to me? I'm just the leader he wants!'

'I don't think,' said Atreus carefully, 'Jason is seeking a leader; he's doing the job himself. He badly needs outstanding warriors like you – but he's a very selective man.'

'Selective?' Hercules spluttered. 'He can't have doubts about *me*! He'll jump for joy if I join him. It's a chance to add to my laurels, and Tiryns is damnably dull. If you'll release me for a while I'll interview Jason and tell him I'm coming.'

Eurystheus kept his face impassive. 'It can be arranged. Come to the Hall and take a cup of wine.'

There, relaxing in a chair, surrounded by admiring nobles, I first met Hercules. I had expected a giant, and found instead a person of middle height, almost as broad as he was long; tremendous muscles knotted a bulky body. He wore a lion skin – summer or winter he never changed – and carried a knobbled vine-staff. A shaggy man: tousled rust-coloured hair fell to his shoulders, the beard cascaded across a barrel chest, a furry mat swathed legs and arms. You could hardly see his face for all the hair, only mad blue eyes that stared between the tresses. His voice was high and squeaky, a chicken's cackle mouthed from the frame of a bull.

I poured him wine in a golden cup and waited close beside him: a moonstruck boy adoring a famous Hero, the remembrance of Atreus' criticisms gone like mist at sunrise. Hercules drained the goblet at a gulp. As I refilled it I asked, in reverential tones, the history of the tawny hide he wore.

'Ha!' he squawked. 'Have you not heard of the Nemean lion, my lad? Where have you been all your life? A monster which killed cattle, men and horses, and nobody would face him. So, naturally, they sent for me. The creature must have known I was on his track, and went into hiding. Took me days to find him. Cornered him at last on a rocky hillside, strung my bow and shot. By The Lady, the brazen barbs glanced off his hide like raindrops! I charged and swung my club; the wood splintered on his ribs. Nothing left but my hands, so I closed and strangled the brute.'

Hercules drank deeply, wiped his mouth. 'Not too difficult, really, for a man of my courage and strength.'

Atreus entered the Hall, Jason rolling by his side, and interrupted Hercules' fascinating discourse. The Marshal said, 'Here, Jason, is the Hero who wishes to sail in *Argo*. I promised you'd be surprised – it's Hercules, no less!'

Hercules waved his cup. 'Ho, Jason, well met! I'm told you want a champion to stiffen your force, set an example, provide initiative and guts. You've found him! When do we start?'

Jason's face showed none of the pleasure and gratitude befitting the occasion. 'Hercules, blast my eyes! Be damned if you step on my deck! Anyone but you! Are you aware,' said Jason tautly, 'that Neleus of Pylos, whose city you looted, whose sons you slaughtered, is my uncle?'

16

'I didn't know,' said Hercules.

'Nor I,' Atreus murmured despondently, seeing the stratagem he had woven shredding about his ears.

Hercules recovered his poise. 'Unfortunate, I admit, but these things happen. Chances of war, my good fellow, chances of war!'

Jason's weatherworn features suffused. Atreus seized his elbow, led him aside and whispered energetically in his ear. The sailor angrily shook his head. After a long confabulation Atreus brought him back to Hercules who, between great gulps of wine, bragged loudly about a gigantic stag he caught and killed in Arcadia.

'I have persuaded Jason to overlook the – um – unfortunate accident at Pylos. He agrees you should return with him to Iolcos, and voyage in *Argo* to Colchis.'

Hercules belched. 'Can't do without me. Bound to fail unless you have the strongest and bravest Hero in Achaea to lead the way. That's me. I'll find you your gold.'

He buried his nose in the goblet. Jason turned on his heel and stamped from the Hall.

Atreus smiled contentedly as we crossed the Great Court together. 'I had to promise Jason a sheep-flock's price in treasure. Well worth it. But fancy voyaging to the ends of the earth on the word of a wandering Thracian! These Argonauts will vanish without trace – and we're rid of Hercules.' Atreus chuckled. 'Pity about Jason, though. I like the chap. Now to dispose of another nuisance.'

His eyes discouraged the question that trembled on my lips.

* * *

Hercules, Jason and the Heroes the king had chosen departed for Iolcos. When Hercules tried to insist on taking his ragbag following Jason tersely specified *Argo*'s strict capacity: fifty men and stores were all she could embark. Hercules growled and submitted. Hyllus and Iolaus led their retinue to Tiryns; Atreus watched them go and tweaked his beard. 'We'll have to evict those rascals before many moons have passed,' he reflected aloud. 'Shouldn't be too difficult now the figurehead has gone.'

The linchpins of Eurystheus' realm were Tiryns and My-

cenae. Tiryns now lacked a Warden. The king accepted Atreus'
suggestion and nominated Thyestes.

Menelaus was one of Thyestes' squires and must accompany
him to Tiryns. We had never before been separated; both of us
felt the wrench. I asked him, while he packed his gear, whether
he enjoyed serving Thyestes.

Menelaus shrugged. 'I don't. Damnably free with his whip if
you make a mistake. He's surly and unapproachable, and keeps
his household nobles at a distance. Even his family fears him.
The only person Thyestes likes is a ten-year-old daughter,
Pelopia, and he dotes on the brat.'

I said, 'That curious creature Plisthenes lives in his household.
Do you ever see him?'

'Now and again. Most of the time he stays secluded in his
rooms. He's going with us to Tiryns – and I'd rather he wasn't.
Fellow gives me the creeps.'

Thyestes and his retinue departed on a beautiful springtime
day, warm and glorious, the light so clear you could see spears
glint on Argos' faraway hilltop. Atreus stood on the tower that
guarded the Northern Gate, and contemplated a vanishing dust
cloud pluming the Argos road. Thyestes' migration plainly
brought to a fruitful conclusion some devious design he concocted, and I expected him to be pleased. Atreus' demeanour,
on the contrary, was grave and forbidding. When the column
disappeared from sight he murmured under his breath, 'Thyestes and Plisthenes gone. The way rolls clear ahead. The time
has come.'

He turned and laid a hand on my wrist. 'You believe me to
be your father?'

I stared, astounded. 'Of course. What else —'

'Such was my intention. So I have ordained it over the years
since Plisthenes...' He stopped. His grip tightened, vivid blue
eyes held mine.

'Prepare yourself for a shock, Agamemnon. I am your grandfather, and I'm going to marry your mother.'

My throat went dry, my legs were straws. 'You're my ... I
don't understand. Then ... who is my father?'

'My son Plisthenes.'

Atreus guided me firmly down the steps. The compassionate
tone he had used to soften the revelation melted from his

voice, and he said brutally, 'Pull yourself together! The heavens haven't fallen; nothing is changed. Sit on this bench – and stop snivelling, boy!'

I collapsed on a stone bench some long-forgotten builder had provided at the foot of the tower's steps. Atreus propped his shoulders against the rampart's massive stones, and looked at me balefully. 'Feeling better? Nothing, as I said, has changed. Since infancy you have believed me to be your father. In all but name I am. One generation divides us. What does it matter?'

'But ... Plisthenes,' I stammered. 'Why have you ...'

'Shut your mouth, and listen. When I was sixteen years old I married a woman called Cleola, who bore me Plisthenes and died before she saw him. I brought him up – as I've brought you up – and taught him all the elements of statesmanship and war. He was tall and strong, radiantly handsome and, unlike your typical Hero, extremely intelligent. He was born to be king – or so I decided. Even Thyestes liked him, and made him something of a protégé.'

A chariot rolled past on its way to the gate. Atreus absently acknowledged the Companion's salute.

'I looked round to find him a suitable wife, and settled on a daughter of the Cretan royal House: Aerope, Catreus' child. I brought her back to Plisthenes, and she bore him you, Menelaus and that girl – what's her name? – Anaxibia. Then I let Plisthenes go with Hercules to Thrace to buy horses for Eurystheus. It seemed a harmless expedition – but I hadn't allowed for Hercules. Rather than disgorge the ox-hides and bronze the king had provided for payment he decided instead to raid the herds, swooped with his ruffians and stole what he could and fled. Not fast enough – a warband overtook him. Hercules won the fight that followed and escaped unscathed.'

Atreus paused and bit his lip. 'Plisthenes was not so lucky. He returned as you saw him, grievously wounded, the wits bashed out of his head. The years I spent in teaching him were wasted.'

'Is he quite ... mad?'

'No. Plisthenes has lucid moments when he's apparently sane as you or I. He has become entirely biddable, and will obey to the letter any command you give him.'

19

Atreus levered his shoulders from the wall, put a hand beneath my chin and glared into my eyes. 'Get this into your head, Agamemnon: I intend one day to rule Mycenae!'

'But,' I gulped, 'you ... we ... are not of the reigning House. King Eurystheus has five sons. How can —'

'You're damnably obtuse today, young man! Wake your ideas up! Don't you see? Backed by the Host and influential nobles I shall seize the reins of power when Eurystheus dies, banish his sons — I may have to kill them — and rule in his stead. There'll be a dynastic upheaval: except for the sons and that villain Hercules — who doesn't count — Eurystheus is Perseus' last descendant. An alien ruler will take the throne, a man of Pelops' line. To make the usurper acceptable his successor — a suitable heir — must be assured.'

'And Plis ... my father is —'

'An imbecile who had to be hidden from the sight and memory of man. Thyestes was still fond of him and pitied his condition. I persuaded my brother to accept him in his household; and then re-cast my ideas. My obvious successor was one of my grandsons, either you or Menelaus, boys just out of infancy. I kept an eye on you both, and made my choice.

'*You* are that heir, Agamemnon!'

I held my head in my hands. An ant crawled over my sandalled foot, and bit; I hardly noticed the sting. 'And the centrepiece,' I said, 'of a horrible and dishonourable design.'

'You're talking nonsense! Scrub these stupid scruples from your mind! Any expedient, any ruse, every crime in the catalogue justifies the enterprise of kings!'

'And you propose to wed my mother. Why? I don't understand. ...'

'It looks better,' said Atreus patiently, 'if a man is married to the woman who has borne his heir. Besides, whatever you or anyone else may think, I'm very fond of Aerope.'

Atreus stood, and patted my cheek. The grim expression faded from his face. He smiled, and said, 'The shock has numbed your brain; you simply aren't thinking straight. I shall send you from Mycenae, and give you time to recover.'

Chapter 2

BRISKLY and efficiently Atreus organized the arrangements. He bent the rules a little and obtained the king's permission to grant Heroic status to Diores. A Companion, strictly speaking, cannot become a Hero until he has killed his man in battle: always a difficult feat because unless a charge is broken and he has to fight on foot a chariot driver seldom meets a foeman blade to blade. Although Diores had been a Companion for several years – he drove for a Hero who held an estate near Argos – he had not yet won his greaves.

The Marshal also persuaded Eurystheus to grant Diores Rhipe, an out-of-the-way demesne in the foothills which owed an annual tribute of three oxen, thirty sheep and a jar of olive oil. When the king called a levy of arms the holder had to provide three spearmen, a scout, his Companion and himself both fully armed and armoured.

The reason for so paltry a tribute lay in the manor's remoteness: a factor of little account in olden days before the Goatmen started seriously encroaching. Now they regularly decimated Rhipe's flocks. Eurystheus, and King Sthenelus before him, sent warbands to comb the area; after every expedition the troubles stopped for a while and then recurred. The Hero last holding Rhipe had begged the king for a demesne in easier reach of Tiryns or Mycenae. He was not alone; the majority of outlying estates suffered similar depredations.

The king granted Rhipe to Diores with injunctions to restore the farms and make it pay. Being a reasonable man he recognized the dangers and drawbacks and, because the holding had been abandoned for several years, provided breeding stock and seed corn, twenty sturdy freemen and a band of male and female slaves. With an eye to my safety Atreus added from his retinue a half-dozen seasoned spearmen who normally worked on his lands. He also gave me some personal slaves and, unusually, a Scribe: a youthful, serious fellow named Gelon. 'He'll keep Rhipe's accounts,' the Marshal said, 'and teach you the economics of husbandry. Gelon's a clever young man; if you listen to him carefully you may learn a good deal more.'

I took my concubine Clymene. About a year before I had begun to experience the usual sexual urges. Lightly-clad slave girls serving in the Hall or encountered in palace corridors excited fervid pricklings which resulted, on occasion, in hurried secret gropings and fumblings in corners. Someone must have reported these skirmishes to Atreus. I had been allotted a separate room in the squires' wing – a cubby-hole just large enough to accommodate a cot – and a lovely seventeen-year-old whom Hercules took at Pylos and sold in the Nauplia market. Though still a little shaken by the shock of a violent sack in which her family perished, Clymene became in time much more than a sheath for tumescence; she stayed for years my counsellor and friend. She was the first of a long procession of concubines, and the only one whose memory I cherish to this day.

On a windy dawn in spring we departed for Rhipe, a long column of men and carts and animals. I rode with Diores in a travelling chariot, for he had not yet chosen a Companion. 'Nice to be made a Hero, though I almost feel ashamed to wear my greaves. Everything has happened in a rush,' he explained, smacking his whip at a fly on the offside horse's withers. 'I've barely had time to collect a household, let alone find a decent driver who's willing to live in Rhipe.' He wriggled his shoulders beneath a new and shining cuirass. 'Damned bronzesmith has boxed the job: shoulder plates don't fit. Cost me forty fleeces and eleven jars of oil. Take me years to breed enough sheep and press enough olives to pay him.'

We followed the road till noon – a military way between strongholds, and therefore paved – and diverged on a stony track which led to Rhipe. Derelict byres and tumbledown walls signified the outer fringes of Diores' new estate. Glumly he surveyed the evidence of neglect: winter-withered weeds choking the vines, olive trees unpruned, ploughland smothered in deep rank grass, undrained pastures reverting to marsh. 'Enough work for a multitude,' he declared. 'I'd hoped to teach you driving, but there won't be a chance for moons. We'll all be labouring from dawn till dusk.'

Diores touched a sore point. His promotion and my relegation to Rhipe had ended for a time my training as a warrior at a most important stage: the art of handling a chariot in battle. Any fool can drive on a road; to swerve and turn and check at a gallop and lock your wheel with an enemy's is a different slice off the joint. But I was old enough to realize the transition Atreus ordered likewise belonged to a Hero's education. From boyhood they herd flocks on the hills, graduate later to care for precious cattle and learn the skills for tending vines and olives, ploughing and planting and reaping wheat and barley.

Husbandry is really a Hero's life; to the end of his existence he spends more time in shepherding than riding battle chariots. During daylight hours in peacetime it is hard to find a Hero; they are all away working the land or watching flocks. By nightfall at any season your Hero, like his peasants, is gobbling lentil broth in a ramshackle stone-built farmhouse and wondering where the blazes his missing wethers have gone. Royal household men fare better, of course; they can use the palace amenities. But this humdrum side of a Hero's career the bards don't often sing.

Rhipe proved to be an extensive domain. We marched till sundown before reaching Diores' manor perched on a rocky hillock protruding from a plain. Forested ranges cleft by valleys surrounded the plain; beyond them soared the mountains. A massive wall of rocks girdled a two-storied house hugged by thatch-roofed hutments like a hen among her chicks. The place resembled a minor fortress, an appearance common to every settlement sited far from a citadel.

Diores looked more cheerful. 'Solid defences at least; no one will break in easily.'

We led our retinue through a gate whose oaken doors sagged tiredly on the hinges – 'That's the first job,' Diores commented – and assembled in a crowded mass in a courtyard before the house. Diores stamped through the buildings and allotted quarters. 'Offload baggage, turn the animals out to graze, mount guards. Clear the place up. Get moving!'

Before darkness fell we were fairly well settled and eating a meal. Robbers had ransacked every building. All metal articles the former holder may have left were gone – cauldrons, tripods, pots and pans – but a scattering of plain wood furniture remained. We found some wooden ploughs, hayforks and the like still littering the outhouses.

Goatmen don't use chairs and tables, nor do they till the land.

After posting a sentry on the gate tower Diores returned yawning to the Hall and stretched himself on a fleece-covered cot his slaves had found. The rotten twine fragmented and thumped his rump on the floor. He swore like a Hero, snuggled into a cloak and lay beside the hearth.

'Tomorrow,' he said sleepily, 'we start putting Rhipe to rights!'

*   *   *

At the first whisper of dawn Diores and I rode out to explore the demesne; freemen appointed as bailiffs followed the horses on foot. Diores allocated fields to be ploughed for the sowing of barley and wheat, selected cattle pastures, hillside grazing for sheep and, on the higher slopes where trees began, foraging grounds for swine. He defined an extensive tract as common land where peasants would grow subsistence for themselves and the slaves and craftsmen – bronzesmiths, weavers, carpenters, potters and fullers – who must help make Rhipe self-sufficient.

It took us all day to ride the whole perimeter. Back at the manor I found Gelon, using a goose quill dipped in ink distilled from charcoal, scratching mysterious marks on a sheet of the paper Egyptians make from reeds. 'I'm working out the daily ration scales for our workmen,' he told Diores, 'in the proportion of five to two to one for men, women and children respectively.' (A babble of brats accompanied the slaves, and some of the freemen had brought their families.) 'Do you approve, my lord?'

'Whatever you think best,' said Diores. 'I've no head for figures. Tally the supplies we've brought and fix your calculations to make them last till harvest, four moons hence. Then, if The Lady is kind, we'll start living on what we produce.'

'Very well.' Gelon compressed his lips. 'I warn you, my lord, we shall have to live frugally through the summer.'

24

Intrigued by my first acquaintance with scribal skills, and remembering Atreus' injunction, I craned over Gelon's figuring although, like anyone not a Scribe, I had no slightest knowledge of writing and considered the art to be something approaching magic. Scratching and squiggling busily, tongue between teeth, Gelon assured me the calculations were simple: he applied to Rhipe in miniature a system which prevailed throughout the realm. 'Every person below noble rank receives a fixed allocation of barley, wheat and oil based on the kingdom's total resources divided by the population count. Achaea, densely peopled, can't grow the food she needs; hence corn is shipped from Sicily and Crete.'

'I had no idea,' I said in wonder. 'Surely, on a country-wide scale, a most complicated business?'

'It is. That's what Scribes are for. Without us the economy would collapse.'

Gelon uttered a simple truth. Scribes are ubiquitous; a coterie exists in every city and town. They control administration and regulate the economy; every ruler depends on a senior Scribe's advice – I remembered King Eurystheus' Curator at Mycenae. Their power resides in knowledge of writing, a jealously guarded monopoly whose mysteries outsiders are never allowed to learn. (Not that Heroes nurse any desire to master an art so horridly cabbalistic.)

It is commonly averred that the Scribes' origins are Cretan, although in appearance and characteristics they are very unlike that good-looking, easy-going race. The distinguishing mark of a Scribe, besides the long grey robe he always wears, is a hooked nose dominating swarthy features. They forbid marriage outside the sect, and worship a private god whose name, so far as I can pronounce the throat-stopping syllables – Gelon told me this – is something like Jahwah. Which worries nobody: all sorts of obscure divinities are honoured in rustic Achaea. In urban neighbourhoods the Daughters, not surprisingly, severely discourage unorthodox cults: on The Lady's pre-eminence depend their own estates, granted by kings for Her worship. They also fight a tendency, mostly in the cities, to elevate as deities our ancestors: those mighty Heroes of olden time, founders of royal Houses, Zeus and Poseidon.

But I digress – a tedious vice belonging to ageing men.

25

Within a couple of days Diores and Gelon between them organized the running of Rhipe out-of-doors and in. I was given a hundred sheep and banished to grazing grounds a morning's march from the manor: my realm for seven moons, a spreading river valley ramparted by hills. My companions, besides the sheep, were two spearmen and a surly-tempered dog: the spearmen a condition that Atreus commanded; he had told Diores I was not to be left unguarded while shepherding the flocks. We repaired dilapidated folds and huts which commanded grazing areas, rebuilt walls and roofed the huts with tamarisk fronds on olive-wood rafters.

So began an idyll I gratefully remember, a happy, carefree interlude never to be repeated. I saw to the year's first mating, ensured the rams shirked none of their work and favoured all the ewes. Spring drifted into summer, hot sunlight faded the flowers – hyacinth and crocus, violet and lily – and sucked aromatic scents from herbs and grasses. I discarded my woollen tunic, wore deerskin boots and knee-high leggings to guard against the thorn scrub of Rhipe's rocky hillsides. A short spear and dagger completed my equipment – everyone, slaves excepted, always has a dagger at the belt: an all-purpose implement for shaving, hair-cutting, carving food and whittling during idle afternoons.

At every dawn and sunset I inspected and counted my charges, collected stragglers and rolled silly fat ewes to their feet. Otherwise I basked in the sun or drowsed under shady trees. The hillsides' grassy slopes, dotted by white fleeces, fell from forested heights to a willow-tasseled stream meandering through the valley: a fragrant sun-drenched kingdom I regarded as my own. Occasionally I bade the dog – an obedient creature despite his snarls – to retrieve a wandering wether. I cut flutes from streamside reeds and piped melodious tunes that tinkled in the still clear air like raindrops falling on water. I rolled dice with my guardian spearmen, breakfasted on wheat-cakes spread with honey, dined on cheese and barley-bread and figs washed down by rough red wine. At night, cloak-wrapped against the dew, I lay on a couch of grass beneath a sky black-purple and counted the glittering stars. Doubtless it rained from time to time, but my memory pictures days that were ever bright and golden.

26

Every seventh day Diores paid us visits and brought baggage-laden slaves to replenish our supplies. He examined every sheep, prodded pregnant ewes and ran fingers through their fleeces. Early in the summer I was warned to prepare for shearing, and spent laborious days washing struggling sheep in the stream. Then Diores arrived with a shearing team and ox-carts to carry the wool. 'We'll have a good crop,' he said contentedly, sitting beneath a willow and watching the knives at work. 'In high summer you'll be lambing; send word to the manor before it starts and I'll send you men to help.' He paused, and frowned at the forests that canopied the hills. 'You've seen nobody in the woods?'

'Nobody,' I said, surprised. 'Why? Whom would you expect?' Diores beckoned a spearman and led him aside. Intrigued by his question I strained my ears to hear what he said.

'You scout the forests, Echion, as I instructed?'

'Regularly, my lord, and find not a soul. They were there last winter: you can tell by the bitten-down saplings.'

'Um. They shouldn't be down from the mountains for many moons yet. Keep a sharp watch, Echion, when the leaves begin to wither.'

'I will, my lord.'

When Diores and his workmen went I questioned Echion, who shrugged and muttered something about boar attacking the flock. I thought the fellow stupid: I had walked every pace of the grazing grounds and found neither droppings nor slots which mark the passage of boar.

For reasons of health I journeyed periodically to Rhipe, leaving the flock for the day in the spearmen's charge. Clymene greeted me ecstatically, and speedily administered the medicine I sought. Afterwards, lax and satiated, we strolled around the manor. Diores had transformed the place, thatching roofs, plastering walls, restoring gaps in the ramparts and generally tidying up. Workmen had entirely refurnished the house, providing chairs and tables, cooking pots and gaily patterned hangings. Gelon weighed the wool crop and calculated, quill in hand, the proportion due for tribute and set it aside in store rooms; weavers worked at looms to convert the rest into cloth. Clymene informed me proudly she had taken command of the household, ordered the slaves and kitchen staff and kept Diores happy.

'Your solicitude stops at his stomach, I hope?'

'How could you say such a thing? I am yours, Agamemnon, body and heart and soul. Besides,' she pouted, 'Diores is besotted with a fat Euboian slut. How he abides the girl is beyond my comprehension. She waddles like a pregnant cow and washes once in a moon.'

During these hasty visits Clymene cooked me a midday meal: a haunch of mutton grilled on the spit (we never had meat while herding), gravy and savoury herbs and spices – cumin, fennel and mint – which Clymene gathered at daybreak. Then I gave her a farewell tumble in the little cubicle Diores granted – a singular privilege; but Clymene, though a slave, belonged to me, and her blood was noble – and departed on the long tramp back to the flock.

A midsummer sun blazed high in the sky; the stream dwindled and the grass turned yellow and brittle. I folded the sheep in different valleys to alternate the grazing, and idled away the burning days in the shade of parch-leaved trees. When the summer lambing started I despatched a spearman for help and for days was frantically busy. We did well, losing only twelve ewes and twenty lambs; Diores was pleased. With the size of the flock near doubled I had to shift ground more often, and hoped the end-summer rainstorms would freshen the grass.

Clouds like pale transparent shreds drifted across the sky, gathered above the peaks, slid lower and misted the hills. Lightning crackled and thunder rumbled; the deluge fell like spearshafts.

'Autumn advances her banners,' said Echion the spearman while we sheltered beneath a crag. 'We shan't stay here much longer.'

Diores, on his next visit, agreed. He kicked a clump of grass and said, 'There's little goodness left in the grazing here. Start mating the ewes for winter lambing, and then we'll bring you down to the manor pastures.' Again he scowled at the hilltops, where rain-mist shrouded the trees. 'Maybe sooner. Here, I've brought you this: wear it wherever you go.'

He handed me a sword in an oxhide sheath attached to a

leather baldric. I protested in astonishment. 'Why? A sword will clutter my movements and' – I patted my kilt belt – 'I always carry a dagger.'

'Do as I say – and keep it sharp.' Diores turned to the spearman. 'Anything, Echion?'

'Nothing, my lord.'

'Good. Tell your dog to round that wether, Agamemnon: if he falls into a gully he'll surely break a leg.'

Diores waved farewell and strode away.

*   *   *

I mated the ewes, and wore a cloak while I worked; the days were growing shorter and the wind had a bite like knives. Winter's onset turned my charges restless; they wandered far in search of richer herbage. Dawn and evening counts revealed sheep gone astray which had to be retrieved with much scrambling and searching. One morning, dog at heel and Echion in tow, I followed a missing ram along a steeply slanting gully which cleft the hill from forest-line to valley. Clambering up the rocks was wearing work; I paused to regain my breath.

Echion eyed the thick-set trees which crept down the slope a spear-cast distant. 'Give the ram best, my lord. He'll return of his own accord.'

The dog sniffed the scree ahead, and whined. 'Look – he says it's close in front. We'll search in the fringe of the forest.'

We resumed a scrambling climb, the dog panting eagerly in the lead. I reached for a jutting rock to steady my balance, heard a sound like the whup of a whip and Echion's choking cry. I turned quickly, slipped and fell. The spearman writhed on his back; an arrow transfixed his shoulder.

Hairy creatures closed on me and bayed; my nostrils flinched from a frightful stench. Wild animals, I thought in panic, and tugged at my sword. Hands twisted the hilt from my hold, flung my body over and ground my face on the rocks. I was dragged by the legs uphill; jagged stones scored gashes on face and ribs.

The agonizing haul seemed endless; my head struck rocks which knocked me dizzy; I crashed like a log from ledge to ledge and the air was slammed from my lungs. I saw nothing but the ground scraping painfully past my face, heard only the animal grunts of those who held me fast.

Foliage closed overhead and screened the cloud-smeared sunlight. My captors flung me against an oak tree's bole. Blearily I wiped away the blood that stung my eyes. I lay in a glade on level ground, a giant step which nature had carved in the hillside, and at last saw the enemy clearly. Men in the guise of beasts, clad every one in goatskins. Thirty or forty in all. Matted filthy hair and tangled beards, bare furry legs and calloused feet. Their stink was almost palpable, a solid essence of goat.

They gathered round me, babbling. A spear point pricked my chest. Weakly I thrust it aside. One of the creatures stooped and shouted in my face; I flinched from a blast of rancid breath. He spouted a torrent of speech; dazedly I strove to understand. A word here and there was familiar, the rest incomprehensible as the bray of the goats they herded. I tried to vanquish terror, and swallowed the bile in my throat.

They ripped away my kilt and left me naked. Somebody grabbed my genitals and wrenched; I squirmed and yelped in agony; the brutes guffawed. A body thumped beside me, an arrow shaft protruded from the shoulder. Echion, conscious and in pain, eyes bulging and affrighted in a face like a bloody mask. A savage trod on his chest, grabbed the shaft in both his hands and pulled. The barb came free attached to a gobbet of flesh. Echion shrieked and fainted.

One of the creatures dragged by the tail the carcass of my wretched dog, squatted on the ground and quickly skinned it. He used, I noticed dully, a knife of stone ground sharp at the edges. All their weapons were stone, daggers and spearheads and arrows. He cast the pelt aside and hacked the corpse in pieces, tore out liver and guts and handed chunks to his fellows. Greedily they devoured the raw flesh, tearing with their teeth and champing, blood smearing greasy beards. The dog, though large, could not feed all; the men deprived gesticulated angrily and growled like hungry wolves.

The man who had questioned me before – or so I assumed; so hairy-featured were they all you could not tell them apart – vigorously prodded his spear on my breastbone and yelled unintelligible words. Numbly I shook my head. He reversed the spear and slammed the haft across my skull. The treetops reeled in a crazy dance and the day went dark.

Sense and feeling filtered back; I forced my eyelids apart. The stinking brutes had withdrawn some paces distant; a trio squatting on the ground rubbed sticks to make a fire, others filled up waterskins from a trickle that ran through the glade. I saw clean-shaven faces, blinked away the mist that hazed my sight and realized they were women, filthy uncouth harridans clothed in goatskins like the men. A multitude of goats browsed scanty herbage between the trees and stood erect with forefeet against trunks to strip the lower branches. There was also a tribe of rangy, half-starved dogs, yellow-eyed and ferocious. Neither they nor the goats strayed beyond the tree-line to open ground below – whether by chance or training I never discovered.

A man leaning on an ash stave watched my return to consciousness. It is hard to describe him. Withered, stringy, emaciated, bent beneath the weight of countless years. Long dirty-white hair fringed a smooth bald pate. A wispy beard, the upper lip shaven, the nose a wedge of gristle, sunken violet eyes in caverns beneath white brows. In contrast to the stigmata of age the skin of his forehead and cheeks was smooth, unwrinkled, pale as polished bone. He wore a linen tunic once dyed green, now sun-bleached, torn and stained; his arms were sinew-corded stalks, dead ivy clasping twigs. And yet – which is why I find it difficult to depict him properly – an aura hung about him of dominance and dread.

He spoke sharply to a spearman standing at his shoulder, a man different from the Goatmen as he himself – stocky and blond, hair and beard trimmed short, rocky weather-tanned features and eyes like burnt black wood. His only garb was a leather apron; a fold pulled through his crotch was gathered in front and buckled to the belt like a codpiece of times gone by. A bracelet of lead-coloured metal decorated a wrist; he grasped a heavy spear. Stepping smartly forward he wound fingers in my hair and jerked. The pain brought tears to my eyes and cleared the fog from my brain.

The old man said, 'You come from Rhipe. Who are you?'

A gentleman's voice, the timbre deep and clear, the voice of a man in lusty middle age, the accent indefinable. All the inflexions of Achaea and lands across the sea overlaid his tones, as though our tongue was one of many he could command at will.

He kicked my leg. 'Answer, lad! I have ways of finding the truth.'

I had realized directly I saw them that these were the dreaded Goatmen, the scourge of all Achaea and the bane of civilized men. To me, hitherto secluded in impregnable Mycenae, they were nothing more than a legend, a fairytale nursemaids told to frighten children. I knew little of their history, and never troubled to learn. But now, like an icy douche, I recalled something Atreus had once said: 'Better to cut your throat than be taken alive by the Goatmen.'

Should I tell this decrepit old cripple my name and rank and lineage? He was clearly the Goatmen's leader, despite his age and frailty. Perhaps if I did he would shrink from the repercussions – a warband after his head. Or maybe the spilling of royal blood would simply add spice to his sport. No – whoever he was, deny him the relish of knowing the prize he held.

I gathered a little spittle from a mouth as dry as a kiln, and spat. A smile infinitely evil curved the grey cracked lips.

'Turn over.'

Was this to be the death-blow? He carried no weapon; his spearman lolled negligently on the shaft. Painfully I obeyed, and rolled on my face. The tip of the stave touched my shoulder.

'As I thought. The mark of Pelops.'

I wear on my right shoulder an ivory-coloured birthmark: a heritage borne by every male descended from Pelops of Elis. (And a wonderful story the bards have concocted to account for *that*!) Even under the stress of pain and fear I wondered how this freak, a companion of outcast Goatman, should be familiar with the fables of Achaea's noble Houses. I turned on my back, and croaked from an arid gullet, 'Very well. I am Agamemnon son of Atreus. Who the blazes are *you*?'

'Dionysus.'

He uttered the word proudly, like a title borne by kings. Remembrance stirred: some half-forgotten tale which connected the name with Thebes. (The source of everything vexatious, Atreus had said.) A legend of olden days when Electryon

32

still ruled. Surely this crazy creature, ancient though he was, could not be *that* Dionysus?

With insolence wefting the words I said, 'The name means nothing to me.'

'No?' He sighed. 'You youngsters have no memory for fame. And impertinence, my lad, does not become your situation. In these two hands' – he held out skinny claws – 'I hold your life.'

Echion stirred and groaned. Dionysus' hooded eyes rested on him briefly. 'I regret to say that one of you has to be sacrificed. The choice, Agamemnon, is yours.'

'Sacrificed?'

'Yes. To the Goat God who rules the forests and mountains. The people lately' – a touch of smugness – 'begin to call him Dionysus. You see, they have just migrated to the foothills from summer pastures in the mountains, where game is scarce. They have not tasted meat for moons – and your dog was a paltry snack.'

I glared at him in horror. 'You will not....'

'Indeed. One will suffice for today; my band, as you see, is small. Which shall it be, Agamemnon? You must decide: your man is still unconscious. Think it over and let me know.'

With a word to the loinclothed spearman Dionysus hobbled away. I stared across the glade, my mind in turmoil. The sun slipped behind the mountains' cloud-draped peaks, the corridors of trees were growing dark. Raindrops pattered a carpet of leaves that autumn wove on the ground. The Goatmen built fires, and balanced spits across them on forked sticks. Occasionally they looked my way, gestured obscenely and laughed. I closed my eyes and held an aching head. Was I to take seriously the abominable decision tossed so casually into my hands?

In desperation I addressed the spearman. 'Is it true? Will they ...' I touched my chest, raised hand to lips and pretended to chew.

'It is true.' A guttural intonation, the pronunciation strange, but I caught the sense. 'These people live like animals, roving in packs and always hungry. Don't be afraid – they will cut your throat before...' Grinning, he repeated my little mime.

I rested my head on the oak tree and contemplated a darkening sky. I was deathly afraid – who would not be?

If I survived the night I would probably die next day – but dawn might bring salvation. The second herdsman had certainly reported my disappearance to Diores, who would hunt the hills with spears. Echion was resolute and loyal, but for all that a lowborn freeman – thousands like him served Mycenae. And I? A direct descendant of Zeus through Tantalos and Pelops I was heir – so Atreus said – to Perseus' throne. Sprung from a line of rulers, born to rule.

A common spearman or a future king. Could there be any choice?

Dionysus tottered from the trees. 'Have you cast the lots, Agamemnon?'

I turned my head away, and gestured blindly to the form that lay beside me. The old man cackled. 'Congratulations, lad – a wise decision.' He called across his shoulder; Goatmen came running and hauled Echion away. The lolling head bounced on fallen leaves. I do not think he knew what was happening.

They dragged him into a cypress grove beyond my sight. All the skin-clad creatures followed; the glade was suddenly empty save for dogs and goats and fires flickering redly in the dark. I heard the mumble of voices, and a kind of rhythmic chanting. Dionysus sat crosslegged beside me, and prodded his stave in soft brown earth. The mysterious spearman who spoke my tongue so badly rested on his weapon and hummed quietly to himself.

Dionysus pointed a bony finger. 'You call them Goatmen. I call them the Dispossessed.'

The chanting swelled in volume, male and female voices blended in strident discord. A dog nuzzled the spearman's foot; he kicked it away.

I said dully, 'The Dispossessed?'

'The people who held the land before it was named Achaea, who lived here peaceful and prosperous before Zeus brought his warriors from Crete.'

The singing rose to a shriek which shivered the drifting woodsmoke. Goatmen burst from the cypresses. I saw the things they carried, and closed my teeth on the vomit that surged in my throat.

'Which,' Dionysus continued in conversational tones, 'hap-

34

pened a long time ago. Zeus came with chariots and men in armoured panoply, and found unwarlike people who were easily subdued. Some submitted: their descendants today are slaves. Others fought to defend their homes, and died in droves. The survivors fled to the mountains.'

Chattering and laughing, the Goatmen ringed the fires and speared collops on the spits. A sickening stench of grilling flesh assailed the air. Dionysus regarded the scene benignly, like a father indulging playful children. The spearman shifted his feet, and hawked and spat.

'There they have remained. Achaeans seized the productive plains and fertile valleys; the Dispossessed were penned in desolate hills. Only goats can pluck a living from barren soil, so Goatmen they became, and wandered the slopes in search of grazing, moving on when all the grass was eaten.'

A Goatman left the fires, knelt before Dionysus and bowed brow to ground in obeisance. He tendered in both hands a chunk of smoking meat. I lowered my head and spewed between my knees. The old man smiled, showing blackened, rotted stumps, and waved the offering away.

'My food is cheese and honey,' he said when the man had gone. 'My drink spring water and goat's milk.' He picked a flea from his beard and cracked it between his nails. 'I swilled much wine in my youth, but you can't grow vines on mountains, and nomads cannot stay to see them fruit. Instead they make hydromel from wild honey, and get inordinately drunk. An immensely potent brew, but no substitute for wine ten years in jar.' Dionysus heaved a regretful sigh. 'Ah, me! Wine and the juice of the poppy – how easily I have mastered men with the aid of nature's gifts!'

I brushed leaves across my puddle of vomit, and croaked, 'You and your crew are ordure befouling the earth! Kill me now, for The Lady's sake! I cannot bear —'

'The Lady? In the hills I have taken Her place. She will not help you here, Agamemnon. Only I can save you, and I think ...' He murmured to the spearman, creaked to his feet and limped into the dark.

A rain-wind gusted the trees, rattled branches and spattered drops which hissed in the dying fires. The Goatmen finished their horrible feast, crouched near the embers and talked in guttural voices. One of them seized a woman, rolled her out of the circle and openly humped her. The audience grunted applause; several followed the pair's example. Buttocks heaved and rammed around the fires. Dogs skulked past carrying blood-smeared bones. A party at the end of the glade broke branches from trees and built a lean-to shelter. When the work was done they trooped into the shadows and reappeared with Dionysus and led him to the shelter like reverential acolytes conducting a priest to the altar. He lifted his arms in blessing, crooned an unintelligible dirge, dropped on hands and knees and crawled inside.

The fires died and darkness deepened. My captors slept where they had dined; snores mingled with the soughing of the wind. No watch was set; presumably the dogs provided an adequate protection. Only my loinclothed guardian stayed alert, sitting on his haunches close beside me, spearpoint slanted a hands-breadth from my throat. The cold of an autumn night chilled my naked body; dried blood caked the scrapes and cuts of my trawl across the hillside; thirst was a growing torment – but the thought of food was enough to make me retch. I closed my eyes and tried to sleep; ghastly pictures raced behind my eye-lids. Nightmare jerked me awake and I gasped aloud.

A spearpoint touched my neck. 'Quiet!' the sentry hissed.

I lay back trembling and oozing sweat. A form crept from the darkness and crouched beside me, bearded lips approached my ear. I smelt rank body-stink and fetid breath. 'I have re-solved,' Dionysus murmured, 'that a son of Mycenae's Marshal is a prize too hot to hold. If you disappear Atreus will hunt us down with every man in the Host. Regretfully I return you to your friends. My spearman will guide you from the forest. Go quietly!'

I clambered to my feet, swayed and almost fell. The spear-man held my shoulder and roughly hauled me erect. Dionysus gripped my arm; nails like talons dug into my flesh.

'Useless to search for us here; we shall be gone by dawn.' He cackled under his breath. 'Tell Atreus Dionysus lives!'

We crept from the encampment, threaded recumbent goats half-seen in the dark, passed dogs which lifted heads and growled in their throats but forbore to bay alarm – perhaps they were trained to signal intrusion: departures could go unhindered. The descent began: a journey I prefer to forget. Repeatedly I stumbled, slid on screes, bumped invisible rocks and trees, collapsed in numbed exhaustion. The spearman, mouthing curses, tugged me up and thrust me on.

Dawn breathed behind the hills when we left the forest's valance. Shadowy scrub-speckled slopes slanted away to the valleys. I searched for landmarks to guide me home, and recognized none. The man had brought me from the forest into unfamiliar territory; and I lacked the strength to hunt around for a path that led to Rhipe. The spearman silently pointed and turned to retrace his steps.

'Lead me farther,' I begged, 'until I can find my way.'

He hesitated, turned and pushed me on. We entered a narrow cleft, rock-walled and bordered by bushes. A shout, and sliding feet, stones clattering, and a rush of bodies. My guardian lifted his spear too late, men trampled him into the rocks. A shield rammed my chest and knocked me flat; the bearer clutched my throat and peered into my face. The choking fingers loosened.

'Agamemnon!' Diores breathed. 'Thanks to The Lady! We've found you!'

*　　*　　*

'Dionysus?' Atreus said. 'Impossible! You must have been dreaming!'

'Then,' I said huffily, 'it was a nightmare which I pray will never recur.'

The Marshal spread his hands to the hearth-fire's blaze, and doubtfully shook his head. I lay on a pallet in Rhipe's Hall. Bandages swathed my chest and shoulders; healing balms soothed scratches on my face. Clymene sat on a stool alongside, stroked my hair and fed me honeyed bread. I swallowed a morsel and said, 'Why are you here, my lord?'

'Why?' Atreus murmured absently. 'Oh, Diores sent a message. Your second herdsman tracked your trail to the forest's edge, wisely went no farther and returned to the manor. Diores armed every freeman he had, despatched a runner to Mycenae and searched the hills all night. I left at noon with a hundred men and arrived the evening after you were found.'

'I hope you won't blame Diores.'

'No. He did everything I ordered. It was that fellow's fault –
what's his name, Echion? I'd have had his head for letting you
enter the woods. Your fault too – you should have known
better. Damned lucky to be alive: very few men survive an
encounter with the Goatmen.'

'Horrible people!' I shuddered. 'Dionysus told me —'

'Dionysus, my arse!' Atreus snapped. 'The bastard's been
dead for years. Your chum assumed the name to bolster his
importance.'

'Who *is* Dionysus?'

'He is – was – a bleeding menace. Theban in origin, needless
to say, son of Cadmus' daughter. He took to drink and drugs,
dropped out from society and wandered half the world. Wherever he went he attracted degenerates of similar bent who
gathered in sects and indulged in disgusting orgies. Stayed for
years in Naxos; to this day the island is unsafe for decent
people. Tried to settle in Thrace, and was kicked out smartly.
Then he returned to Thebes and introduced his revolting rites
to the younger palace set, most of whom responded with
alacrity. Thebans would, of course. King Pentheus tried to stop
it; a pack of drugged and drunken women tore him in pieces.
Even the Thebans thought it too much, and Dionysus had to
leave. Reappeared in Argos where, I'm sorry to say, he perverted some of the women who built him altars high in the
hills and worshipped him as a god. His secret was the art of
distilling mind-maddening drugs, brewing wine of astonishing
strength, a handsome face, a seductive personality and a most
enormous prick. Could pleasure twenty women between one
sunset and the next.' Atreus chuckled. 'A fortunate man – if it's
true. The sect, I believe, still lingers secretly in Argos. Eventually the Argives got rid of him, and the last anyone heard he
was snatched by Tyrrhenian pirates and sold as a slave in Asia.
Damned good riddance!'

'How long ago was this?'

'Years and years. His mother was Semele, sister of Cadmus'
successor. Let me see.' Atreus counted on his fingers. 'If your
dotard claims to be Dionysus he must be all of ninety years
old. Hardly likely, d'you think?'

'The man seemed old as the hills he trod.'

'Pigs' wings! Anyway, whoever he is he and his gang are

gone: I sent a warband to scour the place. Far more important is this.' Atreus lifted a spear. 'The weapon your escort carried. Look at the barb.'

I fingered the grey metal, the needle-keen point, and nicked my hand on an edge ground fine as a hair. 'What is it?'

'Iron,' said Atreus morosely. 'The man also had this.' He dropped on the bed a bracelet which I recognized as the one my sentinel had worn. 'Iron. A precious metal.' The Marshal touched a ring on his second finger. 'We use it for jewellery, the few who can afford it. How the blazes does a Goatman buy enough to make a weapon?'

'He wasn't a Goatman. Quite a different stamp, different colouring, more civilized. What happened to him?'

'Dead,' Atreus said discontentedly. 'He was badly hurt in the scuffle, and Diores brought him back. I took one look at his spearhead and put him to the question. Fellow muttered something about Doris, called himself a Dorian. Quite willing to talk, but the inquisitors were much too rough, and he died. I've hanged the fools responsible – imagine using red-hot tongs on a man who's barely alive! – but that won't help in tracing his connections.'

The scrapes and gashes stung beneath the bandages, my body ached all over. Clymene's soothing fingers stroked my brow; I felt my eyelids drooping. The Marshal, I considered vaguely, made an unwarranted fuss. Through mists of encroaching drowsiness I listened to him talking as he strode about the room. He had heard rumours of the Dorians: a mysterious race which over the years had filtered into Achaea from unknown lands beyond the Euxine Sea. Though hustled out by the inhabitants of every realm they entered, a clan was permitted to settle in the neighbourhood of Doris on a bleak infertile tract the Locrians didn't want. A harmless people, small in numbers, outwardly inoffensive, not given to marauding and lifting their neighbours' cattle. Why was a Dorian wandering with Goatmen? Where did he find enough iron to use it as we use bronze? There was iron in Euboia, a little, rare as gold: the Euboians guarded it closely. Had they found a secret source elsewhere?

Atreus' monologue and Clymene's gentle caress almost lulled me to sleep. I forced my eyelids apart and said, 'What does it matter, my lord? The Dorians probably barter iron for cattle and corn – which they must badly need if Doris is so barren. Otherwise —'

The Marshal stopped his pacing and stood beside my bed. 'Your wits are fuddled, lad! Wake up! Don't you see? Any people who possess enough iron to forge it into swords and spears can cut through bronze-armed soldiers as sickles mow down grass. Iron will slice the best wrought bronze as though it were mouldy cheese. Give me a thousand iron men and I promise to conquer the world!'

'You've found one – and he's dead.'

Atreus glowered. 'We found him with the Goatmen. If they and iron-armed Dorians combine we shall really be in trouble. I'll send emissaries to Elis and Arcadia and across the Corinth Gulf to find out what's going on.' His voice softened, a hand stroked my hair. 'You're tired, Agamemnon, not recovered from your hurts. Sleep now, and restore your strength. I had intended you should stay at Rhipe another year, but ... In a day or two you'll return with me to Mycenae, where you can start again where you left off – learning a Companion's work and driving battle chariots.'

*   *   *

Atreus left ten spearmen at Rhipe to help Diores guard his stock; and grumbled expansively. 'A steady attrition of manpower: over the past two years I've had to leave detachments at other outlying farms which suffered attacks from Goatmen. The men I lose are husbandmen and soldiers both, so Mycenae's tillage declines and her defences shrivel. The Goatmen have been a pest for years; they're quickly becoming a danger!'

I bade Diores a sorrowful farewell, and clasped Gelon's hand. Atreus remarked my friendship with the Scribe, and said approvingly, 'A first-class accountant, Diores says, and an excellent organizer. I'll soon have him back at Mycenae to teach you administration, auditing stores and trading returns, excise duties and profit and loss – a damned complicated business which I've never quite mastered myself.'

I found Mycenae outwardly unchanged; within the palace there were minor alterations. Atreus and my mother now occupied an extensive suite overlooking the Great Court, the rooms so splendidly furnished they surpassed the royal apartments.

Shortly after I left for the outlands the Marshal had married Aerope. Weddings in Achaea are sedate and simple affairs, the ceremony common to every rank of society. Atreus provided a banquet in the hall for King Eurystheus and his Council while Aerope, heavily veiled, waited with her ladies in a corner. With the final collop swallowed and beaker of wine gulped down the bride removed her veil, a Daughter cut a lock of her hair and dedicated it to The Lady. Atreus bowed to Eurystheus on his throne, faced the assembled nobles and took my mother's wrist. 'I declare this woman my fond and willing wife.' The king said, 'It is approved,' and that was that.

Plisthenes – my father and Aerope's living spouse – might never have existed. The marriage cancelled him out. Even had he been present and hammering at the doors the union would still have been valid.

The king approved.

I believe Egypt and Phoenicia have permanent laws which govern people's conduct and relations. But except for the scales of murder fines no prescriptive laws exist anywhere in Achaea: the kings and the lords of citadels make day-to-day directives affecting their subjects' welfare; they alone decide disputes and punish malefactors. Councils may advise, if asked. Eurystheus occasionally allowed the Councillors' arguments to influence his judgments; Atreus, later, never. From these decisions there is no appeal; the king's word *is* the law.

I paid my respects to my mother, who looked beautiful as ever. She informed me she had abandoned her hunting and chariot driving as inconsistent with the dignity of Mycenae's paramount lady – and the sun was browning her face. (Ladies, particularly palace ladies, take pride in preserving a pale complexion; lesser females have to brave the sun in performing their daily tasks; so you judge a woman's status by the colour of her skin.) She chattered trivialities, solicitously examined my half healed scars and recommended a salve she had got from the palace physician – a son of Aesculapius, the quack who ran a medical school at Epidauros. She listened brightly to my adventures and lost interest when a beefy, handsome Hero entered the apartment with a message from her husband.

Aerope fluttered her lashes; the Hero dithered adoringly.

I sidled out. My mother could never resist a man, and it did her no good in the end.

I resumed my chariot driving under the tutelage of Atreus' Companion Phylacus, a dour, taciturn man but a first-rate hand with horses. I had often driven travelling chariots, heavy, lumbering vehicles. Battle chariots are different as hawks from herons, the carriage builder's art brought near perfection, strength and lightness delicately balanced. Drawn by two fleet horses – some experts added a trace horse, which Phylacus thought dangerous – the body is very light: oxhide or wicker-work covers a bentwood frame; you stand on a floor of plaited oxhide strips. A stout leather thong runs from a figwood guard-rail to the yoke end of a single pole and supports the weight. Four-spoked bronze-tyred wheels are naved on a beechwood axle centred beneath the body.

Battle chariots are gaudy vehicles, painted blue and yellow and crimson, frames gilded and inlaid with ivory and decorated by silver plaques. Ivory medallions sometimes adorn the reins – stupid and risky, Phylacus growled, shaking a grouchy head.

A Companion has to master more than driving. I learned the art of selecting horses by make and shape, the blood-lines, breaking and training, grooming, feeding and stable routine – every aspect of horsemanship. I spent more time in stables then racketing round the Field of War behind two pulling Kolaxians, and soon acquired the distinctive smell which hovers around Companions. Aerope, when I visited her, ostentatiously nosed a phial of scented oil; Atreus sniffed and laughed. 'A fine healthy reek, Agamemnon. No matter – Phylacus allows you'll make an exceptional driver: you have the gift of hands. And so you should, with your pedigree – Pelops gained his kingdom by winning a chariot race!'

My instruction continued throughout the stormy winter months; neither cold nor rain nor sleet deterred a hardy, waterproof Phylacus. With the coming of spring he put me through the aspiring Companion's test: a narrow serpentine course marked by fragile earthenware jars which culminated in a low mud bank and the Field's twin watercourses raging in spate. I took it all at a searing gallop, broke two jars and finished triumphant, chariot and horses intact.

42

'You'll do,' Phylacus said. 'Not bad at all, after only five moons' training. Some take as many years to pass the test. Don't think,' he continued grimly, 'you know it all. There's a lot to learn yet, which only battle can teach you.'

I was eager to be appointed Companion to some Hero, preferably at Tiryns or Corinth – I longed to see new faces and taste a fresh environment; Mycenae had cloistered me too long. Atreus, when I broached the matter, shook his head. 'You're an important person, Agamemnon, and likely to become more so as time goes by. Unfitting you should serve a petty lord. No – I shall make you one of my Companions. What greater honour' – a wide grin – 'than to drive the Marshal of Mycenae into battle? Sooner than you think, perhaps. You never know with that Hercules mob in Tiryns. They behave worse when their leader's away – drowned by now, I hope – than they did when he was Warden.'

Atreus explained. Thyestes had sent him bitter complaints about the conduct of Hercules' followers. Since all were landless men they subsisted on Tiryns' resources and drained the citadel's store rooms. Thyestes quoted a list of offences: they entered the palace precincts unbidden, demanded the choicest meat and oldest wine, became uproariously drunk and invaded the ladies' apartments – one ruffian had been killed by an outraged husband, and a full-scale riot barely averted. They looted merchants' shops, raped the peasants' women and stole their sheep and cattle. Finally, a few days since, a gang commanded by Hyllus raided a herd of horses on one of the Argos estates. King Adrastus of Argos threatened reprisals. Thyestes humbly apologized and sent to Mycenae for help.

'It seems fantastic,' Atreus commented, 'that a scant two hundred rascals can stir up so much trouble. Of course they're tough and ruthless, desperadoes to a man, every one recruited by Hercules himself for just those nasty qualities. A mistake to treat them lightly – but they have to be removed.'

When the Council discussed Thyestes' tirade Atreus recommended a punitive expedition be sent immediately to Tiryns, there to join the garrison in exterminating the Heraclids – as Hercules' kin and followers were generally called. King Eurystheus demurred. He felt the bonds of service and the obligations he owed Hercules forbade killing his relations while the man himself was away on the *Argo* venture: an act of shocking treachery the whole world would condemn. Moreover, he continued, descending to practicalities, Hercules sprang like himself from the ancient House of Perseus, and through his father Amphitryon had powerful kinsmen in Thebes. A massacre might lead easily to war. The king allowed that the Heraclids be banished from the realm; any severer measures were politically unwise. Atreus argued that to leave the brood alive merely postponed a crisis: it left the Heraclids free to gather allies at leisure and descend upon the kingdom when they judged the time propitious.

Eurystheus, however, would not be moved.

Over the next few days Atreus perfected his plans. Surprise was the key; he therefore shunned a levy of arms which would disturb the entire countryside, make Hercules' followers wonder and put them on their guard. He decided on a warband formed from the palace Heroes and those who owned estates around Mycenae. To provide an invincible force – odds of three to one, he judged, should prove decisive – he sent to Argos requesting similar action. Adrastus, smarting under Hyllus' outrage, willingly agreed. On an appointed day the warbands would meet at Argos, swoop together on Tiryns, seize and disarm the Heraclids and escort them to the Isthmus north of Corinth. Thyestes was informed and told to warn his Heroes, providing he could do so without alarming the enemy.

Menelaus had arrived with Thyestes' deputation. Since last we met my brother had gained both weight and height – even so I topped him by half a head. At sixteen years he was already full-grown, chested like a wine jar, broad and brawny. I kissed his cheeks and pulled his auburn hair and asked him how he did in rocky Tiryns.

'Well enough. I'm no longer Thyestes' squire, The Lady be praised. I passed the tests a moon ago, and one of the palace Heroes took me as a Companion.'

'I also. I drive for Atreus.'

'Lucky man. When shall we win our greaves? Any hope of a fight, do you think, when we sling the Heraclids out?'

I hunched my shoulders. 'Doubtful. The Marshal aims to take them by surprise.' I hesitated, and said carefully, 'Do you see

44

anything of Plisthenes? How has he taken our mother's – um – re-marriage?'

A sentinel paced behind us, slanted spear on shoulder. (We were standing on the rampart walk above the northern postern, overlooking an ancient oak tree which sprouted from Zeus' tomb. A peasant deposited an offering on the surrounding circle of tall stone slabs.) When the sentry passed beyond earshot Menelaus said, 'You can't really tell: he shows no outward signs of knowing it's happened. Maybe he doesn't. He lives in Thyestes' apartments; the pair are thick as thieves. And, to Thyestes' credit, Plisthenes has become much more ... sane. He dines frequently in the Hall, and seems perfectly aware of all that's going on.'

'Atreus kept him secluded in Mycenae. Perhaps mixing in society restores the balance of his mind.'

'Perhaps. It doesn't matter any more: the Marshal has got what he wanted. And yet ...' Menelaus tickled an embryonic beard. 'Plisthenes gives me the shudders. So harmless, almost pathetic – but you feel there's something sinister about him.'

'He's our father, Menelaus.'

'Yes. I still find it hard to believe.' Menelaus slapped the stone that bonded the rampart's crest. 'A gloomy conversation, Agamemnon, and we won't be long together. I leave for Argos tomorrow with the embassy to King Adrastus. Let's go to the stables and admire your stud. They say Atreus' teams are the envy of all Achaea!'

I linked an arm with my brother's, and we sauntered to the palace.

*   *   *

Ten days later Atreus led a warband from the portals of Mycenae. Proud, excited and a little apprehensive I restrained the frisky stallions which pulled the Marshal's chariot. (A frowning, sulky Phylacus drove his second car in the rear.) Atreus in full panoply of war – plumed boar's tusk helmet, thrice-skirted brazen armour, a ten-foot spear and treble-hide waisted shield – quizzically eyed my handling of the reins. I wore a Companion's mail of the time – the convention of sparing Companions in battle was rapidly wearing thin – a metal skull-cap, bronze-studded leather corselet and a short stabbing sword.

45

The company numbered a bare four hundred: thirty-odd Heroes in chariots, each with his personal spearmen, and a handful of Cretan bowmen. Scouts on shaggy-coated ponies trotted in the van. We took neither baggage carts, pack mules nor donkeys; a minimum of slaves to wait upon the nobles shambled at the tail. This was a quick in-and-out expedition, Atreus declared; and for the journey to the Isthmus we would find supplies in Tiryns.

I still remember the thrill of my first approach to war: the column swathed in dust, a smell of thyme and horses' sweat, the sun-shot glint of spears, gleaming brazen armour, helmet plumes like rippling flames, the crunch of wheels on the ill-paved road King Sthenelus had fashioned over fifty years before. ('Time we re-laid these roads,' the Marshal remarked as the chariot lurched on the flags, 'and you could have avoided that hole with a scrap more care!') He smilingly regarded my unconcealed enthusiasm and damped my aggressive hopes. 'No greaves for you today, my lad – we're simply rounding up a mob of scoundrelly bandits!'

We reached Argos before noon. King Adrastus greeted Atreus at the gates; a warband half our strength mustered in the citadel's streets to avoid attracting attention. The king, a wizened man whose jutting beaky nose curved to a chin like a warship's ram, had passed beyond the age of leading whirlwind raids. He presented his Leader of the Host, Tydeus, a black-bearded black-browed warrior very short in stature and nearly broad as he was long. An immigrant from Calydon, he had won Adrastus' favour and married his daughter.

Tydeus presented a fourteen-year-old stripling clad in Companion's armour. 'My son Diomedes,' he said. 'He keeps pestering for adventure, and I judged this little foray a gentle introduction for a youngster green in war.'

I liked Diomedes on sight. Short, square and stocky, with the promise of strength and agility in wide-framed shoulders and supple hips. Corn-coloured hair, a snub-nosed, square-jawed face and honest brown eyes. An engaging directness in speech and manner concealed, as I learned in after years, a mind as keen as a newly honed blade. He walked to my chariot, grasped the rail and examined the restless horses.

'As lovely a pair as ever I've seen.' His voice was husky, the

46

tones abruptly changing, obviously recently broken: a contrast to the resonant bellow which later made his war-cry famous. 'Venetic blood – they must be a handful to drive! You are ...'

'Agamemnon son of ... Atreus.'

'Ah, yes.' For a moment Diomedes' eyes held mine; the glance warned me he knew all about my parentage. Which was hardly surprising: family trees and lineage are among the subjects most discussed by men of noble blood. 'We heard rumours of your trouble with the Goatmen. You —'

His father and Atreus ended a low-voiced colloquy. 'Diomedes, you ride with the Marshal's Companion Phylacus. Get mounted!'

'Oh, dear.' Diomedes sighed heavily. 'The old boy coddles me like a new-born lamb. Atreus' reserve chariot, I suppose? Nurse-maided in the second rank, as I expected. Well, maybe one day ...' Smilingly he climbed to the empty place beside Phylacus and engaged that dour character in sprightly conversation. Atreus mounted, lifted his spear. Scouts trotted ahead; the column clattered and crunched the stony road to Tiryns.

Flat and open countryside extended on either hand until, some hundred bowshots short of the point where the citadel's ramparts climb into view, scrub-stippled hills closed in on the road to make a narrow, twisting path just wide enough for four men marching abreast. I handled the horses gingerly: drainage ditches bordered the track and stunted olive and tamarisk bushes leaned from the banks and brushed our shoulders. At a bend that was tight as a fully-crooked elbow a drooping clump of myrtle overhung the way.

A white-clad figure leaped from the leaves, a spearhead flashed in the sun.

A Companion is taught, when a footman attacks from a flank, to swing instantly towards him to shorten the length of his lunge. Instinctively I obeyed the tenets instilled in months of training, and hauled savagely on the reins.

The turn, though slow – the horses moved at a walk – was enough to deflect the aim. The point scored the Marshal's lifted shield, glissaded past his helmet. Quick as a falling thunderbolt Atreus lunged his spear. I heard a high-pitched scream that died in a bubbling wail.

I reined the horses sliding on their hocks. Atreus tugged his spear out, jumped from the car and lifted it high and plunged it down.

A single shriek, and sounds like an animal crying.

Shaking at the knees, I controlled my frightened horses. Atreus straddled a squirming form that scrabbled hands on stony earth and jerked in the throes of dying. The body arched and crumpled. Atreus leaned on his bloodied spear, both hands clasping the haft, and watched his attacker die. His head was bowed; he stayed curiously still and silent.

Phylacus' chariot rounded the bend. He halted, flung reins to Diomedes and pelted sword in hand to help his lord. I craned to see the body, half hidden by myrtle boughs, and glimpsed a white contorted face, glazed eyes fixed and staring.

Plisthenes.

The chariot's leather-thonged floor rocked beneath my feet like the deck of a storm-tossed ship. I clutched the rail. The horses stamped and sidled; numbly I felt the bits.

Atreus roused himself. 'Quick, Phylacus! Take his arms, help me drag him under the bushes.' A snap in his voice like breaking sticks. 'We must hide this unfortunate corpse lest the men imagine omens and refuse to travel further.' Together they bundled the body into a cleft between rocks which oleanders shaded. Phylacus scuffled earth across a scarlet puddle. Atreus plucked a handful of leaves and scrubbed his spearhead clean, brushed his hands together and remounted.

'Drive on!'

I flicked the reins, wheels grated on grit. Atreus stared straight ahead, and spoke between lips that were set and stiff.

'You saw who he was?'

I nodded dumbly.

'I have killed my son. The Lady will demand requital. I must sacrifice....' The sinewy hand that held the rail clenched till the knuckles whitened. 'He could not have hatched this ambuscade alone. Someone pricked him on. Not difficult to guess....'

The road debouched from the pass; Tiryns' greystone towers reared on the horizon. I glanced back. A vulture circled lazily over the slopes where Plisthenes lay.

He was my father. I searched in my heart for sorrow, and found no emotion at all.

*   *   *

We met little opposition from the Heraclids. Ostensibly to celebrate Hercules' birthday Thyestes entertained them with a feast in the palace Hall. By mid-afternoon, when our warbands arrived, they were mostly screeching drunk. Atreus halted the chariots at the ramp that climbed to the gate, dismounted all the Heroes and led them at a run through forecourt and palace courtyard. They burst into the Hall and surrounded the stupefied Heraclids. Spearmen followed fast, blocked the doors and lined the painted walls.

Men do not go armed to palace banquets, so there was virtually no resistance. Iolaus, dagger on high, tried to rush Tydeus; the Argive commander butted his shield and bruised the attacker's ribs. Hiccupping and winded, he vomited his meal. Hyllus, owlishly dignified, protested incoherently; Atreus told him amiably to save his breath. The captives were herded into Tiryns' echoing galleries where, with exits closed and guarded, they huddled cramped and crowded in the dark.

From crannies in the citadel and town spearmen rounded up a handful of lesser followers who had not attended the banquet. Some bore weapons and tried to resist; slaves buried them outside the lower citadel. By evening all were accounted for in one way or another; and the Heroes of Argos, Mycenae and Tiryns gathered in the Hall to recover from their exertions and swallow food and wine. The occasion developed into a celebratory revel; lamps and torches were lighted and the feasting went on till late at night.

Diomedes, the only witness to Plisthenes' killing besides Phylacus and myself, was not of course aware of his identity and tried to elicit a reason for the corpse's hurried disposal. 'Unlucky omens my foot!' he declared. 'Who cares when a brigand dies?' I was more than a little sozzled for the first time in my life – that agonized squealing sang in my ears like a threnody heard in dreams – and answered roughly. 'Do you question the Marshal's wisdom? You saw a robber get his deserts – that's all. So keep your mouth shut!'

Diomedes looked at my eyes, and said no more.

Thyestes hardly shared in the general merriment. His manner distrait, the sunken sea-green eyes wary as a wolf's, he answered shortly Atreus' cheerful banter. His mind seemed elsewhere, brooding secret problems. Often I caught him shooting puzzled glance at the Marshal. Atreus refused to respect his brother's reserve, and persistently and boisterously engaged him in conversation. Finally he clapped Thyestes' shoulder.

'What ails you, man? I've rid you of an irksome pest! Aren't you glad to see me?'

Thyestes answered tonelessly, 'Of course. I'm only sorry you have to go so soon. You leave at dawn?'

'At dawn. An easy march to Mycenae, then a longish haul to Corinth the following day. We'll have to guard our villains carefully when the road goes through the mountains.' He sent the Warden of Tiryns a friendly smile. 'Those passes can be dangerous.'

Thyestes, face inscrutable, traced with a fingertip the graving on his goblet: a winged and hawk-beaked griffin. 'So? You have a sufficient force to discourage intruders. Neither Goatmen nor cattle raiders ever attack strong warbands.'

'True. But,' said Atreus genially, 'you'll hardly believe the things some idiots try. A lone bandit jumped our vanguard on the Argos road. Killed him at once, of course. Fellow must have been mad!'

Thyestes raised the goblet, drank deeply and set it down. 'Undoubtedly.' He scrubbed the back of a hand across his mouth. 'With your pardon, I must go. I have business to attend: arrangements for the transport accompanying you to Corinth.'

Atreus watched him stride from the Hall. The smile had left his lips, his features hardened in ruthless lines and his eyes were cold and cruel.

*   *   *

The column left at sunrise. The pace was hampered by baggage carts and mules and the wives, concubines, relatives and slaves belonging to the Heraclids – a rabble that outnumbered the prisoners themselves. Thyestes had suggested selling the lot; they would fetch good prices in Nauplia's slave market. Atreus, remembering Eurystheus' strictures, reluctantly dissented. He confiscated their chariots, hounds and horses – a mediocre assortment – and divided them among the senior Heroes.

We reached Mycenae in late afternoon and corralled our captives in the citadel for the night. After a weary march through mountains the following day – each Heraclid escorted by a vigilant spearman – we passed by Corinth and halted near to nightfall on a cliff-hung road that traverses the Isthmus. Atreus herded the Heraclids to the front. 'From here you're on your own,' he told Hyllus and Iolaus. 'Keep walking – and don't come back!'

Hyllus' angry eyes glittered in the dark. 'Don't imagine, my lord, that you've seen the last of the Heraclids. We will return!'

Atreus made a contemptuous noise, turned and remounted his chariot. 'To Corinth, Agamemnon, fast as you can make it in the dark.' I whipped the tired horses and drove very carefully indeed: the road was carved in a cliff side, and a precipice fell like a wall to shoreline crags.

Atreus roused himself from silent meditation. 'Hyllus is probably right. Depends on what support they can find in Megara and Athens. And Thebes is always ready to stir up trouble. I foresee a fight in the future.'

The Marshal shook his shoulders. 'Ah, well, that will be another day. Remind me, Agamemnon, to sacrifice a white barley-fed bull to The Lady as soon as we're safe in Mycenae!'

Chapter 3

ATREUS strode from the Throne Room and met me in the Great Court. He said curtly, 'Come on, Agamemnon, I'm going to have a bath. It might wash away ill-humour.' I followed him to the palace's single bathroom. Slaves removed his cloak and boots and kilt; he stepped into a polished marble bath: a stone of unusual colour, pink and streaked with red. Two buxom female slaves sluiced him with steaming water; he sat in the bath and vigorously plied a sponge. I stood against a wall – he had not invited me to sit – and listened while the Marshal, in terse and angry sentences, enlarged upon a crisis.

'Those damned Thebans are strangling our corn supplies from Lake Copais, and the Council is flapping like old wet hens.'

He squeezed water on his hair; a woman scrubbed his back. In days gone by, the Marshal explained between wallowings and splashings, the people of Orchomenos drained Lake Copais, a sunken stretch of land which streams flooded every winter to create a shallow lake. By a system of dykes and embankments and underground drainage channels – a major engineering feat – the Orchomenians reclaimed the area and secured for themselves a large and fertile tract that grew abundant crops of wheat and barley and rye: the most extensive granary in Achaea.

Mycenae established a regular trading connection, bartering bronze, slaves, wine and fleeces for corn: after every harvest a train of ox-drawn wagons laden high with grain trundled from Boeotia to Mycenae. But for three years past, the Marshal grumbled, the convoys returned half empty and the agents full of excuses that Theban bailiffs invented: a poor harvest, exceptional home demand, diverting supplies to a famine in Thrace – and so on.

'Hercules,' said Atreus sourly, 'is the original cause of the trouble. His attack, years ago, on Orchomenian tribute gatherers started a war which ended in Theban victory. Now Thebes controls the Copaic cornlands and imposes blockades at will.'

I swallowed a sigh. The Marshal was off on a lecture, one of several about politics and economics he had inflicted on me lately. It was wise to feign interest: his way with inattentive youngsters tended towards brutality. I said, 'Surely very short-sighted? Why? We've never warred against Thebes.'

'Don't you know any history? Sit down, lad, sit down! Don't stand there like a cornfield dummy planted to scare the crows! Thebans are foreigners, outlanders. Cadmus came from Phoenicia, and alien blood flows thickly in the veins of his descendants. Always they've been hostile to their neighbours, always ready to foster dissension, do us harm. They are insatiably ambitious, and aim at dominating the whole of Achaea. Their hobby and pleasure is sodomy, a vice imported by Cadmus which flourishes like a poisonous weed in the decadent climate of Thebes. They've actually raised a chariot squadron manned entirely by buggers, calling itself the Scavengers – The Lady preserve us! – which does nothing but train for war. We have pederasts in Mycenae, I'm sorry to say – but nobody holds it a social virtue, and if you're caught in the act you get impaled!'

The Marshal paused in his diatribe, and added darkly, 'I shouldn't be surprised to hear those Thebans help the Goatmen in every way they can. Your Dionysus may be bogus – but the real one came from Thebes!'

Atreus surged from the bath, a wave of water raced across the tessellated floor. A woman wrapped him in soft woollen sheets and dabbed his body dry. 'Those greybeards of the Council suggested an ultimatum. I persuaded Eurystheus to think it over and give a decision tomorrow.'

I said, 'Ultimatum?'

'Yes,' said the Marshal, scowling. 'The idiots think we're capable of making war on Thebes. Half haven't seen the place. I have. Immensely strong fortifications, a curtain wall so long it warrants seven gates. It can draw on all the resources of a rich and fertile country. I don't say the citadel can't be taken – it can – but it needs thorough organization and the military support of all the allies we have. Now is not the time: Mycenae has other troubles simmering in the stew. Pylos for one: another heritage that scoundrel Hercules bequeathed. I hope *Argo* tips him overboard and drowns him!'

Skilful stroking fingers massaged the Marshal from forehead to feet; an aroma of scented oil pervaded the steamy air. 'Pylos,' he growled, 'is preparing for war. Neleus saw his family killed and his city sacked by a rogue he regards as King Eurystheus' hit-man. He doesn't believe that Hercules acted without orders – and who can blame him? The ruffian has done some unspeakable jobs for Eurystheus in his time! I hear Neleus is expanding his fleet – Pylos, by her situation, was always a maritime power – and intends to raid our seaboard. He'll do a lot of damage, and we shall have to retaliate: overland, of course, for we can't face the Pylian galleys. Marching a Host through Arcadia is no damned joke! And who the blazes *wants* a war with Pylos?'

Atreus traced his toe on a floor-tile's zigzag pattern. 'That's not all. The Heraclids are busy. Iolaus and Hyllus are concerting an alliance with Athens in the hope of getting support for an invasion across the Isthmus. Athens doesn't much matter: a bunch of yellow-bellied rats. But you can bet your bracelets they've also consulted Creon, Regent of Thebes, and he's not the man to miss an opportunity. I foresee a thrust on Corinth and an attempt to invade the Argolid – and not too far in the future.'

'So,' I said sagely, 'as Mycenae faces a war on two fronts an expedition against Thebes is obviously out of the question.'

'At the moment, yes. Sooner or later Thebes must be destroyed – but we must choose our time and not loose arrows from half-drawn bows. Neither a Pylian nor Heraclid war,' said Atreus savagely, 'will fill our depleted granaries. Already we import all the corn they can spare from Egypt and Crete. The Curator says we're heading for famine within a couple of harvests if we don't break the Theban blockade or find a new source of supply.'

'Does one exist?'

'It does. I suggested to the king in Council we annex Midea and Asine.'

Atreus interpreted. Midea stands inland midway between

Argos and Mycenae; Asine, its port, lies on the coast a half day's journey distant. The land enclosed between them, notably fertile and bearing heavy corn crops, made Amphiarus of Midea a very wealthy man. Hence, though Mycenaean rulers from Perseus on had cast covetous eyes on the pair, none hitherto had ventured to attack them. They remained an irritation, like a thorn adrift in your boot; and because of their strength were bold enough to loose occasional forays on the cattle herds of Tiryns.

'But that,' I exclaimed, 'means yet another war!'

The woman draped a robe around his shoulders; Atreus pulled it close and sat on the bench beside me. 'Not necessarily. I have a plan which I believe will do the trick. Highly unorthodox, and the trouble will be to extract the king's consent.' Atreus sighed. 'Eurystheus, I'm afraid, has a very conventional mind.'

A slave removed the drain plug, water gurgled in the runnels. 'I feel much better. Nothing like a good sluice.'

Pensively I contemplated the red bath, and agreed. 'But,' I added, 'I always get a strange sensation whenever I sit in that tub – a feeling of terrible danger. Quite without reason – and I can't think why.'

'Nor I,' the Marshal said. 'Safest place in the palace!'

* * *

Although Atreus often confided to me his reflections and ideas – and never asked my opinion – I was of course not present at the private consultations between the king and his Marshal. Atreus summarized the interview for me afterwards. Eurystheus flatly refused to sanction his proposal. Ludicrous, he stated. It had never been done before, and that was enough for him. Atreus persisted; Eurystheus then suggested discussing the plan in Council, and was delicately persuaded that secrecy was vital. At last the attractions – if not the feasibility – of the project dawned on the king: it was just the sort of venture fit for Heroes; and he insisted on a condition that, if he accorded leave, he personally must lead the expedition. Doubtless he saw himself, in the evening of his days – Eurystheus was then past fifty – wallowing in the glory of a feat the bards would sing for years to come.

Atreus hid his dismay. He had promised the plan was bound to succeed; he could not now dissuade the king by dwelling on the consequence of failure. Instead he emphasized the physical hardships involved and swore that, barring himself, not a warrior over thirty would be included in his force. Eurystheus saw reason – you don't become king of Mycenae without hard-won recognition of the realities of war – and reluctantly gave consent.

The Marshal's thorough preparations disclosed to me the genius which won him his high position. In a late autumnal dawn I drove him from Mycenae on the road that led to Argos. The travelling chariot he had ordered was a battered, rickety vehicle, the horses low-bred hairies; we both wore shabby clothes; a mysterious rope-knotted bundle reposed on the chariot's floor. When the road forked to Midea he directed me to a gully and stopped on the bank of a brook that was bordered by alders and aspens. Atreus dismounted, untied the bundle and dressed himself in a soiled linen tunic, a patched cloak and a strap suspending a leather box of the kind that pedlars carry. A floppy ferret-skin hat completed the disguise. He knelt beside the water and smeared mud on face and arms and legs, disarrayed his beard and said, 'How do I look?'

I had watched these preparations in goggle-eyed astonishment, and could only stutter. He flipped the box open and displayed a jumble of trinkets and carved bone figurines of the kind that women buy for offerings at The Lady's shrines. 'Personal reconnaissance, Agamemnon – essential for a hazardous venture like this. Stay here and keep under cover. If some wandering herdsman finds you, cut his throat. I shall be back before dark.'

He smiled broadly and shambled away, crouching on a staff to reduce his commanding stature: an itinerant pedlar wandering from town to town to scrape a living. I unyoked and tethered the horses, propped the chariot on its pole and wrapped myself in a threadbare cloak: it was cold in the shade of the trees.

The sun crept slowly across a cloud-fleeced sky. Sheep bells tinkled remotely, a shepherd's distant piping was a threadlike whisper of sound. Nobody came near. I tramped to and fro on the bank of the rill to keep myself warm, and wondered what I would say to the king if his Marshal failed to return. When the sun touched the rim of the farthest hills I put the horses to and waited in gathering dusk, trembling with cold and misgivings.

Atreus entered the grove, discarded his leather box and jumped into the chariot. 'Off you go, Agamemnon, to Mycenae as quick as you can!' He sounded gay and confident. 'A very successful trip – had a good look round and learned what I wanted. Learned something else as well: I'm a most persuasive huckster – sold nearly all my stock! Perhaps I'm in the wrong job! Dammit, boy, you're cold as an icicle! Here, take a pull at this.' He handed me a bulging wineskin. 'Payment for a necklace I flogged to a housewife as genuine silver. They're a gullible lot in Midea!'

He spoke no more during the nightbound journey except, when we saw Mycenae's shadowy bulk, to say in a sword-edged voice, 'You will tell no one of our expedition, Agamemnon, do you understand? Nobody at all!'

During the days that followed I expected a call to arms, an assembly of the Host – and found myself mistaken. Atreus warned a number of palace Heroes, all young and proven in battle, to be ready for a foray against Stymphalos, a troublesome nest of robbers on the borders of Arcadia, and gave similar instructions to certain selected lords of Mycenae's home demesnes. The Marshal was obviously collecting a handpicked force: the toughest and the bravest of all Eurystheus' Heroes. At the end he had chosen fifty, and said he did not require their retinues of spearmen.

'Are you proposing, my lord,' I said incredulously, 'to throw a handful of men against a fortress like Midea?'

'Just that,' he said cheerfully. 'And we won't take chariots either, so Companions are superfluous. Which includes you, Agamemnon!'

I protested violently. 'Whatever you intend, my lord' – and not a soul except himself and, presumably, King Eurystheus knew what he *did* intend – 'my place is at your side. I'm eighteen years of age, as strong and deadly a man-at-arms as any you've picked. Am I *never* to have a chance to prove myself in battle?'

I was near to tears. After a long pause Atreus said, 'You're a loyal and faithful creature, Agamemnon – and I see your point.

57

Very well. Tomorrow we'll start training. You'll have to sweat, my lad!'

Atreus spoke truth. For fourteen grinding days the chosen band of fifty exercised on the Field of War, running, jumping, hurling discs, wrestling and fencing. He forbade spears, the regnant weapon in battle. 'Unnecessary for your task,' he said obscurely. 'Come on, get moving! You're horribly unfit, you gaggle of flab-muscled farmers!' A smile purged offence from the words – you can't treat Heroes like fledgling squires. He also prohibited armour and heavy shields, those tall half-cylinder towers or waisted walls of hide which distinguish Heroes in war. Instead he issued leather corselets and light round targes of the kind that spearmen carry. The company wondered, and argued a little – but it's hard to argue with Atreus.

Every second day he led the men on a fast long-distance march across the roughest tracks and steepest hills in the neighbourhood. This almost caused a mutiny. Heroes ride to war and ride in battle: they see no point in walking when chariots stand in their stables. Some complained. Atreus said icily, 'The king has so commanded – do you question his authority?' Visions of forfeited estates floated before rebellious eyes, and the rumbles subsided in silence.

At the fortnight's end he tried them higher by taking them out at night. Warriors are accustomed to moving around in the dark, herding flocks and hunting strays in nights as black as a Theban's heart. But no one had hitherto bothered to move *noiselessly* in the dark, which now became the object of the Marshal's stringent training. He chose the stoniest hillsides, and swore like a master mariner when a boot sole scraped on rock or a pebble clattered the slopes. We began to see the reason – though not the eventual object – for his interdict on armour and cumbrous shields: you can't climb hillsides quietly in accoutrements meant for chariots. So, dressed in helmets, corselets, short swords and round hide shields, fifty sweating warriors learned during moonless nights to mount boulder-littered slopes as silently as mice.

I began to have an inkling, then, of what Atreus intended, and the realization hit me like a blow between the eyes.

Nobody fights at night: an idea unprecedented in all the

annals of war. (I do not include Hercules' night pursuit to Pylos. Sheer opportunism – and anyway the man was a maniac.) Atreus' purpose dawned slowly on his warriors – Heroes, by and large, are never lightning thinkers – and one or two started to mutter. Atreus looked them over. They saw the menace in his cold blue eyes, and the mutterings ceased.

Winter advanced her vanguards, gales and rainstorms scoured the land. On a particularly vile afternoon – clouds scudding across a lowering sky, wind howling over the mountains – Atreus led his party out on yet another exercise – or so everyone imagined. We crossed the hills on cart tracks leading south until, at the fall of a stormy night, we reached an outlying manor on Mycenae's farthest borders held by an elderly nobleman. Here, surprised and perplexed, we gladly halted. Torches lighted the Hall and meat and bread and wine stood ready on the tables. 'Eat up,' the Marshal said. 'You haven't long.' Rain-sodden warriors devoured the victuals and crowded round the hearth-fire: the night was chilly besides being wet. Meanwhile Atreus, chewing a leg of mutton, watched servants heaping rubble in a corner of the Hall. Squatting on his haunches he arranged pebbles on the top like a toddler building houses in his playground. The audience gazed in amazement; behind the Marshal's back a Hero solemnly tapped his forehead.

Atreus rose and slapped dust from his knees. 'Gather round, gentlemen. This mound represents Midea, which we will occupy tonight. Here is the citadel crowning the top of the hill. From the foot a track just passable for wheels winds thus' – his sword point traced a crooked line – 'to the main gate – here. An easy approach – and under observation top to bottom from the gate. We shall not take it. At the side directly opposite a postern pierces the walls – here. There's no pathway to the postern, and the hillside below is decidedly steep. That is the route we will follow.'

Only the roar of wind on the rooftop broke a stupefied silence. Atreus smiled genially.

'The wildness of the night will cover our approach, but when we start to climb go quietly as worms. I shall lead, you follow in single file, each man touching the one in front. A spearman in my pay has drawn the postern's bars. When we're inside the walls you, Imbrius, with Cteatus, Philetor and Peirus will mount to the rampart walk and go right-handed killing any sentinel you meet. You, Pylaemenes . . .'

Sketching the routes on his model, Atreus detailed every man by name: parties to sweep the ramparts clear, seize the main gate guard tower, occupy a bastion which jutted on the east. He himself would lead a twenty-strong detachment to the palace, cut the sentries down and capture Amphiaraus. 'I want him alive. Whoever else you have to kill, don't harm a hair of his head!'

Atreus repeated his instructions and ensured that every Hero understood his part. He stood and settled the helmet firmly on his head. 'Can't see the stars on a night like this, but it must be nearly midnight. I intend to take Midea before the break of dawn. So, gentlemen, let's march!'

We filed into the dark. A rain-gust slapped my face, the gale snored past my ears. We followed our confident leader on a stony invisible pathway which only he could see.

*　　*　　*

A flickering light in a byre where some farmer, perhaps, attended a calving cow betrayed the little town that clustered at the foot of Midea's mount. Atreus skirted it widely, trudging miry fields that squelched dismally underfoot. The citadel-crowned eminence loomed blackly from the night. The Marshal changed direction; mud yielded to boulders and rock; the ground began to climb. Atreus halted and waited while the warband closed around him. He called the roll, pitching his voice to clear the moan of the wind. Footsore, weary, rain-soaked Heroes answered their names. (Perhaps they recognized, then, the wisdom of those unpopular long-distance marches.) Everyone was present except a warrior who had tumbled in a ravine and broken a leg; and some idiot lost in the dark.

'Right. Form single file. Follow close!'

I tracked Atreus a step in rear. For a hundred paces or so the slope was fairly gentle; then the steeps began. I crawled round enormous jagged crags, scrambled over smaller boulders, slipped on screes the winter torrents gouged. Thorn scrub whipped from the dark and clawed my face and legs. For most of the way, shield slung aback, I crept on hands and knees. The climb seemed endless; every sinew ached and my chest heaved like a bellows. I heard during lulls in the wind-blast the scrape of feet and painful gasps from the men who clambered behind me.

Atreus, barely visible in front, made no sound at all.

I bumped his back. He hissed in my ear, 'Stand still!' Like sable curtains draping the dark the walls of Midea reared from the crest. The Marshal felt his way along huge rain-slippery blocks. The man behind me hauled himself up and started to mouth a question. I clapped a hand on his teeth.

Atreus returned, a spectre black in the darkness. 'I've found the postern. Come on!' Like beads on a jerkily moving string the file traversed the base of the wall. I kept my fingers touching the Marshal's back. A small dark cavern opened in the glimmer of the stones; he stooped and disappeared. A narrow tunnel twenty steps long pierced Midea's massive wall; a rock roof brushed my helmet, elbows scraped hewn rock. Atreus rasped his sword from the scabbard. I drew my own.

I shuffled from the tunnel. This was the moment of greatest peril. Wriggling through the postern's shaft like a worm that a bird has mauled, half in and half outside, we faced the chance of discovery by watchers on the walls. Atreus guided his men into place directly each emerged. With backs to the rampart's inner face we stood in a slender alley between the wall and a row of houses. Not a light showed anywhere. Serrated rooftops leaned against a grey tempestuous sky. Ragged racing clouds, faint as flying phantoms, sped across a heaven like tarnished lead.

Dawn was not far off.

The Marshal faced his forlorn hope. With a parade ground snap he said, 'You know what you have to do. Go!'

Feet gritted on the steps which climbed to the battlements. I glimpsed the sheen of helmeted shapes running the rampart walk. A compact block of twenty Heroes followed Atreus. We twisted and turned in canyoned streets and climbed to the citadel's summit. A flight of broad stone steps, a flagstoned court and a figure which jumped from the shadows. A shout that choked on a squeal as Atreus' sword went home. A spear rattled on the flags and almost tripped me up. We crashed into the portico.

61

Men sleeping behind the pillars struggled from their cots and died before their feet could touch the ground. There were more inside the vestibule and Hall – and women too – spearmen of the guard, guests who slept where the wine had felled them, slaves and serving-maids. In tumultuous semi-darkness we killed anything that moved. The first person I slew in my life was a woman: my blade slid smoothly into her belly and slipped as smoothly out. She yelped and fell at my feet.

I faced a shadowy form and caught the gleam of armour, a spearpoint raised for the thrust. The guard commander, I later discovered; a conscientious Hero who slept in all his panoply but had forgotten to find his shield. I lifted mine and lunged full stretch. The sword point gouged his eyeball and pierced the back of his skull. He crashed to the floor, his armour clanged on the paving. I set a foot on his throat and tugged the blade free.

That ended all resistance in the Hall. Atreus bounded through an inner doorway, kicking ahead a wretched cowering slave. 'Where is Amphiaraus? Take me to the king!' The tumult had aroused the denizens of the palace: frightened figures flitted from doors and ran along the corridors. I jumped ahead of the trotting slave and cleared the way, ruthlessly cutting down anyone slow to move. Speechlessly our guide gestured to a curtained entrance. Clotted sword in hand, Atreus burst into the room. The naked Lord of Midea sat bolt upright in his bed, eyes starting from his head. A middle-aged woman beside him opened her mouth and screamed.

Atreus wiped his blade on a wolfskin coverlet adorning the bed. 'Well, Amphiaraus,' he said pleasantly, 'I have taken your city. Shall I kill you, or do you yield yourself my prisoner?'

A half-dozen panting warriors bustled into the room, saw the situation under control and hurtled out. Shouts and the clash of blade on blade echoed from the corridors where the raiders quenched the flickers of a rapidly failing resistance: gummy-eyed palace Heroes who snatched the nearest weapons and tried to fight the terrors that sprang from the night.

Amphiaraus resignedly spread his hands. 'I am at your mercy.' Atreus said in an undertone, 'Agamemnon, go swiftly to the ramparts. If we've taken the gate tower find wood and fire a beacon. Run!'

Dawn light paled a sullen sky; pandemonium thrashed in the streets; terrified citizens scurried like ants in a nest which a boar has rooted. I mounted to the ramparts, ran along the walk, skipped over bodies and reached the tower. Familiar faces peered from the top. I climbed the ladder quick as a squirrel and repeated Atreus' order. They hacked the guard-room furniture and built a fire. Flames leaped redly in daybreak dusk.

On the peak of a distant mountain a light like a lambent star answered the beacon's signal.

I struggled through tumultuous streets to the palace. Atreus had mustered his Heroes in the Hall. Four had died in the fighting. With Amphiaraus and one of his sons found hiding in a store room we formed a wedge, forced through seething mobs and gained the gate tower. A little band of Midea's Heroes, rallying from the shock, gathered in an alley and prepared to rush the ramparts. Atreus put his swordpoint to the small of his prisoner's back, forced him to the edge of the walk and shouted in his ear. Amphiaraus lifted his arms and spoke with the feverish passion of a man on the verge of death. His gallant followers lowered their spears and retreated into the houses.

The Marshal leaned arms on the parapet and gazed across the mist-hung plain surrounding Midea's mount. A noise like a tumbled hive buzzed from the town far below; a column of spearmen crawled up the zigzag track. 'They haven't a hope,' he said. 'No one can take Midea by storm. All we do now is await reinforcements.'

At midday a watery sun gleamed on the trappings of chariots, on twenty-score spears and brazen mail crowding the road from Mycenae. King Eurystheus led his Host through the gates his Marshal opened.

*　　*　　*

The Warden of Asine, pressed by his captive Lord, looked at the force Eurystheus brought and prudently surrendered. Within the space of a day a rich and fertile territory fell into Mycenae's hands. Because there had been no sack of either town, and consequently no looting, the king ordered confiscations and awarded every Hero who survived the night attack two female slaves apiece, a talent of bronze and fifteen head of cattle.

Atreus received a dozen farms, and immediately gave me half. 'You've killed your man and won your greaves, and a Hero must have a demesne. You'll be an absentee landlord, I fear: no question of your rusticating on a Midean manor away from the hub of affairs. As the Marshal's heir Mycenae's the place for you until you're old enough to warrant an important post in government. I'll have to see about that.'

Atreus flayed alive the spearman he bribed to open the postern, and nailed his skin to the wall above the gate. 'A warning to traitors. Treachery is a terrible crime. Unless we make it expensive,' the Marshal asserted gravely, 'nobody can feel safe.'

Eurystheus ceremonially bestowed on me a pair of silver-limned greaves. Immersed in the blissful euphoria of joining the Heroes' ranks I shared happily in the glory which aureoled Atreus' reputation. Heroes throughout Achaea discussed the operation, dissected it step by step and wagged their heads admiringly. A night attack – unprecedented! May be something in it after all!

Thus emboldened King Augeas of Elis hurled his Host in the dark at a stronghold in Arcadia – and was bloodily repulsed. In the slapdash way of Heroes he neglected the rigorous training and meticulous planning – a meal before battle, a soldier suborned, the chain of beacons summoning Eurystheus – which made Atreus' exploit such a shattering success. Augeas' defeat discouraged a repetition: commanders reverted to orthodox habits and fought their battles in daylight.

I have lingered over this episode for two reasons: it introduced me to combat and, more important, invigorated the expansion of Mycenae's power which began when Electryon stormed Corinth sixty years before; continued when King Sthenelus laid Nemea under tribute; and had wilted since in Eurystheus' languid hands. The escalade at Midea helped to found the mighty empire Mycenae rules today.

It also had another curious aftermath. A quarter-century later, brooding on Scamander's banks, I remembered Atreus' tactic and devised the fall of Troy.

* * *

As a newly-fledged Hero I abandoned my palace quarters near Atreus' and my mother's apartments and started a separate establishment in a commodious house by the northern gate. Supported by revenues from my Midean estates I furnished the rooms luxuriously, buying marble tables inlaid with rosettes of ivory and gold, cedarwood chairs intricately carved, bronze cauldrons and tripods, vases of dark green mottled stone from Laconia, patterned rugs and hangings woven in the town. Tunics and mantles and gaudy robes filled beechwood chests in store rooms, and jars abrim with fragrant oil and mellow vintage wine sentinelled the walls. Clymene was pleased, but not so pleased when I sent to Nauplia for slaves and she found herself sharing favours with a brace of willowy Cretans: good house-maids, handy at the looms and remarkably agile in bed. Clymene sulked.

'Who expects one woman to satisfy a Hero?' I asked her brusquely. 'You run the house and order the servants. Isn't that enough?'

'Common peasant bitches,' she sniffed. 'I wonder you bear the smell!'

'It's part of your job to see they wash – and don't be such a snob. When next we sack a city I'll take a royal daughter. That'll put your nose out of joint – your father in Pylos was only a lordling!'

Clymene feigned humility. 'My breeding is coarser than yours, I know – who can match Pelopian blood? – but all my arts in love I learned from you.' She smiled demurely. 'Is Agamemnon's pupil less versatile than a couple of Cretan sluts?'

I laughed, and fondled her breasts; and hastened out to inspect a pair of thoroughbred sorrels a dealer had brought from Euboia.

Besides providing myself with horses I had to order armour from the smiths. While tradition governs warriors and war, and accoutrements remain unchanged through many years, in the matter of mail two schools of thought contend. One swears by the ancient fashion – somewhat modified – our ancestors brought from Crete: a leather corselet, helmet and greaves – all of which depend for proper protection on a body-length shield of the waisted or concave kind. (The bards insist that Zeus and his followers fought naked, disdaining even corselet and greaves.) This school – the traditionalists – say a soldier so equipped is quicker and more active than one weighed down in mail.

Their opponents hold the opposite view: Heroes riding chariots don't jump around like fleas; a warrior wounded is a warrior the less, so protection is of paramount importance. Hence they wear the strongest armour that hammer and bellows can forge, virtually impenetrable by any brazen blade. These clanking Heroes deride the conservative school and pride themselves on moving with the times – though the type of mail they favour was introduced, so Atreus said, by a former Lord of Midea far back in Perseus' time.

The fossilized thinking of military minds was a factor that hindered me later.

I held no strong opinion either way and followed the example of Atreus, a convinced 'modernist'. The smith forged me backplates and breastplates, chin-high gorget, shoulder-guards and arm-shields and a knee-length skirt descending in triple overlapping flounces. All were solid metal, tried and tested bronze. The leather-workers' guild constructed a close-fitting oxhide casque and sewed upon the outside boars' tusks ranged in rows. Interwoven straps lined the helmet's interior and rested on a skullcap made of felt. A horsehair plume dyed scarlet bannered the crest. I favoured a waisted shield five hides thick, a ten-foot spear and thrusting sword, and brazen greaves fastened at the back by silver wire. The whole outfit cost fifteen oxen; and until I grew accustomed I waddled beneath the burden like a pregnant woman eight moons gone.

Though Eurystheus did not evict the men who held the Midean manors, their tributes flowed to Mycenae; Atreus became a richer man and the king extremely wealthy. Over-ruling his Marshal, who advised for dynastic reasons that the man was better dead, he banished Amphiaraus. He went to live in Argos; it was rumoured he had foretold Midea's fall, and thereafter earned a reputation as a seer. Following a lenient policy – pointless to sack towns and devastate land whence he intended to gather tribute – Eurystheus allowed Amphiaraus' son Alcmaeon to rule Midea in his stead. Everyone was reasonably happy; and ox-carts from Midea's cornfields swelled Mycenae's granaries.

'Which removes for a time the threat of famine,' Atreus said, 'but the people will still go short. Sooner or later we'll have to break the Theban hold on Orchomenos.'

About this time – or perhaps a little later; nowadays my memory is apt to go astray – Jason returned from Colchis. Word arrived from Tiryns that *Argo* had anchored in Nauplia's bay. Jason, the messenger added, resolutely refused to beach his ship or allow anyone on board: he held a cargo for delivery to none but King Eurystheus in person. Rumours of his return had reached us from Iolcos where he first made port; stories of his exploits during a two-year expedition multiplied like maggots in a corpse. He, his ship and crew were names in everyone's mouth; men wanted to meet the mariner and hear the truth from his lips.

Eurystheus renounced dignity – you don't normally summon kings – and escorted by palace Heroes drove to Nauplia.

Galleys bristled a sandy beach in rows; every owner had his own particular slip. A wharf of quarried stone jutted from the tide mark a bowshot out to sea; here ships were moored to offload heavy cargo. Seamen clustered in groups on wharf and beach, squatted beside the galleys and cobbled sails and cables, planed the oars. Away to the left reared Nauplia's natural breakwater, a rocky arm of land two hundred foot-lengths high; on the seaward face a cliff fell sheer to the sea. (Aerope's Leap, the people called it, after a doom-laden day in the future.) Solitary in the bay a long black penteconter rocked lazily on the swell.

Eurystheus drove down the beach till the wheels sank deep in sand, dismounted and greeted Thyestes who, surrounded by attendants, waited to receive him. The Warden of Tiryns wore a gold-embroidered cloak and a vindictive expression, and gestured angrily towards the galley.

'The harbour master commanded the fellow either to beach or moor at the wharf; he refused both. Spearmen went in a boat to enforce the orders; Jason, damn him, manned the bulwarks and fended them off Is his cargo too precious for ordinary men to see?'

67

'It wouldn't surprise me,' Eurystheus said quietly. 'Call to him, my lord: tell him the king is here.'

Thyestes cupped hands and bawled across the water. The anchor thumped aboard; oars rattled on tholes and paddled *Argo* to the wharf. Sailors whipped ropes round bollards. Jason leaped ashore and saluted, back of the hand on forehead.

Sun had burned the mariner's features brown as plough-turned soil, sea rime cindered his beard. Smilingly he said, 'I come to repay my debt, sire. Half of all I brought from Colchis awaits you in the hold. Care to see it?'

He handed king and Marshal on deck; a jerk of Atreus' head signalled me aboard. Thyestes stayed on the wharf, muttering in his beard and eyeing with growing interest a vivid appari-tion sitting in the sternsheets: a remarkably beautiful woman, red-haired, red-lipped, fierce green eyes in a face like flawless marble. Seamen lifted planks which covered the hold. Leather sacks reposed on the garboard strakes. Jason unknotted thongs, opened wide the mouths. Gold dust glittered like sun-rays in the darkness of the hold.

The king's mouth opened; silently he counted. 'Fifteen sack-loads. And this is only half?'

'Exactly half. The rest, after rewarding my crew, I deposited at Corinth's port.'

Atreus scanned the sailors who busied about the ship, stack-ing oars, coiling ropes, lowering the mast. 'These are not the Heroes who sailed with you to Colchis?'

'No. They left me at Iolcos and later landfalls in Achaea. I recruited ordinary seamen in their place.'

'Where did you leave Hercules?'

'That blasted nuisance! He behaved like a thundering pest from the start. Never, to my knowledge, been to sea before. Didn't stop him trying to interfere. You'd think his strength would help the rowing. Not so. Clumsy lout kept breaking his oar. After clearing the Hellespont we beached one day in Mysia. I told the crew to stay by the ship – the natives can be hostile on these unknown foreign shores. Hercules defied my orders, wandered into the woods. When he hadn't shown in the morning I re-embarked and left him.' Jason grinned. 'We all felt better afterwards.'

'You marooned him?' asked Atreus, startled.

'Just that. Mysia's not very far. The bastard will find a way back. Unfortunately.'

Atreus, like his brother, had not failed to notice the woman aboard. He nodded in her direction and said lightly, 'A slave you bought on the way, or perhaps a captive taken from the enemies you encountered? She's extraordinarily lovely!'

Jason made a face. 'My wife Medea, daughter of the King of Colchis. I meant to leave her in Iolcos, but a palace revolution killed my brother Pelias and we had to sail in a hurry. She won't let me out of her sight. Medea is not,' said Jason ruefully, 'a lady to be tampered with.'

(The mariner, I learned later, told less than half the truth. Medea, hoping to put her husband on Iolcos' throne, had instigated Pelias' murder in a rather horrible way. His son, discovering the facts, chased her and Jason out. Undoubtedly a woman worth avoiding!)

Slaves off-loaded the precious cargo and piled it into wagons under Atreus' watchful eye. Thyestes detailed an escort; oxen strained at the yokes and the convoy trundled away on the Argos road. Eurystheus invited Medea and Jason to dine in Tiryns' Hall. Thyestes swiftly ousted his Companion from the chariot, mounted the lady instead and took the reins. Jason, riding in my car – I had not yet found a Companion and drove myself – missed none of this little ploy, and observed wryly, 'I wish the Lord of Tiryns luck – but really he hasn't a chance. Medea won't look at another man, and she's jealous as a lioness in whelp.'

Jason described during dinner the hazards of his unique voyage to Colchis: adventures since renowned, embroidered and exaggerated, a favourite epic sung by the bards in every palace Hall. Eurystheus listened entranced; Atreus showed more interest in the mercantile side of the quest.

'I understand these Colchians are more or less barbarians?'

'Fairly savage, yes, but endowed with primitive cunning.' Jason drained his cup, and appreciatively smacked his lips. 'Vintage Pramnian, if I'm not mistaken – a change from the muck I've been drinking lately. They have little idea of their gold dust's value but are keen as knives when it comes to barter. Cleaned out all my trade goods, and demanded more. An ugly crisis developed, but Medea calmed them down. She'd fallen arse over tip in love, did anything I wanted. So I married the girl and promised to return. Otherwise we mightn't have escaped.'

The woman from Colchis sat stiffly erect in her chair, baleful viridian eyes like gems in an ivory face. Thyestes assiduously plied her with food and wine and conversation; he might as well have talked to the wall. Her attention and regard stayed immovably fixed on her husband.

Jason smiled sardonically. 'Medea's mastery of our tongue is slight as a harlot's virtue. I fear my lord of Tiryns wastes his breath.'

Atreus laughed. 'My brother's a vaunted seducer – boasts that he never fails. Do him good to assault an impregnable fort. Will you go back to Colchis?'

'Not flaming likely! I've made my pile and crave a quiet life. Settle in Corinth, perhaps – a pleasant town.'

Atreus, deep in thought, drummed fingers on the table, swallowed a honeyed fig and said, 'You've found an opening for trade, and a perennial source of gold.' He addressed the king. 'I believe, sire, we should emulate Jason's cruise, and equip an annual expedition to bring the gold from Colchis. Not a single ship, but several, all laden with the goods the Colchians want.'

Eurystheus looked doubtful. 'Surely a risky venture? You encountered many perils on the voyage?'

'Nothing insurmountable. Quite straightforward for well-found ships and capable seamen. Only one genuine obstacle. The Hellespont.' Jason wetted a fingertip in wine, traced lines on the cedarwood table. 'A narrow strait and a day's hard rowing. The entrance is a problem: tortuous and full of reefs. Northerly four-knot current and strong north-easterly winds three-quarters of the year. A proper brute.'

Atreus looked disappointed. 'Is there no way round?'

'You don't know the geography, my lord.' Jason sucked wine from his nails. 'No way round, but one across. You could disembark here' – a finger stabbed – 'at a promontory abutting the entrance, carry your cargoes over the projecting peninsula, thus, and re-embark at a bay – about there – within the Hellespont.'

'Which means,' said Atreus, 'a squadron stationed permanently at the re-embarkation bay and a fleet of wagons ashore to carry the goods.'

'Exactly. Worth it, I'd say.'

Eurystheus said uncertainly, 'The overland route crosses Trojan territory. Should we not get leave from Laomedon of Troy?'

The Marshal nodded. 'It might be wise. I can't see him raising objections. Do you consider the project feasible, sire?'

'It sounds possible, certainly – and we want that gold. The plan demands a lot of ships. We can hire galleys from Crete, and perhaps —'

'No!' said Atreus strongly. 'Let's not depend on foreign fleets. Far wiser to build our own in Nauplia's yards. It is time, and more than time, Mycenae sailed a navy of her own! How otherwise can we guarantee safe passage for our gold ships against pirates roving the seas from Phoenicia and Caria? Would Pylos threaten our shores if we had a fleet in being?'

His Marshal's vehemence shook the king. An obstinate expression crossed sere and wrinkled features. 'You urge an ambitious programme, my lord – and a considerable change in policy. This is not a matter for decision during gossip after dinner. Tomorrow, at Mycenae, we'll discuss the scheme in Council.'

Eurystheus rose from the throne. Everyone stood respectfully. Attended by squires he left the Hall. Atreus lifted a golden goblet, drank deep and winked at Jason. 'I'll sway him, never fear. You'll see regular voyages to Colchis before three years are out!'

(Atreus kept his word. A fleet navigated the Hellespont in the second year of his reign; every spring thereafter a convoy lifted anchor and sailed from Nauplia's harbour, transhipped at the Hellespont's mouth and awaited return of the gold ships. Every captain, in Jason's honour, named his galley 'Argo', and many notable Heroes crewed the first and subsequent trips. They all liked to pretend they had braved the original voyage with Jason; and the tactful bards who enshrine our legends never contradict Heroes.)

Thus was born the genesis of Mycenaean sea power – and a cardinal cause of the war we fought against Troy.

*　　*　　*

At the King's command Scribes recorded Jason's instructions for sailing a ship to Colchis, noting landfalls, tides and currents, stellar observations, the friendliness – or otherwise – of inhabitants on the way. Jason and his formidable wife then departed for Corinth, where King Eurystheus granted him a manor. (They lived in Corinth for several years and bred a brace of children; until a harried and henpecked Jason skipped to Thebes and married Creon's daughter. Medea's smouldering savagery flared in a blaze of vengeance. She immediately killed her children, followed her errant husband and contrived to poison his bride. Escaping to Athens she bewitched old King Aegeus, who installed her in his palace as a concubine. Nobody seems to know what became of her thereafter; she may be alive today – a frightening thought.)

Atreus devoted himself to building a powerful fleet. Woodmen roamed the forests, felled cypress and oak and pine; waggoners in hundreds hauled the logs to Nauplia; shipwrights adzed and sawed and planed; sail- and cable-makers laboured from dawn until nightfall. The Marshal journeyed often to the port, supervised construction and hurried on the work. Combined with his other duties – adviser-in-chief to the king, Leader of the Host, ambassador-at-large – the task became a burden heavier than even Atreus could bear.

He conceived the idea of a deputy to lighten the load at Nauplia. 'At the moment I'm forced to depend on the harbour master, and the man's a fool, and idle as well. I need someone entirely reliable to whom I can depute authority. A Master of the Ships, in fact.' He eyed me speculatively. 'You're young, Agamemnon, but I think you'd fit. Do you fancy the job?'

'Not I,' I answered fervently. 'I know nothing of ships and the sea!'

Atreus looked unconvinced, and I feared – with reason – the intention remained in his mind.

News from the north brought further distractions. The Heraclids, successfully concluding alliances, had gained an Athenian contingent, some Locrian slingers and detachments from Boeotian territories which Thebes controlled. A tentative raid on the Isthmus ravaged an outlying demesne a Corinthian Hero held, and the Warden of Corinth expected further forays.

King Eurystheus in Council considered the pros and cons

and, after long and wordy argument, proposed a pre-emptive strike. Levy the Host, he said, burst across the Isthmus, bring the Heraclids to battle and smash them into fragments with an overwhelming force. The Council's greybeards croaked agreement; Mycenae, they reminded the king, had not waged full-scale war for years, and Heroes were getting soft.

Atreus heatedly demurred. A campaign demanded a bulky train which would absorb draught animals, wagons and drovers and deprive the transport hauling timber for the fleet. A trifling delay, the Council murmured; the war would be over, the Host returned before the moon waxed full.

Very well, said Atreus; then what about Pylos? – an immediate threat they could not ignore. Intelligence sources declared King Neleus' armada crowded Pylos' beaches; only a contrary wind prevented him from sailing. The Council's recommendations delayed the launch of galleys to oppose the Pylians; would they also strip the kingdom's shore defences when an enemy was poised to wreak destruction from the sea?

Eurystheus would not be deterred. Atreus opined later (I did not attend the meeting) that the king in his declining years craved a glorious and not too difficult victory before the grave engulfed him. But he could not stay blind to the challenge from Pylos, and concocted a proposal to counter his Marshal's warning.

'We will make peace with Neleus,' he told the Council, 'and offer generous restitution for the destruction Hercules wrought. You, my lord Atreus, will lead an embassy to Pylos, taking valuable gifts, cattle and horses, slaves and gold and bronze. Offer the king our friendship, plead our deep contrition for the wrong that he has suffered.'

'You will humble yourself to Neleus?' Atreus asked.

'A wise political gambit, my lord. Pylos can do us enormous harm; we'll find it hard to retaliate. Of course, when you've built your fleet ... Meanwhile let us extinguish Hercules' troublesome brood.'

'Are you seriously suggesting,' Atreus raged, 'that I, Marshal of Mycenae, Pelops' son, sprung from Zeus through Tantalus, should crawl like a beggar to Neleus, Thessalian Tyro's by-blow?'

'He claims descent from Poseidon. It's statecraft, Atreus,

statecraft. Take when you're strong, bluff if you're weak, yield when you must. We are forced, for a time, to yield.'

'Then who,' demanded Atreus, 'will lead the Host? I can't be in two places at once!'

'I am quite capable,' said Eurystheus warmly, 'of conducting a campaign. You will make arrangements immediately for the embassy to Pylos.' He addressed the Curator. 'Provide the Marshal with an opulent treasure. I shall call a levy of arms and march when the moon is new. That is all, gentlemen. The Council is ended.'

You can't, without losing your lands, defy a royal command. Atreus brooded in sullen fury, recognized realities and the urgency of the mission, recovered his temper and quickly collected a wagon train and escort for the journey. I expected to accompany him, and made my preparations. He entered my house, brusquely dismissed the slaves packing accoutrements and baggage and said, 'You go with King Eurystheus and the Host.'

A cuirass I was holding clattered on the floor. Clymene retrieved the piece and polished a smear on the bronze. 'Why, my lord? Surely —'

'Excellent reasons. Come!' The Marshal beckoned me outside. 'I want somebody whose judgment I can trust to scrutinize palace politics when I'm gone, and also observe the Heraclid war. With Eurystheus in charge I have an ugly feeling things could easily go wrong. He's never led a major campaign, and is getting on in years. You'll watch like a hawk, Agamemnon, and send me word in a flash if anything untoward happens.'

I was not altogether displeased. A Hero far prefers the chance of a fight to a dull diplomatic mission. The Marshal watched my face, read my thoughts and said coldly, 'No false heroics, if you please. Don't get yourself stuck on some asinine Heraclid's spear. If we look like being defeated move out fast. There's no disgrace in running when the odds are turning against you.'

Atreus left in the morning. He held Mycenae's throne when next I saw him.

*   *   *

Heroes flocked to the citadel in response to the royal levy, each bringing his Companion, a troop of spearmen and slaves, and ox-carts to carry his baggage. Almost every nobleman answered Eurystheus' call; a few exceptions – sick or elderly, perhaps, or engaged in private quarrels with unforgiving neighbours – paid fines instead. Though King Adrastus of Argos offered a detachment Eurystheus declined allied aid : he reckoned Mycenae's vassals alone could beat the Heraclid gang. Two hundred chariots and two thousand spearmen encamped around the city : a considerable Host by any standards before the Trojan War. The rasp of grindstones whetting blades and bronzesmiths' clanging hammers resounded from dawn till night.

When kings go warring they delegate administrative powers to one of their principal Heroes. The machinery can't be allowed to grind to a halt. A flow of petitioners daily besieges the Throne Room, ranging from importunate Daughters seeking extended estates to humble freemen disputing a boundary fence. Wrongdoers have to be punished, and the kingdom's accounts inspected. Someone has to carry on the work.

Eurystheus summoned Thyestes.

I began worrying directly his bull-necked figure swaggered into the Hall. For an indefinite time the man would control Mycenae, his machinations only obstructed by a dotard or two on the Council. From the Marshal's dissertations I knew Thyestes' ambitions were unlimited and pitiless, his capacity for mischief beyond all calculation. He profoundly hated his brother and, since Plisthenes' death, hungered for revenge. I pretended to myself that while the king went warring he couldn't do much damage : he had no troops at his command save a slender palace guard; neither Argos nor Sparta, friendly neighbours both, were likely to lend their Heroes to further his designs. Pylos? He might be in touch with Neleus, but Atreus hurried to draw that serpent's fangs.

Neverthless I remained uneasy.

A series of minor incidents added to my anxieties. Thyestes was quartered in chambers adjoining the Marshal's staterooms where my mother kept her court. He strolled in and out of her rooms all day, his visits far more frequent than courtesy required. I managed to be present at several of these meetings –

75

Aerope declared her surprise at her son's unwonted attentions – and disliked the glint in Thyestes' eye, the responsive gleam in my mother's. She had always had a weakness for burly, muscular men – Thyestes was certainly that – and I called to mind unhappily a long-forgotten scandal dating from her spinster days in Crete. Catreus had surprised his daughter in bed with a lusty Hero, and was only just dissuaded from selling her to slavery. (The unfortunate Hero he burned alive.) They hushed the matter up; perhaps Atreus had never learned of it. Perhaps he had, and the knowledge of her frailty incited him to seduce her while Plisthenes still lived. Yet I was tolerably certain she had never horned the Marshal since her marriage.

But Atreus travelled Laconia's distant roads, the court would shortly remove to war – and my mother's fragile defences faced a redoubtable foe.

I debated the problem. Should I send the Marshal a courier urging a quick return, a warning suitably veiled? – you couldn't be blatant with verbal messages. Difficult. Atreus obeyed a royal command: nothing short of Eurystheus' seal would turn him back. Least of all a young man's callow counsel based on grounds no stronger than foreboding and suspicion.

I abandoned the thought – which proved unfortunate. From my weak-kneed dereliction flowed a torrent of catastrophe whose scars endure today.

*   *   *

Menelaus, still a Companion, arrived with the Tiryns contingent. A brisk argument and a hearty bribe – three jars of olive oil – persuaded his Hero I could take him as my driver. (While seeking a Companion among Mycenaean gentry I found nobody very anxious to share my chariot. A driver and his Hero grow very close; most of the younger men believed me the Marshal's son and feared – I wouldn't say wrongly – I might betray their confidences.)

On a morning in late summer, the harvest safely gathered, the Host started from Mycenae. Eurystheus and five sons – he seemed determined to make the campaign a family affair – rode in the van behind a sprinkle of scouts, a brilliant sight despite his age in armour washed with gold. Palace Heroes followed, then noblemen from Tiryns and our tributary cities. Every chariot, including mine, trailed a troop of slaves and spearmen, carts and mules and donkeys: the Hero's personal entourage. A long disjointed column straggled into the hills.

I saw nothing singular in the order of march, for this was my first campaign. (Atreus, when I described it, almost threw a fit. *His* chariots invariably led, all spearmen in a body marched behind; he sternly relegated transport to the rear, and a rearguard closed the column. Such uncomfortable innovations imposed by a great commander who thought in advance of his times met with nobody's approval. With his presence removed, the Heroes – King Eurystheus included – happily reverted to the old chaotic ways.)

The sun blazed down in fury, dust clouds scarved the column and gritted your teeth and nettled your skin. I sweated like a bullock beneath my newly-wrought bronze; Menelaus, lightly armoured, fluttered his whip and smirked. 'A Companion has advantages you'd never suspect in peacetime! I hope, in the coming battle, you'll order your course in a way that'll win me my greaves! Where do you think we'll find Hyllus and his friends?'

'The Lady and, I presume, Eurystheus knows.' I wiped a dribble of muddy sweat from my chin. 'I'm told we halt at Nemea tonight and Corinth late tomorrow. Slow progress. Atreus, herding the Heraclids, did Mycenae to the Isthmus in a day!'

'So I heard.' Menelaus reviewed the noisy rabble rambling through dancing dust. 'We could do with a modicum of discipline and order. A pity he isn't here.'

Menelaus spoke more truly than he knew.

After a restless night in the open at Nemea – the palace so small it could house only the king and his sons – the Host absorbed the Nemean levy (five chariots and fifty spears) and followed a mountainous road that led to Corinth. The slender sinuous track which alternately climbed and fell as the bones of the hills dictated played havoc with the column's brittle cohesion. Wagons toppled down bluffs, lost wheels and blocked the way. The vanguard entered Corinth's gates in early afternoon; the last of the stragglers plodded in by starlight.

Spies from Attica reported the enemy at Eleusis, the strength estimated at less than a thousand all arms: the Heraclid band, detachments from Locris and Athens, a Theban contingent and various odds and ends. Eurystheus called leaders to a council in the Hall. There followed a heated discussion under the flickering light of torches amid the debris of a meal, servants clearing tables, a bard crouched in a corner and crooning to himself. Gelanor of Asine and Alcmaeon of Midea advised that the Host remain at Corinth and await the Heraclids' onset, thus fighting on ground of our choosing with a firm base at our backs. The king's eldest son Perimedes, supported by Tiryns' captains, advocated seizing the initiative by an advance across the Isthmus to catch the foe unbalanced on the Eleusinian Plain. Eurystheus, normally the most cautious of men, uncharacteristically resolved on the latter course. (I am sure his greed for belated glory nurtured a rash decision.) The Host, he stated, would march at dawn to Megara, encamp there for the night and advance to battle the following day. He declined to take the Corinthian levy – which proved a fortunate judgment.

We marched before sun-up and straggled along the Isthmus track, the most horrible road in Achaea. On one side a precipice sheers to the sea, on the other are vertical cliffs. The road itself gives a goat to think. At a place called Sciron's Rocks the mountainside in ages past had fallen into the sea, the track weaves through jag-toothed boulders big as houses. Charioteers dismounted and warily led their horses. (The pass is named after a bandit chief whose band of rogues and outlaws, years before, lived in the crags and murdered solitary travellers; until a Corinthian warband sent by Eurystheus wiped them out. Afterwards, happily ignoring dates – the man was a babe at the time – Athens fostered a tale that Theseus killed Sciron. A typical Athenian invention to collect some undeserved credit – but The Lady knows they need every scrap they can filch.)

The Host emerged from Sciron's Rocks in considerable disorder. Alcmaeon exhorted the king to halt for a while and allow the column to close. Eurystheus refused; incandescent sunlight rebounded from the rocks and enclosed his ageing body in a heat like an over-stoked oven. Megara beckoned, half a day's journey ahead. The troops rambled on, sometimes twenty bowshots separating chariots.

Hillsides retreated on either hand, the Isthmus road debouched on the Megaran Plain, a featureless scrub-blotched flat-land patched by cultivated strips and isolated farmsteads. Menelaus sprung his horses for the first time since Mycenae. 'Slow down,' I told him. 'Give our retinue a chance!' I scrutinized my sweating spearmen and troupe of slaves and carts – one missing over a cliff at Sciron's Rocks – the scattered clumps in rear, each trawling its private dust cloud. We closed on Eurystheus' bodyguard marching in the van.

Dust plumes feathered the plain in front, came near and resolved into galloping scouts who reined in a spurt of pebbles and gestured towards the sun-hazed flats. Eurystheus halted abruptly, Heroes jostled around him.

'Enemy in sight!'

Menelaus hauled on the bits, the chariot rocked to a standstill. He mopped his brow and said, 'Blasted scouts can't tell a spearman from a swineherd. Ruddy nonsense – the Heraclids were reported last night at Eleusis, a day's march further on!'

Though Eurystheus likewise doubted the scouts' unlikely news his innate prudence directed precautions. He issued hurried orders: Heroes wheeled about and galloped to hasten laggards. All the chariots present – roughly half the total – formed a ragged line, each with attendant spearmen tramping behind. Baggage detachments were left where they stood, forlorn blobs on the tawny plain.

I dubiously watched a scrambling deployment, and told Menelaus to station the car on a flank. 'There'll be horrible collisions when this mob starts to move – let's keep clear as long as we can!' The Host – such as had made their ground – halted in line of battle and waited for the dawdlers to arrive.

'I hope the king won't keep us extended all the way to Megara,' Menelaus observed. 'Damned difficult driving in thorn-scrub.'

I shaded my eyes and stared into the haze. A shimmering curtain of dust banded the horizon. The sun flicked slivers of light on the mist like gold-specks scattered in sand.

'Scrub or no scrub, brother, your driving is going to be tested. The Heraclids have stolen a march and sprung a surprise. We're only half assembled, and they're closing on us fast!'

Commanders had seen the enemy; orders and counter-orders

79

rattled along the line. Indecision and argument eddied like leaves on a flooded stream. The discussion continued far too long: an elderly palace Hero solemnly quoted encounters from wars Electyron waged. The majority wanted to stay where they were till the Host was fully mustered; young hot-headed Heroes advised an instant attack. Gelanor of Asine – a most impetuous youth – ordered his chariot forward, his spears obediently followed. Others copied his example, chariots bowled from the ranks. Eurystheus shouted commands that were drowned in the crunch of wheels, struck hand to brow despairingly and pointed his spear to the sky. Like a wavering breaker spent on shoals the battle-line advanced.

'Incline to the left,' I told Menelaus. 'Keep well on the flank if you can.'

I settled my helmet firmly, tested the chinstrap, fronted shield and hefted the ten-foot spear, scrubbed a sweaty palm on the warm dry figwood rail. From a throat that was suddenly dry as a stone I instructed the spearmen to close on the chariot's tail.

A wheel lurched over a boulder, Menelaus cursed. I recovered balance and planted my feet on the plaited leather floor, screwed eyes against the sun-glare. I distinguished garish helmet plumes, and silvery harness-trappings; a line of cantering chariots fronted a rolling dust cloud.

The enemy were nearer than I'd thought.

It is hard to recall impressions on the threshold of your first big battle. From epics sung by bards I cherished vague conceptions of chariots charging in rank, thundering hooves and singing wheels, warriors bellowing war-cries and maddened horses neighing, an ear-splitting clash when they met. Then a furious, swirling mellay till one or the other broke, a galloping pursuit and killing, killing, killing.

It was not like that in the slightest.

Companions curbed their horses for fear of outstripping the spearmen running behind. The line dissolved in fragments before it had gone a bowshot; Heroes examined the enemy ranks for details of horses and mail, forms and faces – maybe seeking personal foes in order to settle scores, or fighters famously formidable to be avoided at any cost – and directed their drivers accordingly. Chariots swerved, criss-crossed, scraped hub against hub in flurries of violent language. Panting troops of spearmen followed the erratic tracks.

The leading cars clashed wheel to wheel, spears lifted, hovered and plunged.

The combatants dispersed in individual duels. Chariot circled chariot, Heroes hacked and stabbed, spearmen battled spearmen – holding the ring, as it were, while their principals fought it out. Companions adopted traditional tactics and manoeuvred to take opponents in the rear where spears met shieldless backs; their opposite numbers wrenched on bits to counteract the moves. Vehicles swirled in circles like puppies chasing their tails. Dust-towers spiralled from every fight and mingled in a canopy. Triumphant yells and death-shrieks resounded from the murk.

Whatever I expected, it was certainly not this.

Menelaus edged far to the wing and overlapped the Heraclid line. No immediate enemy presented himself in front. I ordered my brother to halt, and tried calmly to assess the scene. King Eurystheus gave battle with barely half his troops, and kept no reserve in hand – an elementary error Atreus had often condemned. The individual duels ensured a protracted struggle. A very untidy battle, the outcome most uncertain. Prudent to hold my hand and see how affairs turned out.

A contest an arrow-shot distant came to a gory end. A Mycenaean warrior – I recognized Gelanor's piebald horses – pierced his adversary's guard and skewered him through the buttock where cuirass jointed brazen skirt. The spearhead spitted bowels and bladder; the Heraclid lurched from the chariot and his armour clanged around him. His Companion dropped the reins and ran; the dead man's spearmen sheltered his flight and then, their Hero killed, fled like hunted deer. Gelanor and his retinue stripped the corpse's armour, piled it in the enemy car and trotted with his prizes briskly from the battlefield.

Similar little scenes were everywhere repeated. Victors in the duels on either side quickly collected booty while spearmen stood on guard. Triumphant loot-laden Heroes drove from the conflict in both directions; the scattered personal tussles grew noticeably fewer. Did the result, I wondered, depend on the ultimate duel? – or on which side won the heaviest load of plunder? Only round Eurystheus, conspicuous in gilded armour, did organized fighting continue: he and his sons, a compact brand, battled a cloud of chariots.

'Get moving, Agamemnon,' Menelaus growled impatiently, 'else we won't win any booty, and I'll never win my greaves!'

So *that*, I concluded dimly, was why Heroes fought so heroically. Remember I was young and extremely inexperienced.

A violent interruption whipped decision from my hands. A chariot whirled from the dust-fog, the Hero brandished a spear and bawled at the stretch of his lungs: 'Who'll fight Theseus of Athens, Theseus of Athens!'

I surfaced sharply from a stupor the weird manoeuvres had induced. 'Take him, Menelaus! The idiot's out of control. Whip up and turn behind him!'

Theseus thudded past, the naves of his wheels whirred a foot from our own, an ineffectual spear-jab thumped my shield. Menelaus swung his team in a tight two-cornered turn, and flailed his whip. The chase led across the battlefield's front, we swerved round interlocked chariots, skirted bunches of spearmen and slowly gained on Theseus whose driver wrestled the reins to curb his bolting horses. We crashed through a group of Locrians swinging slings of fine-spun wool; a stone bounced off my helmet. Menelaus closed on the quarry, guided his chariot abaft the nearside wheel. Theseus frantically twisted about, tripped on the rocking floor-thongs, cowered behind his shield. I lifted my spear for the thrust.

'The Lady save us!' Menelaus howled. 'Look to your left!'

I turned my head. A solid wall of chariots raced like a tidal wave, a roaring, thundering breaker galloping wheel to wheel. Long hair streamed in the wind of the charge, tawny naked bodies – absolutely naked – manned the hurtling chariots, a bugger and his catamite in each, and every one hell-bent on death or glory. They wore neither helmets nor shields; a menacing cable of spears glittered like frost in the sun.

The Heraclids' hidden reserve flung in at the critical moment: the Scavengers of Thebes.

My spear haft slid from a paralysed hand. 'Run!' I shrieked. 'Turn right! Drive like the wind!'

Menelaus needed no telling. We tore from the field of

Megara like men possessed by furies, overtook panic-struck Heroes who had also seen the horror, scraped past slower drivers, jolted over corpses, smashed through scrub and bushes. Like a gathering storm behind us we heard the Thebans' war-cries, the roll of drumming hoofbeats and strident bronze-tyred wheels. Menelaus flogged his horses, I gripped the rail and struggled to keep my feet, glanced fearfully over my shoulder.

Gradually but certainly our fast Venetic thoroughbreds outstripped the Theban horde.

We left the plain in a welter of flying vehicles that crammed the hill-girt funnel gating the Isthmus road. Ruthlessly my brother thrust sluggish teams aside, tipped in the ditch a lumbering three-horse chariot – an artful trick, nave lifting nave – and overhauled satisfied Heroes who had left the battle early with chariot-loads of plunder. The track, approaching Sciron's Rocks, made overtaking difficult; I pretended I carried to Corinth the king's victorious tidings, and demanded right of way. Grumbling, they shuffled aside. Having gained the lead I shouted that the Scavengers were loose; if they wanted to save their skins they had better move like lightning.

Menelaus cracked his whip; we hurriedly drove on.

He passaged Sciron's Rocks at an unbelievable trot. I averted my eyes from a vertical cliff which plunged below the nearside wheel to rocks like fangs and a boiling sea. The track thereafter seemed level and broad as a highway newly paved. In the glow of a crimson sunset we saw Corinth's grey-walled citadel perched on its craggy mount, and walked our weary horses up the serpentine track to the gate.

Conveying bad news is always unpleasant, and often highly dangerous if the recipient loses his temper. Bunus, Warden of Corinth, became neither flustered nor angry. He seated us in the Hall and offered watered wine – I emptied a double-handled cup without drawing breath – and heard our tale in silence. I confessed we had fled from the fight and therefore could not describe the finish of the Scavengers' tempestuous charge. I surmised that the attack, so furious and surprising, must have swept Mycenae's forces from the field.

Bunus summoned his captains; trumpets on the watch-towers blared alarm; spearmen manned the walls and Heroes donned their armour; messengers ran to the town below. A long procession – men, women, children, cattle, sheep and horses – ascended to the citadel for refuge. By sundown Corinth was ready for escaladers.

None appeared. Instead the gates admitted a trickle of survivors: exhausted, staggering warriors, many badly wounded. Among them my old tutor Diores, his forearm gashed from elbow to wrist. I embraced him almost in tears – delayed reaction was setting in – fed him meat and wine and bound the wound. Remnants of a defeated Host crowded the palace Hall; torchlight conjured movement from leaping boars and lions painted on the walls and sculpted the faces of grave-eyed Heroes listening to Diores' tale – a story that crowned calamity.

King Eurystheus was dead.

'They caught him at Sciron's Rocks, pulled him from the chariot and hacked him in pieces,' Diores said tiredly. 'I was driving a bowshot in front, and saw it happen. Hyllus cut off his head and stuck the skull on a spear – which so delighted the bastards they sang a paean of triumph and danced around the trophy. Checked the pursuit. Only reason I escaped.'

He dragged his hand across a dusty sweat-caked face. 'Some of our Heroes dismounted and fled on foot through the hills; but there won't be a lot of survivors – you don't get quarter from the Scavengers. The Athenians' prisoners might ransom themselves if they're lucky. Otherwise...' The hand that lifted a cup to his mouth shook like a leaf in the wind.

I strove to collect my shattered wits. The king's death changed the disaster's whole complexion: from a military defeat now stemmed a political vacuum whose implications were serious indeed. The chance Atreus awaited fell unheralded from heaven – and he was far away and unaware. I recalled through mists of fatigue his appreciation, years before, of the course events would take when Eurystheus died: a short sharp bicker between Marshal and royal sons, the Heroes supporting Atreus and a peaceable accession.

Were they alive, those sons – my friends Perimedes and his brothers whom last I had seen fighting around the king? I put the question sharply to Diores.

He opened drooping eyelids. 'Can't say for certain. Damned unlikely. Probably killed with Eurystheus.'

Which, if true, opened without hindrance the Marshal's path

to the throne – or the way of any Hero bold enough to seize it, someone on the spot.

Thyestes.

The name rang in my ears like a death-cry. I must summon Atreus from Pylos; not a moment could be lost. I forced jaded limbs from the stool and addressed the Warden. 'Lord Bunus, I want fresh horses. I go at once to Mycenae.'

Bunus eyed me searchingly. 'The Heraclids might be anywhere. You will travel the road tonight?'

'Tonight.' Menelaus sagged in a chair; I shook him awake. 'Come, brother – let us try your driving in the dark.'

*   *   *

Moonlight silvered the track, carved sharp-edged ebony cloaks from clefts and crags. Menelaus drove in a daze, ready to drop from fatigue – nothing is so dispiriting as defeat. Periodically I relieved him at the reins, and sombrely reflected on the reverses a day had brought. My baggage and spearmen lost – but easily replaceable – the throne at risk, a battle incompetently fought, Heroes contending like brigands hunting loot, Mycenae's Host destroyed.

Our methods of making war warranted speedy reform. A vision of the Theban charge flashed on moonlit scarps: an irresistible onslaught combining velocity, vigour and order.

That was the way to win battles.

The horses, mettlesome and frisky, tugged my aching arms. The armour weighed like mountains on my shoulders. 'Menelaus,' I said, 'there was something horribly wrong with our tactics today!'

Menelaus, asleep on his feet, snored gently in reply.

Chapter 4

WE reached Mycenae at cockcrow. Figures flitted like wraiths in the half-dark heralding dawn: peasants carrying mattocks, women bearing pitchers for filling at the Perseia spring, ploughmen driving ox teams to the fields. The long night's journey had subdued our horses, which hung on the bits and plodded up the hill to the citadel. A sleepy guard was unbarring the gate, the chariot rattled through. I tumbled tiredly out.

During the journey from Nemea onwards I kept wondering whom I could trust to carry the news to Pylos. Neither Menelaus nor I had slept from one sunrise to the next; battle-strain and incessant driving had taken toll; we were in no condition for a whirlwind non-stop trip across Achaea. Moreover I had to stay in Mycenae and try to control events till the Marshal arrived. I could not entrust the message to anyone guarding the citadel; he might inform Thyestes – the very last thing I wanted.

A young squire crept furtively past, clearly hoping to escape our notice. (He was returning, he told me afterwards, from bedding the wife of a merchant away in Argos, who lived in a house overlooking the Chaos Ravine.) I knew him well; for moons he had dogged my footsteps, silently adoring, and asked me once to take him into my household. I refused because his pedigree was not entirely noble – an unfortunate mésalliance between his grandfather and a slave girl – and only men of the purest blood should serve the Marshal's heir. But he was likeable and dependable – and this was no time for priggishness.

'Talthybius,' I called. 'Come here.'

Torn between guilt and eagerness he shuffled from the shadows. I said, 'Talthybius, I am entrusting to you a mission of vital importance. On you will depend Mycenae's fate; you must not fail. Take this chariot to my house, yoke fresh horses from my stables – the Kolaxian greys are the best – ask Clymene for food and a wineskin. You will drive to Pylos as fast as the horses can go. Change horses at Sparta; leave the greys in payment. Go like the wind till you're climbing the mountains past Lerna – by midday you must be beyond pursuit. At Pylos give Atreus my signet ring and tell him: "King Eurystheus is dead. Thyestes holds Mycenae. Return at once." You will not mention this to another soul; and I expect the message to be delivered within two days.'

I slipped from a finger the ring with my personal seal – a jasper bezel portrayed my ancestor Zeus grappling a lion in either hand – and made the lad (he was just fifteen) repeat the instructions word for word. Talthybius made no bones about it, asked no questions. Serious and slightly portentous, a youth abruptly cloaked in a mantle of responsibility, he grasped the nearside bit to lead the chariot off. I added, 'When you return, Talthybius, I'll take you as my squire and, after you pass the tests, make you my Companion.'

His countenance glowed scarlet, tears started in his eyes, he slapped a horse's neck to hide his emotion. (Later on, at Troy, Talthybius drove me to battle.)

I had to move quickly. It seemed to me essential that news of the Battle of Megara should not be known in Mycenae – carried, perhaps, from Corinth by a runner across the hills – before my messenger to Atreus was well on his way. After that the outcome lay in The Lady's lap. I guessed Thyestes would act directly he heard the battle's result. He had brought from Tiryns twenty or so retainers: Heroes, Companions and spearmen. Against these stood the citadel's slender guard: sick or elderly lords and young Companions. Thyestes' men would obey his commands; whom would the palace people support when they heard of Eurystheus' death? Unwise to assume they would back the Marshal. Even if they did so I doubted victory in a fight between Thyestes' stalwart Heroes and a leash of youths and dotards.

The focus of loyalty centred on Aerope; as the Marshal's wife and Mycenae's paramount lady she might command obedience from men on either side. Long enough, maybe, to confuse the issue and hold the fort till Atreus returned.

Four days to wait, I reckoned. I must see my mother at once and convince her of the role she had to play.

Tersely I briefed Menelaus. He looked perplexed – my brother was never quick in grasping a new idea – and, so tired we could hardly put a foot in front of the other, ascended the road to the palace. Dust and wind and weariness had stung my eyes to tears, daybreak's crimson streamers danced across the sky like banners whipped in a gale. A palace sentinel's spear-shaft barred the gate; then recognition dawned and spear and jaw both dropped. We crossed the Court and shuffled along dim corridors, climbed stairs to Aerope's apartments. A fat old dozing maidservant squatted against a door-jamb. She floundered to her feet, backed against the door and stammered, 'No, my lord, no! I pray you, do not enter....'

My mood allowed no sympathy for conscientious slaves. Thrusting the crone aside I tapped on the doors and pushed them open.

The room was all but dark, heavy woollen hangings covered a window opening on a balustraded balcony. Furniture loomed like rocks in a gloomy sea. I paused to accustom my eyes, and looked towards the bed: a foursquare ebony frame inlaid with gold and ivory, covered by purple rugs and snow-white fleeces.

Something heaved and plunged on the bed. Strangled animal grunts and a piercing feminine squeal.

I ran to the window, sent a table flying and wrenched the curtains apart. Grey dawnlight flooded the room. Hand on sword-hilt, blade half drawn, I faced the bed.

Thyestes sprawled atop of Aerope, both stark as their mothers bore them.

He pulled himself free, rolled to the bedside and stood, prick rampantly erect, a look like nightfall on his face. Aerope lay on her back, thighs obscenely spread, eyes wide in a terrified stare.

I felt angry, sick and fearful. Menelaus stopped on the threshold, breathing gustily through his nose, a horrified snarl on his lips. For ten heartbeats the tableau froze, and no one moved.

Thyestes searched for a weapon in one quick glance, saw none, and stealthily as a prowling cat padded towards the window. He crouched like a wrestler, arms wide and fingers

88

clawed. Muscles rippled his hairy frame and sweat-drops beaded the skin. I waited paralysed, more afraid than ever in my life. He came so close I could smell his body, and spoke in a rasping whisper.

'This is death, Agamemnon.'

Menelaus streaked from the shadows, flashed sword from sheath and rested the point on Thyestes' spine.

'Stand still, my lord!'

Thyestes lowered his arms, turned slowly about. 'So. The second fosterling cub of Atreus' brood. Confronting an unarmed man, and therefore brave as lions. Why are you here? Has warfare frightened you back to your den?'

Menelaus prodded his navel. He said tightly, 'Shall I kill him, Agamemnon?'

Aerope screamed. 'For The Lady's sake, for the womb that bore you ... I beseech ... do not ...'

My blade came out. I crossed to my mother, wrenched back her head by the hair and laid the edge on her slender neck. Veins laced the skin like faint blue threads. 'You whoring bitch!' I choked. '*You* above all deserve to die. Betraying the Marshal —'

'If you harm Aerope,' said Thyestes in even tones, 'I will slay you in turn with my naked hands.'

I believed him. He would kill us whatever the cost. I rammed my mother's head on the pillow, stood behind Thyestes and let him feel my sword. (A sword-point pricking his belly and another on his backbone would make a normal man believe his end had come. Not the smallest quiver betrayed any fear.) I tried to think. A bloody massacre in Aerope's room would not help Atreus' cause, for Thyestes' crime would never be known with all the protagonists dead. His infamy must be blazoned abroad, his punishment come from the Marshal's hands.

We had to leave the adulterers alive. Talthybius by then was away on the Argos road, having told the guard commander his intended destination – a mandatory precaution lest travellers failed to return. Thyestes must assume we had sent a message to Atreus and would try to intercept it. The squire needed time to drive beyond his reach.

For as long as we could manage Thyestes must be penned.

You may think I made a stupid, muddled decision. With

89

hindsight you could be right: my brother and I should have taken the risk and killed the couple at once, thus saving much grief in the future. Remember I was tired, my brain fuddled by fatigue – and still sufficiently youthful to flinch from desperate measures.

However much you hated her, would *you* despatch your mother?

I said, 'Menelaus, stand guard on the door. Let nobody enter. I'll call when I want you back.'

Menelaus scowled, viciously prodded his point in Thyestes' stomach and left the room. Alone with the enemy I considered ways and means. I had to keep the lion at bay, prevent a leap for my throat. I jabbed his spine and said, 'Lie on the bed.'

Thyestes walked unhurriedly to the bed and lay beside Aerope. I backed beyond his reach, felt for a stool and changed my mind. A man was a fool to be sitting when a wild beast waited to spring. I cradled sword on forearm, and listened to the thumping of my heart.

Sunrise slanted yellow shafts on the bedroom's wall, silhouetted the balustrade's convoluted pillars. The citadel wakened; feet clattered in the Great Court, voices rumbled, a bucket jangled on paving. A day guard relieved the night watch; commanders shouted orders; a steward scolded laggard slaves. Footsteps in the corridor, muffled inquiries and my brother's gruff replies. Dogs barking persistently from the direction of Zeus' Tomb; a distant crunch of wagon wheels, the drover cursing his beasts.

Inside the room it was dim and cool and quiet. I kept my eyes on Thyestes, and felt the lids begin to drop. Fiercely I gripped the sword-hilt and forced myself awake.

He looked at me slyly. The pair of naked bodies – his deep brown, hers white as the rumpled fleeces – lay side by side on the coverlets. His hand crept to Aerope's belly, wandered to her hip, caressed the tuft of hair between her thighs. My mother went rigid, and gasped. His fingers probed more deeply, worked busily in the cleft, his weapon climbed revoltingly erect. Aerope closed her eyes and clutched her breast, breathed deeply in jerky spasms, spread her legs.

Thyestes held my eyes, and leered.

I gulped the bile that clogged my throat. Sword aloft I strode to the bed, detected a sudden stillness and the tensing of his muscles – and stopped in time to elude the lunge. Slowly I withdrew, and rested blade on forearm. Not a flicker of expression betrayed the failure of his gambit. His fingers went on delving. Aerope moaned.

My body ached with tiredness, every sinew cried for rest. Despite the spectacle performed before my eyes sleep enveloped my mind like a soft and soothing cloak. I stamped my feet, rapped blade on ribs, studied familiar furniture: ebony chairs and marble tables, a silver sewing basket running on castors, crystal jars and phials littering a chest, ivory combs and brazen mirrors, an earthenware pitcher for drinking water embellished with black and red octopi, a lionskin rug by the bed. Flies buzzed monotonously and settled on my face. I let them rove; the irritation helped in keeping me awake.

Thyestes watched me intently, his eyes like splintered ice. Even when he ejaculated his gaze never wavered a fraction.

Time crawled past. The sun climbed high in the sky, the pillar-patterned square of light retreated from the wall and spread a golden carpet on the bedroom's marble paving. Near noon, I thought exhaustedly, and time to move.

I called Menelaus.

He came in at a run, sword outstretched, checked at the sight on the bed and muttered imprecations. I beckoned him close and whispered in his ear, 'Harness a chariot, the fastest team you can find. Bring it to the palace gate. Be quick, Menelaus!'

He strode out. I backed to the door, shot the bolt by its leather thong: a means to discourage intruders with my brother no longer on guard. Thyestes rolled on his side, propped chin on hand and spoke for the first time since my long ordeal began.

'You can't keep us here for ever. What do you hope to accomplish, piglet?'

I levered shoulders from the door – far too restful, I nearly slept standing – and said, 'Your death, Thyestes, your death. Not today, not tomorrow – but one day I will kill you slowly, slow as the vigil I spent in this room.'

Thyestes laughed, and made to rise from the bed. I advanced a pace and pointed the sword. He laughed again, rolled on his back and closed his eyes. Aerope lay still as a log and gazed blankly at the spiralled whorls that decorated the ceiling.

The door rattled, Menelaus shouted. I whipped the bolt free and leapt into the corridor without a backward glance. 'Run, brother!' We sprinted along passages, brushed past wondering Heroes, ladies and gaping servants, hurtled across the Court and jumped in the waiting chariot. 'Argos,' I snapped, 'and use your whip!' The vehicle rattled dangerously down narrow swerving streets, stormed through the citadel gate and out on the Argos road.

Menelaus settled the horses to a steady rhythmical gallop. He said, 'The Lady knows what you're at, Agamemnon – but if I don't sleep soon you'll be driven by a waking corpse!'

*   *   *

A chamberlain conducted us to the Hall where King Adrastus relaxed on the throne and chatted to Tydeus, his Leader of the Host, and a little group of Heroes. Announcement of our names chopped talk like a falling axe. I saluted the king and said, 'Sire, I pray an interview in private.'

Adrastus' nutcracker features advertised astonishment. 'Agamemnon! Menelaus! I thought you gone with your Host to scupper those troublesome Heraclids! Is the war decided? Sit beside me, have some wine and tell me all the wonderful deeds your Heroes performed!'

An old-fashioned man with old-fashioned ways, heroics dear to his heart, ceremony in his blood, averse to haste. Numbly I resigned myself to guest-and-host politeness, conventional exchanges and formal conversation. You do not hustle kings. Tydeus, luckily, was a more perceptive man beneath his forbidding appearance. He said, 'These fellows are out on their feet, sire. Best hear what they have to say before they collapse completely!'

'In private, my lord,' I begged.

Adrastus clicked his tongue. 'Most unmannerly. Can't we finish our wine? Young men nowadays are always in such a hurry. Very well.' He waved a hand; his Heroes unwillingly withdrew, leaving only Tydeus. 'Courtesy yields to your wishes, my lord. What is your news?'

I had come to Argos on Atreus' behalf to find him help and

fighting men. I must use every possible plea, even reveal the horrible episode in Aerope's bedroom – a private family affair I would rather have left unsaid. It had to be told. Adrastus, notorious for his archaic views and adherence to outworn codes of Heroic behaviour, could conceivably be swayed my way by Thyestes' treacherous adultery. (After Helen and Paris eloped I used the same incentive to rouse Achaea's Heroes.) No ruler likes to interfere in foreign dynastic quarrels, but Aerope's evil seduction might inflame his chivalrous instincts and spur him on to punish the guilty man.

Or so I hoped. I had yet to learn the covetousness of kings.

In short strain-blurred sentences I told the entire story, beginning at our defeat and Eurystheus' death. Adrastus tut-tutted and waggled his hands. When I described my discovery in Aerope's room his face went stiff and he listened in stony silence. I swore that Thyestes would seize the citadel, usurp the throne and oppose the Marshal's entry.

Tydeus said, 'What are Thyestes' forces?'

'A score of spears he brought from Tiryns. Roughly a hundred men if the guards in Mycenae support him.'

'How many men has Atreus taken to Pylos?'

'His household Heroes, and fifty spears.'

'Fifty spears won't take Mycenae,' Adrastus said. 'Thyestes, I fancy, holds the whip. Why appeal to me, Agamemnon?'

'To beg a favour on Atreus' behalf. The Marshal will arrive here in four days' time. Sire, I ask you to reinforce him with a warband from your Host.'

'H'm. Why should I? A purely Pelopid dispute. I'm not sure it's politic for Argos to meddle. These family quarrels —! Besides, your Host has been defeated and there's nothing to stop the Heraclids crossing the Isthmus. Hyllus may be tempted to invade the Argolid – and I'll want my warriors here, not galli-vanting to Mycenae. Very difficult.'

'The Heraclids,' I pleaded, 'suffered casualties in the battle, and are probably licking their wounds.'

'Supposition, Agamemnon – a dangerous base for action. I'll have to think it over. No immediate hurry.'

'Sire,' I said desperately, 'there is urgent need for haste. Apart from Thyestes' garrison, survivors from Megara's battle will be dribbling back to Mycenae. Defeated men don't look for further fighting. They'll probably resign themselves, accept the situation and bow to Thyestes' rule.'

Tydeus spoke long and earnestly in Adrastus' ear. A cunning expression puckered the king's lined features. He nodded sagely and said, 'Agamemnon, I am inclined to grant your request. Thyestes' crime deserves most condign punishment. A gentleman, so-called, who dishonours his brother's wife —! Revolting behaviour!' A flush tinged shrivelled cheeks. 'You request a warband – when Atreus arrives he can have my entire Host. I'll order it to be mustered and ready.' Adrastus cleared his throat. 'There's one condition.'

'Which is, sire?'

'Argos henceforth holds in tribute Midea and Asine.'

I rocked on my feet. Menelaus wedged an arm behind my back and whispered hoarsely, 'Tell the old fool to jump in the sea!'

I said wearily, 'How can I give such an undertaking, sire? I am not king of Mycenae!'

'You speak for Atreus who, if I support him, will soon be king. *If* I support him, Agamemnon. Otherwise ... not. Thyestes wins the throne.'

My brain refused to function. I closed my eyes. Menelaus said, 'If my brother agrees to your condition how can we guarantee the Marshal will approve?'

'You'll both accept my hospitality in Argos,' Adrastus said kindly, 'until Thyestes is sent packing and a compact written by Scribes bears Atreus' seal and mine. Hostages, my dear Menelaus. Somehow I don't think Atreus will sacrifice his grandsons. Dammit, what am I saying? I mean his sons, of course!'

I met Adrastus' gaze. He smiled benevolently, his eyes were hard as stones. I said dully, 'You leave no choice. I promise that Atreus King of Mycenae will grant Argos the tributes of Midea and Asine.'

'Well said!' Adrastus exclaimed. He clapped his hands. 'Bring cups and flagons! Let's celebrate the compact!'

My legs gave way. Despite Menelaus' supporting arm I sank slowly to the floor, and pulled him down as well. We sagged there shoulder to shoulder like a pair of broken dolls. Tydeus laughed out loud.

'It's not wine they need, but sleep. Ho, Diomedes! Fetch litters, and take these gentlemen to bed!'

*　　*　　*

We slept like carcases till next day's noon, and woke in a palace bedroom superbly furnished. Squires attended our wants, conducted us to a bath where attractive female slaves sluiced away sweat and grime and oiled and anointed our bodies. Ravenously we devoured roast venison and pork, baked octopus and cockles, beans and lentils, cheese and figs and pears. Bloated like bladders we fell on the beds and slept again. In the evening cool I sauntered out to take the air in the Court; an affable palace Hero, armoured, sworded and shielded, appeared from a passage and strolled beside me.

'I regret,' he said, 'you may not pass the gates. Otherwise the citadel is yours to go where you will.'

Our confinement was not unpleasant. We dined in the Hall and talked with Argos' Heroes, all agog to hear the details of Mycenae's rout at Megara: the Scavengers' performance caused several valiant warriors to worriedly scratch their heads. Adrastus was all benevolence; his Leader of the Host heard courteously my theories on tactical reforms. I met again his son Diomedes and fascinated him by demonstrating the battle with pebbles and twigs on the portico floor. He concurred in all my criticisms – a most percipient youth.

An insect soured the honey: a nagging anxiety about Atreus' reaction to the undertaking promised in his name.

On the fourth day's forenoon the Marshal, outstripping his scouts, rocketed through the gates and reined outside the palace. Floured by dust and rank with sweat he clanked into the Hall and saluted the king on his throne. Adrastus mouthed the polite banalities court conventions demanded, ignored Atreus' testy impatience and beckoned me forward.

'Your – ah – son, my lord Marshal, will tell you all you should know.'

Atreus' eyebrows climbed in surprise; he swung on me and said, 'Agamemnon! Why are you in Argos?' His face beneath the grime was set in hard harsh lines, blue eyes fierce and cold as a wintry sky. He gripped my arm and led me from the group around the throne, pushed me on a bench and said, 'Now. Your messenger told me Eurystheus is dead. Thyestes holds Mycenae. That's all I know. Details, please – and fast!'

For a second time I sketched the sorry tale. Atreus stood rock-still, one hand grasping sword hilt, the fingers of the other traced a moulding on his cuirass – a boar's head, viciously tushed. When I came to the scene in Aerope's room I stammered, the words sticking in my throat. I sent him a nervous glance. A look like death rampaging ravaged his face.

I described the compact agreed with King Adrastus.

In a voice like the hiss of sword from sheath Atreus said, 'The doom I devise for Thyestes shall make men shrink from the telling. Aerope ...' His face twisted. Visibly he controlled himself, lifted his chin and stared at a garish wall-frieze of warriors battling bulls. 'You bartered away the cities we took. You did right. Adrastus shall stand by his bargain.'

He left me on the bench, returned to the throne and said, 'Sire, I honour the agreement Agamemnon made. Now, where is your Host?'

Adrastus said smoothly, 'Mustered, as I promised, in the citadel and town, ready to march at dawn.'

'At dawn?' Atreus looked at the sunlight shafting clerestory slats. 'At dawn? Half the day remains, sire. Sound the trumpets, assemble your men. I lead them to Mycenae directly they've yoked the chariots!'

The king turned helplessly to his Leader of the Host. A wondering admiration crossed Tydeus' swarthy features. 'It shall be done, my lord. We'll be hammering Mycenae's walls before the day is out!'

*   *   *

The Host marched; and I remained in Argos. Courteously but adamantly Adrastus refused to let me go: until Atreus as King of Mycenae ratified the treaty I must remain his guest. The king relented enough to permit Menelaus' departure. 'You're the valuable hostage, Agamemnon,' he confided, 'the son Atreus cherishes most. He doesn't give a damn for Menelaus.'

Guardian Hero alongside I anxiously paced the ramparts of Argos' deserted citadel and saw nothing of Mycenae's bloodless taking. Thyestes viewed the approaching Host, armour gleaming in westering sunlight, counted more than a thousand men and considered the hundred-odd spears he commanded. He collected his family, including Pelopia and a son named Tantalus, and fled by a secret postern above Perseia's stream. They vanished in the mountains and were lost in evening dusk.

Submissive Heroes opened the gates; Atreus strode to the palace, told Tydeus to man the watch-towers and post strong guards on the walls. He summoned to the Throne Room every nobleman in Mycenae – a handful had run with Thyestes – and extracted from the treasury Eurystheus' crown and sceptre. Under the wavering light of torches he seated himself on the throne, removed his helmet and donned the golden crown and proclaimed himself King of Mycenae, Tributary Lord of Tiryns, Nemea and Corinth and lesser cities under Mycenae's sway. The nobles loudly acclaimed him – Tydeus' Heroes, grimly alert, lined the Throne Room walls – and Daughters sanctified the ceremony by burning a lock of his hair.

A son of Pelops ruled the realm that Perseus founded.

Menelaus described all this at Argos the following day. Adrastus smilingly signified I was free to go where I would and loaded me with gifts – a gold two-handled cup, bronze three-legged cauldrons, jars of oil and seven fleeces. The cunning old rascal might well be generous: the tributes of Midea and Asine henceforth flowed to his store rooms. Including, I remembered sourly, those from my own demesnes.

Driving back with Menelaus I broached a topic we had sedulously avoided – an unpleasantness tucked to the backs of our minds. 'Is our mother ... safe?'

The road descended a slope in a series of bumpy shelves; Menelaus pulled to a walk and made a face. 'Thyestes refused to take her. Left her to face the music alone. The man's an abomination!'

The gradient eased; Menelaus whipped the stallions to a trot. I said, 'Has Atreus seen her?'

'No. She's confined to her apartments, allowed one servant to attend her wants, and a guard has been set on her door. Nobody dares to mention her name to Atreus. I wouldn't either, if I were you. He has changed greatly, Agamemnon, very taut and grim, all the sparkle gone. Thyestes, by the way, is declared officially banished.'

My brother had something else on his mind, some wretched

news he could not nerve himself to tell. He made a business of guiding the horses round an insignificant pothole. I said, 'Come on, Menelaus. What's worrying you?'

He flicked an imaginary fly from the offside stallion's quarter and said, 'You won't like this. Directly we ran from Mycenae Thyestes sent spearmen to sack your house and kill everyone inside. All your slaves are dead.'

I hung on hard to the chariot rail. 'Clymene?'

'Clymene also.'

I could not speak. The rest of the drive has gone from my mind like frost in noonday sun. I remember at journey's end Mycenae's grey-gold walls, spearheads gemming the ramparts, a picture blurred in tears. I prefer not to dwell on my feelings. You might well deride such weakness: sensible men don't grieve for slaves; they are nothing but cattle and often less valuable. I will say only this: of all Thyestes' crimes it was sweet Clymene's killing which drove me to a vengeance that horrified the world.

I found Atreus in the Throne Room; he was tense, unsmiling and very busy. 'A job for you, Agamemnon. Interrogate survivors from Megara, and give me a casualty list – killed, missing and prisoners. We must reconstitute the Host, replace dead men with sons or kindred, re-allot lands which have lost their lords, negotiate prisoners' ransoms. Adrastus wants his troops returned, and we can't have Mycenae defenceless.'

'Have we so much time before the Heraclids attack?'

'Do you think I'd be sitting here if Hyllus and his ruffians were pouring across the Isthmus? No. They haven't appeared in force. Raiders are savaging Corinth's fields, but the citadel's safe. No sign of a strong invasion – yet. They'll be back, so the sooner we recoup the better.'

(It transpired that we gave the Heraclids so rough a handling before the Thebans sent us flying that King Aegeus of Athens, mourning losses, forbade his levy to advance beyond the battlefield. Hyllus was hot for invasion, the Scavengers indifferent. After bitter disputes the troops dispersed. Hyllus left a detachment under Iolaus at Megara to harry Corinth; the rest of the Heraclids retired to Thebes.)

Not a word did Atreus say about my mother, though the scandal itself was common knowledge – chamber-slaves learn everything, and you cannot stop them gossiping. He had vacated the Marshal's apartments and moved to the royal quarters: a splendid suite which occupied the topmost floor of a wing above the Great Court. I was told he went to Aerope only once – a short, low-voiced interview – and nobody knows what passed, or ever will. She stayed immured, invisible but somehow palpable, like a decaying corpse in an upper room whose stench pervades the house.

I met Gelon, come from Rhipe with Diores, cataloguing oil jars in the palace store rooms, and enlisted his help. I cross-examined returned Heroes and Companions while Gelon noted their statements on papyrus sheets. Though much of the information was sparse and confused – you don't see much in a fight but your enemy's threatening spear – I was able to tell King Atreus the losses were less than we feared. Roughly a third of the Host was either killed or enslaved; the remainder – Heroes, Companions and spearmen – eventually returned to their manors. In one way and another the king restored Mycenae's first-line strength, and the average age was younger – no bad thing.

Atreus gave Menelaus his greaves, and land on the Argive border. He granted me a rich estate a short ride from the citadel, and another demesne near Tiryns. 'You'll still have revenues from your Midean farms, but it's wrong for my successor – not for a long time yet, so take that smirk off your face – to hold only tributary lands. Incidentally, I haven't had a chance to discover what Eurystheus did wrong, and I want a detailed report.'

During the hectic days that followed Atreus' enthronement I annexed Gelon as my personal Scribe (Rhipe ran like a well-greased wheel, and Diores declared him superfluous) and visited my new domains, listed animals, freemen and slaves, arable fields and pastures, manors, byres and ploughs, and calculated the annual production. Gelon conned the records he made and announced, 'You've become a wealthy gentleman, my lord. You own nine cattle herds, four of goats, ten droves of pigs and twelve flocks of sheep. I believe that only the king has more.'

'We're all landowners, more prosperous or less,' I answered, 'and the king is simply the richest. Atreus has taken all Eurystheus' demesnes, and his possesions must be ten times mine at least. So they should be – otherwise why be king?'

I gave Atreus, as commanded, my views on Megara's battle, emphasized the orderless approach march and the extraordinary – to me – conduct of the fighting. 'Is it *really* customary,' I inquired plaintively, 'for gentlemen to leave the field when they think they've won enough booty?'

'Yes,' said Atreus. 'It is – but they're supposed to return to the conflict when they've disposed of it somewhere safe. Why else do Heroes fight? For honour, allegiance, glory, renown? Nonsense! Forget the ballads our bards recite – those songs depicting Heroes as they like to think they are: valiant, proud, magnificent. Fish-feet! Your average Hero at bottom is a rapacious, self-seeking, treacherous sod. The only sanction that controls him is the threat of losing his lands. So he'll follow his king on campaign, and make it a source of profit.'

This scathing portrayal scarred my illusions badly. I groped for palliation. 'I think you're unjust, sire. War – and farming – is the Hero's way of life. Gentlemen spend moons in practising skill at arms and exercising their bodies.'

'Of course. You can't grab an enemy's armour unless you kill him first. You've got to be good or you don't win loot.'

I reflected dismally on the bitter cynicism clouding Atreus' outlook, so unlike his satirical good-humour before he went to Pylos. He had indeed changed. 'At Megara,' I admitted, 'booty seemed everyone's main object. The Scavengers had different aims.'

'Theban bugger-boys!' the king snorted. 'Uncontrollable fanatics! Tactics based on theirs will lose nine battles out of ten!'

The Scavengers' aggression, control and discipline had won the Battle of Megara. I kept the thought to myself: the king's demeanour discouraged dissent.

'The affair was a shambles,' Atreus continued, 'because spearmen crowded on chariots as they did in Perseus' day. Fatal. Always, when I led the Host, I ordered spears and chariots to manoeuvre as separate bodies. When I saw the enemy I advanced my mobile armour, spearmen in rank a bowshot behind, a reserve of both in the rear. If our chariots broke the enemy line spears followed and exploited. Were the armour repulsed it rallied behind a spearmen screen.'

'Which,' I murmured, 'is the sort of sensible tactic I had in mind. You have never lost a war, so it must have worked.'

'Not once. Directly the chariots began to move the spearmen broke into separate squads which followed their personal lords. Exactly like Megara. They share in the plunder, you see – and nobody in Achaea fights for anything else. It's hard to break a tradition dating from Zeus' time.'

Except the Scavengers. From this depressing discussion was born a resolve to form, whenever the means arrived, a body of disciplined charioteers bent on winning battles before they scrambled for booty.

       *   *   *

I had buried the bits of Clymene's body Thyestes' murderers left. He had sent Stymphalian axemen, men notorious for their pitiless ferocity. (Fifteen years later I burned Stymphalos, slaughtered the men and enslaved the women and children.) I shifted from my ruined house to quarters in the palace, but seldom set eyes on Atreus. He immersed himself in work and travelled extensively, visited Corinth where Heraclid raids had ceased and husbandmen rebuilt burned-out manors; and inspected demesnes he had granted to newly made Heroes. Because he had not appointed a Marshal he personally supervised training on the Field of War, and led a warband to Arcadia to chastise cattle thieves. Curator at heel he scrutinized store rooms, tallied enormous jars of olive oil and corn, checked fleeces, hides and bales, counted sacks of gold and brazen ingots stored in musty basement chambers that contained Mycenae's power, the wealth that she imported and the goods she traded abroad, all centralized in the citadel, directed by the king and inventoried by Scribes.

The bribe delivered to Pylos, Atreus once grumbled on return from probing the treasury, had made somewhat of a hole in the realm's resources. None the less, he conceded, Eurystheus had judged rightly: the gifts and the Marshal's diplomacy persuaded King Neleus to abandon his intention of raiding Mycenaean shores.

'Neleus is failing,' Atreus told me. 'Sixty if he's a day, and the Hercules raid quite broke him up. Nestor, his only surviving son, is running Pylos. *He's* no chicken, either – twice your age.'

Dogmatic and full of bounce, but an intelligent man with un-usual ideas. He is rebuilding the palace and citadel on a differ-ent site inland on a hill overlooking the bay – and is leaving the place unwalled. Nestor declares that fortifications didn't save old Pylos from Hercules' destruction; and in future his navy replaces walls.'

'Like Cretans in olden days,' I ventured.

'You know that much history? I suppose you're picking Gelon's brains. Nestor may be right, but Achaeans conquered Crete despite King Minos' ships. A long time ago: Acrisius, I believe, commanded that invasion.

'Pylos,' the king continued, 'can never be allowed to black-mail us again. Far too expensive. So our navy must be more than a match for theirs. I visited Nauplia's yards a fortnight ago and sacked the harbour master – an idle layabout. Now nobody is properly in charge, and I'm sending you to supervise the shipwrights.'

Atreus surveyed the sculpted bulls' horns cresting the palace building – we were sauntering in the Great Court – and added, 'There's another question. Since . . . Thyestes went, Tiryns lacks a Warden. I considered Copreus, my most experienced noble-man, an outstanding warrior, holds a lot of land – and is bent as a bowstave. I need a strong administrator: he'll be re-sponsible both for Tiryns and the whole shipbuilding pro-gramme.' (That hesitant reference to Thyestes was the nearest he ever came, until Aerope's end, to mentioning the disgrace that burned him like searing brands.)

Atreus entered the portico and sank on a marble seat. His escort – a Hero guarded the King of Mycenae wherever he went and sentried his chamber at night – leaned against a pillar discreetly beyond earshot. I said, 'You need a Hero who can think – rare enough, I allow – and a Scribe to keep his records.'

'Quite so. You and Gelon. I'm proposing your name to the Council tomorrow. A formality, of course.'

'Your older Heroes will make me a target of jealousy. Is it wise to arouse enmity?'

'Do you care? You're unscrupulous, ruthless and tough, Agamemnon, and one day you'll be king. You'll have enemies in plenty before you've finished: better start learning to cope with them now. You'll take over Tiryns and Nauplia before the old moon sets, so make your preparations.'

(I disagreed, then and afterwards, with Atreus' brisk assessment of my character. All Heroes in these hard times have to be tough to survive, and some are perfidious crooks. I do not believe I am worse than most. A forbearance afflicting my nature – as, for example, tolerating Achilles' tantrums during the Trojan siege – has often proved pernicious. In politics and statecraft – the dirtiest of games – I played the hands as I found them, and who can blame me for that? In war I obeyed the prevailing rule: no mercy for those who resisted – why should I be condemned for behaving as everyone does? I have come to the conclusion that a frightening reputation rests largely on my appearance: from Atreus I inherited an impressive stature, eagle features, blazing blue eyes and a cruel mouth. And for one who became the most powerful king in all Mycenae's history it was fortunate indeed that very few men – perhaps Menelaus alone – have ever discerned the kindliness a forbidding exterior hides.)

I duly informed Gelon, who was gravely enthusiastic. We strolled the ramparts by the north-west postern and discussed the problems arising from assessing and accounting the revenues of Tiryns: a much more complicated matter than auditing Rhipe's receipts. As for the shipyards, he confessed his inexperience in maritime accounting, hazarded a guess that affairs were in a muddle and asserted a belief we could sort the business out. I confided my scheme of raising a chariot squadron, and asked him whether systematic payments were a feasible alternative to dependence on battle-plunder.

Gelon rested elbows on parapet and gazed across the sun-soaked valley. 'You mean a force of paid professional soldiers? It has never been done in Achaea, my lord, although his forefathers' – he pointed his chin at Zeus' tomb in the foreground – 'kept a standing army in Egypt.'

I stared, astonished, at the ancient oak tree shading the mound. The usual offerings that peasants deposited – dead doves, small pottery figurines, wheat-cakes – littered the ring of standing slabs. 'Zeus, the first of the Heroes? An Egyptian?'

Gelon looked equally surprised. 'Didn't you know, my lord? Zeus' family certainly came from Egypt, though not of Egyptian breeding.'

Leaning on the wall while a sentry paced behind us he related a history I suppose I should have known; but nobody bothered to tell me and, a man of the moment, I seldom delve in antiquity. Moreover I doubt whether many Achaeans outside the Scribal sect learn more of the past than their pedigrees. Four hundred winters ago – for me an unimaginable aeon, to Gelon as but yesterday – a dynasty of foreign kings, sprung from nomadic shepherds, governed the lands of the Nile until the Egyptians rose and expelled them. Some of them crossed to Crete: the Cretans, a peaceable race, unwisely allowed the refugees to land. They promptly fortified a place called Gortys, which to this day remains the island's only fortified city.

'These exiled kings,' Gelon explained, 'had ruled Egypt from fortresses guarded by monstrous walls and therefore felt uncomfortable without ramparts. The limestone walls which girdle Avaris, their capital in Egypt, soar higher than the tallest in Achaea.'

From Gortys the aliens, within fifty years, captured neighbouring Phaestos, then Malia and Knossos, overran Crete and established rulers in all the cities.

'Impossible!' I protested. 'Cretans can fight if they have to – remember their record at sea.'

'The men from Egypt,' Gelon said, 'brought chariots and horses, both unknown to Cretans. Chariots, my lord, were decisive then, and later in Achaea.'

Towards the end of this period Zeus, grandson of a deposed shepherd king, first saw the light on Mount Dikte where his parents found temporary refuge from a palace uprising in Knossos. ('In fact his name was User,' Gelon interpolated, 'taken from a king in ancient Egypt. Cretan tongues soon twisted the word to Zeus.') He grew to manhood, peerless in war and cunning in counsel, valiant and wise, a paladin and paragon who held all Crete in fee.

Then fire fell from heaven.

An insignificant island called Thera lay a day's sailing northward from Crete. A volcano humped from the island's centre; intermittent earthquakes tumbled houses. (Manifestations of dread Ouranos, who lives in the bowels of the earth, whose name nobody speaks. Indeed to *think* of him invites disaster. I will hurry on.) On a summer's day three centuries ago an appalling eruption buried Thera under twenty spears' lengths depth of ashes. Successive shocks carved clefts in the crater's sides. Sea gushed into the blazing hollow.

The entire island exploded.

The sound stunned people in distant Colchis, desert dwellers in far Sumeria trembled at the thunder. Masses of molten rock, burning ash and debris whirled to the roof of heaven. Ash and vapour blackened the sky and plunged the world in darkness from Thracia to Egypt – one of many plagues afflicting the country around that time. A poisonous blanket fell on Crete and smouldered three feet deep.

Worst of all were the waves.

The speediest horse ever foaled can gallop just so fast: the waves came four times faster. Walls of water from sunken Thera battered the Cretan coast. They were fifty feet high, so Gelon averred, and utterly engulfed the towns on the northern shores. Blackened, cracked and cloaked in ash, inland Knossos alone survived.

I listened enthralled. A memorial of catastrophe in days beyond man's memory lingered faintly in bardic lays; Gelon told the story as though his eyes had seen it. I said, 'How can you know of happenings which are so remote in time?'

'My ancestors were there, and wrote it down. We have the records still.'

'Ancestors? Are you then of Egyptian or Cretan blood?'

Gelon sniffed. 'Certainly not. Long ago my people, defeated in war and enslaved, were taken into Egypt by the victors. We brought the art of writing, and found employment in the palaces. When the shepherd kings were evicted they carried away their Scribes. Part of my tribe – called Dan in our tongue – arrived in Crete.'

I glanced at his crow-black hair, nutbrown hook-nosed features, the long grey robe all Scribes affect. Undoubtedly he and his fellows, both in character and appearance, seemed different as Phoenicians from the fair-skinned men of Achaea.

'Go on. What happened next?'

King Zeus and his surviving kindred surveyed the ravaged island. A crust of virulent ash blighted the earth. Nothing would grow, the people starved. Zeus decided to cut the ties and begin again in a different country. He salvaged broken ships from the fields where the waves had flung them, scoured the southern harbours which had suffered lesser damage. Embarking all the descendants of those who came from Egypt seventy years before, the Scribes and chariots and horses, he sailed northwards to Achaea.

Simple rustic husbandmen inhabited the land, peaceable and unwarlike, dwelling in open villages. Zeus and his warriors destroyed them like a holocaust. Thousands died, more became slaves; many fled from the fury and sought shelter in the mountains.

'Where their children's children are present-day Goatmen,' I remarked.

'Even so. Implacable enemies, my lord, ever seeking vengeance for the wrongs their forbears suffered. As you well know.'

Before Zeus died, Gelon continued, his followers ruled in Pylos, Elis, Argos, Sparta, Mycenae. Arcadia became a no-man's-land where the old race fought the new. (It remains so in part till now.) They fortified the towns, bred multitudinously over the centuries – 'Achaean families are always large,' Gelon commented wryly – and extended their sway to the realms we know today.

'Zeus died peacefully in bed, and there he lies: Mycenae's earliest king, the founder of your line.' Gelon pointed to the oak-surmounted mound. 'He and Hera his queen, his sons and other relations. All wear masks of beaten gold, their bodies encased in gold and silver. And nowadays' – a tinge of contempt – 'the common people believe him a god.'

'Much to the Daughters' annoyance.' I dredged my memory. 'Haven't I heard of a brother Poseidon, a famous mariner who founded the House of Perseus?'

'He led Achaea's navy three hundred years ago. Pylos claims his grave and the royal line his blood. I think they err in both: our records show him lost at sea while fighting Sicilian pirates. None the less the lower orders worship him in Pylos.'

An ox-cart squealed up the road from the town, laden with jars and hides and cloth – some outlying manor's tribute. Children played 'catch-if-you-can' among the burial ground's stone mounds, their voices muted by distance like mosquitoes whining at dusk. A peasant trickled a handful of corn in the dust of Zeus' Tomb, folded his arms in prayer, seated himself with his back to a slab and drowsed in the oak tree's shade. I said wonderingly, 'So I'm descended from Egypt's kings. You've certainly opened my eyes to the past! The bards sing none of this.'

'The bards!' Derision was plain in Gelon's tone. 'They come to us for history, then embroider and distort. They sing to flatter their patrons; and only in chanting pedigrees which Heroes know by heart do they tell the approximate truth. Even then they often invent to hide unsavoury gaps. If you'll forgive me, my lord . . .' Gelon finished in some confusion.

'What do you mean?'

The Scribe hurriedly disclaimed any reflection on my ancestry which, he swore, the documents traced generation by generation through Pelops back to Zeus. But, he added uncomfortably, the Perseid line was not so well attested. Perseus' mother Danae certainly had no husband: in Argos when her pregnancy grew obvious her angry father, Acrisius, immured her in a watch-tower. Perseus later founded Tiryns and rebuilt Mycenae's crumbling walls. His descendants asserted their distinguished progenitor could not have been misbegotten; so the bards concocted a story that Zeus' ghost raped Danae – when it comes to protecting the blood line the bigger the lie the better.

Gelon quoted similar tales to cover lacunae in noble descents. 'You see, my lord,' he ended apologetically, 'nobody likes bastards dangling like rotten fruit on the family tree.'

'No one does,' I agreed. 'In my own genealogy I've occasionally doubted the line from Zeus to Tantalus. Some odd names. . . .'

'I promise you, my lord,' Gelon said earnestly, 'your line is quite unsullied, each ancestor truly attested. You can see them in our records, if only you could read.'

(Years afterwards, when Gelon became my trusted Curator and friend, he confessed that my lineage from Tantalus back was almost entirely bogus. I laughed and smacked his back; I'd suspected it all along.)

'Which you refuse to teach me,' I smiled, 'because Scribes won't share their skills.'

'We are forbidden. A short-sighted policy. When we and our writings are gone, what will remain to tell Mycenae's splendour, the prowess of her warriors, the mightiness of kings?

Naught but minstrels' lying songs handed down by word of mouth, increasingly warped as the centuries roll, perverted and encrusted by unbelievable tales until, in a thousand years, people might easily doubt the Heroes ever existed.'

I laughed. 'As a man who lives in the present, Gelon, you can't expect me to worry a thousand years ahead. We have idled too long by this sun-warmed wall, and I'd like you to check the stores I am taking to Tiryns.'

Side by side, grey-robed Scribe and kilted, bare-bodied Hero, we climbed the rubbled path to the palace gate.

*   *   *

The citadel of Tiryns stands on a jagged mound in the plain within sight of the sea. Walls of tremendous hewn stone blocks rise from natural rock, the mightiest rampart on earth, fifty feet thick and thirty high. The resonant galleries piercing the walls – where Atreus prisoned the Heraclids – lead to magazines and store rooms which are second in the wealth they hold only to Mycenae. On top of the mount the palace buildings stand three storeys tall, plastered and painted white, a beacon for mariners entering Nauplia's harbour. Twisting streets and steep stone steps weave between houses and workshops; and a walled enclosure juts from the northern ramparts: a shelter for refugees in times of danger. Around the hillock's foot homesteads, hovels, shops and byres spread like a mottled apron.

Tiryns became my home, and during the next few years I seldom saw Mycenae. The palace Heroes – some twice my age – obediently accepted me as Warden: they recognized in Atreus' son their future king. Midean cattle raids had ceased on Atreus' conquest; our friend Adrastus of Argos allowed no dissensions within his realm; so nothing marred the harmony of my peaceful life in Tiryns. I expected some disturbance when Adrastus sent an embassy demanding tribute from Epidauros – an inoffensive city notable only for the medical clinic Aesculapius founded. But Argos and Mycenae had reached an understanding about their respective spheres of influence: Atreus' eyes henceforth were turned to the north, to command of the Isthmus and dominion along the Corinthian Gulf.

Epidauros conceded an annual tribute and asked Adrastus in

return to sweep the mountains clear of robbers and rustlers who for years had pestered their lands. Which Adrastus did, and so began the extension of Argive influence that Diomedes in years to come so vigorously continued.

The construction of ships at Nauplia progressed in a desultory way. Twelve lay beached and ready; twenty more were building in the yards. All were triaconters, thirty oars a side, the largest craft afloat. (Because you may be ignorant of maritime affairs I explain that triaconters are longships painted black, shallow-draughted for beaching, brazen beaks for ramming, sternposts carved in outlandish shapes: a lion-head or seahorse. The captain has a cabin in the sternsheets, a flimsy wooden hut whose walls are gaudily painted; amidships rises a mast of fir stepped in a hollow box. To shelter the rowers from sun a collapsible oxhide canopy supported on poles runs fore and aft. Cargo is carried in coffer-like holds between the rowers' benches.)

I bought slaves to augment the work force, trebled wagons and woodmen hauling timber from the forests, chased carpenters and shipwrights. I needed seventy galleys to match the Pylian fleet. The yards disgorged triaconters to swell the ranks on the beach; I then faced a shortage of crewmen. While you can teach any idiot to row – except perhaps Hercules – you must have sailors to navigate, steer and handle sails and sheets: the experts who keep a ship afloat when storms and reefs are about. I shipped pressgangs to Crete, whose maritime traditions reach far into antiquity, and obtained the men I wanted. Force was seldom needed; with Cretan overseas trade in the doldrums unemployed sailors were glad to find work.

I embarked on my maiden voyage in a galley beached at Nauplia. Rowers ran the vessel to the sea, put mast and sail aboard, trimmed the ship, fixed oars in leather slings. The master, a red-haired ruffian, face blackened by sun and salt, straddled a monstrous steering oar and hoarsely bellowed orders. Sixty oars struck the water together, the galley leapt like a startled horse and glided into the bay. The coxswain piped on a flute to mark the rowers' rhythm.

In ruffled water outside the bay the crew shipped oars and hoisted sail: layered squares of linen stitched together. The sun dashed sparks from dancing waves, the galley rolled and plunged, spindrift sprayed my beard. The crimson prow climbed high on the combers, pitched in the troughs between. A strange sensation invaded my guts. I clutched the backstay and swallowed. A grin exposed the master's yellow teeth. 'Over the lee side, my lord, if you please.' I knelt at the low beech transom and voided into the waves, the first of many tributes I paid the sea.

(In all my many voyages I invariably spewed while the ship still sighted harbour, and never felt the smallest qualms thereafter.)

After wading ashore from this short trip and driving back to Tiryns I met Menelaus in the Hall. I seated myself on Perseus' marble throne, ordered wine and food – I was ravenously hungry, my breakfast gone to the fishes – and inquired his news. My brother said he brought a message from the king, pointed an elbow at noblemen and ladies who loitered within earshot, and pursed his lips. I stuffed cheese in my mouth, led him to the hearth and mumbled, 'If you now feel we're sufficiently private will you kindly tell me what Atreus wants?'

'He is going to kill Aerope.'

I choked on my mouthful, sprayed crumbs and gulped down wine. 'How? When? Where? By The Lady, he's taken long enough to make up his mind!'

Menelaus said wretchedly, 'The king has decided on a public execution, and is bringing her to Nauplia to throw her into the sea from the cliff above the harbour. He sent me to bid you choose the place and make arrangements. And other matters.'

I found, to my annoyance, the wine cup shook in my hand. 'Why drag her to Nauplia? If he demands that kind of death why not the Chaos Ravine?'

'It's the place of execution for common criminals. Aerope is noble, a daughter of Minos' line.'

I felt both shattered and numbed. Atreus' belated vengeance seemed unnecessarily cruel, like a cat that plays with a mouse before the claws unsheathe. (I did not know, nor Menelaus, he had sent searchers after Thyestes, hoping to kill them together – hence the delay.) 'A public execution. Atreus will bring spectators from Mycenae; Nauplia and Tiryns will gloat upon her dying. I'll have no hand in this. Tiryns' gates will be closed, the garrison confined while the procession passes by.'

Menelaus attentively examined the pleatings of his kilt. 'I said there were other matters, Agamemnon.'

'You did. What do you mean?'

Menelaus took a breath, and looked me in the eye. 'Atreus ordered me to watch our mother's killing. I refused. He then offered me the choice of banishment or death.'

My mouth sagged open in stunned disbelief.

Menelaus said, 'Yes – I couldn't believe it either. Since you left Mycenae the king has changed for the worse – solitary, brooding, dangerous. I believe his lust for revenge is driving him demented. Nothing but the deaths of the couple who dishonoured him will purge the venom poisoning his mind.'

'He's got Aerope. Does he know where Thyestes has gone?'

'Elis. King Augeas gives him sanctuary.'

I pressed fingers to throbbing temples. Heroes wandered in groups in the Hall, conversed in undertones and sent us speculative glances. My squire Talthybius, flagon in hand, came to fill our cups. I waved him away.

'You agreed to see our mother flung to her death, or you wouldn't be here. She deserves her fate. How can I blame you for accepting Atreus' ultimatum?'

'I bring you much the same conditions, Agamemnon.'

'What! The king commands my presence on the cliff?'

'You, and all the noblemen of Tiryns.'

I hurled my goblet in the fire. 'No! It's abominable! I'd rather quit Tiryns, live exiled in Sparta or Pylos and never set eyes on Atreus again. I will leave before night!'

Menelaus said wearily, 'I said *much* the same conditions. Atreus offers you one choice only: obedience or ... death.'

I supported my shaking frame on a hearthside pillar. 'The king is undoubtedly mad! And, if I refuse, does he think I shall stay in Tiryns to await his retribution?'

'His executioners have travelled in my train. Unless I tell them otherwise they will come for you by sundown.'

I am ashamed to say I burst into tears. That Atreus, whom I worshipped, was ready to destroy me opened a bottomless void that swallowed my soul. For one dark frantic moment I considered calling on Tiryns' Heroes, barring the gates and challenging the king. But who would support a youthful Warden against his formidable sovereign?

Menelaus gripped my hand. 'Don't torture yourself, Agamemnon! Aerope is doomed whatever we do – why should we sink in the welter? Remember the scene in that dreadful room! Can you truthfully say she hasn't earned her punishment?'

'I don't give a damn for Aerope,' I gulped. 'But Atreus....'

'Atreus at the moment is not quite sane. He believes that if Aerope's sons witness the execution people will think her condemnation justified. He feared you'd disobey him – and he loves you, Agamemnon. He can't bear the thought of you defying him, turning against him, hating him. He'd rather you were dead.'

'Small comfort for me in that. And you, my brother? Prepared to tell the executioners —'

'Not really.' Gently, with the back of his hand, Menelaus brushed tears from my cheeks. 'I reckoned you'd be shrewd enough to see the light. Senseless to sacrifice life and land in the cause of a faithless slut who happens to be our mother.' He paused. 'I take it you agree?'

I nodded miserably.

'Good. Now we both need a drink.' He signalled Talthybius, who came running. 'Your oldest vintage, lad, and fill the cups to the brim!'

*   *   *

The procession left Mycenae at daybreak. From Argos it collected a rabble of curious spectators – tradesmen, peasants, slaves, women, even children – and reached Tiryns by early afternoon. Spearmen marched in the van, followed by Heroes in chariots. Then a solitary ox-drawn four-wheeled wagon used for carting hides – your nostrils shrank from the stench as it passed. Four strapping Thracian slaves – Atreus' executioners – walked behind the wagon. The king in a gilded travelling chariot, his palace Heroes, more spearmen in the rear.

Aerope rode in the wagon, her seat a bale of hay. She dressed in the height of fashion. Naked rose-tipped breasts thrust from a short-sleeved bodice of transparent azure linen scalloped by silver threads. A girdle of solid gold suspended a quilted apron studded with gems and striped by golden sequins. Seven separate flounces of a gaudy embroidered skirt flowed gracefully to her feet. Carefully waved hair clung to her skull like an ebony cap, a tress in a bandeau across the top. Carmine stars adorned her cheekbones, the mouth a scarlet wound in a face the colour of chalk. She clasped her hands in her lap; wide dark eyes stared trancelike straight ahead.

She had never looked more beautiful.

Menelaus led Tiryns' contingent to follow at the tail, driving tight-lipped through the chattering mob from Argos, riff-raff rapidly swelled by trash that spewed from the town and harbour.

I waited at the place of execution, and gazed across the sea.

The day was sultry, breathless; from horizon to horizon clouds blanketed the heavens. Thunder muttered remotely, flashes sheared the skyline. A grey and oily sea breathed out sluggish surges which broke in splatters of foam at the foot of the cliff. Gulls spiralled across the surface like snowflakes flurried by wind.

Just below a watch-tower perched on the summit an ancient landslide had sliced a rocky platform broad enough to hold two hundred men. I stepped to the edge. The cliff fell sheer for fifty feet, bulged on a rampart of rocks, dropped like a plumbline to wave-washed crags which the height made small as pebbles. Tufts of grass and withered bushes mottled the face of the fall. At the brink of the ledge lay a red-striped woollen rug.

This was the place I had chosen for ending my mother's life.

I left Talthybius and my spearmen escort, climbed to the watch-tower and viewed the procession approaching the precipice's landward face. From the shoreline a path crept upwards, stony, steep and tortuous, impassable for wheels. The column halted, riders dismounted. The executioners guided Aerope to an open litter borne on the necks of four strong slaves.

The procession crawled up the zigzag track.

I stumbled from the watch-tower and waited on the ledge. The cloud-pall floated lower, tendrils of mist stroked the crest of the ridge. The air was oppressive, hot in my lungs. Lightning gashed like a sword, thunder rumbled and crashed. Far away on a leaden sea, moth-like in the gloom, a galley ran for shelter in the harbour.

Spearmen rounded the ridge-top's scarp, marched to the platform, halted. Heroes and Companions tramped behind. The litter appeared, and swayed to the red-striped drugget. A Thracian murmured commands, the bearers lowered their burden. Aerope stayed on the rough wood seat, blank-eyed, lost in a dream.

Atreus strode forward, folded his arms and stood at her back. He wore Mycenae's royal regalia: golden crown, purple gold-hemmed cloak, gold-and-ivory sceptre slanted on his shoulder. His face was a mask of stone, blue eyes sunk in the pockets, the brilliance somehow faded. Greyness powdered his hair like rime. He had aged ten years in the moons since last I saw him.

Noblemen and spearmen thronged the platform. The rabble scattered and climbed the slope, chattering and yapping, and found convenient viewpoints. I felt a touch on my arm. Menelaus. His auburn beard framed ravaged features pale beneath the sunburn.

The executioners, not unkindly, raised Aerope from the litter and supported her between them. She swayed a little, and shuddered, red lips parted and quivered. For an instant our glances crossed. I looked away.

There was terror in her eyes, and that I could not bear.

The executioners led Aerope to the brink. Atreus, close behind, followed step by step. She bent her head and looked at the sea two hundred feet below. She lifted her gaze to the sky, and closed her eyes. Thunder rolled in a roaring crescendo, a searing flash of lightning split the clouds.

The mob on the crest was quiet and tense and still.

The executioners shifted their hold. Each put a hand on my mother's shoulder, the other spread on her back. They looked at Atreus, questioning. He said something I could not hear. The men dropped their hands, and left her free.

Atreus levelled his sceptre, rested the golden eagle between Aerope's shoulders and lunged with all his might.

She uttered a strangled cry, forlorn as a night-rail's call. The body hurtled out and down, curved in the air and smashed on the bulge of rocks. It bounced and plummeted down, broken and limp as a rag, and plunged to the sea. A transient fountain spouted, small as a raindrop's splash.

The gulls circled and squawked and swooped on Aerope's grave.

Chapter 5

THE Heraclid War had delayed the expedition to Colchis. I assembled ships and crews and collected trading goods in warehouses near the wharf. We still needed Troy's permission for transhipment at the Hellespont and use of the overland route. Atreus decided I should head an embassy to King Laomedon, and provided royal gifts – gold and bronze and scented oil – to smooth negotiations.

I took three triaconters. With a following wind and tranquil sea we beached at dusk successively in Andros, Chios and Lesbos, and on the fourth day lowered sails at the Trojan shore. Lookouts had reported our approach; a warband barred the beach. Rowers paddled my ship to the shallows; I jumped overside and waded ashore alone. A youthful, handsome commander introduced himself as Hector son of Priam, son of Laomedon.

'Who are you, my lord?' he asked. 'From what country have you sailed across the highways of the sea? Is yours a trading venture, or are you pirates roving on chance?'

'I salute you, Hector son of Priam,' I answered formally. 'My name is Agamemnon, son of Atreus of Mycenae. I come in peace to seek a boon from Laomedon King of Troy.'

The punctilious greetings over, Hector accorded permission to beach the ships and disembark my followers. His warband stayed alert, shields fronted, spears on guard. They outnumbered us two to one: a wise precaution on a coastline frequently raided. (A pity it failed disastrously when Hercules made his landfall.) I introduced my Heroes, detailed a guard on the ships and mounted in Hector's chariot. We drove across a windy plain and saw Laomedon's mighty ramparts towering in the distance.

In fact the walls he built on the ridge were not as straight and steep as those at Mycenae or Tiryns; nevertheless their aspect was forbidding. Guard towers pillared the battlements above each of Troy's four gates, the tallest the Tower of Ilion beside the Scaean Gate.

We forded the Simoeis river, and Hector delicately probed the reason for my mission. His peculiar dialect was difficult to follow: Trojan pronunciation grates on Achaean ears. I made myself agreeable; apart from being a very pleasant fellow Hector, as Priam's eldest son, would succeed in time to Laomedon's throne, so his favour was worth pursuing. I came in truth as a suppliant from a lesser king to a greater, because Troy then governed dominions more extensive than Mycenae's. As the bulwark of a prosperous kingdom her power was felt in Thrace, along the Euxine coast, and south to the Lydian borders.

We drove through a sprinkle of houses – as in Achaean cities most of the population dwelt outside the walls – and dismounted at the Scaean Gate. The houses within the citadel crowd more closely than Mycenae's, the streets narrower and steeper, impassable for vehicles. At Laomedon's palace Hector summoned squires who escorted me to a bath. Clean and smelling of perfumed oil and clothed in fresh white linen I was conducted to an audience in the Hall.

The reception of an embassy is a formal state occasion. Again I presented my half-dozen Heroes, and spread at Laomedon's feet the gifts we had brought. The king, though full of years, hair and beard foam-white, was apple-cheeked and hearty, lean and straight as a spear. After the usual courteous cross-talk he wasted no more time and directly inquired the reasons which had brought me across the seas.

I answered him as straightly: Laomedon was not a man to tolerate prolixity.

He heard me out and said, 'Let me summarize. Mycenae wants to open a seaway to Colchis through the Hellespont, which is under my control. Therefore you seek two concessions: permission to station permanently four ships within the straits, and my warrant for overland wagon trains to tranship goods on the outward voyage and gold on the return. Am I correct?'

'You are, sire.'

'We levy duties, of course, on merchandise crossing our territories. I assume you have no objection?'

'None, sire – provided the charges you put on are not unduly heavy.'

A grey-haired man at Laomedon's side stooped and spoke in his ear. The king frowned. A whispered argument followed. I waited patiently, studied the nobles, Scribes and servants crowding the Hall – smaller than Mycenae's – a frieze of painted horses galloping on the walls, ladies gossiping in a corner, a huge Molossian boar-hound asleep beside the hearth. Laomedon gestured the greybeard to silence, sucked in his lips and said, 'My son Priam dislikes your proposals, my lord. He objects to the idea of Mycenae monopolizing trade to Colchis; he sees menace in the squadron harboured permanently in the straits. What have you to say?'

I glanced at Priam. Watery blue eyes, mouth turned down at the corners, an obstinate expression. A weakling trying to assert his authority as heir to Laomedon's throne. I bridled irritation, and spoke in conciliatory tones.

'Four ships are hardly a threat to Troy's command of the Hellespont. I am ready, if you insist, to reduce the number by half. We pioneer a trade route traversed only once before, difficult and possibly dangerous, and feel entitled to reap the rewards. We do not mind if others follow our wakes – monopoly is far from our intention. All trade is beneficial, sire. We in Mycenae send you goods – weapons, pottery, oil – in return for your horses and hides. The gold from Colchis will profit us both by expanding that trade, and some will reach your treasury in payment for your exports. Mycenae takes the risks – you can only gain. Surely, on these grounds, the concessions we seek are not extravagant?'

The king rubbed his cheekbones with finger and thumb. 'You make a good case, my lord. I shall state your views to the Council and give my decision later.'

He pointed the sceptre downwards to signal the audience ended. 'Hector, have you shown our visitor the stables? I'll wager, Agamemnon, you haven't seen such thoroughbreds in Mycenae!'

There, for a time, I had to leave it. As I have remarked before, you do not hustle kings.

I remained at Troy for eleven days, was entertained at banquets, visited noblemen's houses and hunted frequently with Hector. We shot galloping deer from chariots and speared boar on foot in the hills. The more I saw of Hector the more I liked him; of all the men I have known Diomedes alone was his peer. He seemed the epitome of all that Heroes ought to be and seldom are : chivalrous, valiant, honourable and strong. Like all Trojans an exceptional driver, horseman, and horsemaster he was also a brilliant shot – I saw him, near Scamander's marshes, bring down a duck on the wing – and a match for any warrior with sword or spear. He revealed during our conversations a sparkling intelligence and shrewd judgment of the political scene both in the lands of the Hittites, which closely affected Troy, and in Achaea, which at the time did not.

A man born to be king, the greatest Troy had known, overshadowing even Laomedon. A tragedy he died as he did.

His father Priam, in contrast, was cantankerous, suspicious and spiteful. I knew from Hector's hints that Priam argued passionately against the concessions I sought and even suggested the Hellespont be closed to Achaean ships. Mulish, irascible, stupid, he chafed beneath the harrow of frustration : as Laomedon's eldest son and heir he saw time and advancing age shortening the length of the reins of power a long-lived father held. Meanwhile, as an anodyne for discontent, he interfered in affairs of state and begat nearly fifty children : nineteen by his lady Hecuba and thirty-odd from concubines. The legitimate brood and bastards lived together in the palace – or so Hector said. I marvelled at the tolerance of Trojan wives.

Laomedon, despite his years, impressed me as equal to Atreus in all the arts of kingship. He spoke seldom, shortly and to the point; and brooked no opposition. His joy and recreation was to drive across Scamander's plain and inspect the herds of horses which, exported far and wide, were a fount of Trojan wealth – an innocent hobby eventually causing his death. In foreign politics – again, Hector told me this – he handled his strong and menacing neighbours like a skilled Companion managing an ill-matched team.

A clever, prudent, far-seeing king. If Hercules had spared him there'd have been no Trojan War.

Though I met several of Hecuba's offspring I did not encounter Paris – twelve years old at the time – who was away on Mount Ida herding his father's sheep. Hector's grimace when his name cropped up demonstrated a slight aversion for Priam's favourite son.

At last Laomedon summoned me to the Throne Room and, while Priam glowered in the background, announced he was pleased to grant Mycenaean ships free passage through the Hellespont, a harbour within the straits and transhipment overland, all goods both ways being subject to customs duties. He limited the inner harbourage to three ships – a concession, I felt, to Priam – and left the Scribes to haggle over details. (Because Scribes alone can properly conduct these mercantile transactions I had brought Gelon, who in long confabulation with Laomedon's Curator fixed reasonable duties : a twentieth of each cargo's value forfeited in kind, and hiring charges for wagon teams.) We removed to the Hall and sealed the bargain in wine. Successive cups, like links in a lengthening chain, bound the king, myself, his Heroes and mine in a frivolous carouse which continued half the night. Priam sulkily sipped heavily watered wine, his emaciated, pale-skinned face a disapproving death's-head.

King Laomedon gave us a ceremonial send-off; all his Heroes – Priam excepted – drove to the beach to bid farewell. I saluted him hand to forehead and promised King Atreus' everlasting amity : a promise, as it happened, never broken. I clasped Hector's hand, and invited him to visit me in Tiryns.

I never saw Laomedon again; Hector, when next we met, did his level best to kill me.

At Tiryns I organized a six-ship Colchis convoy. While I was embarking crews and cargo Amphiaraus, lately Lord of Midea and exiled thence to Argos, arrived and offered his services. Because he was a nobleman of presence and personality and experienced in commanding men I gave him general charge of the expedition – for which, in his role as a seer, he promised success.

Thenceforth, for several years, ships sailed every spring and beached at Troy. Only the Colchis galleys bore the honourable title *Argo*; only the men who went to Colchis could properly call themselves 'Argonauts' – though several, naming no names, swaggered around as such who had been no farther than Troy.

*   *   *

The king said, 'Thyestes has gone from Elis to Sicyon, and so puts himself within my reach. I will go secretly to Sicyon and take him.'

He, Menelaus and I conferred on a balcony of the royal apartments. Bidden to Atreus' room directly I arrived I was immediately told my presence must not be advertised. Atreus, grim as death, tersely explained his purpose.

'At Elis I could not touch him; nothing short of war would wrench him from King Augeas. Thesprotus rules at Sicyon, the petty lord of an autonomous city which one day I will take. He's unlikely to fight Mycenae's king on behalf of a house-guest.'

Menelaus said, 'Are you taking a warband, or do you muster the Host?'

'Neither,' Atreus said. 'Haven't you any sense? You can't hide warriors marching the roads; directly Thyestes hears they're coming he'll leave like a scalded cat. No – we'll go there quickly, secretly, raising no alarms.'

'We?' I inquired.

'Just the three of us, journeying unescorted as ordinary travellers, our baggage on a mule. This is a family affair, an account to be settled in blood, and we are the men to do it.'

I tried to visualize the King of Mycenae plodding the tracks and leading a mule; and admitted sadly to myself that Menelaus' judgment of Atreus' sanity was turning out exact. His mind was fixed intractably on vengeance for Aerope; anything else, from politics to war, seemed to him comparatively unimportant. How could the king vanish suddenly into the blue? Who would conduct affairs while he was away?

Atreus watched my face and read my thoughts. 'I have told Copreus and the Curator to take charge – their heads are the price of silence. We shall not be gone for long: Sicyon is only a two-day walk. You'll need a cloak and a sword apiece; provisions will be loaded on the mule. We leave tonight by the north-west postern.'

I said baldly, 'Will you kill him when you find him?'

Atreus bared his teeth. 'What is death to Thyestes? An occupational hazard belonging to every Hero, a chance we face each day. I'll kill him in the end – but before he dies he shall drink to the dregs the cup that I have drained.'

I averted my eyes from the naked savagery contorting Atreus' face.

Heroes are chariot men; none walks if he can help it. I did not enjoy the journey. To avoid encountering travellers Atreus shunned the road and followed mountainous trackways. We camped for the night in a valley, where it rained. The mule, a bloody-minded brute like all his tribe, objected to being re-burdened in a grey and watery dawn. Atreus, morosely taciturn, wrapped in desolate thought, said hardly a word in the two whole days. Menelaus cursed monotonously and nursed a blistered foot. I tugged the mule's halter, and was heartily glad when Sicyon's walls climbed from evening mist.

We announced ourselves to the gate guard as noblemen from Corinth – no use pretending otherwise; despite the humble garb Atreus' arrogant bearing proclaimed his royal blood – and asked for Lord Thesprotus. Thankfully I abandoned the mule to wander where he liked. We crossed a smelly, ill-drained Court, passed a portico where slaves spread blankets and fleeces on cots, and entered the smoky, torch-lit Hall. Heroes and their women drank and roistered noisily; servants cleared the litter of a meal. My hand was on the sword beneath my cloak; Atreus, tense as a bowstring, peered around the room.

He ignored an officious steward who inquired our names, and whispered curt commands. Menelaus and I circled the Hall in opposite directions, sidling along walls and keeping in shadows, and examined bearded faces flushed by wine. Few of the boisterous company remarked our presence; a reeling reveller forced a wine cup into my hand. We returned to the king, who shook his head.

Thyestes was not in the Hall.

Atreus strode to a bald-headed man who sprawled on an elmwood throne. The king unpinned his cloak and dropped it on the floor.

'Atreus son of Pelops greets you, my lord Thesprotus. I have travelled from Mycenae to taste your hospitality.'

Protuberant red-veined eyes blinked at the visitor's creased wool tunic, earth-stained leather kilt and muddy boots. 'Whassat? Atreus? Ruddy nonsense! Trying to pull me leg? My dear chap, you must be drunker than I am! Atreus never stirs without a warband at his back, and dresses in gold and jewels. Look at you! Have another drink and sober up!'

A bodyguard in half-armour who lounged on his spear beside Thesprotus' throne stiffened and widened his eyes. He spoke quickly to his lord, stood to attention, saluted. 'I once served Lord Bunus at Corinth, sire,' he mumbled, 'and saw you there.'

Thesprotus struggled to his feet. 'Your pardon, sire,' he spluttered. 'Didn't recognize you ... should have known...' He gesticulated to squires, bellowed for chairs and tables, meat and wine. 'Please make yourselves at home. I can recommend this wine, the grapes from Mount Hymettos....'

Atreus seated himself and accepted a goblet. His name was whispered rapidly through the crowd; men craned to see Mycenae's king. He exchanged polite pleasantries, inquired after the harvest, the health of Thesprotus' family. Spearing a hunk of meat on his dagger he added, 'I understand my brother Thyestes is a guest in your house, my lord.'

Thesprotus' plump face sagged, the loose lips quivered. Aerope's crime and death had been blazoned throughout Achaea; everyone knew of the enmity that sundered the sons of Pelops. Nobody wanted a part in the feud, caught like a nut between hammer and anvil – certainly not a petty lord ruling an unimportant city. When lions fight the foxes run for cover.

He stammered, 'Lord Thyestes came to Sicyon, sire. Now he has gone.'

'When?'

'This morning, suddenly and in haste. I believe he returned to Elis.'

Forewarned of our coming, I thought, despite the precautions we took. Who had sent the alarm? Copreus? The Curator? Improbable. More likely one of the guard who had seen us leave the postern, a spy in Thyestes' pay. Inquiries must wait but, from the look on Atreus' face, someone was going to hang.

The king relaxed, popped pork in his mouth, swallowed and sipped wine. He stroked the arm of his chair and inspected the Hall, men talking in undertones and glancing over their shoulders, women whispering, servants moving noiselessly as ghosts, a bard quietly thrumming his lyre. He said genially, 'You've been having quite a party. Some particular celebration?'

'Nothing special,' Thesprotus quavered. 'Merely my birthday. How may I serve you, sire? I hope you will honour my humble abode for many days to come.'

Atreus ignored this blatantly obvious lie. His gaze, idly roaming the room, settled on a trio of ladies seated near the hearth. I followed his stare. The fire lit their faces clearly. Two were middle-aged and plain, the third young and darkly beautiful. She was listening eagerly to something her companion said. Atreus leaned forward, intent as a hawk that sights a guileless mouse. His teeth were clenched, the hollows in his cheeks like shadowed caves. I wondered at his interest. An attractive wench – but several in Mycenae's palace, both concubines and ladies, surpassed her looks by far. The king was no great lecher; and I had heard, in roundabout fashion, that since Aerope's betrayal he seldom took a woman to his bed. Perhaps continence afflicted him, and any pretty face aroused a sudden lust.

Idly I viewed the girl. Something vaguely familiar about the tilt of her head, the upward slant of eyebrows, the way she used her hands. Who did she remind me of?

The cup in my hand jerked sharply, wine-drops splashed the table. Icy fingers stroked my spine.

Of course – Aerope.

No close resemblance, the nose sharper, mouth fuller, face more rounded. More an elusive likeness in the way she moved and spoke.

Atreus lifted a hand and pointed. 'Who,' he asked Thesprotus in a strained, unnatural voice, 'is the woman beside the hearth?'

The simple question shattered the Lord of Sicyon. His eyes bulged, pendulous jowls quivered, lips shuddered so much he could hardly speak. 'W-which one, sire?' he yammered. 'The g-grey-haired lady is wife to —'

'No,' Atreus grated. 'The girl. What is her name?'

Thesprotus looked wildly around the Hall, dragged a hand down a sweat-dewed countenance. He said huntedly, 'P-Pelopia, sire. My d-daughter.'

123

A common enough name in our family. Was the shaking, corpulent fellow somehow related? I raised an amused eyebrow at Menelaus across the table. His expression froze the question I meant to whisper. He looked shocked as a man confronted by imminent death.

Atreus said, 'Bring her here.'

With a kind of resigned terror Thesprotus sent a squire. The girl threaded gracefully between people and stools and tables and stood before her father, who presented her to Atreus in a voice that was a shadow of his usual unctuous boom. She bent her head and murmured formal phrases. When you saw her close you found a haunting sadness in her face, suffering in the wide brown eyes, memories of bitterness and hurt. And also, rigidly repressed, a fear of the haggard, grey-haired king whose gaze devoured her like flames.

Atreus reached out and took her hand. He said softly, 'My lord Thesprotus, I wish to marry your daughter.'

Thesprotus, gulping wine, choked as he swallowed and crashed to the floor. Menelaus started to speak, changed his mind, thumped crystal cup on the table and shattered it in shards.

*   *   *

'She's Thyestes' daughter, Agamemnon. I saw her often when I squired him in Tiryns years ago. He must have left her in Thesprotus' charge when he fled. What the blazes shall we do?'

We lay on adjacent cots in the portico, our whispers drowned by the snores of Sicyon's Heroes. A sentinel tramped the Court beyond the pillars; starshine speckled his helmet with flashes of silvery light. The night was hot and breathless; I kicked away the coverlet.

'We'll say nothing at all. Atreus is infatuated, fallen flat on his face. If he learned the truth he might do anything – to himself, Pelopia or Thesprotus. He balances on insanity's edge; the knowledge could push him over.'

'But why Pelopia in particular? A good-looking girl, I'll admit – but hardly a raving beauty.'

'Surely you recognized the likeness?'

'What likeness? Whose?'

I slapped a whining mosquito; the little murder soothed a

momentary irritation. Must my brother *always* be so dense?

'Aerope's.'

'Can't say I did.' Menelaus ruminated. 'You think that's why Atreus wants to marry her? Very strange, considering how he treated our mother.'

'He always adored Aerope. The Lady knows what anguish he's suffered since. Pelopia replaces the woman he loved and killed.'

A sleeper thrashed his arms and gabbled dream-talk. Menelaus said, 'Too complicated for me, I'm afraid – but the results are going to be horrid. That lunatic Thesprotus! Why did he tell such a thumping lie?'

'He was given charge of Pelopia. How could he betray her to her father's bitterest enemy?'

'What he has done is very much worse. Atreus intends to wed her tomorrow – unless we warn him first.'

The sentry's spear-butt prodded a snuffling shape that scavenged on a midden in a corner of the Court. The dog yelped and scuttled into the dark. I said, 'No. The king might have a brainstorm, possibly murder Pelopia. His reputation won't stand it. Even for kings there's a limit to the female relations they kill.'

'He's bound to find out. I'm not the only man who will recognize Pelopia. The scandal will spread like a forest fire and someone, some time, will tell Atreus the truth.'

I laughed without amusement. 'Can you visualize anyone who values his life informing Atreus he's married his niece and his enemy's daughter? I can't.'

'What about Thyestes?'

'He won't persuade any messenger to face the king with *that* little titbit; and he's unlikely to visit Mycenae himself. Thyestes is a callous, malevolent scoundrel. When he learns that Atreus has married Pelopia believing her Thesprotus' child he'll probably keep his mouth shut and pick the tangle over in search of some advantage he might win.'

Menelaus made an exasperated noise. 'What a damnable muddle! These blood feuds have a habit of embroiling innocent people. That wretched Pelopia!' He jerked upright on the bed and smacked his brow. 'Burn my belly and bones! She *knows* what she's doing!'

125

I sighed. Really my brother was sometimes a most bone-headed ass. 'Of course. What choice has she? Tell all, and face Atreus' fury, possibly her own death, and prove Thesprotus a liar? I bet Thesprotus has begged her to stick to his tale, and deployed the very arguments we have used.'

'So. We hold our tongues and hope for the best. No point in arguing ourselves silly any more. I'm going to sleep.' Menelaus pulled the blanket to his chin, and added sombrely, 'I foresee a bucket of trouble spilling from this night's work.'

*   *   *

Atreus held Pelopia's wrist and married her in the presence of Thesprotus and his Heroes. (Thesprotus later received a gener-ous bride-price – oxen, chariots, horses and gold – a cynical twist Thyestes must have enjoyed.) The king and his bride drove to Corinth in borrowed chariots, and he lay with her that night. Next evening they reached Mycenae, and Atreus presented his queen to an assembly of nobles in the Throne Room. I saw astonished expressions, heard whispers murmured in slanted ears. Pelopia had been recognized; before the sun had risen twice the scandal would be broadcast throughout Achaea.

Atreus that day had ten years to live. In all that time I was never certain he discovered her real identity. Certainly no one told him, but a truth universally known is hard to conceal from the person most deeply concerned. Any little incident could have given him an inkling – a change of conversation heading for dangerous channels, a stilted avoidance of awk-ward connotations, incautious remarks overheard. If so, he never openly betrayed his knowledge.

I speculate on this because, as time went by, his attitude towards Pelopia subtly altered. Although his loving lacked the cheerful abandon Aerope had destroyed he was always, in the early days, kindly and attentive. Gradually his manner changed; he saw her less, avoided her company, discouraged her from dining in the Hall and confined to state occasions her appearances in public. Towards the end he quitted the bedroom they shared and slept in a chamber at the farther end of the royal apartments. Frequently he summoned concubines to his couch.

An enduring air of sadness lingered around Pelopia, a constraint in all she said, a guarded watchful manner as though hidden dangers lurked. She seldom smiled; the vivacity I had glimpsed when she spoke with her ladies in Thesprotus' Hall had gone for good. I believed I knew her reasons for unhappiness. I could not have been more wrong.

Eight months after the marriage Pelopia bore a son. A bonny, bouncing baby, I was told. A pity no one strangled him before the cord was cut.

* * *

Before returning to Tiryns I had a long discussion with Atreus and his Curator; they reminded me most forcibly that the ships being built in Nauplia's yards must go trading overseas directly keels touched water. (Merchantmen and warships are identical in build, their functions interchangeable at the peep of a hostile sail.) Though Mycenaean ships from Nauplia already voyaged the seas from Sicily to Rhodes the commerce must be expanded and additional markets sought.

We had arranged for Colchian gold to replace the trickle from Egypt the Hittite wars had throttled; similarly we must tap fresh sources for other products: tin from Etruria, ivory, silver and cloth from Phoenician Sidonia; and establish trading stations far to the north in Thessaly, southwards in Cyrene. Atreus assured me our mariners and merchants needed no encouragement: predatory and adventurous by nature they asked only for ships and cargoes – which the kingdom would now provide.

I wiped my brow, and demanded more Scribes to help keep Gelon's accounts. Hardly the kind of job, I groused, a Hero wanted chucked in his lap. Atreus said sternly, 'This is your introduction to the business of ruling a realm. Kingship doesn't solely consist of galloping into battle and battering your enemies to bits. Very little, in fact. Most of the time you sit on your buttocks totting up debits and credits.'

Because my new responsibility entailed control of all Mycenaean fleets Atreus granted me the title of Master of the Ships: a style not borne since Poseidon, Gelon averred. An empty reward, I told him grumpily, for a task demanding the knowledge and skills of seaman, Scribe and merchant combined.

127

We returned to Tiryns, and worked for many moons from dawn to dark. I shall not bore you with the details. Gelon and his assistants kept the accounts; I consulted master mariners, navigators and traders; chose sea-routes and destinations; sent commercial envoys – reluctant noblemen from Tiryns – to negotiate with rulers in distant lands across the seas. I voyaged myself to the nearer islands, Crete and once to Sicily; and built a second wharf in Nauplia's harbour.

Before two years were out Mycenae had a hundred ships at sea.

These maritime concerns were sometimes interrupted. A warband I sent to harry Goatmen in the Arachneos Mountains returned at half its strength. The commander, a saturnine Hero nursing a bandaged arm, informed me morosely he had not only been heavily outnumbered – which did not matter much with Goatmen – but Iron Men in quantity reinforced the nomads. He showed me his shield. 'Hand-to-hand fight on a hill, and a Dorian bounded down like a boulder loosed by a landslide. I fronted my shield to ward his slash. Look at the results.' I fingered a cleft in the treble-hide shield from upper rim to waist. 'I tried to parry the swipe that followed; his sword lopped my blade like a leek. Iron, of course. I didn't wait for more.'

The incident confirmed information from other parts of Achaea. Elis, Sparta and Argos reported increasing numbers of Iron Men stiffening the Goatmen. Chasing the hairy savages was ceasing to be a sport. Hitherto they had raided unprotected herds, occasionally but rarely attacking a carelessly guarded manor. Strengthened by Dorian allies they no longer waited for winter to descend from their mountain fastnesses. The character of the hit-and-run warfare Goatmen normally waged was changing for something more dangerous.

Soon afterwards a hysterical runner from Lasion reported an outlying manor burned to the ground, the occupants massacred, stock driven off or slain. Lasion was in the Arachneos foothills; the town paid tribute to Mycenae; so I mustered every fighting-man available in Tiryns and force-marched through a sweltering summer's day. The Warden had manned the walls; the gates were closed and barred. I considered these panicky precautions surprising and displeasing. Lasion is a tiny fort, the garrison small and defences weak – but fancy a citadel standing to arms for Goatmen roaming loose! The Warden received us gladly, and crowded the warband within walls already packed by husbandmen and animals from the countryside.

I demanded details.

'They came on here after burning the manor,' the Warden said. (I've forgotten his name; Goatmen killed him a year or two later.) 'Normally, as you know, they raid and run for the hills. A shepherd warned us, and judged their strength around three hundred. In Lasion,' he added defensively, 'I have three Heroes and fifty spearmen. So I sounded Alarm and closed the gates. As well I did.' The Warden pointed. 'We haven't much of a town; they destroyed the little there was.'

I looked at a scattering of ruined, burnt-out houses, wisps of smoke still drifting. 'Did they storm the citadel?'

'No. Stayed beyond arrow-shot and yelled abuse – gibberish we couldn't understand. Then they went. If ever they try an escalade I doubt we'll keep them out.'

'How many Iron Men did you count in the pack?'

'Fifty or so. Easily distinguished: short leather corselets, small round shields, bronze or iron helmets. Stand out from the Goatmen like falcons among sparrows.'

When a citadel, however puny, was forced to close its gates, warning beacons flared in tomorrow's skies. I recalled my experience near Rhipe, where a Goatman band of forty contained a single Dorian. The proportion had increased alarmingly over the years and indicated a Dorian emigration, an effort to settle permanently in Achaea's mountain wilderness. If their aggressiveness was anything to reckon by they would not be content to remain in the hills for long.

I abandoned my gloomy reflections and said, 'We'll chase the brutes at daybreak. Meanwhile keep your garrison standing to arms.'

In the greyness of early morning we easily followed the trail – all warriors are herdsmen, accustomed from childhood to tracking wandering cattle or predatory beasts. The swathe the Goatmen beat was plain as a stone-paved road. We crossed the flatlands below the Arachneos foothills, left chariots under guard – Companions and twenty spearmen – and ascended steep forested slopes. Climbing rocky mountainsides in armour is a pastime worth avoiding. Even in the tree-shade I broiled in a brazen cuirass, tripped on my body-length shield, tangled the ten-foot spear in bushes and branches. Leather-clad spearmen skipped ahead; sweating, swearing Heroes clambered behind.

A hill crest won from a morning's toil revealed the trail – broken twigs and flattened grass, cattle-hoof scrapes on rock – dippping to a valley and soaring to another crest beyond. Successive ridges in forested tiers mounted to peaks still streaked by winter snow. I unbuckled my helmet strap, wiped sweat from my temples and said, 'I'd hoped the Goatmen would camp in the hills, but they must have marched all night. Too long a start – high in the mountains by now. We'll have to give up.'

Disconsolate and hot, the warband retraced its steps. While crossing a fan of shale to the gully where the chariots were harboured I heard a shout and slid down the slope in a shower of stones. Companions and spearmen surrounded the chariots. Men and horses dying and dead littered the ring like fallen petals.

'A rearguard ambush,' Talthybius said. 'Forty-odd Dorians.' He pressed a hand to his cheek; blood trickled through his fingers from a gash that bared the bone. 'They hid in a ravine. Waited till you were gone, then rushed us. We weren't ready; chariots and horses dotted all over the place. They did a lot of damage before we could rally and close. We formed a circle round the chariots and fought for our lives.' Tears diluted the blood on Talthybius' face. 'Your bay stallion is dead, my lord. Panicked and broke his yoke, and one of the bastards speared him.'

I comforted my young companion, tore strips from a dead man's tunic and bound his jaw. I counted casualties: five horses and seven men killed and twice as many wounded. Four Iron Men lay dead. I examined a long grey sword, cautiously thumbed the edge and winced from a hairline cut. A terrible weapon. It rendered our bronze blades obsolete as the Goatmen's chipped-stone spearheads. I sheathed the sword and gave it to Talthybius as recompense for his wound. (He sold it to a Tiryns goldsmith and received ten sheep for the iron's value. I told him he'd been swindled.)

We rearranged horse teams (you can't drive one-horsed chariots), loaded badly wounded men, towed the horseless cars behind and shambled back to Lasion. Our reverse frightened the Warden, who demanded reinforcements from Tiryns or Mycenae. Bad-temperedly I answered that, to judge by our experience, every citadel in Achaea would shortly plumb its resources to stem the Goatmen's attacks. I inspected Lasion's walls, and recommended he set workmen to increase the height and breadth, build a tower above the gate, dig a well within the citadel, construct fortified watch-towers on surrounding hills to observe the Goatmen's approach.

'You make it sound, my lord,' he bleated, 'as though Lasion will be permanently under siege.'

'Not only Lasion,' I said sourly. 'Within fifty years there won't be a citadel standing if the Dorians aren't stopped.'

I may have been wrong; I hope I am. Today, in effect, the Iron Men hold Arcadia. I hurried to Mycenae to impress the peril on Atreus.

*   *   *

A maidservant tilted a silver jug, dripped water over my hands and patted my fingers dry on a soft woollen cloth. Squires brought baskets of wheaten bread and poured wine from golden mixing bowls. Carvers beside the hearth-fire sliced roasted pork and sirloin; a slave slid a loaded platter on the table under my nose. My dagger tested the tenderness. Satisfied, I said, 'The Goatmen, sire, may make our outlying citadels untenable.'

A cheerful, noisy company thronged the Hall. The king feasted Echemus, Lord of Arcadian Tegea, passing through Mycenae to visit a physician in Epidauros who guaranteed curing piles. The guest of honour, taciturn, craggy-faced, stocky and strong, sat on Atreus' right; Pelopia on his left; I occupied a footstool at his feet. Noblemen and ladies ate at tables placed, as usual, in widening rings from the hearth, leaving a lane from throne to fireside so that the king could see the fire and feel its warmth.

Atreus rested his head on the throne-back, and picked his teeth with a fingernail. 'I am quite aware of the problem,' he said, 'and one day I shall hack it by the roots. The Goatmen

131

alone are merely a nuisance; supported by iron-armed Dorians they're a menace to civilization. Dorians are the people we have to exterminate. Not easy – and there's a catch : Thebes protects Doris and encourages the Iron Men's raids. So, to tear the roots, Thebes must be destroyed – which won't be done by wishing, Agamemnon. Thebes ranks near Mycenae in influence and power. Our preparations must be thorough, our strategy faultless, our forces overwhelming. You can't mount major wars in a day. It will all take time.'

'Meanwhile,' I said, 'the Iron Men leave Doris in droves to settle in Arcadia.'

Echemus belched and patted his stomach. 'I agree. They swarm in the mountains north of Tegea. I hear – can't vouch for the facts – Dorians have occupied small towns in the depths of Arcadia. May be nonsense. Sinister if true.'

'For the time being we'll have to contain them,' Atreus said. 'I've another stew on my plate which is tougher than this beef.' He scowled at his platter and pushed it aside. 'Those damned Heraclids are gathering at Marathon and intend to invade the Argolid. I shall have to muster a Host and beat them back.'

I said, 'They missed a chance after Megara when Athens ratted. Hyllus is remarkably persistent. Have they found stauncher allies?'

'Don't you see?' said Atreus impatiently. 'Warfare in Achaea has two causes: economic or dynastic. Sometimes the two combine. This is a dynastic war. Perseus' blood flows strongly in Hyllus' veins: his great-grandfathers on both sides were Perseus' sons. Perseus in olden times held Argos and Mycenae: the blood line, in Hyllus' view, supports his claim to kingship. I must admit,' Atreus added broodingly, 'from the genealogical aspect his right to rule Mycenae is better than mine: we Pelopids, after all, are rank usurpers. Hence Hyllus looks for redress by force of arms.'

'Are the Scavengers,' I inquired gingerly, 'among their forces?'

'You sound terrified of those buggers,' said Atreus severely. 'No, my spies say not. Thebes is having troubles in the palace: Polyneices and Eteocles, Oedipus' sons, are quarrelling about succession to the throne. Each seeks the Heroes' backing; neither is disposed to send warriors to war on anyone else's behalf. Convenient for us, and long may it continue. The Heraclids – Hyllus and Iolaus – have mustered their own followers plus warbands from Athens and Locris, a thousand or so in all.'

'What about Hercules himself? Isn't he taking the field to support his kindred?'

'I wish he were. The fool would insist on taking command – and make my task much easier. No. He found his way back from Mysia – after marvellous adventures and quite astounding deeds, according to his stories – and lives in Thessaly. Hercules is getting old; incapable, I hope, of inflicting more disasters.'

A bard in a long white robe embroidered with bands of brown and yellow squatted on a stool beside the hearth, plucked a seven-stringed ivory lyre and looked inquiringly at the king. Atreus nodded permission. The bard burst into song: an epic ballad of long ago describing the taking of Knossos by Acrisius and his Heroes. The king tetchily twitched his beard.

'I can't stand this new-fangled music. Why in The Lady's name can't bards play decent tunes?'

Privately I considered the modern melodies a vast improvement on those mournful dirges I remembered from my childhood. They had a swing and rhythm that set your fingers tapping.

Echemus said peevishly, 'I agree. Disgusting row. Can't imagine who invented these horrible yowls.'

'Orpheus,' said Pelopia unexpectedly.

'Really, my dear?' Atreus said. 'Orpheus? Surely not the fellow who sailed with Jason in *Argo*?'

'The same, my lord. A wonderful composer, a superb poet. His music,' said Pelopia dreamily, 'is stilled for ever, his lyre broken, the player dead.'

'How so?'

'Orpheus lived in Thrace, and opposed the cult of Dionysus. He taught gentleness and love instead of orgiastic revels and sacrificial murders. In revenge a sect of Maenads waylaid him in the forests and tore him limb from limb.'

'Damned good thing,' Echemus muttered. 'No more ghastly noises.'

'I didn't know, my dear,' said Atreus kindly, 'you were interested in verse and music. Your father's palace at Sicyon seemed an improbable environment for fostering the arts.'

Pelopia folded hands in lap and retreated into silence. Atreus regarded her worriedly, shook his head and said, 'To return to the Heraclid problem. I'm not taking any risks. Eurystheus mustered only Mycenae's Host, advanced too far and was caught unprepared. I have sent to Adrastus of Argos for help, and will give battle near Corinth on ground of my choice with twice the enemy's strength. Corinth shall be the mustering place. You'll get detailed orders later, Agamemnon; meanwhile mobilize your warband and be ready to march from Tiryns at two days' notice. The corn won't be cut for a moon as yet, which gives us plenty of time.'

(Perhaps I should explain there are three campaigning seasons: early spring before sowing; summer between sowing and harvest; and autumn after harvest. You *can* campaign in winter; I have done it – a cold and wet and miserable business.)

Echemus said, 'Mind if I bring my men? I can raise two hundred spears.'

'Certainly, my lord,' said Atreus, surprised, 'but Tegea isn't tributary to Mycenae.'

A grin split the coarse black beard. 'Doesn't matter. My warriors are sick of chasing Dorians and Goatmen. Do them good to see some proper warfare.'

'I am grateful.' Atreus beckoned a chamberlain, who called above the babble. Voices stilled. The king rose from the throne, and everybody stood. Leading Pelopia by the hand, Echemus at his side, Atreus left the Hall.

Menelaus overtook me in the Great Court. 'Did you find the king well?' he asked anxiously.

I shrugged. 'Grim, humourless, hard-headed and sharp as a sword. An odd question, brother. You live in Mycenae: you must know his temper better than I. Why weren't you in his company at dinner?'

Menelaus grimaced. 'I keep out of Atreus' way as much as I can. Knowing what we know it's difficult to behave normally in his presence. How did he treat Pelopia?'

'Politely, kindly, as a gentleman should his wife – at any rate in public. Why not? You don't believe he suspects —'

'Not for a moment. I was only afraid Pelopia's attempt to expose her son might have turned the king against her.'

'Expose her—? I've heard nothing. What did she do?'

Menelaus explained. Soon after the baby was born and the festivities celebrating a royal heir were over – the child's line of descent led to Mycenae's throne – Pelopia bribed a midwife to conceal him beneath bushes in the depths of the Chaos Ravine. Fortunately – or otherwise – a wandering goatherd found the infant and he was suckled by a she-goat. Meanwhile the disappearance caused uproar in the palace. Atreus could extract no sense from Pelopia, who relapsed into a half-conscious trance and disregarded his questions. He put her slaves to the torture; the miserable midwife confessed. Search parties ranged the countryside, and found the goatherd cherishing his squalling prize.

Pelopia received her missing son with a kind of silent resignation, as though she admitted defeat in a battle against fate; and afterwards displayed all a mother's loving care. Although flabbergasted by his wife's unnatural behaviour Atreus gladly believed a physician's advice that she had been affected by the temporary madness which sometimes afflicts women after childbirth, particularly in premature births. He replaced her slaves, sent the women to sailors' brothels in Nauplia, men to stone quarries near Mycenae, and appeared to put the episode out of his mind.

'He hasn't, in fact,' Menelaus ended, 'as the name he gave the brat testifies: Aegisthus means "goat-strength".'

I could make neither head nor tail of this peculiar story, and considered the physician's solution valid. What else could I have done? Who could have guessed the terrible truth?

*   *   *

King Atreus summoned the levies from every tributary city. King Adrastus needed no urging to mobilize his Host: he perceived the Heraclid threat as being dangerous to Argos as to Corinth and Mycenae.

Atreus revealed the administrative genius which marks outstanding captains. Aware that troops and transport, uncontrolled, would congest the road to Corinth and cause unspeakable confusion (I ruefully remembered King Eurystheus' march) he sent Adrastus a movement table, written by Scribes and deciphered by Argos' Curator, which ensured that warbands from both cities, marching on different days, would not obstruct the narrow mountain roads. He went himself to Corinth and arranged with the Warden Bunus for each detachment's reception, encampment and supplies. (Armies moving in hostile territory live off the enemy's lands; Atreus intended to fight on friendly soil, so men and animals had to be fed.)

I led the Tiryns contingent – twenty chariots and three hundred spears – on a leisurely, trouble-free march, and reached Corinth on the third day's afternoon. As a Warden I was quartered in the palace; less eminent Heroes found bedrooms in the citadel; the rest, and all Companions, spearmen, grooms and servants lived in an encampment at the foot of Corinth's mount. I met again King Adrastus, the leathery Tydeus, Leader of his Host, and Tydeus' son Diomedes strutting proudly in Hero's armour.

Diomedes, bouncing with youthful zest, could talk of nothing except the coming encounter, his first affray-at-arms. I found his ardour engaging and, from the heights of experience and age (he is two years younger than I) offered sage advice, probed his Companion's driving skills and criticized his accoutrements. 'Your left shoulder-guard chafes the cuirass,' I told him. 'Tell the smith to loosen it a finger's breadth. Why a brazen helmet? Boars' tusks give better protection. I prefer a waisted shield myself; this tower affair can hinder your low-line thrusts. An ivory-hilted sword? Very fine and fashionable – but slippery when your hand begins to sweat. You'll find a silver grip safer.' I smiled cheerfully. 'Too late to change now, but I dare say you'll survive.'

Diomedes absorbed my counsel like oracular commands delivered by the Selli at Dodona. Echemus of Tegea, listening to my discourse, said caustically, 'Armour's perfectly useless if the man inside can't fight. Strength and skill and courage are the only things that count.' Hard grey eyes looked us up and down. 'Don't worry – I believe you have all three.'

Atreus' scouts roved far beyond the Isthmus, and his spies in Megara and Athens informed him of the Heraclids' strength and movements. They said the Scavengers were safely away in Thebes, and also that our Host – ten-score chariots and two thousand spears – outnumbered the Heraclids three to one. Hyllus marched his warbands from Marathon to Athens where he awaited reinforcement by a levy of Boeotian bowmen. Iolaus led a reconnaissance in force which reached no further than Sciron's Rocks, where Bunus had stationed spearmen who drove the intruders back.

In the meantime Atreus exercised his mingled Hosts, Argive and Mycenaean, on the Corinthian Plain. It was an unwieldy mass, incapable of doing much more than charge to the front. Atreus strove to teach the Heroes to shift ground to a flank by wheeling in threes to the right or left; tactics resulting, often as not, in colliding naves, broken poles and tangled harness. Companions who individually could turn their teams on a platter semed incapable of wheeling round in concert. The confusion arose from inexperience; close-order drill had never been tried before.

Hyllus advanced from Athens to Megara and headed for the Isthmus, whereupon the king took Tydeus and every warband leader to reconnoitre battle positions. He chose a line confronting the Isthmus' narrow neck; a river secured his flank on the left, a bluff on the right fell sheer to the sea. A thousand paces of bush-pocked ground sloped gently away in front, sufficient for a charge to gain momentum; the slant would speed the pace. When Bunus, a would-be tactician, suggested our force be concentrated like a stopper on a wine jar to block the Heraclids' deployment from the pass Atreus looked at him coldly.

'Fight on a narrow front, and waste our superior numbers? You deceive yourself, my lord. I shall let the enemy deploy, then charge and envelop the flanks, cut his line of retreat and massacre every man.'

On a cloudy midsummer's morning our outpost at Sciron's Rocks, hustled from position, galloped into Corinth and reported Heraclids pouring across the Isthmus. The Host was already under arms – Atreus insisted on chariots being harnessed, arms and armour donned at sunrise every day – and warbands marched to the stations Atreus had appointed. Adhering to his principle of separating spears from chariots he grouped the heavy armour in a two-rank line of battle at fifty paces' distance, and placed all spearmen in a third line in support – thus preventing retinues from trailing their Heroes' chariots. Mycenaeans held the van: Tiryns in the centre, Tegean chariots under Echemus on their right, Mycenae's on

137

the left. Corinth and Nemea guarded the wings. Behind them Tydeus marshalled Argos' ninety chariots. King Adrastus' advancing years confined him to a place in the rearmost line, where he hammered his chariot's rail and shrilly abused the spearmen's untidy dressing.

I glanced along the ranks. An array of tossing horses' heads, manes plaited in pointed locks, scarlet, blue and yellow chariots, bronze and boars'-tusk helmets plumed in flaring colours, glistening armour and tall hide shields, a forest of upright spears.

Enemy outriders, specks in the distance, trotted from the cliff-hung Isthmus road, checked and stared, whirled round and disappeared. 'Could they be surprised?' I murmured to Talthybius. 'Surely Hyllus' spies have told him we are ready?' Chariots in single file swung quickly right and left, formed a ragged line and advanced at a walk. Then spearmen running, Locrian bowmen and a scurry of naked slingers. I glimpsed the head of a transport column halted on the road: asses and mules and ox-carts, drovers and sutlers and slaves. Slowly and uncertainly, vehicles opening and closing on the vagaries of the ground, the Heraclids' chariot line approached until, three hundred paces away, you could tell a chestnut horse from a bay.

There it halted.

Warriors dismounted and gathered in a group. They were obviously conferring, waving arms and shouting, the air so still their voices carried like starlings' chatter at roost. Behind them climbed the Isthmus' mountainous spine; tamarisk, pines and scrub-oak patchworked jagged ridges, precipices split the foliage like waterfalls of rock. Arrows of sunlight pierced the clouds, slashed transient gilded scars on a grey-green sea.

Atreus moved his chariot four horses' lengths ahead; every Hero from wing to wing could see him. A sun-ray gleamed on his armour and bathed him in fleeting fire. I shifted my shield a fraction and rubbed my feet on the webbing. Talthybius poised his whip and shortened reins. Atreus looked to right and left, and lifted his spear.

When the point swooped down we would go.

The enemy's conclave ended; warriors remounted. A lone chariot trotted towards us, oxhide frame dyed crimson, wheel-spokes limned in silver, prancing sorrel stallions. The Companion wore a leather skull-cap and studded linen corselet, the Hero beside him a brazen helmet; cheek guards curved to a point at his chin.

Atreus frowned and lowered his spear.

The chariot reined a spear-cast away. The Hero swept his helmet off and showed his face. Straw-coloured tousled hair, a short fair beard, smouldering dark-blue eyes. 'Hyllus son of Hercules whom Amphitryon begat,' he called in rasping tones. 'Alcaeus fathered Amphitryon, and Perseus Alcaeus.' (While custom requires that strangers announce their pedigrees I felt that, on a battlefield, the rigmarole was rather out of place.) 'I demand audience of King Atreus.'

'You see him,' Atreus growled. 'What have you to say? I come for war, not words.'

'I also. I offer single combat against any noble warrior from Argos or Mycenae. I will not,' said Hyllus sharply, 'fight one whose blood is base.'

The distance between the speakers compelled both to raise their voices, so the centre of our line could hear the conversation. A surprised murmuration travelled along the ranks, horses lunged at bits, chariots see-sawed back and forth, drivers tautened reins and swore. Talthybius soothed his restive team. 'Let's kill the bastard now,' he breathed. 'Give the word and I'll charge.' 'Restrain yourself, Talthybius,' I reproved. 'We must start the battle like gentlemen – the dirty work comes later.'

Atreus said, 'Lord Hyllus, any of my Heroes would be happy to cut your throat. But I see no purpose in your challenge, for we mean to kill you all. Return to your Host and get ready to die.'

'Is your blood-thirst so insatiable you will sacrifice three thousand lives, your followers and mine? We'll fight to the death, King Atreus, make no mistake. I offer an escape from needless slaughter.'

'Do you mean,' asked Atreus incredulously, 'you're willing to gamble the battle's outcome and your claim to Mycenae's throne on an individual duel?'

'You heard me,' Hyllus said. 'Will any of your cowards dare to meet me blade to blade?'

Heroes shouted and brandished spears, chariots surged from

the ranks. Atreus faced them and raised his arms. 'Be still!' he thundered. He turned to Hyllus. 'If you are slain, am I to understand your Host will retire from the field?'

'If I die,' said Hyllus tartly, 'the sons of Hercules will not return along this road for another fifty years. This I swear on my mother's womb. If I win, let your throne and realm be mine.'

Atreus bowed his head in thought. At last, 'I will consult my captains.' He dismounted, sent a messenger to summon warband leaders, walked beyond Hyllus' hearing. Adrastus, Tydeus and Diomedes galloped from the Argive Host in rear. Echemus of Tegea, Bunus, Alcmaeon of Midea, myself and other Heroes clustered round the king.

He said, 'Hyllus is the fire and fount of Heraclid dreams of conquest. We want him dead. In a general engagement he might escape – so I'll accept the fellow's challenge. His Host won't honour the compact, of course, and then we can set about them.'

I said, 'Are *you* going to fight him, sire?'

'Who else? It's my throne he wants.'

'Madness!' Adrastus squeaked. 'Why should Mycenae's king fight a landless outcast vagabond and wager his dominion on the result?'

Atreus stared. 'Wager my dominion? Are you serious, my lord? Should Hyllus cut me down, directly you see me fall you'll charge and sweep that rabble to perdition!'

'Ah, yes, I see.' Adrastus tried to scratch his armpit, met bronze and wriggled his shoulders. 'Still, it's out of the question for you to risk your life. Nonsensical!'

'You'd do him overmuch honour,' Tydeus snapped.

'Eagles don't fight rats,' said Bunus.

I took a breath and said, 'Sire, we cannot forbid you, but I beg you to choose another.' I looked him in the eye. 'Should the worst befall, no one yet is ready to succeed you.'

Atreus held my gaze, and gave a tiny nod. 'Very well. You all seem damnably certain,' he added irascibly, 'that Hyllus will chop my head off. Then who will take my place?'

'Let me fight him!' Diomedes pleaded.

'Shut your mouth!' his father grated. 'Hardly out of the nursery – Hyllus would carve you in pieces!'

Every Hero clamoured for the honour. I said, 'It's fitting your son should stand in your stead. You'll find no better champion in the Host.' I shouldered my shield and turned to go.

'Stop!' The king's voice cracked like a whip. 'We'll decide the issue by trial of arms. He who casts his spear the farthest shall take his chance against Hyllus.'

The butt of his spear traced a long straight furrow. 'Toe this line, gentlemen, and throw when I give the word.'

Hyllus, I suppose, watched the performance in wordless astonishment. Thirty-odd Heroes formed in line and threw their spears. Atreus walked to the weapons, some slanted in the ground, some flat where they skidded from stones. One quivered a stride ahead of the rest. 'Mine!' exulted Echemus. He grabbed the haft and trotted towards his chariot.

(Did I put every bit of my strength in the cast? I like to believe so – but it's difficult to remember after so many years.)

'A moment, Lord Echemus,' said Atreus. 'The bargain needs Heraclid witnesses.' He spoke to Hyllus, who galloped to his ranks and returned with two Heroes alongside: Iolaus and another. The king presented Echemus. Hyllus sneered. 'Is this your valiant champion? Does your kingdom, Lord Atreus, depend on the spear of a dwarf?'

Indeed the duellists in appearance provided a remarkable contrast: Echemus stumpy, dark-haired, broad, bull-shouldered; Hyllus slim and lithe, nearly as tall as Atreus, straw-haired and fair-skinned.

Echemus growled deep in his chest. 'My body is short but my spear is long and thirsty, Hyllus, and avid to drink your blood.'

'Enough,' said Atreus. 'You trade blows, not words.'

He made Hyllus repeat his vow, and testified agreement. Echemus tightened his cheek-guards, hitched shield-strap over his shoulder, hefted spear and mounted his chariot. He spoke laconically to his Companion, swarthy, tough and muscular, a replica ten years younger of himself. The chariots cantered away, turned midway between the opposing Hosts and faced each other a hundred paces apart.

A great shout rolled from our ranks, answered by a resounding roar from the Heraclid line of battle.

The chariots sprang to a gallop and hurtled on converging courses, offside meeting offside. Echemus tucked shaft under armpit in the old-fashioned Pylian style; Hyllus lifted his spear on high for an overhand thrust. In a sudden explosion of dust the chariots met. The Heraclid's point scored his enemy's shield.

Echemus speared Hyllus' Companion from nipple to spine and hooked him from the chariot like a fish.

Angry yells went up from the Heraclid Host; chariots shot forward from the ranks. Iolaus whirled round and flourished his arms and ordered them back.

'I'm not surprised they're furious,' I told Talthybius. 'You shouldn't deliberately kill Companions. A foul if ever there was one. They must have different standards in Tegea.'

Hyllus cradled his spear and grappled the reins and hauled his team about in a dust-feathered arc. Echemus whipped round and darted, galloping hard, to strike his opponent's flank. His spear was lost, embedded in a body threshing in agony, the shaft flailing like a sapling lashed by gales. He drew his sword and slanted blade on shoulder.

Hyllus won control of his bolting horses and tugged desperately to face his foe head-on. The chariots closed at an angle, Echemus galloping belly to ground, the Heraclid barely cantering. Hyllus dropped reins and lifted his spear. The cars met wheel to wheel in a splintering crash. Echemus' pole snapped short, his nearside stallion ploughed to the ground. In a flurry of reins and tumbling horses the chariot whirled end over end and flung the occupants out.

Hyllus' chariot swung in crazy circles, the nave of a shattered wheel gouging trenches in the dust.

He jumped to the ground. His horses fled, dragging the broken chariot in bumpy lopsided leaps until the yoke straps broke and it scraped to a stop on its side. His shield dangled by the strap; frantically he retrieved his spear, jerked from his hand in the crash. He plodded towards Echemus, who climbed to his feet, fronted shield and waited, sword withdrawn for the lunge. His Companion, half stunned in the fall, propped himself on hands and knees in the Heraclid's path, drooping his head and trying to recover his senses.

Hyllus paused beside him, plunged spear in the driver's back, stood on the spine and tugged it out. His weight drove the dying man's breath from his lungs in a rasp like a corncrake's cry.

'Spear against sword,' Talthybius observed. 'Hyllus has the advantage.'

Immediately he lost it – and I never understood why. Nobody in his senses throws heavy thrusting spears unless the enemy is shieldless or lightly armoured. Then, naturally, it pays to cast your spear before you close with the sword. Echemus peeped over a tower-shield's rim and wore three-skirted brazen armour. Yet Hyllus halted ten steps distant, straddled his legs and balanced the spear and flung with all his strength.

The point glanced the Tegean's helmet and the shaft clattered harmlessly on the ground behind him.

Echemus staggered slightly, recovered his poise and shuffled forward, one foot behind the other, each stepping in turn and feeling the ground. Hyllus' sword hissed from the sheath, he fronted a waisted shield and crept to his left, trying to approach his foe on the unprotected side. Echemus stopped moving, and shifted stance to meet the angled attack. Hyllus came within sword-length and slashed at the bull-hide shield.

Technically it was an interesting contest. The Heraclid wielded a short cutting sword some four spans long, while Echemus used a ribbed thrusting blade a good span longer or more. Heroes in Halls and encampments waste a deal of breath in argument as to which is the deadlier weapon – futile discussions, I maintain, since each has a different function. If you're unlucky enough to be fighting on foot against a warrior wearing a helmet, gorget girdling neck, body cased in armour and a tower or waisted shield, then the only vulnerable part is his face: to reach this you must have a longer sword. For chariot fighting, however – assuming your spear is lost – speed and a jolting platform don't allow accurate aim; so a damned good clout with a cutting-sword's edge is often effective.

Hence, everything being equal, Echemus' rapier held the advantage – but the Heraclid was taller and had the longer reach.

They circled each other, stabbing and hacking in turn. Shields took the brunt, and neither was hurt. I heard the thuds as bronze met hide, the fighters' laboured breathing, saw the spurts of dust their feet kicked up, cloud-light flashing from blades. Neither could gain the upper hand; the duel became a trial of endurance.

The opposing Hosts cheered their champions on, yelling and shouting and screaming like spectators at the games. Atreus, erect in his chariot, watched the unending struggle; the fingers of his spear hand impatiently tapped the shaft.

Single combats between Heroes on foot are fairly rare in Achaean history and so become a theme of bardic lays. I was watching a fight from days gone by, chronicled blow by blow and sung in Halls, a contest like a solemnly stylized dance: cut and thrust, lunge and parry, slash and ward: the kind of conflict I had seen engraved on a golden goblet Atreus owned. According to the artist both duellists fought naked, their sole defences body-length shields. If the engraving depicts the truth – poets and artists care little for accurate detail – the men must have moved more freely than Echemus and Hyllus who, weighted by heavy armour, shuffled around like ponderous mobile trees.

By unspoken consent the fighters drew apart, thrust swords point-down in the dust and leaned panting on their shields. Echemus' horses, still yoked to the splintered chariot, peacefully cropped the sun-bleached grass; the Companions' bodies hunched in puddles of blood. The audience's uproar swelled, throats bellowed lusty encouragement.

Wearily the champions grasped hilts and hefted shields and hobbled within sword-reach.

Hyllus tried a lateral cut; his sword clanged the shield's bronze rim. Echemus' riposte was oddly slow, a faltering jab that ended in air. He tottered and his shield swung wide. Hyllus shouted hoarsely, sprang forward, sword aloft. Echemus dropped on a knee, gripped hilt in both his hands and thrust upwards beneath his enemy's armoured skirts.

The blade pierced genitals, bladder and guts. Hyllus collapsed writhing round it like a beetle spitted on a pin. Echemus dragged out the sword, Hyllus screamed in a high thin voice. Echemus put a foot on his chest, rested the bloodied point on his teeth and rammed the blade down hard.

Hyllus arched his back, kicked legs out straight, lay still.

The Heraclids moaned, a rasping noise like shingle raked by a comber's backwash. Argives and Mycenaeans brandished spears and bellowed triumph. Atreus spoke to his Companion; the chariot rolled forward and halted within earshot of the stricken pair of Heroes who had seen from near at hand their leader die.

144

'Will you honour the agreement?' Atreus called. 'Hercules' son is dead. Your vow demands that your Host immediately retire.'

Fury distorted Iolaus' sullen countenance. 'Your man fought foul. Companions are inviolate in battles between gentlemen. The compact is void.'

'Hyllus didn't stipulate conditions – and you know very well that that archaic convention is nowadays seldom observed. Do you mean to break your oath? The idea of the combat, I gather, was to avoid unnecessary slaughter.' Atreus swung an arm to the serried ranks behind him. 'If you insist on battle, Iolaus, who do you think will come off worst?'

Iolaus studied the double line of chariots, wings projecting far beyond the Heraclid flanks, the spearmen massed behind. Horses don't stand still, they are always shifting and stamping; movement rustled and shimmered the ranks like the waves of a glittering sea, a bronze-tipped cataract poised to engulf all creatures that stood in its path.

He turned his head and looked at his Host; and bit his lower lip so hard blood trickled down his beard.

'Well?' said Atreus gently.

'I abide by the oath,' Iolaus said in muffled tones. 'No one alive today on this field will ever see Heraclids south of the Isthmus.' Eyes like points of fire glared into Atreus' face. 'I swear by The Lady, sire, my descendants will raze Mycenae and obliterate her site from the memory of man.'

He rapped an order. The Heraclids lifted Hyllus' corpse and crammed it in a chariot, turned and galloped away. After much disputation, gesticulation and shouting Iolaus persuaded his reluctant warriors to observe the vow their leaders had made. Slowly the Host dispersed; the backs of the rearguard faded from sight on the Isthmus road. Atreus watched them go, his countenance still as stone.

Adrastus' chariot rattled from the rear and pulled up alongside the king. 'What's all this?' he huffed. 'I thought we were going to attack whether Echemus won or lost. Now you're letting them go!'

'Changed my mind,' said Atreus. 'All promises made by a Heraclid are made on Hercules' behalf. And however much I dislike that bombastic, braggart ruffian he's never been known to break his word. In our lifetime and our sons' I believe we'll be free of the Heraclids. For the price of three men's lives,' Atreus ended sombrely, 'the boon is cheap.'

(I always thought it a barren excuse for Atreus' mental somersault. During one of the king's approachable periods – rare in his later years – I ventured to ask his real reason for sparing the Heraclid Host at Corinth. 'You don't think Hyllus offered single combat from the goodness of his heart, do you?' Atreus inquired acidly. 'He saw himself outnumbered and out-manoeuvred, and tried to retrieve the situation by an appeal to ancient traditions, to the duels fought when Zeus' sons were carving out shares of the land. Could have made sense when they led two men and a boy apiece. Three thousand troops paraded on Corinth's plain, and battles aren't decided that way any more. But Hyllus' proposal handed me a diplomatic victory. Public opinion is very strong in our warrior society. However shifty and treacherous Heroes actually are, they all pretend they adhere to gentlemen's codes. If the Heraclids break the pact and try to mount an invasion they won't find a single ally, not a Locrian or Athenian, not even a swine-faced Theban. I had Iolaus pronged on the fork of Heroic honour – so why waste Mycenaean lives?'

'And if Echemus had lost?'

'I'd have charged directly he hit the ground.'

'But ... Heroic honour ...'

Atreus sighed. 'I had something Hyllus hadn't – power. Power and honour don't share the same bed, Agamemnon.'

*   *   *

There was a mighty feast in Corinth that evening. Echemus, the guest of honour, sat on the king's right hand. I have never met a modest Hero; the Tegean was no exception. He recounted the struggle cut by cut; with every cup of wine his adversary grew bigger and stronger, his own feats more amazing.

'Never thought Hyllus would fall for that old trick,' he hiccupped. 'Pretend to be tired and lower your guard – hoary as the hills. If I'd been him I'd have backed away, not charged like a drunken bull. Otherwise he fought damned well – doubt anyone else could have beaten him.'

146

Corinth's resident bard hastily composed some adulatory verses and sang them in the Hall. Verbose and far too long, but the tune had a rhythmical beat; I recognized Orpheus' hand. I have heard the poem sung often since, round campfires and in Halls; exaggerations swell with every telling, Echemus' deeds grow miraculous.

I wonder whether, in ages to come, poets will recite huge lies about me?

Next morning Atreus drove a queasy, blear-eyed Bunus to the Isthmus' neck where it joins the Corinthian Plain. He demarcated a line eight thousand paces long, and commanded the Warden to build on the line a wall from shore to shore. The wall would be twenty feet high, a tower at every hundred paces, a fort in the centre and one at each end. 'Set every slave you have on the work,' said Atreus. 'I'll send you more from Mycenae. The wall will be finished within two years – or Corinth will get a new Warden.'

Bunus blinked, and massaged throbbing temples. I said, 'You told Adrastus, sire, you accepted Iolaus' promise. If so, why raise these massive fortifications? No one except the Heraclids threatens Mycenae.'

'Their terms have a limit – fifty years. I build for posterity, Agamemnon, against the day the Heraclids return.'

The huge grey stones are standing now, a barrier pierced by a single gate, watch-towers manned day and night, forts garrisoned by spearmen. Wasteful in troops and stores, and nobody dreams of attacking the wall. I often wonder whether it's worth the expense. The Heraclids have settled in Doris – native Dorians nowadays live mostly in Arcadia – and give us no trouble.

With Thebes and Troy destroyed and Heraclids contained perhaps I shall evacuate the Isthmus Wall.

Perhaps.

Chapter 6

SOON after Hyllus' death I received disturbing reports about threats to our overseas trade.

Piracy is an ancient profession and has a respectable history. When your ships on a trading voyage seize a galley more weakly manned or land to sack a village and capture slaves you call it tapping new markets; when somebody does it to you the crime is condemned as piracy. So long as the practice is kept within bounds losses and gains are roughly balanced – but things get out of hand when inconsiderate ruffians make piracy a whole-time occupation.

This was happening now; and the offenders came from Crete of all unlikely places.

Gelon says that in ages past, before the kings from Egypt landed, Crete had ruled the seas. After Zeus' forbears conquered the island they maintained Crete's naval supremacy until Thera's devastation destroyed their ports and ships. Zeus crossed to Achaea, and afterwards Phoenicians ruled the waves. Knossos, however, revived, and under Minos – a Cretan royal title; similarly Pylos calls her rulers 'Wanax' – defeated Phoenician fleets and gradually restored her ancient maritime mastery.

In Achaea her resurgence passed unnoticed: Zeus' sons were busily establishing their kingdoms, fighting the natives and one another for shares of the land. Around Acrisius' time, when life had settled down, they found Cretans raiding Achaean coasts and waylaying ships.

Such maritime bullying was more than Heroes could tolerate. Acrisius mounted a seaborne invasion, chose a time when Minos had taken his fleet to wage war on Sicily, landed unopposed and burnt Knossos to the ground. The Sicilians slew Minos and sank his ships; so Acrisius had no difficulty in placing Asterius, an Achaean noble, on Knossos' throne and thenceforth ruling Crete as a tributary kingdom.

Asterius placated native Cretans by assuming the Minos title; then raided a Phoenician town and carried off Europa, a local chieftain's daughter. From these two spring the Cretan Royal House. The ruling Minos, third since Asterius and an aged man who sired my maternal grandfather Catreus, was therefore Achaean by blood. Though Mycenaean hold on Knossos loosened over the years, and tribute has been remitted, he naturally kept on friendly terms with his powerful Achaean neighbours.

Hence, when a battered penteconter – a twenty-five-a-side oared galley – limped into Nauplia's harbour and her master related a running fight against ships undoubtedly Cretan I found it hard to believe him.

Other sources confirmed his story. Survivors described a roving Cretan squadron raiding islands lately colonized by settlers from Mycenae. Ships voyaging on the Rhodian route mysteriously disappeared: a surviving crewman swore the enemy Cretan. I reported the tales to Atreus, who sent an embassy to Minos protesting against his seamen's depredations.

Minos denied responsibility. He said a band of pirates occasionally used Malia as a base – a shanty town arisen on the ruins of a city the earthquake waves engulfed centuries before. He had sent warbands to evict them; but the pirates embarked at sight of a spear and fled beyond the horizon.

Atreus summoned me to hear his delegates' reports. 'All very unsatisfactory,' he declared. 'Minos, if he wanted, could easily crush the nest. They probably pay him a share of the loot for beaching their ships at Malia, and the king makes a nice little packet.'

I said, 'Shall I take a squadron and burn the place?'

'Nothing much to burn, from what I hear – a scatter of huts among fallen stones. Besides, Minos would certainly take umbrage, and we don't want to start a war. Knossos can launch a powerful fleet.'

'By all accounts the pirates have only three galleys. With your approval, sire, when next I hear of a strike I'll sail a triaconter squadron – six fast ships – and try to intercept them.'

149

'Yes. You may be lucky. Blasted nuisance, though – six ships less on the trade routes.'

I returned to Tiryns, and hadn't long to wait. One of our galleys beaching at Cythnos found a fire-wreathed town and three sails disappearing in sea-mist on the skyline. A dying fisherman confirmed the raiders Cretan. (You can always tell a Cretan by his accent: they speak our tongue with guttural intonations derived from the native language.) The news was two days old. I launched my triaconters and, hoping the pirates were heading for Malia, set a course for Melos in hope of cutting them off. Thanks to a following wind we reached Melos four days later, and saw not a sign of a ship except a peaceable galley from Troy.

Hunting pirates at sea is like searching for an amber grain in sand. They might be anywhere. In spring-bright days we cruised across sunlit seas, sailed from island to island and landed to make inquiries. At nightfall we hauled the ships ashore and lighted driftwood fires to cook our meals, afterwards reposing on soft warm sand, sipping from wineskins and watching the stars swing slowly across the heavens. A carefree life untrammelled by conventions governing life in citadels: no audiences or parades or ceremonial dinners, no Scribes or stewards or slaves, my sole attendant a fourteen-year-old squire called Eurymedon.

Nowhere did we find word of Cretan pirates. We sailed round Naxos and put in at a shelving, sheltered strand where ships could be safely beached – not so easily come by on these rocky island coasts. A large fishing village clustered round the haven, boats bottoms-up on the beach, nets spread out to dry, a penteconter tilted on her keel. The appearance of a six-ship squadron roused frenetic activity: spearmen ran to guard-towers and gathered on the shore, women and old and young hastened towards a rock-built fort on a hillside above the town. In those days Mycenae's maritime grip had hardly begun to close; no dominant power ruled the sea; coastal settlements constantly feared attack.

Within six years I made the seaways safe.

The rowers of my triaconter – *Aithe* was her name – backed water beyond arrow-shot; her leather-lunged master bawled our identity and asked permission to land. Rowers grounded keels, jumped overside and hauled the hulls ashore. I splashed to the beach, greeted a greybearded elder clad in a leather cuirass which drooped on his skinny frame like a windless sail, and shortly related our mission. No – he had neither seen nor heard of Cretan pirates.

The stranded penteconter was being prepared for sea. Crewmen ran the hull to the water, put mast and sail aboard, fixed pinewood oars in leather slings, waded waistdeep carrying victuals – bleating foot-tethered goats, corn sacks, bulging wineskins. A man in a calfskin kilt directed operations from the beach. Intending to ask news of our elusive pirates I crunched across the shingle, introduced myself and politely inquired whence they had come and whither they voyaged.

'From Amnisos in Crete,' he said. 'We sail for Athens. I am Theseus son of Aegeus son of Pandion.'

The Hero I had chased at the Battle of Megara. Short, deep-chested, muscular. A countenance all features: bulging forehead, beaked thin nose, a gash for a mouth and square blunt chin. Grey wideset eyes; sun-bleached hair and beard. No longer a youth; past thirty, I guessed.

He had not recognized his late opponent, nor I him: helmets and battle-excitement blur your enemy's face. I thought it tactful not to remind him, and offered a share of my wineskin.

We sat side by side on the sand. Theseus described a journey to Knossos where he had sought remission of a tribute Athens paid. 'An iniquitous imposition,' he declared, 'which dates from an unfortunate accident years before I was born. One of Minos' sons visited Athens to compete in the annual games – the man was a notable athlete – and got himself killed in a robbers' ambush. Minos in revenge disembarked a warband, raided Megaran territory and ravaged Attica. We can't mobilize much of a Host,' Theseus admitted, 'so my father agreed on a stiff indemnity and a nine-yearly tribute of slaves. I accompanied the last consignment and tried to persuade Minos that Athens had paid enough compensation for a killing not her fault.'

I remembered tales of the episode, and knew Theseus lied: politics lay at the root of a deliberate slaying. Minos had sent his son to encourage Athenian dissidents who aimed at removing Aegeus. Aegeus discovered the plot and conspired with Megaran bandits to have the Cretan killed. I was not surprised:

Athenians are liars by nature. Their city is small and unimportant, yet they call the ruler king: a title properly kept for powerful kingdoms like Pylos, Argos and Elis, Sparta, Mycenae and Thebes.

'Were you successful?' I asked.

'Indeed,' said Theseus smugly. 'I am, as you probably know, a mighty wrestler and gymnast. In Knossos they leap bulls for sport, and train acrobats to somersault over the horns. Extremely dangerous, I promise you. I'd never done it before, of course, but easily outshone the Cretan experts. Minos was so impressed he wanted me to stay and teach his performers.'

'A risky profession.'

'Being braver than any man I've met, risks to me are enjoyable. It wasn't that. My charm and personality persuaded Minos to cancel the tribute, and he liked me so much he insisted I wed his daughter Ariadne.'

'An advantageous marriage, uniting Athens and Crete.'

'Maybe. She fell head over heels in love with me but,' said Theseus frankly, 'the old hag has a face like the backside of a bullock. I prevaricated and made excuses, and eventually skipped to Amnisos, hoisted sail and slipped away by night.'

Theseus tilted the wineskin and drank, wiped his mouth with the back of a hand. 'A day out from Crete I found a stowaway hidden under sailcloth in the hold. Ariadne,' he ended despondently.

I ran an eye along the people thronging the beach, gathering round my crewmen with presents of fruit and honey. 'Is she here?'

'No.' Theseus glanced furtively over his shoulder. 'I told Ariadne we're sailing tomorrow, and she's gone to the hills for the day with a bevy of women. Wild looking creatures: probably a sect Dionysus founded, bent on some feminine orgy. I couldn't care less. I'll be well away before she's back.'

A heartless, vain and bumptious man, I reflected, and foolish as well: Minos' offended pride might look for reprisal. (In fact Minos died of extreme old age during the time we harboured at Naxos. Catreus, his son and successor, disliked his sister Ariadne and let the matter drop.) Belatedly I remembered to ask Theseus whether he had seen any sign of our quarry during his voyage.

'Very likely. We passed three penteconters a day's sail out from Naxos going southward fast under sail and oars. I didn't like the look of the blighters, and sheered away. As I must now, in case the woman returns before she's due.'

Theseus ran to exhort his sailors. The last of the baggage was handed aboard, rowers settled on thwarts and the coxswain trilled his pipe. Oars thrashed water in gouts of foam, the galley slid from the shore. Theseus in the sternsheets waved farewell; the gilded sternpost vanished behind a headland.

I had to cope with Ariadne when she returned to the town that evening. Minos' youngest daughter was well past mark of mouth – my aunt, in point of fact – thin, sallow and highly strung and, as Theseus had hinted, excessively plain. She was more than a little drunk, her breath wine-rank; and blood flecks stained her flounced blue skirts. (One has heard hair-raising stories of gory drunken orgies in which Dionysus' female acolytes, commonly called Maenads, indulge in secret places in the hills.) Finding the Athenian galley gone Ariadne threw a fit of hysterics and clung weeping to my shoulders. I comforted her as best I could, delivered her in charge of the local chieftain's family and retired to sleep on the beach among my men. The Naxians seemed harmless enough, but you can never be too careful.

I slumbered wrapped in a cloak, and was woken by a naked woman entwining her limbs with mine. In darkness and half asleep I could not recognize my visitor and gratefully accepted the gift that fate bestowed. She proved passionate, expert and tremendously exhausting; except for the moans which signalled successive crises she never uttered a sound. (Just as well: my crewmen snored on the sand not far away.) When I failed to respond to her fifth assault she removed her hand from my weapon and whispered in my ear, 'Now, dear Agamemnon, will you take me on your ship?'

I must admit I was shocked. 'Ariadne, this is disgraceful! How could you —'

'You enjoyed yourself, didn't you? Take me with you, dearest, and we can make love every night when the ships are beached. There's a lot I can teach you yet!'

I pushed her off and reached for my cloak. 'Impossible. We're hunting pirates and have no place for women aboard.'

'I promise to keep out of the way. You can land me at Nauplia when you return and I'll travel to Athens' – her voice hardened – 'and confront that runagate Theseus.'

'No. You must wait for a passing galley.'

Ariadne started weeping. I groped fruitlessly in the dark for her clothes: apparently she had stolen from the chieftain's house stark naked. A coppery sheen tinged the eastern sky; distractedly I besought her to go before daylight disclosed her shame. At last, still sobbing, she stumbled away.

I reclined tiredly on the sand and reflected on the oddities of women.

We launched the ships at sun-up and loaded provisions bought in the town. Everyone gathered on the strand to see us off. I looked for Ariadne among the serried faces and failed to find her. With something akin to remorse I signalled coxswains to trill their pipes; oars flashed in the rising sun and we rowed from the harbour in line ahead. In wind-rippled water beyond the headland I ordered masts to be raised, and was struck by a devastating thought.

Hailing the ships I instructed masters to search thoroughly for stowaways in the holds.

None was found. I breathed a sigh of relief. Sailors stepped masts in hollow boxes, hoisted sails and sheeted home. A following wind swept the squadron south on tumbling seas to Crete.

I never discovered what happened to the unfortunate Ariadne. Rumours abounded later: that she married Dionysus in Naxos (quite ridiculous: the ancient I met near Rhipe must then have been dead for years); that she was accidentally killed by a hunter's arrow; that she emigrated to Cyprus and died in childbed. (I hope I had nothing to do with *that*.) Years afterwards when, as king, I conducted the long sea war against Troy I harboured at Naxos. They still remembered Ariadne on the island; I was shown a shrine where Maenads worshipped her memory. Bards have seized on her tragic story; men will remember her name, I feel, for generations to come.

Theseus returned to Athens, found his father dead and assumed in his place the grandiloquent title of 'King'. I never cared for the fellow, and he gave me, indirectly, a basket of trouble later. Though he spurned the wretched Ariadne he

154

never could keep his hands off women; and his rape of Spartan Helen begat the lunatic Iphigeneia whom Helen's sister Clytemnaistra successfully foisted on me. Killing Iphigeneia damned near cost my throne. But, as they say, I anticipate.

*　　*　　*

Our navigators set course for a landfall near Malia. The sea stayed calm, a fair wind rested the rowers. On the second morning the Cretan coast heaved above the horizon, a long grey line like stormclouds stroking the sea. The galleys sailed line abreast within hailing distance; the slowest periodically unshipped oars in order to keep her station. I drowsed on deck in the cabin's shade; the master leaned on his steering oar; rowers lounged on benches, dozed or gossiped or diced; the coxswain piped lilting melodies; seamen idled in handy reach of the sheets. Waves slapped strakes, *Aithe* pitched gently and rolled, the wind played tunes on mast-stays.

A lookout hailed from the prow.

Three white specks like wisps of wool drifted on the haze where shore met sea. I peered beneath the sail and shaded my eyes. Impossible at that distance to decide the course they set, whether they moved towards us or away. The master resolved my doubts. 'They're crossing our course, me lord. Sailing slow with the wind abeam. Could be the ships we're after. May be peaceful merchantmen. Can't tell yet. Shall I alter course to intercept?'

'Yes – and make all speed!'

Orders volleyed from galley to galley. Sailors jumped to sheets and trimmed the sails. Oars rattled from thwarts, dropped and struck. Pipes shrieked a quickening beat. The line of triaconters leaped like hard-whipped horses, smacked foam from bows and flew.

I clutched the backstay and watched faraway sails which seemed to draw no nearer. Then, remembering the chase could end in a fight, I called my squire and ducked inside the cabin. You don't wear chariot mail on ships; I donned a bronze-studded leather cuirass and plumeless metal helmet, strapped on a slashing sword, put arm through grips of a round hide shield and picked up a throwing-spear. Thus armed I stood in the sternsheets. The sails looked distant as ever. For one accustomed to swift and sudden clashes on land the nerve-twanging slowness of battles at sea was disconcerting.

The master tugged his steering oar and said, 'Pirate galleys, me lord. Unless they go about we'll cross their course.'

As he spoke I saw the broad white flecks of the corsairs' sails shrink to a finger's breadth and billow again like wings. 'Gone about,' the master spat. He screwed his eyes and peered at the peaks that soared above the coastline. 'I reckon they're making for Malia. We'll have a job to catch them before they beach.'

He hailed the triaconters a spearcast on either beam. Steering oars dug froth from wakes, seamen sprang to sheets and hauled. The galleys, turning together, set course for a straight pursuit. Oars swung in a faster cadence. The ships raced on like running stags: black hulls and crimson prows, tall beast-headed sternposts, the honey-hued flash of bronze-sheathed rams jutting from waves as they pitched in the swell, oarbanks rhythmically lifting and dipping, sails bellying and straining on masts.

In *Aithe* the rowers' oak-brown bodies swung forward and back like a single machine. Men crouching at sheets trimmed sail to the shifts of the wind. Sailors spliced stout ashwood staves to make a forty-foot bronze-barbed pole. 'Fending-pole,' said the master shortly, answering my questioning look.

Steadily we overhauled the fleeing ships.

I distinguished their oars, a helmsman's figure at the stern, the foaming furrow carved by his sweep. Beyond them soared the mountains, clefts like giant gashes shading tree-clad slopes, snowfields streaking the peaks. A yellow-sand bay was a bite in rocky cliffs. Buildings clustered inland, small as a handful of pebbles cast on the spring-green grass.

'Malia,' the master stated. He calculated distances, glanced at the sail, shifted slightly the slant of his oar. 'We might just catch the bastards. They row twenty-five oars a side; we have thirty, and larger sails. Going to be close. Cox'n, speed the strike.'

The tempo climbed to the battle-stroke, a pace no oarsman can hold for long. Sweat-streams coursed down the rowers' naked backs; above the screech of the wind I heard their gasping breaths. (I wondered for a moment how these overtasked men could possibly fight when we closed the enemy ships.) The gap shrank fast; three spearcasts divided hunters' prows from hunted sternposts.

We entered the arms of the bay. Rollers curved and broke on the sand; serried reeds like olive-green lances palisaded the mouth of a stream.

A penteconter lagged three lengths behind her sisters, her oarbeats ragged and faltering. 'We'll get that one at least,' the master promised. Faintly I heard orders shouted; the pirate's sail whipped free from the sheets; the helmsman hauled on his oar with all his strength. Larboard oars dripped clear of the water, starboard dug in short quick strokes. The galley spun in her tracks. Timed by an urgent pipe both oarbanks drove her straight for *Aithe*.

'Down sail! Down mast!' our master roared. 'Out pole! Prepare for ramming!'

The penteconter's bows were aimed at our starboard quarter. Our helmsman pushed his sweep; *Aithe*'s bows swung larboard, angling away from the enemy. I watched the threatening prow approach, bow wave frothing, ram like a shark's fin slicing the waves. Why, I dithered, mouth gone dry, expose our beam to the ram? I braced myself for the shock of collision. At arrow-shot range the master shouted 'Ship starboard oars!' and flung his weight on the steering oar.

Propelled by the sweep of the larboard oarbank *Aithe* turned like a pony. Her starboard rowers slipped oars inboard, grabbed spears and swords from straps. In a crash of riven timbers and splintering oars our ram gouged the pirate's hull. Her mast snapped short and the flying sail smothered her crew in the stern. Our seamen lifted the fending pole, butted beak on enemy strakes and thrust to release the ram.

The impact had flung me flat on the deck. I climbed to my feet and lugged out sword. Cretans swarmed over the sides and tumbled aboard. Our rowers rushed to meet them, and a savage little battle erupted in the forepart. I scrambled over benches, mast and sail and oars. A burly naked Cretan lunged a spear-thrust at my head; I lifted shield and parried the point, plunged blade to the hilt in his belly.

I needn't have doubted the oarsmen's endurance; inside a hundred heartbeats they had hurled the assailants back or overside into the sea. The sailors' weight on the pole pushed

Aithe clear; with a creak and a crack the ram came free and we drifted away. Water surged through the shattered hole in the penteconter's hull. She listed and started to settle. Bowmen appeared at the side rails, arrows whirred and thumped in wood. A seaman shrieked, and tore at the feathered shaft spiking from his stomach.

'Damned Cretan bowmen!' the master grumbled, 'Out oars! Back water!' *Aithe* retreated crabwise and paddled beyond range. He eyed the sinking ship, men jumping overside and swimming for shore. 'She's done for. What d'you want now, me lord?'

The two remaining penteconters had rowed themselves on the beach, keels ploughed deep in sand. Crewmen raced for the dunes. *Aithe*'s sister galleys, following hard on enemy sterns, were likewise preparing to beach. I remembered Atreus' warning about raiding Cretan coasts. Be damned to that. The pirates were in my grasp and I meant to close the fist.

'Get under way. We'll beat those fellows to shore and kill them as they land.'

Spaces in the oarbanks yawned like gaps in teeth: rowers had been wounded in the fight. Keels rasped on shingle, oars rattled inboard and the squadron's crewmen waded ashore, weapons in hand and baying for blood. They swarmed over sand and tussocky grass in pursuit of vanishing Cretans. I ordered *Aithe*'s men to stay on the beach, slay the sunken galley's crew as they swam ashore, and afterwards to fire the two beached penteconters.

Malia lay inland a short way beyond the dunes: the devastated skeleton of a large and prosperous city. Gaunt grey roofless walls, great tumbled stones and fallen pillars, weeds flourishing in cracks of the Great Court's paving, sand-drifts covering floors and piled at the bases of buildings. A brittle coating of ash hurled long ago from Thera encrusted open surfaces and crunched beneath my feet.

Mud-walled, grass-thatched hovels squatted among the ruins and vomited terrified families when swords appeared from the sea. Some of the pirates we chased attempted to rescue their kin; others fled for the foothills; a few made a stand behind rubble and walls and shouted defiance.

We scoured Malia, hunted stone-flagged streets, searched

dilapidated houses, granaries and store rooms, slaughtered every male and burned the huts. Many escaped, dodging between broken houses and hiding in woods on the outskirts. We rounded up women and children, save a handful killed in the turmoil – slaves were in great demand in Nauplia's market. A sprinkle of cattle and sheep and goats grazed on the fields outside: some we took to replenish our larders, the rest we killed. A search in the huts before burning produced cauldrons, bracelets and golden cups: the pirates' loot from merchant ships and pillaged coastal towns.

By mid-afternoon it was over, and our men returned to the beach. Pillars of smoke coiled skywards from burning penteconters. I stayed for a while exploring Malia, wandering desolate streets and poking into the palace's shattered remains, walking beneath tottering archways of tremendous hewn-stone gates and examining an altar surmounted by marble bulls' horns. Nowhere was there a sign of fortifications. I speculated on the nature of Cretans in olden times who dared to live for centuries in undefended cities.

Back at the bay I stripped my armour, wallowed in the shallows and scrubbed off sweat and blood. We buried our seven dead and feasted royally on pirate beef and mutton. The more personable female captives, distributed among galley crews, were taken into the dunes and comprehensively raped. I enjoyed an acrobatic tumble with a dark-haired Cretan filly – a virgin, as I proved – and relished the contrast between her squealing maladroitness and Ariadne's talents.

While rustling rollers lulled me to sleep on the sand I considered the repercussions of our foray. In flagrant disobedience of Atreus' instructions I had sacked a Cretan settlement; and King Catreus would undoubtedly be displeased. Forebodings disturbed my slumbers; and I was glad to board *Aithe* again and feel the clean salt sea-wind blowing my hair, and sway to the thrust of the oarbanks that carried me home to Nauplia.

*   *   *

I described the episode to Atreus: he was bound to hear sooner or later, probably in garbled versions, and I judged it best to tell my story first. He did not seem greatly interested. 'As well you rooted them out: a warning to other pirates, Sidonians and

159

Sicilians,' he observed. 'I'll soothe Catreus' injured pride – send him a herd of horses or such.' His manner throughout the interview was moody and withdrawn, his mind occupied elsewhere. There were more grey streaks in his hair, new lines on the careworn countenance; the beginnings of a stoop diminished his height.

He beckoned me to a chamber above the Throne Room and pointed from a window across the valley. On the crest of a hill in the distance I saw figures aswarm on a tawny mound of newly-dug earth.

The king said, 'I am building my tomb.'

Which did not necessarily indicate a morbid concern with death though, glancing at Atreus' expression, I felt a momentary doubt. Royal tombs from Mycenae's past pimpled the hillsides surrounding the citadel: Sthenelus, Electryon and others before them. (Perseus, who founded Mycenae's glory, lies at Argos.) Every tomb, so far as I know, was built in the occupant's lifetime.

Atreus took me to the site. The scale of the work was enormous. A deep canyon excavated in a hillside led to a vast circular pit dug from the summit downwards, later to be lined with cut stone slabs and roofed by a dome. The sepulchre dwarfed all others, Zeus' tomb a cairn in comparison.

'A new dynasty rules Mycenae,' Atreus explained gravely. 'The sons of Pelops' memorials should not be less magnificent than the Perseids' they succeed.'

I tactfully concurred. An army of slaves and craftsmen worked on a long-drawn task. The Isthmus Wall, then building, also engaged workmen by the thousand. While our expanded maritime trade procured slaves in numbers from abroad these two undertakings together must strain our labour resources. Miletos and other cities provided plenty of slaves, but there was always competition, the supply not inexhaustible. The men would be better employed on the land, in mines and quarries and shipyards.

However, one does not argue with kings, certainly not with Atreus; and my reservations stayed behind my teeth. Nor was it tomb construction (a dismal pursuit, in my opinion: I have not put mine in hand and never will) which troubled his mind and ploughed the bitter lines from jaw to cheekbones. He

160

called Menelaus and me to the Throne Room's deserted antechamber and disclosed the black obsession which gnawed in his
brain like a rat.

'Thyestes remains at Elis. My spies report he is concocting
schemes to oust me from the throne. King Augeas isn't privy
to his plans – he's anyway beyond the age to engage in risky
ventures – but my brother is finding support among young,
adventurous, ambitious Elian Heroes. He is also trying to
suborn nobles in our tributary cities. He has ripped my
honour in shreds,' said Atreus in a voice like a falling sword,
'and now he aims at my crown. Thyestes must be destroyed.'

'Surely,' I protested, 'he reaches for a star beyond his grasp.
How can an exile collect forces enough to defeat Mycenae's
Host – the strongest in Achaea?'

'He has found a tool: Phyleus, King Augeas' eldest son.
Years ago Phyleus and Hercules, then in bondage to Augeas,
started some treacherous intrigue – I can't remember the
details. Augeas banished them both. Phyleus has recently
returned to Dyme, a short day's march from Elis across the
northern border.'

'Another banished outlaw lacking a following,' Menelaus
said.

'On the contrary. Phyleus' relations in Elis consider him
badly treated and strongly support his cause. Thyestes encourages the malcontents, went to Dyme and saw Phyleus.
They've made a pact. In return for fomenting a palace uprising,
deposing old Augeas and putting his son on the throne,
Thyestes has won Phyleus' promise of military support against
Mycenae.'

I said contemptuously, 'Are we afraid of an Elian Host?'

'No – although they can mobilize a formidable array. The
real danger is internal. If Thyestes can rouse a rebellion in
Mycenae and her tributary cities to coincide with invasion
from Elis he has a fair chance of success.'

I said, 'He'll have to dangle tempting rewards in the shape of
treasure and land – neither of which he possesses. So I don't see
how —'

'Thyestes will *promise* rewards,' said Atreus harshly. 'Would
you stake *any* Hero's loyalty against an offer of gold and

demesnes? I can count on my fingers the lords I would trust to resist a big enough bribe.'

Menelaus said, 'Have you no idea who the potential traitors are?'

'Copreus, for one, here in Mycenae. Three in Corinth – not Bunus – three in Nemea, one or two others. Surmise based on intelligence reports; I have no proof. Nor do I need it. I could have them killed tomorrow on the offchance – and consequently make more enemies among their kindred. Until they actually show their hands it isn't worth the trouble.'

The antechamber had not been swept since the morning's audience; a mess of petitioners' litter strewed the chequered marble floor: a shattered wine jar, bits of bread and biscuit, a kilt belt's broken buckle, a cloak crumpled in a corner. I picked up a papyrus fragment some Scribe had dropped, and absently studied an indecipherable scrawl. 'So, sire, what do you intend to do?'

'Send you and Menelaus to tempt him back to Mycenae.'

The paper fluttered from my hand. 'Persuade Thyestes to leave Augeas' protection and enter the lion's den? You must think the man insane!'

'Not so, Agamemnon. Thyestes, like any exile, yearns for his native land. A vulnerable weakness. I shall send him sumptuous gifts, assure him all is forgiven, promise him safe conduct and guarantee his life. His estates shall be restored intact – provided he stays in Mycenae. I believe the bait sufficient. Moreover' – a sardonic inflexion – 'once ensconced in the palace he can more easily weave his plots against my life.'

'I don't understand.' Menelaus rubbed his russet hair. 'You said Thyestes must be – um – eliminated. Yet, having brought him here, you are bound by your oath to let him live.'

Atreus said tonelessly, 'He shall not be killed.'

I said, 'Your purpose, sire, escapes my comprehension. You invite a scorpion to nestle in your boot.'

'I know what I'm doing. Now remember this. Before you meet Thyestes you must learn by heart the terms I offer and, before witnesses, repeat them to him exactly as I have stated them to you. Without the smallest variation, Agamemnon.'

'I shall, sire.'

'If Thyestes still refuses to return you have my authority, then, to offer him joint rule of Mycenae.'

My jaw dropppd. 'You will share —' I met Atreus' look, and stopped. 'Very well, sire.'

'That is all. You'll leave for Elis immediately.'

I summoned my courage and said, 'What *do* you mean to do with Thyestes?'

The faintest hint of a smile touched Atreus' lips, a smile that shivered ice-barbs on my spine. 'I shall make him endure, living, the tortures I have suffered at his hands.'

*   *   *

I detailed a powerful escort for our journey across Arcadia: twenty chariots and three hundred spears guarded a train of mules and ox-carts carrying baggage, provisions and a profusion of valuables intended as gifts for Thyestes. Arcadians are rough mountain folk, inimical to strangers, living in tribal villages clinging to the slopes. Gelon says they descend from Achaea's earliest people, aboriginals who held the land before the Goatmen. Besides these primitive savages, Goatmen and Dorians infest the heights and descend to harry travellers. Men journeying in Arcadia keep swords loosely scabbarded.

Despite the need for incessant vigilance, despite stony rutted trackways and barely fordable streams the march was not unpleasant. Fresh greenery mantled hillsides, flowers speckled the valleys in a gorgeous rolling tapestry splashed yellow and red and blue. I sent chariots ahead to Elis to announce our peaceful advent: Elians were touchy about armed parties from Arcadia and I had no desire to meet a pugnacious warband.

King Augeas received us as hospitably as his infirmities permitted – at this time most of Achaea's rulers seemed doddery old men – provided a hutted camp for drovers, spearmen and grooms, and quarters in the citadel for Heroes and Companions. After greeting Menelaus and myself, and learning the purpose of our visit, Augeas sent a chamberlain to fetch Thyestes, and tottered to his apartments. We saw him no more until we took our leave.

It was easy to see in Elis how young ambitious nobles, chafing under a senile king who refused to die, could easily become a fertile bed for the seed of mutinous plots.

I displayed two ox-carts' loads of gifts in tempting array on the floor of a room the chamberlain provided. Clad in kilt and sandals. Thyestes swaggered in accompanied by two Heroes and a boy about nine years old – Tantalus, his youngest and favourite son. Sunken eyes surveyed us bleakly.

'King Augeas bids me meet you. I defer to my host's commands. I'd rather foregather with swineherds than talk to Atreus' lackeys. Say what you have to say quickly, and return to your master's midden.'

It was not a promising start. Moreover Thyestes' very appearance made gooseflesh pimple my skin. Even today his memory recalls a cringing fear from childhood days fuelled by the loathing my ordeal in Aerope's room engendered. Time had grizzled a stiff brown beard, deeper hollows and harsher planes chiselled the weathered-oak face. I could almost smell the evil he exuded.

I indicated the gifts on the floor. 'King Atreus sends these for your pleasure, my lord, and hopes for a reconciliation. It is not becoming, he says, for brothers to live at enmity.'

Thyestes' foot sent a beaker clattering. 'Damned rubbish! I have treasure enough for my needs. Why this sudden generosity? Atreus wouldn't part with a wooden platter unless he expected a lucrative return. What does the blaggard want?'

I repeated the offer I had learned by rote, varying never a word. Thyestes listened in mounting surprise and, at the end, remained silent for several moments. Absently he unsheathed the dagger at his belt, examined the blade unseeingly, returned it to the sheath and tapped it home. He said abruptly, 'What has caused my brother's astonishing change of heart?'

This was outside my brief. 'The realm is expanding, my lord,' I improvised. 'Mycenaeans are settling in islands overseas; trade is flourishing; and I believe the king is contemplating conquests in Achaea. It's a heavy burden for a man to carry alone. He needs your help to lighten the load.'

'Very plausible – if one could believe a word the trickster says. He promises an amnesty and guarantees my life. Will you answer for that with your head?'

'I will, my lord.'

'And I,' Menelaus murmured.

164

'Then,' Thyestes snapped, 'one of you stays in Elis as hostage for my safety.'

I strove to conceal confusion. 'I regret we have not King Atreus' permission. I must obey his orders faithfully – they were detailed and precise. He made no mention of hostages, ourselves or any other.'

'Of course,' Thyestes jeered. 'So he extends no solid safe-guards, and expects me to take him on trust. He must think me a monstrous fool! Atreus can eat his gifts, the estates he offers, his promises – and I hope they choke him!' He swung on his heel and stamped to the door, scattering tripods, cups and flagons as he went.

'Wait, my lord!' I cleared my throat and said incisively, 'That is not all. Provided you come to Mycenae the king is ready to cede you half his realm in equal rule.'

Thyestes turned in the doorway and rested a hand on the jamb. He gave me a meditative look. Cunning and calculation glinted in hard green eyes. 'So. An offer of kingship. Rather more generous than these trashy gifts. It gives a different slant to the whole affair.' He draped an arm affectionately round Tantalus' shoulders, and crooked a finger at his taciturn brace of Heroes. 'You witness Agamemnon's words, my lords, and you, young fellow? I am entitled, on reaching Mycenae, to share Atreus' kingdom. Repeat the contract, Agamemnon.'

I did so, loathing every word, certain I perjured myself. Atreus, of all people, was not the man to yield a tittle of his power to anyone on earth, least of all to a brother he hated from the bottom of his heart. The king was set on vengeance for Aerope, some horrible requital whose nature I could not fathom – for I fully believed his promise to spare the seducer's life. I almost, against all reason, blurted a warning to stay securely in Elis.

I kept my mouth shut, and disaster flowed undammed.

'In that case,' Thyestes said, 'I'll consider the matter and give you an answer by morning. Come, my lords. Tantalus, dear boy, it's time you went to bed.'

They left the room. Perspiration damped my temples. Mene-laus met my look, and wordlessly rolled his eyes.

At dawn Thyestes, with Tantalus in his chariot, an entourage of Heroes, Companions and squires driving behind, headed the column marching for Mycenae.

* * *

Atreus accorded Thyestes the ceremonial grandeur befitting a reigning monarch. Taking his palace Heroes and four hundred spearmen splendidly accoutred, he drove out to meet him. The brothers dismounted and embraced. Atreus looked brisk and cheerful. For one optimistic moment I almost dared to hope that the king had changed his mind.

Nobody, unfortunately, had remembered to tell Pelopia. While crossing the Great Court attended by ladies she met her husband and Thyestes and a boisterous party of Heroes emerging from the stairway. I thought she was going to swoon. She put hand over mouth and staggered, gave an inarticulate moan and ran from the Court as fast as her skirts would allow. Thyestes watched her going; a malevolent little smile quivered on his lips. The king, surprised and anxious, hastened into the portico after his queen.

When he returned Thyestes inquired easily, 'Who is the handsome lady who has been suddenly taken ill?'

'My wife Pelopia,' said Atreus shortly, 'Thesprotus of Sicyon's daughter. Heat and sun-glare have brought on a painful migraine.'

'Ah, yes — I heard of your marriage. Although I stayed in Sicyon I never,' Thyestes lied, 'had the pleasure of meeting your lady. You have a child, I hear.'

'A two-year-old son : Aegisthus.'

'An uncommon name.' Thyestes' eyes were hooded, his countenance inscrutable. 'Aegisthus. I must remember.'

Pelopia eased an impossible situation by pleading severe sickness and confining herself to her room throughout Thyestes' stay. The scoundrel thoroughly enjoyed his secret joke: he inquired solicitously after the queen's health and regretted he had failed to make her acquaintance. I could have stuck my dagger in his throat. Though most of the palace Heroes were equally aware of Pelopia's bizarre predicament none dared whisper a hint to Atreus, who maintained a serene composure and seemed entirely indifferent to the queen's continued absence from the banqueting and ceremonies.

Atreus royally entertained his brother day after day. Hunting parties went to the hills, bagged many a lion and boar. On the Field of War Atreus organized games and competitions: foot and chariot races, boxing and wrestling matches, javelin and archery contests. A banquet every afternoon, and long evenings in the Hall lingering over wine and listening to bardic caterwauling. Never before, in my memory, had Mycenae seen festivities so prolonged.

I shared in all these diversions and, when the boy was not engaged in squiring Thyestes, acted host to Tantalus: a pleasant enough lad, a thought dim-witted. Thyestes plainly doted on his son – a viper, I suppose, can love his brood – and was for ever stroking his hair and holding his hand. A nauseating spectacle, when you remember the way he abandoned his daughter Pelopia.

I hardly recognized Atreus. His manner had reverted to the debonair carefree habit which prevailed before he discovered Aerope's adultery. Watching him at a feast graciously transferring choice morsels from his platter to Thyestes' I was persuaded he had genuinely forgiven his brother. I said so in an undertone to Menelaus. That hard-headed individual pronged mutton into his mouth and mumbled, 'Don't you believe it. The Lady knows what Atreus is at – but I'd hate to be in Thyestes' place.'

As the days went by Thyestes became impatient. The king showed no inclination to ratify the agreement which had persuaded him to enter Mycenae's gates. Atreus stayed deaf to blatant hints, suggested another hunt – 'a really enormous boar, Thyestes, ravages Midea's crops' – a trip to Nauplia to inspect galleys recently launched; anything rather than formal restoration of forfeited estates and announcement to the Council that he and Thyestes shared Mycenae's rule. Finally, while chatting beside the hearth in the Hall, Thyestes' patience snapped and he loweringly demanded the king discharge his oath.

Atreus kicked a glowing log, and laughed. 'Why, certainly, dear brother. I merely await Mycenae's greatest day, the anniversary of Perseus' foundation. Tomorrow as ever is. Surely it is proper your accession to the throne should fall on such a glorious occasion? A most exceptional feast shall celebrate the event and I'll make the announcement after, provided you are willing.'

'I am,' said Thyestes tersely.

*   *   *

Alabaster lamps and pitchpine torches flared in Mycenae's Hall and dimmed the afternoon sunlight that lanced clerestory windows. On a blazing hearth fire cooks turned spits and basted joints of beef and mutton and pork. Carvers sawed and sliced; servants scurried to tables and handed laden platters; squires poured wine from hammered gold flagons. At the widening circles of tables two hundred noble gentlemen ate and drank, talked loudly between mouthfuls, wagged hunks of meat on dagger points to emphasize an argument. Twenty sheep, twenty boars and fifteen barley-fed oxen had been slaughtered by Atreus' command; baskets of wheaten bread reposed on three-legged tables running on golden castors – only the palace's finest furniture decorated a banquet in Perseus' honour. Fleeces washed to snowy whiteness draped low couch-like seats; torchlight flashed a myriad gems from gold and crystal drinking cups, from gold and silver platters. The din of voices roared like rollers beating rocks; the heat from lights and fire beaded sweat on naked midriffs. A pungent smell of scented oil, roast meat and warm humanity thickened the smoke-hazed air.

Twin dog-headed dragons glared from the wall behind King Atreus' throne. Despite the heat he wore a gold-threaded scarlet tunic, a silver fillet bound his hair, his beard was trimmed to a point and curled. He seemed in uproarious spirits, laughing and cracking jests, repeatedly beckoning squires to fill Thyestes' goblet. In Pelopia's absence my table and chair were placed on Atreus' left: as Master of the Ships and royal heir I ranked next the king in the palace hierarchy.

Beside me Menelaus sent Atreus worried looks.

I was not altogether happy myself. Apart from the king's behaviour, so foreign to his usual grim reserve, I considered it odd that spearmen and armoured Heroes lined the walls at sword-length intervals. All weapons save the dagger used for eating were sternly forbidden at meals in the Hall: gentlemen warmed by wine were apt to become quarrelsome. Over the

168

years I had attended many anniversary banquets; never before had forty weaponed warriors sentinelled the feast.

An unimportant point perhaps; but for indefinable reasons I felt nervously on edge.

I had spent the morning showing Tantalus round the stables. The boy had an eye for horses and sensibly remarked their points. I harnessed a team he admired, drove to the Field of War and allowed him to handle the reins. He was, naturally, unpractised; the horses pulled his arms out, quickened from canter to gallop and incontinently bolted. I took the reins, brought the chariot under control and parried his shamed apologies. 'Nothing to worry about; this pair would test a trained Companion's skill.' We returned sedately to the stables where he insisted on grooming the brutes. A stallion nipped his buttock, a severe and painful bite as I knew from harsh experience, enough to reduce any boy to tears. Tantalus yelped, gritted his teeth and went on wisping the horse's quarters. A likeable child with plenty of guts.

Soon afterwards someone came to fetch him away, and I had not seen the lad since. Nor could I find him among the flagon-laden squires who flitted from table to table.

A carver beside the hearth sliced a sirloin and heaped a platter. A servant brought it to the king, knelt and placed it on his table. Atreus skewered a piece and tasted. 'Not as tender as I like,' he observed pleasantly to Thyestes. 'The cooks won't pound the joints before putting them on the spits. In your especial honour, brother, I have ordered a particular dish prepared in the women's kitchens where the staff are clever in catering for our ladies' delicate palates.'

He spoke to the man who had served him. As the fellow hurried away I noticed his stricken expression – but slaves were often timorous when royalty gave orders.

Atreus attacked his beef and, between mouthfuls, reminisced about a recent hunt when a savage Nemean lion had disembowelled his favourite hound. Thyestes fingered his wine cup and squinted enviously at Atreus' laden plate. Like everyone else he had not eaten since dawn – a light breakfast, figs and honey, barley-cakes and watered wine – and was ravenously hungry. The banquet's opening course, broiled fish and savoury herbs, had merely whetted his appetite.

The servant re-appeared from an entrance opposite the Hall's bronze-plated doors. He carried a big gold charger, knelt in front of Thyestes and proffered a smoking joint.

Atreus said jovially, 'Tender as newborn lamb, I'll warrant, garnished with cumin, fennel and mint, tasty and fit for a king – a king, my dear Thyestes. Allow me to serve you.'

The meat, a haunch of sorts and somewhat underdone, was certainly tender: Atreus' dagger cut the joint like cheese. He spiked slices and piled Thyestes' platter. 'There, fall to. I'll bet you've never eaten so dainty a dish before.'

Atreus resumed his meal, sending his brother occasional sidelong looks. Thyestes' dagger hacked the meat. He crammed a hunk in his mouth, champed voraciously and swallowed. A thread of pinkish gravy webbed his chin. Meanwhile the kneeling slave, still holding his golden dish on outstretched palms, behaved most strangely. Though his head was bowed in correctly servile fashion he gagged as though he was going to be sick; a greenish pallor tinged his face.

The rascal deserved a whipping. I beckoned a steward.

'Does our cookery earn your approval?' Atreus inquired.

Thyestes finished his plateful and cut another slice. 'Excellent. Never tasted better. Veal, is it not, steeped in milk and broiled, then lightly grilled? Thesprotus served me the like in Sicyon, though not so good by half.'

'Not *quite* the same,' said Atreus gently. 'Have you had enough?'

Mouth full and temporarily speechless, Thyestes nodded. The king reached out a foot and kicked the kneeling slave.

'Bring that which I commanded!'

The man shambled from the Hall. I reprimanded the steward for allowing an incompetent servant to wait on the king, and ordered a flogging. The steward hastened through the small side door where the slave had gone, and reappeared a moment later. He threw me a hunted look, and scuttled to concealment on the farther side of the hearth.

What the blazes was the matter with the palace domestics today?

Idly I scrutinized spirals and stars and roundels in variegated colours decorating the ceiling. Above processional stags and lions depicted on the walls a dozen bare-bosomed ladies leaned on the clerestory's gallery rail and watched animated gentle-men feasting and talking and laughing twenty feet below them.

I addressed some casual remark to Menelaus, who answered by pointing a thumb at Atreus. The king's genial, breezy manner had gone. He sat on the throne like a sculpted crag, hands gripping the bull's-head arm rests, staring fixedly ahead, eyes like flames.

Thyestes swallowed wine, patted his stomach and belched. 'What delicacy do you serve us next, brother? Nothing so good as the last, I'll swear – a culinary masterpiece!'

Atreus slowly turned his head. 'My lord,' he said in quiet, formal tones, 'I shall show you the animal which provided your pleasure.'

Thyestes raised his eyebrows. 'Indeed? You'll bring a calf to the table?'

On Atreus' lips there hovered a thin and deadly smile.

My clumsy slave re-entered the Hall, still bearing the golden charger and hacked remains of a joint. Another followed him closely; a cloth was spread on a similar dish he carried. They weaved in file between tables and halted side by side before the throne. Both men looked ghastly, sweat glistened on their fore-heads. The king's hand moved in a downward gesture. They lowered the joint on Atreus' table, the covered salver in front of Thyestes.

Atreus touched the congealing meat. 'This, dear brother,' he said in conversational tones, 'is the flesh you have eaten. Would you care for another slice? No?' He reached for the second charger. 'And here is the beast which furnished your dish.'

Atreus whipped away the cloth.

Trimly arranged on the plate were two hands severed at the wrists, two feet cut off at the ankles, and a neatly decapitated head. The features were drained dead white, a grey tongue peeped between tightly clenched teeth, half-closed eyes rolled back to show the whites.

Tantalus.

My bowels churned. Thyestes stared in disbelief, his face the colour of clay. His mouth juddered and worked on words that would not come. Painfully he twisted his head and met Atreus' savage glare. His chest heaved in uncontrollable spasms. Yellow, lumpy vomit flooded from his mouth and fouled the mutilated horrors which once had been his son. Repeated convulsions racked him, inhuman noises gurgled from his mouth. He tumbled forward in his chair, dropped face-down in his vomit.

Tantalus' head, disturbed, teetered on its neck.

Atreus leaned back in the throne and impassively studied his brother's agony.

A deathly quiet rippled outwards from the throne. Those nearest the king at once recognized the victim. 'Tantalus. Tantalus. Tantalus.' The name whispered across the Hall like a rustle of leaves. Men at the outer reaches stood to view the spectacle, gulped and abruptly sat. In horrified surmise Thyestes' Heroes scanned each other's faces. Some stepped towards their stricken lord.

As if at a signal warriors moved from the brazen ring at the walls. Spearpoints prodded spines.

Atreus, I thought dimly, had taken every precaution.

Thyestes lifted his head and levered himself erect. Vomit clotted brow and beard. He took a staggering pace towards his silent, watchful brother. He groped on the table behind him, feeling for his dagger, and knocked the head to the floor. Thyestes whipped his hand from the salver as though a snake had struck.

Words came, thick and strangled. 'My son ... why ... you promised...'

Atreus said brutally, 'Who are you, you spawn from the depths, to talk of oaths and honour? None the less I will keep my vow – let everyone here bear witness.' Lips curled back from his teeth in a snarl. 'Will you not stay in Mycenae, Thyestes, and share my throne and kingdom?'

For twenty heartbeats Thyestes stood, swaying on his feet and searching his brother's features. He uttered a wordless choking noise, turned and reeled to the doors. Men flinched away as he passed. At the doorway he halted and turned a splotched and ghastly countenance to the king. A terrible laughter racked him, he cackled like a madman.

'My revenge, dear Atreus, lives within these walls. Within these walls, I say, a gift from brother to brother, a son for a son. Farewell.'

His laughter echoed from the vestibule, faded beyond the

portico. Atreus smiled evilly – the last smile I ever saw upon his lips. 'The poor fellow's mind is unhinged,' he murmured. Raising his voice he addressed Thyestes' Heroes. 'Go. Leave Mycenae forthwith, and take away your lord.'

Voices muttered and footsteps shuffled. I stared, fascinated, at the hacked-up joint on the charger. Shallow indentations showed beneath the crust, faint but unmistakable.

The marks of a horse's teeth.

* * *

Everyone agreed Atreus had gone too far.

Cannibalism has precedents in Achaea. Gelon once informed me that Zeus' father, in Crete, was partial to human flesh; and people tell dark stories about the Daughters' sacrifices. The Goatmen's predecessors, whose remnants live in Arcadia, are said to kill and eat old men in time of dearth; Goatmen themselves are not above suspicion. Yet, as Menelaus observed, tricking a man to eat his son went much beyond the odds.

The tale resounded through the land and echoed with embellishments from Thessaly to Crete. Even now, years after, nursemaids tame fractious children by the threat 'Atreus will feed you to Thyestes' – though both are dead. Bards avoid the subject – it reflects no credit on Heroes.

Gentlemen in Mycenae walked tiptoe, fearful of offending a king who wreaked such terrible vengeance. In general they opined, in Menelaus' expressive phrase, that Atreus was off his nut: a belief certainly shared by people near the king, elder Councillors, senior Heroes, Menelaus and me. Atreus wrapped himself in an armour of hard indifference, shielding himself from contact with men who had been his friends. In Council and audience he voiced decrees and decisions without consulting anyone's advice. Nobody dared to protest.

Pelopia, after the tragedy, withdrew entirely from society. Before returning to Tiryns I saw her once or twice taking the air on a rampart walk or hurrying across the Court, always surrounded by her ladies. She gave me the impression of walking in her sleep. Menelaus once ventured to approach her. 'A haunted woman,' he told me. 'Terrified. Frightened to death. And no wonder. How would *you* feel if your father had dined on your brother?'

173

Her relations with Atreus did not bear thinking about. It was at this time he and the queen ceased sharing a bedroom.

Misfortune followed fast. Drought afflicted the land, perennial streams dried up, springs and wells failed. A scourge of ravening insects attacked the corn in ear; famine threatened Heroes and husbandmen alike. Seers and soothsayers cast ineffectual spells, farmers and peasants made offerings to The Lady. Eventually the Daughters in a body sought audience with the king and boldly declared his crimes – Aerope's and Tantalus' killings – had offended The Lady Who now imposed Her penalties.

I have hitherto said little about these women who govern and administer our official religion, or the religion itself, because no man except the king is much concerned. (Until I held the sceptre I never realized how troublesome the Daughters could be.) They are virgins from noble families, dedicated from an early age to The Lady's service. A ministry of Daughters keeps religious tenets burnished in every Achaean city; the king grants rich demesnes which guarantee them wealth and independence.

No one willingly offends the Daughters, servants of The Lady Who gives men life and takes away life and calls them back to the earth from which they sprang. At The Lady's behest burgeon fruit and flowers, trees and herbs, creatures and corn: She gives everything on which mankind exists. All men in a greater or less degree are farmers bound to the soil; so from lordliest Hero to poorest peasant every being – excepting slaves – is dependent for survival on Her benevolence. Therefore men respect The Lady and sacrifice at Her shrines – but the true devotees and worshippers are women.

Like the majority of Heroes I never, before my accession, attended The Lady's rites. Daughters conduct the sacraments at hilltop shrines: usually a small courtyard round a tree beneath which stands an altar surmounted by stone doves and horns of consecration. (The latter, I think, a relic brought by Zeus from ancient Crete's bull worship.) The tree itself embodies The Lady's presence. Here, at midwinter and early spring, they celebrate The Lady's principal feasts involving ceremonial dances, prayers and sacrifices and mystic invocations.

As king I attend these rituals, donate white barley-fed bulls for slaughter in front of the altar, and have learned the Daughters' fundamental belief: Eileithyia, as She is named on these biennial occasions, gives birth to a son in the spring who dies at the winter solstice.

The springtime rites are harmless, gay festivities – unless a crisis looms, when sinister things can happen. I, and all other males, invariably quit the winter celebrations at an understood point in the rubric. The women then take charge. I prefer not to speculate on the course of events thereafter but, from the noises I hear while descending the hill, the subsequent sacrifice is not an animal, nor female; and the women's orgiastic fury transcends Dionysus' Maenads.

For these and other reasons men are seldom active participants in The Lady's Mysteries. Yet people cannot live without divine belief, so men for the most part honour dread Ouranos, Destroyer, Thunderer, Earthshaker, Who dwells deep in the centre of the world. You never mention His name, you never openly worship Him, you try to forget He exists, you cower and beg forgiveness when His wrath convulses the firmament. Every living creature is fated to meet Him face to face; for when The Lady recalls you to earth, and flesh has dissolved from bones, your spirit flies to the Shades where dreadful Ouranos rules, never to return to this world. When men die they stay dead. We have no ghosts.

Dangerous talk, best ended.

The Daughters gave Atreus an ultimatum: the king must purge his crimes by travelling to Dodona, there to consult the Oracle and seek The Lady's forgiveness; otherwise the famine would decimate his people. The Daughters, in effect, exacted a penance: Dodona in Epiros lay twenty days' hard travel from Mycenae through rugged mountainous country and unfriendly tribes. Civilized cities customarily allow safe passage for pilgrims through the territories they control; but some of the folk on the way were far from civilized. Moreover the King of Mycenae's person might prove an irresistible prize.

There were no witnesses to the colloquy between Atreus and the Daughters. Though the king, I am told, was icily furious, they held him on a spearpoint, and he could not refuse. The Daughters carried The Lady's commands: even a king must obey – or face expulsion from his realm. Atreus suggested a nearer Oracle at Delphi where in a subterranean cave The Lady manifested Herself as a python. The Daughters remained adamant: Delphi was an obscure and negligible shrine; only The Lady at Her principal sanctuary might expurgate his offences.

Atreus glumly yielded.

Hearing of his intended journey I suggested he should go by sea rather than risk the perils of overland travel. With favourable winds the passage round Cythera to a landfall at Ithaca where King Laertes ruled would take but half the time. (Laertes' son Odysseus was later my comrade-in-arms at Troy.) Thence a two-day march brought him to Dodona. Atreus agreed; and appointed me Regent of Mycenae in his absence. I chose our fastest triaconter and put the king, his Heroes, squires and servants aboard at Nauplia.

I led a tedious existence in Mycenae. Much business had to be postponed until Atreus' return, for the king alone could take important decisions affecting land tenures and the like. I hunted frequently, spent days inspecting my estates and gloomily examined shrivelled corn, lean herds and arid, powdery soil. Peasants and animals starved, and began to die. I emptied the royal granaries, ransacked store rooms at Tiryns and Nemea, and distributed every grain. Imports from Thebes' Copaic fields had long since ceased. A corn ship arrived from Egypt quarter laden: the Nile harvest had failed. We received no help from our neighbours: Argos and Sparta were also famine-stricken – and blamed Atreus for incurring The Lady's wrath. Only in Pylos and Elis, on Achaea's western coasts, intermittent rainfall nourished a scanty yield; and no inducements of bronze or hides or gold tempted Neleus or Augeas to barter their grain reserves.

On a sweltering sun-scorched day an exultant message from Nauplia sped my chariot to the port. Four galleys from the Colchis convoys moored at a wharf. A master conducted me aboard; incredulously I beheld the holds awash with wheat.

'A tempest, chance and The Lady's grace,' the master explained. 'Gold ships, returning from Colchis, blown grievously off course made harbour, battered and leaking, at a land they call Krymeia on the northern Euxine coast. The people were friendly, and helped to repair our galleys.'

The master stooped, seized a handful of grain and trickled it through his fingers. 'They had this: barley fields and wheat fields stretching far as the eye could see. The captains knew of our famine, bartered a little gold and filled the holds. They transferred cargoes at the Hellespont's overland portage – and here we are!'

'Miraculous! Enough, if severely rationed, to feed the people for several days. If only you'd brought more!'

'On the way, my lord. Lord Amphiaraus commands at the Hellespont, and has diverted all galleys from the Colchis run to Krymeia. He thinks, in this emergency, grain more essential than gold. Is he right?'

'He surely is. Get your cargoes unloaded fast. I'll send wagons to bear them away.'

That night a great wind roared, clouds raced from the west and rainstorms drenched a thirsty land. The tempest blew itself out; rain fell gently for nineteen consecutive days. The crisis passed.

Atreus' galley beached at Nauplia a moon and a half after his departure. I feasted him in Tiryns' Hall, and asked how the expedition went.

'Well enough. A gale off the Thesprotian coast, but Laertes made us welcome in Ithaca and replaced cordage and broken oars. Pigsty of a palace – but I liked his son Odysseus: a crafty rogue if ever I saw one.'

'And Dodona?'

'A marshy, forested place surrounded by mountains. Primitive herdsmen living in huts. The shrine a huge old oak, the priests called Selli. Smelly individuals – sleep on bare earth and never wash their feet.'

'Did the Oracle speak?'

Atreus grunted. 'The tree is full of doves which coo and moo. Wind creaks and rustles the branches. Together they form the oak tree's speech, which the Selli interpret.'

'Favourably?'

'Oh, yes. Had to sacrifice a bull, and donate a flock of sheep – the Selli won't touch metal. Expensive. Lot of damned nonsense, in my belief.'

Struck by a curious thought I inquired, 'On what day exactly did you consult the Oracle?'

Atreus frowned, and counted on his fingers. 'Twenty-two days ago. Why?'

'The very day,' I said, 'when shiploads of grain reached Nauplia, and the rains began.'

The king glowered. 'Coincidence, that's all.'

Coincidence or not, I have always since been careful to propitiate The Lady.

Chapter 7

FOR two years after this I lived an uneventful life.

My experience with Cretan pirates convinced me that Mycenae needed warships. Heavily laden merchantmen depending on rowers for protection could hardly match marauders equipped entirely for fighting. It seemed to me fatuous that, while manoeuvring for position in a battle, half a galley's motive power should have to quit the benches in order to repel boarders. I therefore picked experienced masters, skilful sailors and sturdy, proficient oarsmen to crew eight triaconters launched recently from the yards. In addition to the normal complement I embarked on every ship a fighting element consisting of ten armoured spearmen and four bowmen, about the maximum a ship could carry without becoming crowded and top-heavy.

I enlisted the archers in Crete. Warriors and crews required both for the battle squadron and an expanding merchant marine were found without much difficulty among the younger sons of freemen who, squeezed out from husbandry when subdivided holdings reached their limits of partition, were glad to find employment in the fleet.

In fact the fleet had reached its economic ceiling: over two hundred Mycenaean keels furrowed seaways to Krymeia, to Sicily and Egypt, Ionia and Sidonia. I lowered the monthly building rate from seven vessels to two, sufficient to recoup wastage and provide a small reserve. (We lost on average five ships every year. The seas can be dangerous even in summer, lashed by freakish gales; and rash or greedy masters sometimes prolong their voyaging into stormy winter months when every sensible mariner has beached his ship till the spring.) The saving in shipyard manpower provided still more hands for the galleys.

Gelon mentioned significantly that these discharged ship-wrights, sailmakers, caulkers, carpenters and foresters – all freemen – seldom found work on the land where every tillable strip already supported more than the fields could feed. He hinted at over-population leading to unemployment. I brushed his mutterings aside: such questions did not concern the Master of the Ships. The quandary hit me later, and most force-fully, when Mycenae's economic problems rested on my shoulders.

I appointed Periphetes son of Copreus – a straightforward, venturesome, energetic Hero of a very different stamp from his crooked, intriguing father – to command the battle squadron and gave him a roving commission. Periphetes had a super-natural nose for pirates. During the navigable summer months he destroyed strongholds, sank a Phoenician flotilla at sea and discouraged Sicilian corsairs from passing east of Cythera. In all this fighting he lost only three galleys.

I replaced his losses and increased his strength to twelve triaconters. Periphetes relentlessly whittled piratical ships and bases; attacks on coastal towns and merchantmen at sea be-came remarkably infrequent. The experience he gained pro-vided a foundation for the massive fleet I deployed as king in the nine-year sea war we fought against Troy.

Meanwhile, with the Krymeian cornlands inviting a per-manent solution to Mycenae's perennial shortages I sent with Atreus' authority an embassy to King Laomedon of Troy. Menelaus, who led the deputation, sought an increase in our merchantmen stationed within the Hellespont from three to ten, so that trade in grain and gold might continue simul-taneously. Supported by Hector, opposed vigorously by Priam, Menelaus after long negotiations agreed to pay higher customs duties and secured the concession. Thereafter for three years until Hercules' criminal exploit our summertime corn convoys brimmed Mycenae's granaries and left a useful surplus which we sold to neighbouring cities.

While engaged in these enterprises I received two unex-pected visitors. Castor and Polydeuces, twin sons of Sparta's King Tyndareus and his dotty consort Leda, arrived and asked permission to embark on a ship for the Hellespont and transfer thence on an 'Argo' galley for Colchis. You could not tell them apart: tall, exceptionally strong, blue-eyed and fair haired; lively, gay, adventurous young men. Something of a handful to their father, they expended their energies on boxing, wrestling, horses and cattle-raiding – an occupation which accounted for both in the end. They had walked from Sparta with only a squire and servant apiece, camping at night in the open or sleeping in shepherds' huts, scorning the amenities of baggage carts and chariots.

I found them an amusing and entertaining couple, and readily granted permission to embark in the next ship leaving for Troy. Meanwhile I took them hunting and was often alarmed by their rash behaviour when confronting angry lions or charging boars. They used short stabbing swords and small round targes, considered spears unsporting and refused to let hounds worry the quarry before going in themselves. Withal, unlike most Heroes, they never bragged, laughing off their dangerous feats as nothing out of the ordinary.

I asked them why they wanted to sail to Colchis.

'Boredom. Dull place, Sparta,' said Castor.

'Never been to sea. New pastures,' Polydeuces added.

'Done everything else.'

'Might give us a thrill.'

I refrained from telling them the Colchis passage was now routine, no more risky than any other voyage in well-found ships sailed by experienced crews. I suspect the *Argo* glamour still exercised attraction. Today there are fifty-odd Heroes swaggering around as 'Argonauts', though only a handful can truthfully claim they sailed in Jason's crew.

After pressing me to visit Sparta – a city I had never seen – Castor and Polydeuces departed. I relaxed in undisturbed routine. The clamour of war was muted apart from sporadic cattle raids across Arcadia's borders and counter-attacks which Argos usually mounted. To keep my Heroes busy I sent war-bands to reinforce Tydeus' expeditions.

Between whiles I hunted, paraded Tiryns' garrison, called periodical practice levies of all surrounding landholders, cruised to Lemnos once in Periphetes' galley and manoeuvred my thirty chariots in a battle-drill I formulated. The Companions soon became proficient, wheeling from line to column, forming line to either flank and holding close formation in the charge. This contingent became the nucleus of Mycenae's chariot squadron which afterwards sent Priam's armour reeling.

Chief among my personal entourage of Companions, squires, chamberlains, stewards, concubines and slaves were Talthybius and Eurymedon, Companion and squire respectively. During these tranquil years at Tiryns they became, and have remained, my closest friends excepting Menelaus. I am not, I suppose, by nature a very amicable man and tend to repel an acquaintance from ripening to intimacy. I afterwards developed a comradeship with Argive Diomedes, but politics and war governed our relations and imposed a guarded restraint. My high rank – I speak of the time before I was king – evoked a wary constraint among the citadel's Heroes: they were ever aware that as Atreus' heir my favour would in time become their warrant to hold the demesnes they tilled. Which seldom deterred the bolder spirits from shouting grouses in my face – Heroes are not mice – but wasn't conducive to close and familiar friendships. Moreover, as Menelaus in a rage once ranted when we quarrelled, my manner is cold and severe, my mien harsh and forbidding as a surly-tempered falcon's.

It's in the blood. Men who are born to sovereignty lack gentle, lamb-like qualities.

I kept a dozen concubines in the women's quarters at Tiryns, slaves imported from overseas and bought in Nauplia's market. None captured my affection; all shone dim as rushlights beside the blazing memory of dead, beloved Clymene. They came and went; when a wench's expertise became repetitiously familiar and therefore tedious I sold her in the market or bartered her to a Hero who fancied her looks – four oxen was the accepted price for a woman trained in domestic work. The concubines not only preserved my health but also protected me from dangerous liaisons. The palace swarmed with noble wives and daughters who often cast me loving, lingering looks. Some were very beautiful, salaciously provocative; whenever I felt resolution melting I quickly drained desire within some Lemnian or Carian slut.

A halcyon interlude ended when Atreus summoned his Wardens for ordering a levy of the Host.

*   *   *

182

'After the spring sowing,' said the king, 'I'll lead the Host to Sicyon. When the city has fallen we will attack Pellene.'

An icy wind, a lash on the tail of winter, swirled about the Court. Atreus fastened his cloak, paced to the portico, turned and retraced his steps. The Wardens of Mycenae's chief tributary cities and the principal palace nobles followed like a flock behind the shepherd.

'Sicyon can mobilize barely a quarter of our strength, but the citadel is strong, not easily stormed. I don't intend to exert the usual pressures – burning crops and manors and farms and seizing cattle – which normally persuade an early surrender. This won't be a punitive expedition. Sicyon, when taken, becomes part of Mycenae's realm. Pointless to destroy your own property.'

A sentry beneath the colonnade clashed to attention as the distinguished procession passed him. I said, 'Why not immediately offer Sicyon tributary status, sire, as Argos did to Epidauros? Adrastus didn't need a campaign to bring that city under his rule.'

'In return for Epidauros' submission,' Atreus said in a gravelly voice, 'Adrastus had to clear the mountains of bandits – which occupied his warbands an entire summer. I haven't time for negotiations. Sicyon's taking, and then Pellene's, is only the start. Mycenae is going to enlarge her dominion, and it might take several years.'

The audience murmured happily. The prospect of lasting warfare is always exciting for Heroes. Though Atreus had banned plundering, a captured city invariably pays an indemnity – treasure and slaves and stock – for distribution among the victors.

Bunus of Corinth said, 'What, then, sire, is your ultimate aim?'

'To hold the entire southern coast of the Corinthian Gulf from Sicyon to Dyme.'

Menelaus gasped. 'You will have to take' – he tapped his fingers in turn – 'five cities, besides smaller coastal settlements and inland forts.'

'Exactly. Not beyond our capabilities. Each city taken will augment our warriors and resources. A long-term project, as I said: three or four years at the least.'

I risked a snub. 'Why are you doing it, sire?'

Atreus paused in his pacing and supported himself with an arm outstretched to a colonnade's crimson pillar. Sunken blue eyes examined me coldly. 'Apart from material gain I have two purposes. First, by expanding our territory to make Mycenae Achaea's paramount power. Second, to close the coast to sea-borne Dorians infiltrating across the Gulf. The Wall already bars their passage across the Isthmus.'

'They are crossing in numbers, sire?' Bunus inquired.

'The movement,' said Atreus grimly, 'has attained the proportions of a mass immigration. They land and take to the mountains, where they reinforce the Goatmen. If we don't soon stop it we'll become embroiled in a ceaseless war of attrition. And not Mycenae alone. Every civilized city will likewise suffer.'

Heroes shook doubtful heads. Some smiled behind their hands. Goatmen raids and counter-raids had become a way of life, a repetitive military exercise to keep warriors on their toes, a salutary irritant like blistering a horse. None conceived them a major menace. Atreus' far-seeing vision proved everybody wrong.

The king pulled closer his cloak and leaned against the pillar. 'That's the situation, gentlemen. You'll take this as a warning order. The Host will muster at Corinth when sowing is done; after the next full moon, let us say. I shall send you detailed instructions.'

The Heroes saluted, hurried thankfully into the Hall to warm themselves at the hearth, and in due course departed for their homes. I stayed awhile at Mycenae, dividing my time between residence at a manor I held nearby and sharing Menelaus' quarters in the palace. Crossing the Great Court with my brother one afternoon I met a toddler some five years old who broke from his nursemaid, wrapped arms around my leg and lifted a laughing face in the way that children do. I ruffled his hair, gently disengaged him and returned the boy to the flustered servant.

'Who is the brat?' I asked Menelaus.

'Aegisthus, Atreus' son – and Pelopia's.'

'Oh. A bonny child. How is Pelopia?'

Menelaus shook his head. 'Can't say. Hardly ever see her. Spends all her time in the royal suite surrounded by her ladies, everlastingly spinning and weaving, so I'm told.'

'A queen can have worse occupations.'

'True.'

A melancholy look crossed my brother's face. My chance remark had evoked Aerope's pitiful end. I said quickly, 'Is it true Thyestes has returned to Elis?'

'Yes – after making a pilgrimage to Dodona.'

'Damn my blood! Like Atreus? A good thing they didn't meet! Have you any idea what the Oracle told him?'

'Thyestes puts it about,' said Menelaus sourly, 'that the Oracle promised him Mycenae's rule.'

'What utter non —' I checked, and felt discomforted. The Lady undoubtedly had a habit of keeping Her promises. 'Well,' I finished lamely, 'it doesn't seem very probable.'

'Most unlikely – I hope. To win the throne Thyestes must get rid of Atreus first, then you, then me. A distressing prospect, if the Oracle prophesied truly.'

'Oracles,' I said firmly, 'can be wrong.'

I was on the point of leaving for Tiryns when a courier arrived from Argos and delivered his message, speaking stiltedly by rote, to Atreus in the stables. The king sent for me and said without preamble, 'Adrastus seeks my alliance in a campaign against Thebes.'

'Thebes? The strongest city north of the Isthmus? What makes him think —'

'He doesn't think. The old fool is letting personal pique override polity, and will earn a thumping defeat unless he's lucky.'

Atreus waved away the courier standing stiffly to attention, and summarized a chain of complicated factors. When the Thebans banished Oedipus, his queen's brother Creon had ruled the city as Regent until Oedipus' sons Eteocles and Polyneices came of age. Creon had then surrendered the sceptre and proposed the brothers should rule either as co-kings or alternately year by year. (A more asinine suggestion I cannot imagine.) Naturally the arrangement failed to work; the pair quarrelled violently over protocol and power. Eteocles, the more skilful intriguer, won by bribes the palace Heroes' backing and hunted Polyneices from the kingdom.

Because Polyneices had married Argeia, one of King Adrastus' daughters (the other daughter wed Tydeus and became

Diomedes' mother), he fled to Argos and begged the king's help in restoring him to the throne and kicking Eteocles out. Adrastus decided the slight to his kindred affronted his ageing dignity, lost his temper, started mustering his Host and sent emissaries to neighbouring cities requesting support.

'Adrastus,' Atreus continued, 'says Polyneices still commands the allegiance of important Theban nobles who will change sides directly his Host appears at the gates. I don't believe it. Tyndareus of Sparta has refused. So shall I. Apparently Adrastus has been promised help only by Parthenopaeus, one of King Agapenor's semi-independent Arcadian Heroes, and of course by his own chief Argive nobles Tydeus, Capaneus and Hippomedon. Amphiaraus also, who has lately returned from the Hellespont.'

'Which, with Polyneices and Adrastus himself, makes a total of seven.'

'Yes. Seven against Thebes. Heroes leading warbands raised from their own estates, some numerous and strong, some not. Virtually an Argive Host. Not nearly enough. A successful war on Thebes demands more than one kingdom's manpower.'

I contemplated a groom oiling a roan stallion's mane and plaiting and tying the hair in upright pointed locks. 'It *is* a good excuse for smashing Theban power. Why won't you help Adrastus?'

'Because,' said Atreus irascibly, 'I'm embarking on my own campaign which I don't intend to postpone. Secondly, Adrastus' is a half-baked expedition, thrown together in haste, understrength, cobbled with threads of disaster. You don't make war on Thebes without thorough preparation and the odds heavily in your favour. Senility, I think, corrodes Adrastus' judgment.'

'He's a friendly ally. Won't your refusal anger him? Unwise to rouse a neighbouring realm's hostility.'

Atreus broodingly watched a Companion yoking in his chariot a pair of prancing greys. 'You're probably right – though apparently it doesn't worry Sparta. I'll send him a token force: possibly a dozen chariots and a few score spears.'

I said impulsively, 'Let me lead them, sire.'

The king's brows met in a bristly grey-flecked bar. 'Why? What a damnfool idea! Who would lead the Tiryns contingent to Sicyon?'

'There are plenty of first-class fighting-men among my Heroes. No – I have it! Put Menelaus in command. He has never been given a chance to lead a warband in battle.'

Atreus scowled. I persisted. Striding up and down the stables' stone-flagged yards, peering into stalls and watching grooms at work, I argued that the heir apparent commanding Mycenae's detachment would give the force prestige and mitigate its weakness in Adrastus' eyes. I emphasized the importance of keeping on terms with Argos.

My motives were mixed.

Privately I considered that little renown or reward would be won by anyone but Atreus in subduing lesser cities such as Sicyon and Pellene: the glory of a Theban victory beckoned. I wanted an independent command unconfined by Atreus' strict direction: King Adrastus, I felt, drove Heroes on looser reins. Finally I had never, in Achaea, travelled north of Megara. Fresh pastures drew me strongly as they had Tyndareus' Twins.

Atreus gave way; and grumpily examined a horse suspected of glanders. I hurried off before he could change his mind, and informed Menelaus. At noon we drove to Argos and spent the night in the palace where I told Adrastus tactfully that though Atreus and his Host were otherwise engaged he had agreed to detach a warband to reinforce the Argives. Pouring diplomatic oil on the king's spluttering vexation I promised a handpicked force of proven, valorous warriors. Slightly mollified, he told me to bring my men to Argos within four days.

Deeming it prudent that Adrastus rather than Atreus be annoyed I limited my detachment to seven chariots and fifty spears, collected the usual assortment of baggage carts, drovers, grooms, spare horses, hounds, meat on the hoof and slaves and departed for Argos. Warbands dribbled to the muster. Swarthy, squat Tydeus, Leader of the Host, swore volubly when Parthenopaeus' warband straggled in from Arcadia.

'Never seen such a ragbag bunch! Hardly a cuirass among them, half-starved horses, three ox-carts and no rations. Say they're accustomed to living off the land and will pick up supplies as they go. The idiots seem to think they can pillage their way through Argos, Mycenae and Attica. Damned uncivilized hooligans!'

Amphiaraus, my late commander at the Hellespont transhipment station, further ruffled Tydeus' irascible temper. Married to King Adrastus' sister Eriphyle – the woman sharing his bed on that long-ago dawn in Midea – he had acquired, as I have related earlier in this history, a certain prophetic fame. He now mooned round the citadel disseminating dismay and despondency by lugubriously predicting the expedition's failure. He asserted in hollow tones that of all the seven leaders Adrastus alone would survive. Such defeatism encouraged nobody: I had difficulty dissuading my Heroes from a precipitate return to Tiryns. Adrastus himself was furious and engaged his brother-in-law in a stand-up row. At one time the entire venture looked like coming to pieces. A worried Polyneices, seeing his chance of regaining the Theban throne dissolving before his eyes, persuaded Eriphyle to intervene and reconcile her quarrelling relations.

In view of later events I feel there must be something in this soothsaying after all.

*   *   *

The Host at last set off. I attached my command to Tydeus' warband and travelled most of the way in Diomedes' chariot, relegating his Companion to my own alongside Talthybius. Tydeus lacked Atreus' superb organizational skill. The troops straggling through Mycenae's lands (with Atreus' permission) forcibly reminded me of King Eurystheus' disjointed column years before. Blockages, confusion and delay. An unfortunate incident when we camped at Nemea afforded Amphiaraus a further pretext for prophesying doom. A snake bit the Warden's son, and the child died. Amphiaraus beat his breast and called it an ominous sign. Tydeus, blackly furious, nearly put him under arrest.

We took four days to reach the Isthmus Wall where masons added finishing touches to towers and forts; and threaded the perilous passage past Sciron's Rocks. Slow progress; and I could not resist, for Diomedes' benefit, recalling Atreus' trouble-free high-speed marches. Tydeus' son said crossly, 'That's all very well. Your father is his own Marshal; mine has an interfering, pernickety old man to placate. Adrastus insists on old-fashioned methods: what his father did is good enough for him. And *that* takes you back fifty years. Adrastus is past campaigning; he should have stayed in Argos.'

We crossed the Megaran battlefield. A drift of whitened bones still spattered the plain – skulls mouldering under bushes, golden spires of broom piercing a broken rib cage. I described the battle to Diomedes, traced on the ground my chase after Theseus, indicated the course of that final devastating charge.

'I suppose we'll meet the Scavengers,' said Diomedes pensively. 'Let's hope they don't surprise us as they did' – he flashed me a sidelong smile – 'the Mycenaean Host.'

'They may have disintegrated – bugger boys are temperamental people. Do you know anything about the Theban order of battle?'

Diomedes shook his head.

Nor, so far as I could discover, did anyone else in the Argive Host. We were blundering into Attica, Thebes a two-day march away, ignorant of hostile strength, whether they meant to hold the Cithaeron Mountain passes, assemble on the Asopos plain beyond or concentrate in Thebes itself. An Athenian deputation met us when we camped for the night near Eleusis and politely inquired our purpose in entering Attic territory. Adrastus assured 'King' Theseus' ambassador he was merely passing peacefully through to chastise Thebes – and had he any information about Eteocles' dispositions. He might have been asking a doting mother when her daughter last was raped. The Athenian assumed a shocked expression and asserted no Theban warrior trod Attic soil this side Cithaeron. More he could not say: Athens and Thebes had no relations.

A thorough-paced liar – the cities were close as lovers in bed.

The Host – three thousand fighting men and twice as many followers – set out northward from Eleusis on the road to Thebes: first across flat open country sprouting springtime flowers, then climbing steadily from the lower to the higher ranges of Cithaeron. Scouts rode in the van; seven separate warbands followed, each tailed by baggage and servants: precisely the inept march formation Atreus forbade. The column wound its way across an upland plateau and entered a rocky defile walled by towering crags – the perfect place for an ambuscade. I peered anxiously at ledges and crannies and caves which overlooked the track, nipped from Diomedes' chariot and mounted my own, fastened helmet tight and hefted shield.

Nothing happened. Not so much as a pebble bounced from the heights.

We reached the head of the pass and saw Boeotia spread before us like a patched and chequered quilt. At the foot of Cithaeron's rolling spurs a silvery gleam marked Asopos' course. Far on the horizon, radiant in snowy splendour, soared the peaks of Helicon and Parnassos.

The plain was void of life, the entire river valley stark and empty. Neither goats nor sheep nor cattle grazed the slopes, not a husbandman moved in fields of spring-green corn. A village nestled in foothills below, another humped thatched rooftops in the valley; never a smoke wisp spiralled from cooking fires or kilns. The grey stone huddle of Thebes daubed a smudge on the horizon.

We waited, crammed in the cleft, while scouts scoured the plain, and then cautiously descended a steep and tortuous track. It took a long time. Carts jammed on bends, slithered helplessly over cliffs. A meandering column crossed the valley's floor and camped on Asopos' banks. Meanwhile foragers roved widely, burned villages and tried to fire cornfields – an unsuccessful exercise; the crops being green and damp would only smoulder. They slaughtered a handful of peasants who through age, infirmity or obstinacy had refused to shelter in Thebes: none would have fetched a barren goat from a drunken dealer in slaves.

After posting pickets Tydeus called a council of war. We squatted on the ground outside the king's leather tent, the seven leaders and principal commanders. A wave of Adrastus' bony old hand gave Tydeus permission to speak. He said, 'We shall have to set a leaguer. Thebes is obviously adopting a defensive strategy.'

A threatened citadel may choose one of two military alternatives. It can bring the subject population, flocks and herds within the walls, close gates and await a siege. Against the disadvantages of township and lands being abandoned to destruction is the fact that citadels are difficult to storm and seldom fall unless betrayed by treachery. Or, to preserve her property from depredation a city can give battle outside the walls, staking all on a quick, decisive result.

Amphiaraus said, 'I suspect a trap. They may have forces concealed in woods to attack us while we are advancing.'

'I've sent scouts across the river to search within sight of the walls,' Tydeus replied. 'They've found neither hide nor hair.'

'A siege might take all summer, and we haven't enough provisions,' said Arcadian Parthenopaeus: a hairy, hot-eyed, heavy man, thick red beard fanning over his cuirass. He suffered from some nervous affliction, eyelids, lips and hands everlastingly twitching. 'Let's march at dawn and storm the gates.'

Tydeus gave him a frosty look. 'Thebes has seven gates, and we don't even know where they are. No bull-headed nonsense, if you please. We'll reconnoitre first.'

'I can show you,' Polyneices said brusquely. 'It's my city, and I know every stick and stone.'

'My wish,' King Adrastus quavered, 'is that we first send heralds to Eteocles, demanding he resign his throne in favour of Polyneices.'

Eye met eye in hopeless resignation. 'Ruddy waste of time,' Parthenopaeus muttered. But Adrastus nominally commanded the Host; and a king's wish is tantamount to a command. Tydeus sighed and climbed to his feet. 'I'll go myself.' He eyed a cloud-streaked sun dipping towards the mountains. 'Enough time to get there and back before dark. Ho, there! Harness my chariot! Diomedes, you'll come too.'

The chariots forded Asopos and were lost amid trees and bushes that raddled the slant beyond. Near nightfall I heard from the farther bank a picket's raucous challenge. Chariots splashed from the ford; looking angry as a stormcloud, Tydeus strode wordlessly to Adrastus' tent. His son stooped over a fetlock wound on his offside horse. I inquired how the deputation went.

Diomedes straightened, patted the animal's neck. 'Apply a cold water compress, and tie the skin-flap firmly,' he told his Companion. 'How did it go? Badly. Those Thebans are touchy folk. Greeted us with oaths and arrows, ignoring the olive leaves tied to our spears as a sign of peace. After shouting back and forth they opened a gate and let us in. The citadel's packed; refugees and animals jam every street and court.'

'Many warriors?'

'Thick on the ramparts, and clustered behind the gates. Chariots tilted on poles, teams alongside ready and bitted. They're well prepared to counter anything we do. However. We went to the palace and saw Eteocles. My father put Adrastus' silly proposal. Eteocles was extremely rude.'

'What's he like?'

'A thin, gangling, pale-eyed creature. Loud-mouthed, brash, ill-mannered. Obviously hates his brother. Tydeus replied in kind, and the interview developed into a slanging-match. Creon intervened and told us to go while the going was good.'

'Creon? That's the uncle?'

'Yes. A short deep-chested greybeard who hardly said a word. Watchful and dangerous. Clearly the brains and driving force behind Eteocles and Thebes.'

Diomedes sucked his wrist, and showed me a nasty gash. 'Got this on the way back. The treacherous bastards laid an ambush in the dusk – twenty or thirty men. We had to gallop and cut a way through. I killed one; Tydeus accounted for a couple more. Serves them right.'

'Typical Theban perfidy. What, then, is your father's plan?'

'I don't know. He's in a vile rage, swearing like a spearman.'

Adrastus and his Leader conferred far into the night. Lying cloak-wrapped on the ground among my men, cuirass for a pillow, Talthybius beside me, I watched the yellow lamplight slash the king's half-open tent flap, heard voices rise and fall, Adrastus' querulous tones and Tydeus' rasping growl. A moon like a silver galley sailed the night-sky's purple vault. The camp was a restless sea that heaved in murmurous darkness, starred by crackling fires, stroked by a many-voiced wind: men talking, a sentry's distant challenge, horses stamping and neighing, music from flutes and reed-pipes beguiling the warriors' rest.

I bade Talthybius good night, and dropped into dreamless sleep.

*　　*　　*

Tydeus called a war council at daybreak and disclosed his tactics. Firstly a reconnaissance in force to examine the citadel's environs and establish the gates' locations. That done, he would post a warband before each gate to impose a strict blockade. The plan, he stated – Adrastus wagged an assenting head –

would starve the enemy out and at the same time compel him to disperse his troops at seven different points, thereby diminishing the possibility of his mounting a sally in strength.

I listened in growing horror. Tydeus invited comments. Apart from a minor bicker – Polyneices insisted his warband deserved the honour of facing the principal gate – nobody disagreed. I clambered to my feet, leaned on my spear and said forcibly, 'You invite defeat in detail. The Thebans hold the advantage of interior lines. They can shift their reserves speedily to any gate they choose, and swiftly reinforce a promising sortie. I believe we should concentrate four warbands before the weakest gate. Divide another into pickets to watch all other gates, each supplied with mounted scouts to bring us warning of a break-out. Two warbands in mobile reserve, ready to meet counter-attacks or exploit success. Your scheme, my lord Tydeus, envisages *no* reserve. If the leaguer doesn't compel surrender and we're forced to assault, you have the main body already concentrated at the weakest point, and the pickets can support it by feint attacks.'

'I am told,' Parthenopaeus sneered, 'you've won naval victories, my lord Agamemnon, but your experience of battles on land is limited to a single notorious defeat. On what grounds, therefore, do you presume to advise us?'

'Better grounds by far,' I barked, 'than a Hero whose knowledge of war is confined to cattle-raiding!'

'Calm yourselves, gentlemen.' Adrastus scratched a wrinkled cheek. 'What do you think, Tydeus?'

'I don't like it,' Tydeus muttered.

'Nonsensical,' Polyneices snapped. 'Leaves Eteocles the initiative.'

'Let us settle the argument,' Adrastus said. 'Who favours the tactics I and Tydeus conceived after long debate?'

Six spears were raised. The king blinked at me kindly. 'There you are, Agamemnon. I fear opinion goes against you.' He climbed shakily from his wooden stool. 'Now, my lord Tydeus, whose warband will you send to reconnoitre?'

*   *   *

I attached my seven chariots to the thirty from Tydeus' warband. (Having decided on a swift-moving mounted reconnais-

193

sance we took no spearmen.) We forded the river, and from a grass-covered ridge I had my first close view of Thebes.

A formidable citadel crowned an ochre rock-strewn knoll; towers studded a circuit of dark grey walls. Sunlight sparkled spearheads on the ramparts; the palace's whitewashed buildings gleamed like sails on the summit. The township's swathe of deserted houses curved outside the walls, and isolated dwellings speckled the whole circumference.

Tydeus bunched the chariots within eyeshot of the battlements. Defiant bellows floated on the breeze; arrows whirred and spurted dusty fountains. We drove at a canter round Thebes, skirting the town and avoiding buildings lest bowmen lurked in ambush. The citadel had four main gates (three too many, in my opinion; Mycenae has but one; the unattainable ideal none at all) and three small posterns or sally ports. So much for seven-gated Thebes.

Tydeus completed the circuit, signalled a turnabout and led at a trot in the reverse direction. He slowed to a walk before the four gates and searched them for weaknesses. To me they looked equally strong, all guarded by towers and curtain walls. He chopped a hand in the river's direction and led us back to the camp.

'A supine lot, the Thebans,' he told Adrastus. 'We trailed our cloaks in view of the walls and nobody tried to punish our impertinence. We'll be able to invest the citadel unhindered.'

The Seven gathered in council; Tydeus' swordpoint traced in the earth an outline plan of the city and marked the entrances. At noon the Host crossed Asopos and, when towers broke the skyline, warbands diverged to stations opposite the gates. Tydeus' force, which included mine, halted in close formation four hundred paces short of a main gate facing south. He advanced a screen of chariots while everyone else – spearmen, drovers and slaves – hastily collected boulders and constructed a four-foot breastwork to ring the entire detachment, leaving a single entrance wide enough for chariots. Two bowshots away on the left, Polyneices' band built a similar enclosure, and Amphiaraus' on the right. The remainder, beyond our sight around the walls, likewise fortified their positions according to Tydeus' orders.

A dangerous interlude: with everyone save charioteers engaged on fortifications, and defences uncompleted, we were vulnerable should the Thebans emerge in strength.

By late afternoon the Argive Host ringed Thebes like disconnected felloes of a vast irregular wheel.

Tydeus withdrew his chariots within the perimeter. There was not much room to spare inside a fieldwork seventy paces square. Chariots ranked hub to hub, horses were yoked and fettered by reins knotted to chariot rails. Slaves lighted fires, hooked cauldrons under tripods, slaughtered goats and prepared a meal. My squire Eurymedon untied a wineskin's mouth and brought me a brimming elmwood cup. I propped myself against a wheel (you can't do much relaxing in triple-skirted mail), sipped and sniffed the cooking smells, felt ravenously hungry. A dog howled desolately from the abandoned town, my Molossian boarhound pricked his ears and bayed. I patted his head and soothed him. Rooks flapped slowly to roost across a sky tinged sunset gold; long black shadows flowed from the skirts of trees.

At dawn the entire warband moved out, and spearmen guarded by chariots fired the deserted town. Flames lashed smoke clouds high in the sky and swept an acrid curtain across Thebes' adamant walls. The burning had a tactical use: the houses had half concealed the gate and screened a possible sortie. Now, across smouldering ruins, we could watch every stone of the ramparts.

The Argives withdrew to the forts and waited for Thebes to surrender.

*   *   *

Besieging a citadel, I found, can be a tedious occupation. Beyond manning the towers from dawn till dusk and shouting abuse from the walls, the garrison made no move. Bored Heroes ended their confinement in the breastworks. Leaving spearmen on guard we drove abroad, held chariot races, hunted – provided, on Tydeus' insistence, we stayed within sight of the forts. Gentlemen made themselves shelters outside the boulder-built barriers and started little households of their own.

Water was a problem. The wells of the burnt-out town were in arrow range of the citadel; and a sudden sally annihilated a night-time watering party. So waterskin-laden carts trundled to Asopos; the round trip took all day.

Despite the close investment it was impossible to prevent communication between the garrison and its allies in Boeotia. Messengers and agents repeatedly penetrated the siege lines after dark. Capaneus' warband on the citadel's northern side intercepted a supply train which tried to enter by night. The scuffle roused everyone from sleep; trumpets sang alarm in Thebes and the garrison clattered to battle stations.

Tydeus divided the captured provisions among the Host, for victuals were running low.

After forty days the shortage of supplies became acute. Tied to a ring of forts in the midst of a hostile land our foragers dared not roam too far afield. Meat vanished from our meals, bread was rationed, wine became a luxury. Tydeus prodded the king to calling a council of war. An argumentative session decided the Host must either attack forthwith or raise the siege and acknowledge defeat.

'Monotony must have lulled the Thebans,' Parthenopaeus supposed. 'An unexpected storming will catch them half asleep.'

'You can't mount an escalade without disclosing your intentions,' Tydeus said. 'They'll see our preparations, see us advancing, and man the walls before we're halfway there.'

'Do it by night,' I said.

A flinty silence greeted my suggestion. Parthenopaeus curled his lip. 'On the pattern of Midea? We've all heard about that. Atreus took by treachery a citadel unwarned. Thebes is ready and waiting.'

Tydeus said conclusively, 'Nobody fights in darkness. With your permission, sire, the warbands will mount a simultaneous attack in two days' time.'

'I never thought Thebes would prove so stubborn,' the king bleated. 'Yes – I have to agree. No alternative remains.'

They thrashed out details: construction of scaling ladders assault formations, camp guards, and a starting time when the rising sun tipped Cithaeron's highest peak. The interval was passed in making ladders, grinding swords and spears to hair-line keenness, and in considerable trepidation. Few Heroes in the Host had experienced an escalade against a well-defended citadel; and the precedents were not encouraging. They viewed the twenty-foot walls, calculated chances and pulled long faces. As Diomedes observed, the top of a rickety ladder was not a place where a man felt at his best.

When the sun shot long gold streamers from the summit of Mount Cithaeron Tydeus' warband left the fort and marched towards the gate. Ladders swayed at the heads of six columns led by Heroes. We had discarded body-armour save cuirasses – you can't climb ladders in brazen skirts – and swords replaced long chariot-fighting spears. I tramped at the head of the Tiryns contingent reinforced by Argive warriors; on my left Diomedes' party advanced, Tydeus' men on the right. The target of all three columns was the wall on the left of the gate. Three more parties advanced to the right-hand ramparts. Spearmen in a body marched behind, ready to rush the entrance when the stormers opened the gates; and a leash of Cretan bowmen shot arrows at the defenders.

A dozen chariots – this on my insistence – ranked in front of the camp to deal with unexpected sallies or, if the attack went awry, to cover our retreat. Adrastus commanded these: he was not of an age to scurry up ladders.

We crossed the ruined town, ash and cinders crunching underfoot, greaves rapping blackened beams, kicking up grey powdery dust that stung the eyes. Enemy thronged the ramparts, brandished weapons and howled. Arrows whirred and thudded, slingstones whistled and thumped. I lowered my head and fronted a waisted shield, clenched jaws and plodded on. A bubbling cry behind, armour clanging on rock, a knell for a fallen Hero. Precipitous boulder-strewn slopes, and throwing spears falling like rain. I slanted the shield to cover my head. A spearhead pierced the hide and slashed my arm. I reached sword-hand round the waist and wrenched the shaft away, climbed the last of the slope in a crouching trot and arrived at huge grey slabs that based the Theban wall.

Three Heroes rushed forward a ladder and planted it against the wall. The tip just reached the parapet where enemy faces bellowed. I started to climb. It was damnably awkward. To free my hands I put sword between teeth and slung shield aback by the carrying strap. Helmet and armoured shoulders took the brunt of the missile storm. The ladder rocked alarmingly;

defenders using poles tried to buffet it away. A slingstone struck my cheekguard, stars danced before my eyes. A Hero climbing beneath me hit my calf and swore. 'Get on! Get on!' I clutched the rungs in slippery palms and struggled up.

A frenzied bearded face at the topmost rung, a spear withdrawn for the lunge. I ducked and it missed. Arms outstretched I jumped from the ladder, sprawled on the slabs of a parapet five feet wide. A sword-edge rang my cuirass. I knelt and fronted shield and battled for my life.

Heroes mounted and stood beside me. Weapons clashed and battered, shouting dinned the eardrums. We won the width of the parapet, dropped to the rampart walk and went on fighting. Lunge, shield right and parry, withdraw, shield front and cut. A sword-thrust scraping forearm, a cleft skull spouting brains.

We cleared a space and stood in a bunch, shields fronted facing outwards, backed against the parapet. The Thebans retreated on either side and girded themselves for a charge. Blood slipperied the narrow walk, feet stumbled over bodies. I looked to my left. No sign yet of Diomedes' stormers. On the right a raging fight at the head of Tydeus' ladder. A gate tower blocked from view the farther escaladers.

The Thebans charged, and again we fought, and again we beat them back. I nursed a bleeding hand and counted the cost. Of twelve who had gained the ramparts eight were left. Could we cut a way to Tydeus' men and together reach the gate?

I scanned the fighting where his column's ladder mounted. Tydeus straddled the parapet, swung his sword. A javelin spiked his belly below the cuirass rim. Tydeus dropped his blade, the black beard pointed skywards and he toppled from the wall.

Enough. Whatever happened elsewhere the assault on this gate had failed. I shouted commands. One by one we descended the ladder, an ever-diminishing shield wall warding off assailants. I went last, hastened by a wild-eyed Theban hammering an axe on my shield. I chested the parapet edge, scrambled with my legs to find the rungs. The Theban followed, lifted the axe.

Spreadeagled like a landed fish I closed my eyes and awaited death. An arrow whanged. He dropped the axe and clutched a shaft protruding from his throat. My foot found the rung and I went down fast, skinning both hands to the bone. Arrows, stones and throwing spears whistled about my head. I stumbled down the slope and scuttled with my Heroes to the slender line of chariots.

I paused on the way to recover my breath and congratulate our bowmen. Were it not for Cretan marksmanship I wouldn't be telling this story.

I looked for Adrastus, but the king had gone. Collapsing beside a chariot I surveyed the wrack of defeat. Embers of a battle flickered on the ramparts right of the gateway. All the ladders there had fallen; any Argives on the parapet were bound to be killed. Further away Amphiaraus' stormers streamed back across the plain; Polyneices' warband was also retreating.

Just the moment for an enemy counter-attack. Safer within the fort. Wearily I gripped a wheel spoke and hauled myself up.

Diomedes staggered from the dust and flopped at my feet. Blood smeared his face, he held the hilt of a broken sword. 'You didn't support us,' I croaked. 'Your Heroes left us fighting alone on the wall.'

Diomedes said exhaustedly, 'We hadn't a chance. I reached the top and fought on the ladder. They thrust it away. The fall knocked me out. I think my party tried again but ...' He dropped the useless sword. 'Why is it, Agamemnon,' Diomedes said despairingly, 'that when their leader falls Heroes lose heart so easily?'

'Our Heroes had better not, because —' I stopped, and bit my lip.

Diomedes started to rise. 'I must find Tydeus and report our failure. Have you seen my father?'

I put a hand on his shoulder and pushed him down. 'I'm sorry, Diomedes. I saw Tydeus die.'

He raised a stricken face, buried head in hands and sobbed. Warriors hurried past, spearmen, Heroes, bowmen, wounded carried on shields. The chariot beside me rocked on its wheels. The occupant said, 'Mind yourselves, my lords. I'm retiring behind the breastworks. Not too healthy here, by the looks of things.' His Companion cracked a whip, the vehicle crunched away.

I lifted Diomedes to his feet. 'Come, my friend. Tydeus,

though the noblest, is but one of a host of dead. We'll lament a hundred Heroes before the day is done.'

Borne on a stream of defeated warriors I supported him into the fort.

*   *   *

Every warband had been repulsed, and the losses were heavy Besides Tydeus, the Argives Capaneus and Hippomedon and Arcadian Parthenopaeus were dead. The Arcadians, deaf to Adrastus' appeals, loaded baggage and departed.

Three of the Seven remained. Amphiaraus mournfully reminded us his prophecy was coming true.

Adrastus called a council. The reverse, and Tydeus' death, had totally unnerved the king: he shook all over and stuttered so badly one couldn't sort out what he said. We gathered that he proposed to abandon the campaign. Argive Heroes who replaced the fallen leaders dejectedly concurred.

Polyneices violently protested. Seeing his bid for the Theban throne drowning in a quagmire of despondency he exhorted the king to try again, this time concentrating the Host on a single gate. (Which, I reflected sadly, had been my advice at the start.) A mulish expression settled on Adrastus' shrivelled features. Diomedes said, 'Agamemnon's attack alone won a footing on the wall. Why should a second attempt fare better?'

'After all their casualties,' Amphiaraus moaned, 'I doubt our men will be persuaded to attack.'

'Our victuals are near exhausted,' Adrastus quavered. 'We must march away or starve.'

Polyneices flung out his arms. 'Then,' he exclaimed, 'I'll challenge my brother to decide our claims by the test of single combat! That, my lords, will save you from endangering your shrinking bodies and craven souls!'

Shaking with anger he strode away, his dramatic departure rather marred by tripping over a chariot pole. Adrastus said, 'I have a mind to clap him under arrest.'

I said, 'Let the idiot go. He can't change anything. Whether Eteocles accepts or refuses, whether he or Polyneices wins the fight, we lose nothing and gain nothing. Thebes won't stake her destiny on the life of a single man.'

The king gave Amphiaraus active command of the Host.

After extending the barricades he withdrew the decimated warbands to our enclosure opposite the southern gate and left pickets of mounted scouts in the ring of forts. Obeying Adrastus' behest he started preparations to raise the siege and depart. Amphiaraus followed my counsel and kept these activities hidden from enemy observation, sending baggage carts to leaguer beyond Asopos after dark.

I could not understand the Thebans' inactivity, their failure to exploit the Argive defeat; and feared the slightest sign of retreat would encourage a sortie in force. A fighting withdrawal through Cithaeron's defiles was something I hated to contemplate. I tried to persuade Amphiaraus the Host should also withdraw by night but, abiding by warfare's rigid conventions, he stubbornly refused. It was only decent, he burbled, to stay and watch the duel; and take the road to Eleusis directly it was done. You might have thought he discussed a hunting expedition or arrangements for holiday games on the Field of War.

Polyneices meanwhile sent heralds to his brother, and announced to my astonishment that Eteocles accepted. Heroic codes tempt gentlemen to every kind of foolishness; and I suppose a public challenge could hardly be refused. (Pondering the matter afterwards I concluded that Creon induced Eteocles to risk his life: his nephew's death would leave the throne in the erstwhile Regent's grasp.) The brothers declared a truce for the duration of a contest to be fought on the plain between Argive camp and citadel. The gates would be opened and Theban spectators allowed outside the walls. Moreover, Polyneices said proudly, he and his brother would fight in the ancient fashion, helmeted and naked, carrying only spears and shields.

I disliked the entire programme. The sooner we went the better: why delay to watch a tussle which decided nothing at all? More important, I could not visualize Theban warriors massed outside the walls, gates open to disgorge more, standing passively inert while the enemy marched away. I pressed my views on Diomedes. Grief-stricken, pale and peaked, he accepted my proposals with an air of numbed indifference.

'The war is over. What matter if we leave a day sooner or later?'

'Good. Then warn your warband – the palace Heroes – and be ready to march before daylight.'

'I will.' Diomedes raised his head; the lethargy vanished and he said firmly, 'The king must also leave with his retainers.'

I cursed to myself. You could never predict the wavering bent of old Adrastus' mind. 'Can you persuade him?'

'Yes. For years he has depended on my father to make decisions. Lacking Tydeus' direction he's as pliable as clay.'

I left Diomedes staring wretchedly into space, and found Amphiaraus leaning on a breastwork, glooming at the citadel's sullen walls and talking to his Heroes – including, unfortunately, Polyneices. Ignoring the Theban's lowering disapproval I urged the Host should decamp forthwith, and succinctly stated my reasons. So angry he was almost incoherent, Polyneices blared, 'You haven't much confidence in Theban honour!'

'None.'

'We have my brother's word.'

'Eteocles? Indeed. And if he falls in the fight?'

'His promise binds his people.'

'When has a dead man's mandate bound the living? Have you Creon's assurance the truce will be observed?'

'No – nor do I need it,' Polyneices raged. 'His House and mine are one: he would not dishonour the Theban royal blood.'

The fool was beyond persuasion. Exasperated, I said to Amphiaraus, 'At least draw up the Host tomorrow in battle order before the duel begins. Then you'll be ready for treachery.'

'Impossible,' Amphiaraus said glumly. 'We march directly the fight is finished; therefore we assemble in column of route.'

The man was clearly driven by a death wish; his own dark prophecy lured him to his doom. Lest he should try to dissuade the irresolute Adrastus I forbore to mention that the king's warband and mine would quit the camp before sunrise.

Our departure roused the Host – five hundred men can't steal silently from a crowded camp – and brought a bewildered Amphiaraus furiously protesting. I endured his rating in silence, and gestured to the column's vanguard vanishing in the dark. 'The king leads. It is Adrastus' will.'

Polyneices barred my chariot at the entrance. 'You renegade

rat!' he roared. 'Treacherous deserter! One day I shall find you and slit your cowardly throat!'

'An empty threat. You'll be dead before sundown.' I touched Talthybius' arm. 'Drive on.'

Dawn was breaking when the column reached Asopos and collected its share of the transport sent there days before. 'Keep going,' I told Diomedes. 'Make all speed. Don't halt till you've passed Cithaeron. I shall join you at Eleusis.'

Talthybius turned the horses, and together we retraced our tracks to the grassy knoll whence first I sighted Thebes.

*　　*　　*

The Argive fort traced a crook-sided square on the faraway plain. Formations filtered out, gathered in irregular clumps – Amphiaraus' vaunted column of route – and halted in front of the breastworks. The citadel gates swung open and emitted a crowd which strung the base of the walls. Sunrise sparkled spears – why should spectators assemble armed? There was a long wait. I imagined a murmur of voices carried on a wind which rustled the twigs of an oak tree shading my chariot. Tiny figures moved from the Argive side and the Theban and met on the ground between: presumably heralds concerting the duel's details.

I turned and conned the country beyond Asopos' gleaming waters. Diomedes' column, small as a thread in the distance, mounted Cithaeron's foothills. When I looked again the heralds had retreated. Two specks emerged from opposite sides and merged in a blob like a fallen leaf.

I was much too far away to discern particulars of the fight; a surviving Argive Hero described it to me later. In an untidy, clumsy scuffle neither Polyneices nor Eteocles displayed the dexterous skill at arms expected of a Hero. So determined was each to kill the other they charged and lunged and thrust with little regard for defence, using shields as battering rams rather than protection. Within moments of the start both brothers were badly hurt.

Polyneices weakened first, gave ground and dropped to a knee behind his shield. Eteocles uttered a gasping shout, levelled spear and charged. His adversary in desperation hurled his spear. Although the heavy barb sheared open Eteocles'

203

stomach, his momentum carried him on. He knocked Poly-neices flat, kicked aside the shield and lifted his spear. He smashed his brother's breastbone, broke his spine and pinned him to the ground. Then, mortally wounded and pumping blood, he fell across the body.

Creon regained Thebes.

Nothing of this was visible to me beyond a sudden cessation of movement from the dancing specks I watched. Realizing the fight had finished one way or the other I waited in dread for what would happen next. Suspense did not last long. Chariots burst from the gates and pelted towards the unready Argive Host. Even at that distance I perceived the riders naked.

'Turn,' I told Talthybius. 'Use your whip and drive like the wind. The Scavengers run loose!'

In a welter of foam we forded Asopos and bounced along the stony track that climbed to the pass and safety.

*   *   *

The remains of the Host waited at Eleusis. Adrastus sent sup-pliants to Theseus, sought his permission to stay in Attic ter-ritory and requested he ensure no Theban forces trespassed across Cithaeron. (A fine come-down for Argos to beg Athenian protection!) Theseus, insufferably cocky, visited the camp at Eleusis and scarcely bothered to conceal his satisfaction at Adrastus' heavy defeat. On the king's entreaty, however, he sent a deputation to Creon asking release of the Argive leaders' corpses for burial by their comrades. The body of Amphiaraus, killed by the Scavengers, was never found; Tydeus, Parthenopaeus, Capaneus and Hippomedon were dis-interred from shallow graves and carried on carts to Eleusis.

Survivors of the massacre trickled in. The Argives had fought a battle which hadn't lasted long, and the Scavengers pursued to the mouth of the mountain defile. Few spearmen escaped, baggage and followers were lost; only Heroes driving the fleetest horses eluded the sodomites' spears. Three-quarters of the Host that had marched so bravely from Argos was either dead or enslaved.

King Adrastus, a broken man, stayed mourning in his tent. His Heroes, numbed by disaster, moved about their duties like men walking in their sleep. Diomedes brooded, and nursed a baffled fury. 'The villainous bastards broke the truce!' he gritted between his teeth. 'One day, by The Lady's grace, I'll take a seven-fold vengeance!'

It seemed improbable; and anyone who trusted a Theban's word deserved everything he got.

When the dribble of survivors ceased Adrastus struck camp and marched for the Isthmus. So, in miserable defeat, ended the war of the Seven against Thebes.

*   *   *

At Mycenae I reported events to Atreus, who had recently returned from campaigning. 'No more than I expected,' he observed. 'A badly organized operation, doomed from the start. Now Thebes is cockahoop; the victory has increased her influence and power. Argos won't recover for years. I wonder,' he murmured, 'whether we should try to take over; perhaps send Adrastus an embassy backed by the Host, demand he abdicate and unite the kingdoms under Mycenae's rule.'

'You'd have to fight. Diomedes now is Leader of the Argive Host. Tydeus' death has envenomed him, changed him overnight from youth to man – a man determined, hard and bitter. Not the kind to passively submit.'

'Diomedes? Oh, I remember – Tydeus' son. You think he'd resist?'

'I do. A valiant warrior who'll soon be renowned. Besides, we should avoid entanglements until Thebes' intentions are clearer. Creon may decide to follow up his victory.'

We were talking on a balcony of the royal apartments. Atreus rested hands on the marble balustrade and frowned at a party of nobles crossing the Great Court below. 'There goes that fellow Copreus, always in a huddle with men I loathe. Don't trust him an arrow-head's length. Invasion? Extremely doubtful. Creon isn't a fool; he knows Sparta, Pylos and Elis would come to our aid against a common enemy.'

'We're going to need them. Whether Creon makes war or not the defeat of the Seven has tilted the balance of power, and some day, sire, you'll have to restore the level – a prospect I don't pretend to relish. The Thebans are first-class fighting men. I was lucky to escape.'

'You?' Atreus turned his head and gave me a peculiar look. 'I wouldn't have let you go if I hadn't been certain you'd some-how save your skin. You're a born survivor, Agamemnon – a reason why I chose you to succeed me.'

I disliked the sardonic inflexion in his tone, and changed the subject. 'I gather Sicyon and Pellene are now tributary to Mycenae?'

'They are. An easy war. Thesprotus yielded Sicyon directly he saw my spears. Pellene proved more obstinate. I stormed the gate, imposed a harsh indemnity and enslaved her remaining Heroes. A warning to the rest when their turn comes.'

Atreus left the balcony, entered an antechamber leading to his bedroom and reclined in an ivory chair. A squire brought cups, and wine in a flagon. 'Try this eight-year-old Cytheran – a change from the sour filth you've been drinking on campaign.' He rolled the golden goblet thoughtfully between his palms. 'You mentioned alliances. I agree – the certainty that he faced united kingdoms would certainly deter Creon. But where now-adays may we find reliable allies? Neleus has died, and Nestor rules in Pylos. I don't yet know the bent of his foreign policy. Augeas of Elis' hand lies loosely on the sceptre: his son Phyleus in Dyme conspires with Thyestes' – an ugly spasm of hatred contorted his face – 'to oust him from the throne. Adrastus, from your account, is a broken reed, no longer capable of ruling. Anything might happen in Argos. Sparta remains, a powerful realm firmly in Tyndareus' grip.'

He set down the cup on an alabaster table ornately carved with dolphins intertwined. A sun-shaft stabbed the window and haloed the ash-grey head, shadowed the troughs at temples and cheeks. 'We need a strong confederate to discourage the Theban threat. I want you to go to Sparta and offer King Tyndareus a formal alliance. Then I'll appoint you Marshal, and Menelaus will replace you as Master of the Ships.' He stroked the arms of his chair, his eyes remote. 'I'm getting old; it's time I shed a little of the load.'

I said, 'I am honoured, sire.'

'That's all. Leave as soon as you can.' An upraised hand arrested my departure. 'Something else has happened while you've been away. I considered Hercules incapable of further folly – the fellow's in his dotage. I was mistaken. The madman took ships to Troy and raided Laomedon's horse herds. The king was inspecting his horses, virtually unescorted, and the murderous ruffian slew him, grabbed some mares and fled. I suppose Priam will succeed: you didn't like him, did you? A disgraceful affair – but it can't affect Mycenae.'

Atreus' political prognostications were seldom wrong; but there he made the biggest mistake of his life.

Chapter 8

SPARTA rules a realm called Laconia, a country of fertile plains divided by mountain ranges. There's a lot of room in Laconia: you can travel all day and see nobody except a shepherd watching his flocks, or perhaps a solitary Hero guarding his cattle and horse herds. Natural barriers help to protect the kingdom against invasion: the sea on the south, and the mountain ranges to east and west. Only on the Arcadian border are natural defences lacking. Since Arcadia is incapable of mustering a Host, and Spartans are more competent than most in repelling casual marauders, never within man's memory has Sparta fought a regular war on Laconian soil.

This immunity has set a stamp on Sparta. Unlike all other Achaean cities I have seen (except King Nestor's newly-built Pylos) she has no central citadel, walled and turreted, nor do fortifications girdle the town. In this aspect Sparta resembles Cretan cities; otherwise King Tyndareus' capital has not the smallest affinity with the crumbling decadent splendours of Malia or Knossos.

Security from invasion has not rendered the race effete. Spartans are far from averse to comfort – their bath-rooms are both numerous and superbly appointed, the food, though plainly cooked, delicious – but they disdain superfluous luxuries. Seldom have I encountered men so devoted to physical exercises, to hunting, horses, sports and games. Lacking external enemies they fight among themselves, conducting small campaigns, city against city, of a formal, almost ritualistic character.

King Tyndareus was around fifty years old and looked half his age: tall, spare, deep-chested, russet beard trimmed to an arrow-barb point. A ruddy, fresh complexion unlined except for wrinkles at the corners of clear grey eyes. He ruled Laconia firmly yet flexibly, allowing considerable latitude to the Wardens of widely-spaced cities but stamping ruthlessly on the least sign of opposition to his authority. Earlier misfortunes had taught him the arts of kingship. Descended from Poseidon through Perseus on his mother's side, he had succeeded his father on Sparta's throne only to be expelled by a palace revolt. Tyndareus found refuge in Aitolia, where he married Leda, a local chieftain's daughter, sired on her the famous Twins and two girls: Helen and Clytemnaistra. Then the Spartan usurper died in repelling a cattle raid; and a counter-revolution restored Tyndareus to Sparta's rule.

This was the man, and this the kingdom, whose alliance Atreus sought.

I had travelled in considerable state, as befitted an ambassador from magnificent Mycenae: twenty Heroes in my train, two hundred spears, a multitude of followers and transport, and a wagon load of presents for the king. Tyndareus allotted my retinue an entire wing of his palace, and gave a sumptuous feast within a day of our arrival. There I greeted again Castor and Polydeuces, returned from the Colchis voyage, and asked them how they liked it.

'Rather dull,' said breeder and trainer Castor. 'No decent thoroughbred horses anywhere we landed.'

'Only some pretty rough types,' said Polydeuces. 'Put ashore at Bebrycos on the outward passage. The chieftain, one Amycus, fancied himself as a boxer.'

'Challenged any of our crew to fight him,' said Castor. 'Wouldn't let us water otherwise.'

'Great heavy fellow, muscular and hairy, like a boulder covered with seaweed.'

'Wore brazen-studded boxing gloves.'

'We had to have water, so I took him on,' said Polydeuces. 'Sparred carefully at first, avoiding his bull-like rushes.'

'Then gave him a bloody mouth.'

'And flattened his nose – a straight-left punch – and pounded hooks and jabs to the head.'

'Had Amycus sagging.'

'He grabbed my left fist,' Polydeuces said, 'and swung with his right. I went with the tug and right-hooked in his ear.'

'Followed by an uppercut to the chin.'

'Broke his jaw.'

'Knocked him clean out.'

'We got our water,' Polydeuces ended.

The Twins kept me entertained throughout my stay. I also met their sisters on various social occasions, though ladies on the whole stayed more secluded than was customary in Mycenaean palaces. The elder, Clytemnaistra, was singularly beautiful in a sultry, regal way: full red lips, high cheekbones, black shining hair, green slanting eyes and truly magnificent breasts thrusting above her bodice. Fiery passions undoubtedly smouldered beneath a statuesque and somewhat forbidding appearance.

I thought her most alluring, a citadel inviting assault. So, finding her seated beside me watching games and races the king arranged in my honour, I exerted myself to be pleasant. My railleries rebounded from a polite, restrained formality; not once did I raise a smile. Intrigued and a little put out – I know from experience that women don't find me repugnant – I persisted and grew more daring, offering remarks that bordered on salacity. (But you cannot go too far with noble ladies, at least not in public, and certainly not royal daughters.) Her lips twitched, and a veiled amusement flickered in her eyes.

'Your advances are quite outrageous, my lord,' she murmured, 'and hardly to be welcomed by a woman already betrothed.'

The shadow of a smile assuaged the sting. I hastily assured her I intended no offence and swore her shattering beauty had led my tongue astray. Disappointed, I changed to safer topics. But Tyndareus had been listening, and under pretence of inspecting a winning chariot team led me from the pavilion.

'A peculiar girl,' he observed. 'Never quite know what she's thinking. I see you find her attractive.' Gloomily he ran a hand along a horse's withers. 'Unfortunate. She's promised in wedlock to Broteas of Pisa who visited Sparta a while ago. A distant kinsman of yours, I believe, descended from Pelops. A weak and worthless fellow, but Clytemnaistra fell in love, and he with her. She pestered me into giving consent. I believed it a mistake at the time, and now I'm sure.'

'I've never heard of the man,' I said, 'Pisa's an obscure city. Surely an unworthy marriage for Sparta's royal House?'

'Definitely so – but you don't know Clytemnaistra. She's got a will like granite.' He sent me a speculative look. 'You are ... interested?'

'Your daughter attracts me more strongly than any woman I've known – save one. None the less she's promised to Broteas and you can't break your word ... can you?'

Tyndareus looked at me sideways. 'I suppose not. Broteas has already paid me the bride price. So, however tempting the prospect of a union between our Houses the arrangement has to stand. Most annoying.'

After inviting me to drive the winning team and try its paces he said no more on the subject. Thereafter Clytemnaistra avoided my company, and I was forced to admire her from afar.

Neither then nor later did I love Clytemnaistra in the accepted sense of the word. She was not the kind of woman to arouse such simple emotions. My desire, I believe, rose from pique at her stand-off manner, plain undiluted lust (the sight of her breasts invariably stiffened my weapon) and the advantages of a dynastic marriage joining Sparta and Mycenae – the last certainly being predominant. I made inquiries about this Broteas, Lord of Pisa, tributary to King Augeas of Elis; and failed to understand why Tyndareus wasted his elder daughter on a Hero so inconsequential.

I did not, at the time, appreciate Clytemnaistra's formidable character.

Running about the palace far more freely than the older women was the king's other daughter Helen, an enchanting ten-year-old. Hair like golden sunshine shot with the tinge of autumnal beech, blue long-lashed eyes (and how she could use them!), a heart-shaped face and roses-and-cream complexion. Faultless features: a small straight nose, soft curved lips that you longed to kiss and cheeks deliciously dimpled. (I speak of her as a youngling: she is even more beautiful now; and has added to her armoury the arts of entrancing men.) Tyndareus adored Helen, everybody spoilt her; even Clytemnaistra shed her regal reserve when Helen demanded attention, and frolicked in childish games like a playful kitten.

On reflection, these were the only occasions when I heard Clytemnaistra laugh aloud.

I met Tyndareus' consort Leda only once, at a formal audience in the Hall when our embassy first arrived, and afterwards saw her occasionally when she took the air in the palace courts or walked abroad with her ladies. She was skeletal and grey, years older than her husband, an animated wisp so fragile you might suppose a puff of wind would blow her away. Her eyes, a washed-out blue, were ever lost and vague, fixed seemingly on a point remote in space and time; her voice, on the rare occasions she spoke, a thin and reedy fluting. She had a passion for animals and birds, abhorred any form of cruelty – in Sparta a drover looked over his shoulder before laying whip on ox – and during her wanderings about the city had collected in the palace a menagerie of creatures alleged to have been maltreated. Prominent in the collection was an enormous swan, a cob, which followed the queen wherever she went, indoors or out. A bad-tempered, vicious bird which, hissing and flapping powerful wings, attacked unprovoked any strangers who went near its mistress. Even on ceremonial occasions Leda kept the brute beside her throne, fortunately secured by a golden collar and chain.

(I heard scandalous stories whispered later about the relationship between Leda and her swan: impossible calumnies probably spread by victims whom the bird had pecked and buffeted.)

Pleasant though my social diversions were, however amusing or entertaining the people I met, I kept in mind the serious purpose bringing me to Sparta. In casual conversations during banquets, games or hunting I broached to King Tyndareus the question of alliance. I trod carefully: from a purely Spartan viewpoint Mycenae gained the advantages, Sparta few or none. Her neighbouring kingdoms posed no threat – though Tyndareus, like Atreus, expressed a doubt concerning Nestor's intentions – and quarrels that raged in lands to the north were distant enough to leave her immune. Sparta therefore pursued a policy of armed neutrality and discovered no useful benefits in allying herself to others.

I emphasized the Theban menace, and Thebes' hold on the Orchomenos cornlands, a monopoly now consolidated by Adrastus' defeat. Sparta, overpopulated like other realms, suffered perennial shortages of wheat – a scarcity stressed by the savage

212

famine not so long before. We were driving to a lion hunt when I raised the point; Tyndareus sprang his horses and said, 'All Adrastus' fault. He should have mobilized a proper Host. You can't take Thebes with two men and a boy.'

'The trouble was,' I hinted, 'Argos has no regular allies to call on, no cities outside the realm to help in time of need.'

'Including, if I may say so, Mycenae. Atreus kept well clear.'

'Atreus, sire, as you surely know, was committed to another war. Otherwise,' I lied, 'he would certainly have joined Adrastus' Host and destroyed the power which prevents Orchomenos supplying your granaries.'

'H'm.' Tyndareus fisted the reins left-handed and cracked his whip. 'Are you proposing an offensive alliance for a future joint campaign against Thebes? If so, Agamemnon, you're wasting your breath.'

'Certainly not. King Atreus' strategy is purely defensive. He fears, with reason, a Theban war on Mycenae. Were we conquered, sire, Argos could be overrun in the following year. Then it's your turn. Against separate disunited kingdoms Creon might be victorious; against Sparta, Mycenae and Argos together he has no chance at all.'

Tyndareus steered carefully between gnarled olive trees that overhung the track. 'Has Argos agreed a confederacy?'

'Not yet. Her losses in the war have disorganized the government; Adrastus seems incapable of ruling. Diomedes is restoring order and will undoubtedly see the advantages of a Mycenaean-Argive union. More so if Sparta joins.'

'I'm not afraid of Thebes. Creon would bitterly regret marching into Laconia. But...' Tyndareus thoughtfully scratched the butt of his whip on his jaw. 'If he attempts an invasion, and is thoroughly defeated, we could follow up and liberate Orchomenos. I admit we've felt a pinch since the corn supply dried up. A pinch,' the king said pointedly, 'Mycenae hasn't suffered since she tapped the Krymeian cornlands.'

'We are fortunate,' I murmured, glumly anticipating the favour-for-favour Tyndareus was after.

'If I consent to a defensive alliance with Mycenae will you in return agree to ship wheat annually to Sparta?'

These huckstering kings! I said, 'At market prices, presum-

213

ably? You could hardly expect the cargoes to be delivered as tribute!'

Tyndareus grinned. 'At cost price, shall we say? Our Scribes will calculate details. Provided you agree in principle I'll discuss the proposal in Council.'

I gripped the rail while the chariot bucked on a boulder, and considered the proposition. A trade pact really required Atreus' approval: I had no authority to barter Mycenaean corn. On the other hand the concession achieved my object. I had very little idea of the deal's financial aspects, whether we could afford it, the minimum price to be set. Gelon accompanied my train: I would as usual seek his counsel.

'If you allow, sire, I shall talk to my advisers and give you an answer later.'

'Very wise. Never commit yourself before considering the economic implications – which means consulting Scribes. Heroes can't grasp such tricky problems. Where would we be without our grey-robed rascals?' Tyndareus reined in a grassy gully where hounds and huntsmen waited. 'Here we are. I promise you a snorting chase – Castor says a man-eating lion roams these hills!'

*　　*　　*

I put the case to Gelon, and instructed him to calculate the maximum imports of Krymeian corn we could divert yearly to Sparta without harming our own economy, and a price in hides and bronze which would cover costs. Then he was to settle details with Tyndareus' Curator. Gelon's experience at Tiryns, where he accounted every grain that entered the country, well qualified him to decide a question affecting the balance of Mycenae's trade. Because he had cooperated closely with Atreus' Curator, Gelon also understood the kingdom's overall finances. (As, probably, did Scribes of every degree: so closely knit was the sect that information flowed among them like water soaking a sponge.)

After a couple of days he begged my attendance in one of those stark basement rooms where palace Scribes conduct business: tiny windows shedding a meagre light on white-washed walls, shelves in tiers holding drinking cups and pots and jars by the hundred, oak coffers containing inventories inscribed on small clay tablets, a rough wooden table and stools. Gelon bowed me to a seat and studied a papyrus sheet.

'A satisfactory contract, my lord, involving no net loss. We'll have to reduce slightly our exports of grain to Elis, but the price the Spartan Curator agreed allows a small return which balances the deficiency. If you approve I shall inscribe the conditions on a tablet for permanent record.'

For form's sake I queried a detail or two, particularly the shipping arrangements, being reluctant to use our galleys in a barely profitable trade. Gelon, however, had secured consent for the cargoes to be carried in Spartan hulls. He never missed a trick.

Curiously I conned the spiky squiggles traced on the papyrus he held. 'A wondrous skill. How you can reduce the sounds of words to signs on clay or paper passes my comprehension.'

'Hardly miraculous, my lord. Calligraphy is an ancient art, practised in many lands. Zeus' people originally brought writing from Egypt to Crete.'

'Extraordinary! So you use Egyptian characters?'

Gelon repressed a sigh. 'No, my lord. The Egyptian Scribes lived a hundred years in Crete, and during that time modified their script to accord with the Cretan language – a form of writing which superseded the original Cretan script. When Thera exploded Zeus' Heroes in Knossos spoke a dialect compounding both tongues.'

'So this is a mixture, Egyptian and Cretan?'

Gelon shot me a look which comprehensively expressed a savant's pity for a dunce. 'On the contrary, my lord, these signs express the language you are speaking now. For when Zeus' followers emigrated to Achaea they assimilated the native speech, and his Scribes again adapted the writing. That language' – he tapped the sheet – 'is what I have written here. Pure Achaean, now universal.'

'Except, presumably, in Crete,' I said, pleased to discover a flaw.

'When Acrisius conquered Knossos,' said Gelon patiently, 'he imposed Achaean speech and mode of writing on Cretan Scribes. Therefore they embrace every country from Crete to the Thessalian borders. No Scribes live in Thessaly or beyond, so' – a contemptuous shrug – 'those realms lack enlightenment.

They keep accounts, I'm told, by scratching notches on sticks.'

'Most interesting.' I stood and patted Gelon's shoulder. 'You've managed the Spartan contract very efficiently. I shall tell Tyndareus Mycenae accepts his terms, and conclude the formal alliance King Atreus desires. Draw the documents accordingly.'

The Spartan Council raised no objections – Councillors seldom oppose a king's apparent will. A feast in the palace Hall celebrated the compact. I took ceremonious farewell of Tyndareus and his family: a vague stare from Leda, Clytemnaistra's unfathomable look, Helen's laughing gaiety, the Twins' pressing insistence that I stay for a promising hunt. ('A boar as big as a horse.' 'Tushes two feet long.') Tyndareus took my hand. 'We've made a state alliance, Agamemnon, and both of us, I think, have made a friend. If ever you need help call instantly on me. I shall not fail you.'

Such asseverations being the polite currency of leave-taking I replied in kind. I could not then foresee that the worth of Tyndareus' promise was soon to be assayed.

Three moons since leaving Mycenae I took the homeward road, rejoicing in my mission's success, no forebodings clouding my mind. Unhappily The Lady had not transferred to me the prophetic gift She bestowed on dead Amphiaraus.

(The visit had a curious sequel. After my departure Tyndareus pondered long and deeply; and concluded the Theban peril demanded, not only a Mycenaean alliance, but a confederation of every city which Thebes' ambitions endangered. Over the years he sent emissaries to various rulers, among them Crete, Locris, Salamis and Athens – the last, indirectly, had vexatious consequences for me – and suggested pacts for mutual protection. He invited lords to Sparta and, so it is said, ratified their oaths by sacrificing horses – a binding and expensive kind of vow. Whatever the truth may be, Tyndareus formed a loose confederation which afterwards gave me a foundation for uniting Achaean kingdoms in the year-long land war we fought against Troy.)

*   *   *

Priam was showing the first signs of that intransigence which led eventually to Troy's destruction, as Atreus described on my return. 'Laomedon's murder,' he said, 'made Priam very angry – and no wonder. On the grounds that Hercules once served King Eurystheus Priam pretends he had Mycenaean backing, and that I provided ships for the raid. Rubbish, of course – Hercules sailed from Thessaly. Priam's using the excuse to hinder our Euxine trade.'

'He always opposed Laomedon's granting the passage. What's he done?'

'Forbidden his people to hire us wagons and oxen for over-land transhipment. Extremely awkward. Galleys are having to force the straits in the teeth of winds and currents. At certain times of the year they can't get through at all. And Troy has doubled the Customs duties.'

I whistled. 'That old skinflint Priam! He'll make a tidy packet.'

'I've sent an embassy to protest, and await results. We can afford extra duties. Colchis' gold has made Mycenae very rich indeed – but you can't eat the blasted stuff. Any restrictions on corn imports from Krymeia are far more serious.'

'All this due to Hercules,' I said between my teeth. 'I'd like to find the sod and kill him!'

Atreus shook his head. 'You're too late. He's dead – The Lady be praised. Struck by lightning and burned to death. High time. He must have been over seventy – a wicked old man.'

(A pest happily removed, but the world is far from hearing the last of Hercules. An inveterate braggart all his life who told exaggerated tales about his doings, an expert self-propagandist, Hercules' career has become a quarry whence bardic epics are hewn. Legends multiply faster as years go by, and find accept-ance among credulous Heroes. Some of the stories are so tedi-ously extravagant that I forbid Heraclean songs to be sung in my Hall.)

Atreus, as he promised, appointed me Marshal and gave me quarters in the palace befitting my rank. Hereditary holdings accompanied the post: he relinquished fertile pastures, farms and vineyards into my hands. In territory, wealth and author-ity I now ranked second to the king. My duties embraced the command and organization of Mycenae's entire Host: the same kind of task, on a larger scale, I had done while Warden of Tiryns.

My primary object being to form a powerful chariot squadron capable of fast and flexible manoeuvres I mustered from Mycenae, Tiryns and our tributary cities over two hundred chariots and drilled them on the Field of War in tight close-order formations. At the back of my mind a certainty hovered that sooner or later we had to meet the Theban Scavengers. Only close, controlled manoeuvre could defeat their reckless charge. I had no presentiment the squadron would one day face and slaughter Hector's gallant Heroes.

The reverses the Seven suffered against Thebes set me to considering more effective methods of storming a citadel. I still woke screaming from nightmares where I died on top of a ladder. Never again : there had to be some better way. I put the poser to Gelon. He deprecatingly disclaimed all knowledge of warlike arts, protested that accounting my estates occupied every waking moment – and swiftly produced a sketch. A stout wooden tower, he explained, tall enough to top the enemy battlements, which you moved to the walls on wheels. Protected by the tower's timbers, stormers mounted inside and leaped from the roof to the ramparts.

Sorrowfully I pointed out that every citadel crowned a mound or hill, usually precipitous and rocky – and you could not push heavy towers up steep slopes. Gelon tore the drawing across and confessed himself defeated.

(He must have pondered the problem for the next twelve years. When, confronted by the difficulty of an escalade at Troy, I was nearly reduced to trying those disastrous ladders, he devised a war-winning siegework which, for some queer reason, men called the Wooden Horse.)

I adopted Atreus' methods in ordering column of route and eliminated useless mouths from the baggage train – superfluous slaves and concubines whom certain lords deemed essential on campaign as weapons and armour. Nor did I neglect the spearmen and archers, insisting they drill as regularly as the charioteers they supported. By the time of the second Theban campaign – known as the Followers' War – I reckon Mycenae fielded the most efficient and formidable Host that ever marched to battle in Achaea.

Which was splendid; but because I became absorbed in these

fascinating military matters for nearly two years the Marshal's duties blinded me to the sinister undercurrents stirring in Mycenae.

*   *   *

Pursuing his expansionist policy Atreus led the Host next year to reduce Aegira on the Corinthian Gulf: a quick, easy and unexciting campaign. After a token resistance Aegira surrendered, agreed tribute and escaped a sack. It was still early summer, the corn not ripe for harvest, so I tried persuading Atreus to extend the operations and also capture Aigiai, only a day's march distant along the coast.

The king refused, and bade me prepare for the return march to Mycenae. This was so unlike Atreus – an energetic, thrusting commander – that I dared to remonstrate. He quelled me with a look; and ordered Heroes, sentinels and Scribes from the room – an antechamber in Aegira's squalid palace.

'Sit down, Agamemnon.' A short, uneventful siege could not have graved the trenches in Atreus' face, nor infused the weariness in his voice. I noticed with a shock more white than grey in his hair. 'You wonder why we forgo an easy chance. The truth is this: I dare not stay overlong from home. The palace is a festering sore of sedition.'

'Sedition? Why have I not —'

'You've been heavily engrossed in your duties. Never has Mycenae known a more assiduous Marshal.' A tired irony edged his voice. 'For all our sakes you'd better turn your mind to politics. There's a palace revolution brewing.'

'Who,' I rapped, 'is fostering rebellion?'

'Surely you can guess? My beloved brother Thyestes, of course.'

'Thyestes? Impossible! He's in Elis.'

Atreus pulled a woollen cloak closer around his shoulders. Although the summer warmth dressed everyone in kilts he seemed to feel an imaginary chill. 'My intelligence sources in Elis are dependable. Old Augeas' days are numbered. Thyestes has suborned influential Elian Heroes. Augeas' son Phyleus is poised to march from Dyme. Their plans are laid and ready. A sudden uprising, Augeas killed, Phyleus crowned in his place. The whole affair could finish in a day.'

'And, in return for Thyestes' help, Phyleus will lead his Host to besiege Mycenae?'

'Precisely. I've mentioned this before,' Atreus said exhaustedly, 'and also told you Thyestes hasn't a hope unless Mycenaean collaborators betray the citadel. My brother has found his accomplices: Copreus – the principal instigator – and several others I know of. Probably a number more I don't.'

'Why not accuse them, sire,' I said, 'and cut their throats?'

'No proof except informers' whispers. In ordinary circumstances,' said Atreus strongly, 'I wouldn't need proof to hack off their heads. But they all have powerful connections and I don't want to stir the hive. A man may survive a sting or two: a swarm will prick him to death.'

'You intend to wait on Thyestes' initiative, and do nothing beforehand?'

'Just that. I believe I can contain my palace plotters. They'll make no move till Thyestes and Phyleus march. Then I'll chop them quick, mobilize the Host and appeal to the Heroes' loyalty to repel a foreign foe. Everybody dislikes Elians, and it ought to answer.'

Atreus stood, and poked a forefinger in my chest. 'Keep this under your helmet, Agamemnon – tell no one but Menelaus. Remember: if Thyestes pulls me down your inheritance falls too – you'll never hold the sceptre. We must not give my brother's Mycenaean friends an inkling we're up to their wiles; then a single blow can swat them like flies on carrion. Go now and issue marching orders. Aigiai and the rest will wait till I've killed Thyestes.'

The Host trailed back to Mycenae and dispersed. Atreus' warning buzzed in my head: I was constantly alert for breaths of sedition wafting about the palace, and sniffed the air for treachery like a questing hound. I often sought Copreus' company, engaged him in talk and listened for the smallest hint of treason. All to no purpose. A handsome, grey-haired fellow, well-mannered, bland and polite, he seemed interested in nothing but horses, hounds and vintage wine. I casually mentioned Thyestes and elicited no more than a disapproving sniff and an opinion that his behaviour disgraced the blood of Pelops.

It was difficult to conceive so languid and polished a gentleman taking the slightest interest in power politics.

The embassy's return from Troy checked my search for evidence – which was probably as well: I feel, on looking back, my approaches were too transparent to deceive the artful Copreus. King Priam's answer, though wrapped in diplomatic language, was stark as a slap in the face. He rejected Atreus' denial of connivance in Hercules' raid, and quoted as evidence a certain Oicles, one of Hercules' followers captured by Laomedon's escort who confessed before he died that he came from Lerna. ('These stupid foreigners!' Atreus grunted. 'Oicles was an Argive – Priam doesn't know the difference.') Therefore, the Trojan king declared, he would stop providing wagons for overland transport and revoke permission for Mycenaean ships to harbour within the Hellespont.

'So,' said Atreus grimly, 'our galleys have to struggle through the straits. For most of the sailing season that's a well-nigh impossible feat. Priam imposes a stranglehold which quarters the Euxine trade.'

'His ultimatum,' I said, 'falls little short of a declaration of war.'

Menelaus, as Master of the Ships, had accompanied the ambassadors from Nauplia. He said gravely, 'Troy already wages a limited war. Trojan vessels harry our galleys while navigating the Hellespont. They dart from harbours near Scamander's mouth and crowd our ships towards the reef-ridden western shore. A triaconter lately went aground and sank.'

Atreus sucked in his breath. 'Priam obviously intends to close the straits altogether!'

Menelaus said, 'I've ordered Periphetes to provide naval escorts, which stretches our resources and can't be a lasting remedy. Troy holds the whip hand; in home waters she will always outnumber our ships.'

'Withdraw your warships, Menelaus.' Atreus' face was dark as a winter storm. 'They merely invite an engagement we shall lose. And that means open war. How can we fight Troy? If we mobilize the entire fleet, sail to Ilion's shores and win a naval battle is Mycenae better off? We couldn't sink every Trojan ship: Priam would launch more; half a dozen determined galleys can always close the Hellespont.'

'Perhaps,' I ventured, 'a seaborne expedition might land and capture Troy.'

Contemptuous astonishment creased Atreus' furrowed countenance. 'And you're my Marshal, The Lady save us – my fore-most military expert! Are you insane? Disembark the Host on a hostile coast five days' sail from home to fight its way ashore and then encounter Troy and her allied Hosts: Thracians, Carians, Phrygians and the rest? You'd need warriors and ships from every Achaean city – and probably lose the lot! Either you're drunk, Agamemnon, or touched by the sun!'

'A foolish notion,' I agreed submissively.

'It is. All we can do is send our ships to get through how they can. Tell your master mariners, Menelaus, to avoid aggres-sive tactics. Rather than fight they must run: we can't afford a war. The situation may change: Priam's an old man and Hector may hold different views. You met him, Agamemnon?'

'Indeed, sire. I believe he disapproves his father's policy.'

'Let's hope so. I shall offer The Lady a milk-white bull for Priam's death.'

Not The Lady but dread Ouranos postponed a Trojan show-down. Shortly after this depressing conference a galley flying from the Hellespont under oars and sail brought news of a shattering earthquake which demolished Priam's city. Walls and towers, houses and palace tottered into dust; many people perished. Rebuilding, a gigantic task, engaged the resources of the entire population. Trojans lacked time or desire for mari-time affrays; for over a year our merchantmen voyaged un-molested. Menelaus shipped wagons and oxen to the straits and again transhipped cargoes. Galleys quietly reoccupied the inner harbour; gold and corn flowed southwards from Colchis and Krymeia.

A breathing space for Mycenae. King Atreus' time was shorter.

*   *   *

Every detail of that hideous day is scorched upon my memory.

Clouds mounted from the west and snuffed a watery winter sun. Thunder muttered distantly, rolled nearer like giant char-iots charging across the heavens, crashed and shouted over-head. Blue-white tongues of lightning split the sky. A wind-storm sped on the thunder's heels, a gale whipped trees like grass wisps, rain in teeming lances spouted fountains from the earth.

222

Gentlemen fled indoors from husbandry or hunting: the Hall at dinner was thronged. Rapid little rivulets scoured the Great Court's patterned flagstones, rain battered into the portico and drove sentinels cowering for shelter within colonnades and vestibules. Despite the closed bronze doors wind gusted round the Hall, sent torches flaring like banners and swept tides of light and shadow from wall to wall. Voices clacked like a muffled chorus to the thunder's muted bellowing.

Wrapped in thought and a purple cloak Atreus pecked at his food, glowered at the hearth fire's wind-brushed flames and seldom spoke. I talked sporadically to Menelaus, who had come from Tiryns to discuss his Hellespont strategy. He seemed uneasy, perhaps affected by the storm – nobody enjoys Ouranos' manifestations – tugged an auburn beard and scolded his squire Asphalion for failing to keep his goblet filled. My brother by inclination is a moderate drinker; seeing the fourth cup flood his gullet I said lightly, 'Drowning sorrows? Has Melite spurned your advances?' (Menelaus notoriously pursued – with strictly dishonourable intentions – the attractive widow of a Tiryns Hero killed in a Goatmen skirmish.)

'Damned bitch. No. I feel on edge, tense, nervy. Can't think why. Disaster broods in the air.'

I inspected with concern the most unimaginative man I know. 'Probably indigestion, or overmuch wine. Any particular reason?'

'Yes.' He smacked his empty goblet on the table; Asphalion hastily tilted a flagon. 'I'm worried about those traitors. I feel we're perched on a volcano that will blow us to perdition.'

'So?' Pensively I ran a finger round the rim of my cup. Similar forebodings often nagged my mind. I disapproved of Atreus' decision to leave conspirators at large: postponing an inevitable crisis was strangely unlike him. Likewise he had wobbled over Priam's ultimatum. Privately I considered Atreus was losing his grip: an opinion I would never have uttered aloud. Perhaps the strain of ruling and his sixty stressful years combined to erode resolution.

'Don't fret yourself. Atreus will crush them like grapes when the time is ripe.'

Menelaus snorted, and started on his fifth cup. I looked round the rowdy Hall, identified the men who conspired against the king. Copreus, elegantly dressed in a silver-threaded tunic, gold earrings shaped like bees dangling from his ears, gold and amber necklace at his throat, urbanely stroking the thigh of a simpering squire. If one could catch him in the act, I thought viciously, his schemes would end on a stake impaled in his crotch. I marked some others Atreus had named, swigging wine and gulping food, sun-browned hearty Heroes, replicas of dozens in the Hall, of hundreds more in cities across the land. Were these the type to execute plots designed to topple kings?

On the face of it unlikely; but Atreus' agents – I employ the same spies now – seldom garnered rumours.

The king drained his goblet, touched my sleeve and said in an undertone, 'Come later to my apartment, Agamemnon, you and Menelaus. I have news of grave developments in Elis.' He stood. A chamberlain shouted above the clamour. Voices stilled, the company rose, Atreus stalked to the brazen doors. Thunder crashed as the doors swung open, lightning washed the Hall in lurid light.

When I looked again he had gone.

Gentlemen lolled in chairs, sent squires scurrying for wine. A bard on a stool by the hearth twanged his lyre and intoned the tale of Perseus and Andromeda. (Perseus saved her from drowning when she swam beyond her depth; the song, in typical bardic style, dragged a man-killing octopus into the story.) I listened abstractedly, disliking the pre-Orpheus tune, abandoned attempts to rouse Menelaus from his vinous gloom and exchanged banter with nearby Heroes mellowed by wine. The clamour of voices swelled and drowned the music.

Copreus raised a crystal cup to the light of a torch, admired the ruby glow. He caught my eye on him, smiled and waved a hand. Perhaps, I pondered hopefully, the news from Elis might spark a fire to burn him out of existence.

'Come, Menelaus. Let's find the king.'

My brother lurched to his feet; hand on elbow I guided his steps through crowded tables and boisterous men to the doors. We walked along darkening corridors – the pall of clouds turned day into night – and mounted marble steps to the upper floor. I shivered; winter's chill pierced tunics like knives after the fuggy warmth of the Hall. Passages and stairways were quiet and deserted; thunder rolled more loudly in the stillness. Menelaus tripped and I hauled him up.

'Drunk too much,' he mumbled.

We turned a corner to the wing which held Atreus' apartments. An armoured Hero leaned on his spear beside the cedarwood doors – gentlemen provided the king's guards. I raised my hand to the latch. The Hero said, 'The king is not in his rooms.'

'Hasn't he returned from the Hall?'

'I've been on duty since noon, and the king has never been near.'

'Damn.' I scratched my head. 'Where could he be? Gone to the stables, perhaps.'

'Not in this downpour,' Menelaus mumbled. 'Be soaked to the skin before ... hic, sorry ... he'd gone a step.'

'He may be in the queen's apartments. Steady, Menelaus – hold my arm.'

Dim corridors lit by lightning flashes led to the doors of Pelopia's quarters – the rooms where, years before, we had witnessed our mother's adultery. A bundle like a sack of clothes huddled beside the door post. I tapped on the panels and called. Menelaus, stooping, touched the bundle.

'Agamemnon!'

Bulging eyeballs and gaping mouth, a glistening stain on the marble tiles. A female slave by her garb, one of the queen's attendants. I flung my weight on the doors.

A single oil lamp lighted the bedroom. The flame flared in a wind that soughed through open windows. Pelopia lay on the bed, a lambswool coverlet drawn to her throat. Hair like a flowing black shadow, chalk-white face and dark glazed eyes. She remained so still I believed she was dead. Menelaus, shocked stone sober, rushed to the bedside and shouted, 'The king! Where is the king?'

A sigh faint as a butterfly's breathing trembled Pelopia's lips, her eyelids fluttered. The pupils rolled and fixed on a point behind us. I turned and ran through an archway. A tremendous thunderclap split the heavens, successive flashes drenched the room with light. I saw what I saw, and choked, and stumbled back to the bedroom, Lifting the lamp on high I returned and stood in the arch. Menelaus peered fearfully over my shoulder.

Chairs and tables were scattered and overturned, phials and

vases broken. Blood puddled the floor and splashed the walls, flecked furniture and soaked the woven druggets. A rent and red-stained purple cloak dragged half across a body on the flags, a knee drawn up, arms wide.

Whoever had done it had wielded his sword like a butcher cleaving a carcase. Atreus was unrecognizable. Slashes cut his face apart, spilt oozing brains from the skull, sliced open his throat to the spine, hacked ribs in bloody splinters, slit belly from crotch to breastbone and tumbled the entrails out. A tang of blood and bowels clotted the air.

Menelaus gurgled, bent double and spewed. I shuffled to the bedroom. With a shaking hand I placed the lamp on a table, dripped oil on polished ebony. My knees gave way and I fell on the edge of the bed.

I croaked, 'Who ... did it?'

Pelopia's lips quivered. Her eyes stayed fixed on the painted whorls and chevrons adorning the ceiling. With an effort that shook the slender form hidden beneath the fleece she whispered, 'Thyestes.'

I rubbed smarting eyeballs. 'You are sure? How could he pass the citadel gates? The room is dark, you could be mistaken.'

In a movement barely perceptible she rolled her head from side to side. 'It was ... Thyestes.'

Menelaus staggered to the bed, wiped hand across mouth and rasped, 'Wake up, my lady! The king is dead, your husband murdered. Tell us what you know!'

Pelopia seemed not to hear. Like one who is suddenly pierced by pain her features crumpled. She closed her eyes and breathed, 'He has taken ... his son.'

I looked at Menelaus, saw my thoughts reflected in his face. The terrible shock had addled Pelopia's senses. I said, '*Your* son, my lady. Where did —'

'Thyestes' son ... and mine.'

Menelaus took the lamp and went to a cot in a corner. He examined the blankets and linen trailing on the floor.

'No blood here. No Aegisthus either. The boy has certainly gone.'

Thunder rumbled distantly. The storm receded inland over the mountains, lightning glared less fiercely through the window. The lamp wick guttered and spat.

Pelopia whispered, 'Hear me. I speak ... truth.' She spoke so quietly, in shallow gasping breaths, I bent my head to her lips. 'My father ... drunk ... in Sicyon. Aegisthus is ... Thyestes' son. This I ... swear.'

Horror and fear had so blunted my wits I do not think I realized the abomination she confessed. I stuttered, 'You are overwrought, my lady. Perhaps later —'

'I am ... dying.' Slowly, with infinite effort, she pushed away the fleece. Naked breasts, a dagger below, her hand on the hilt. A sluggish tendril welled from the wound and crimsoned the bedsheet.

Pelopia's eyelids drooped. 'The pain ... I cannot bear ... draw out the blade ...'

Menelaus' eyes met mine across the bed. He nodded once, his countenance grim as death. I unclasped her fingers, gripped the haft and jerked. Pelopia shrieked, her body arched, blood gushed out in a torrent.

We stood beside the bed and watched the Queen of Mycenae die. Her passing was hard and tormented.

*　　*　　*

In faltering sentences broken by long pauses and the diminishing hiss of rain outside the window we decided what had to be done. Menelaus fetched the sentinel Hero, posted him outside Pelopia's room, told him to forbid everyone from entering. I returned to the Hall, now almost deserted, and sent stewards to bring all the Councillors they could find to a meeting in the Throne Room.

There I announced, wasting no words, that somebody unknown had murdered the king and queen and abducted her son. In the stunned silence that followed I glanced furtively at Copreus. He looked astounded as the rest, ashy pale and shaken; unless he was a superb dissembler the news had hit him hard. Perhaps Thyestes' confederates had not expected regicide, perhaps the killing was premature and caught the traitors unprepared. Either factor might give me time, time to sort the faithless from the loyal, to discover the men who would rally behind me as Atreus' successor.

I had to move fast; events were scudding to a climax.

I did not disclose the murderer's identity. Menelaus agreed

with me that any uncertainty we could sow in the conspirators' minds would help confuse their plans. Nor did I mention Thyestes' incestuous rape, the misbegotten consequence, saving such revelations for the critical moment when the Elian Host drew near Mycenae. Then by publishing his crimes I might turn the waverers against him. You must realize I was doubtful how far the rot had spread, which Heroes I could count on, how many collaborators the spies had failed to find.

Menelaus sent parties in pursuit along the roads – whence trackways crossed Arcadia to Elis. Nightfall checked the search; at dawn the hunters baulked at rain-sheared landslides blocking roads and streams the storm had bloated to impassable raging spates. They found no trace of the quarry.

Nor did an investigation among guards on gates and palace disclose how an intruder managed to penetrate a closely guarded citadel. The time of day and the tempest had helped Thyestes: gates were not closed till sundown, and sentries seeking shelter abandoned their beats. A spearman gave a vague description of a man slipping in at the height of the storm, a pedlar by his dress, apparently one of many who passed daily in and out, unremarked and seldom challenged. None had seen him enter the palace; none had noticed a man and a ten-year-old boy slinking from Mycenae.

In my capacity as Marshal I decapitated three spearmen, deprived of his greaves and banished the Hero commanding the gate guard. By then it was past midnight, the palace a humming hive, shocked individuals flitting about the corridors, gathering in corners, lingering in the Hall. I ordered slaves to Pelopia's room to cleanse the carnage, wash and prepare for burial the royal corpses. A flustered chamberlain importuned me about the rites for royal funerals; he could recall no precedents in his lifetime because, he mewed, the Heraclids had interred King Eurystheus' headless body near Sciron's Rocks. Wearily I told him to invent a suitable ceremony and shoved him away. (He consulted the Daughters and an aged Hero who had seen as a child King Sthenelus buried.)

I asked Menelaus to sleep in my room; we kept weapons at our bedsides. Talthybius guarded the door, taking the watch in turns with my brother's Companion Etoneus. I reckoned in this crisis his household noblemen and mine were the only men we could faithfully depend on : a couple of dozen in all.

Slaves disrobed me and massaged legs that felt they had marched the length of the land. Menelaus lay prostrate on his bed and cradled a throbbing head – the aftermath of drinking and disaster. I said, 'Tomorrow I'll post pickets on the Arcadian border crossings to bring word of Thyestes' approach. It will give us a whole day's warning. How do you measure our chances?'

'Slim. Although Atreus proclaimed you his heir in Council, Thyestes, as his brother, can claim equal rights of succession. He's also older than you.'

'Can the Council accept a known adulterer banished from the realm?'

'Atreus invited him back, you remember, and cooked his son. Thyestes won a lot of sympathy from that Tantalus affair.'

'When I disclose he begat a child on a daughter who married his brother, the manner of Tantalus' end will pale to insignificance!'

'Maybe.' Menelaus pulled the blankets to his chin. 'It really depends on the number of Councillors Copreus has subverted. You've lost Atreus' protection, and I'm afraid you're not too popular among the Heroes – particularly the older men who have seen you grow in wealth and power at their expense. You'll have to be very persuasive when you offer yourself as king.' He yawned hugely. 'Blister my balls, I'm tired! Sleep well, Agamemnon.'

*   *   *

Four days later we buried the monarchs of Mycenae.

Embalmers had done their best with the king's mutilated corpse, drawing out brains and entrails, stitching flesh. A mask of beaten gold fashioned in some resemblance to Atreus' living features covered a face beyond their skill to repair. They had arrayed him in a gold-tasselled purple cloak, gemmed and gold-embroidered, sword and dagger by his side; a golden diadem crowned his head. A green silver-threaded garment clothed Pelopia's body from neck to ankles, her face exposed, skin like alabaster daubed scarlet on lips and cheekbones. Heroes carried the bodies on biers across the Great Court, down steps to the

229

palace gate, and laid them reverently side by side on a four-wheeled wagon harnessed to grey Kolaxian stallions, the king's most treasured horses.

Atreus in state regalia started his final journey.

Daughters clad in loose white robes preceded the wagon. A watery sunlight burnished unbound tresses. Among them stumbled a naked man and woman, shivering with fear and cold, wrists shackled in golden chains, heads garlanded with laurel. Royal Companions guided the horses through the citadel gates where an armoured guard saluted, spears aloft. I and Menelaus flanked the wheels. A lengthy cortège followed: Heroes in full mailed panoply, blue and yellow horsehair plumes nodding on tusked and brazen helmets; Companions in studded corselets, squires wearing sleeveless woollen tunics. A group of noble ladies in flounced and resplendent dresses wailed and beat bare breasts. Slaves at the column's tail herded a mingled collection of cattle and sheep, pigs and goats – all picked as the finest specimens the royal herds contained. Behind them a huntsman led on leashes Atreus' favourite boarhounds. Silent, grieving citizens thronged the roadsides: whatever Atreus' faults his reign had afforded them peace and prosperity.

A vast dome of beaten earth, plastered and painted white, pinnacled the hill where the king had made his tomb. The cortège curved round the foot of a spur, entered the mouth of a narrow cutting walled by square stone blocks and hedged by spearmen ranked elbow to elbow. As the procession penetrated the heart of the hill the walls rose higher on either side. The shadows deepened. Serried ranks of slaves silhouetted the crests of the cutting; behind them sloped banks of soil. There was a smell of dank raw earth, and a shuddering chill. Tall stone columns flanked a tremendous doorway. Great bronze doors, gilt-studded, swung wide as the Daughters approached.

Chanting incantations, they passed inside. The wagon halted. Heroes lifted the bodies shoulder high across a threshold sheathed in bronze. Slaves holding spluttering torches ringed the sepulchre's circular floor. The walls leaned inwards like the interior of an enormous beehive, hewn grey stones in course upon course climbing to the peak of a dome lost forty feet above in utter darkness. Torchlight glittered on a thousand gold rosettes which decorated the stones, the brilliance diminishing tier by tier and vanishing completely in the gloom of the upper courses. A golden carpet sparkled in the centre of the floor; here the bearers lowered Atreus' bier. They carried Pelopia into a side chamber walled by alabaster tiles.

Heroes, Companions and ladies thronged the tomb, gazed their last on Atreus' golden mask. Slaves unloaded a cart, brought vessels of food, flagons of wine, jars of oil and unguents, swords, daggers, spears, a waisted shield, bow and arrow-filled quiver and laid them in decent order around the bier. The Daughters' dolorous keening echoed hollowly in the vault. While they sang a hymn of lamentation I stepped to the bier and saluted, back of the hand to forehead, stooped and kissed the mask. I stared at the remains of a mighty king, a magnificent man, and knew a loneliness so desolate the tears ran down my cheeks. A lifelong friend and counsellor was gone, a father I feared and honoured – and realized now I loved. Without his caustic precepts to sustain my resolution the way ahead loomed dangerous and drear.

I took a sword from the pile, set a foot on the blade and bent it, releasing the weapon's soul to battle for its lord in the vulnerable period before the flesh dissolved and his phantom fled to the dark.

Slaves conducted the beasts to a space at the body's feet. A wrinkled white-haired Daughter slew them one by one, cutting their throats with a sharp stone knife. Terrified by the scent of blood the animals bleated and bellowed, plunged against the tethers, tripped the slaves who held them. An indecorous proceeding, I decided, deftly dodging a heifer's flailing hooves.

The Daughters ceased their chanting, went through the brazen doors and ringed the naked couple who drooped beyond the threshold: Atreus' favourite concubine and a trusted slave. Bidden by a gesture they knelt at the beldam's feet; she plunged her knife in turn in the bases of their skulls. When the convulsions ended the bodies were folded heads between knees and propped against the pillars flanking the doors.

Unyoked from the funeral wagon the stallions fidgeted nervously, frightened by the victims' bellowings and a pervading stench of blood. Killing horses was beyond a woman's strength: a Companion swung an axe and severed spines behind the poll. Slaves dragged the carcases to face one another muzzle to muzzle outside the threshold. A huntsman cut the boarhounds' throats and placed them beside the horses.

The mourners filed from the vault, trod carefully round the slaughtered beasts and passed along the canyon between lines of still-faced spearmen. The huge bronze doors clanged shut. Slaves on the tops of the cliffs began shovelling down earth. When the cutting was filled and the entrance concealed only the hilltop's white clay dome would mark a royal sepulchre.

King Atreus and his unhappy queen rested in darkness for ever.

*   *   *

A mud-splashed messenger stopped me as I entered the citadel gate, and reported outriders of an Elian Host crossing the border hills. Their spears could be gleaming in sight of our walls before the next day's noon. The great crisis of my life reared like a racing breaker and carried my fate on the crest.

I gave orders to summon the Councillors, told Talthybius to bring me word when they were ready in the Throne Room and went to the palace to shed my armour. In my apartments a squire unbuckled Menelaus' mail. He listened, frowning, while I told him what impended.

'You'd have done better to assemble *all* the Heroes. Any enemies you have are in the Council; we'll find our friends among the younger men.'

'Traditionally the heir to the throne states his claim in Council.'

'Atreus didn't do it that way. He declared himself king and be damned to the lot.'

'Atreus, if you recollect, had an Argive Host at his back. I have you and our household nobles. Nor,' I added sadly, 'am I Atreus.'

Talthybius ran into the room. He looked tense and alarmed. 'Why so flurried?' I asked. 'Are the Councillors assembled?'

'They are gathered in the Throne Room.' He paused. 'Is it customary, my lord, for men to come armed to Council?'

Menelaus froze in the act of shrugging into his tunic. 'Armed? What do you mean?'

232

'I have seen them. Certain gentlemen – Copreus, and others – wear swords beneath their cloaks.'

My brother said dourly, 'There's your answer, Agamemnon. Are you going to meet them? I doubt they'll give you a funeral so magnificent as Atreus'!'

An icy rage possessed me, shook my body from head to toe. I said between my teeth, 'Re-arm me, Eurymedon, quick!' Concealing surprise the squire clapped greaves on my legs and knotted the silver wires, slipped on breast- and back-plates and fastened straps. Menelaus pulled his tunic off.

'I suppose,' he said lugubriously, 'you intend to fight the entire Council? As good a way as any of committing suicide. Here, Asphalion, give me back those greaves.'

I said harshly, 'No need for you to concern yourself. Find a chariot, go while you can, fly to Argos.'

'Not far enough,' Menelaus grunted. 'Argos hasn't recovered yet, can't possibly resist Mycenae and Elis combined.' He settled cuirass about his chest, fitted brazen skirts round hips. Asphalion's fingers flitted over the buckles. 'Sparta's the nearest haven – provided we get out alive.'

'Shall I arm myself, my lord?' asked his Companion Etoneus.

'And I?' Talthybius said.

'Neither,' Menelaus snapped. 'When we've left for the Throne Room you'll sprint to the stables, yoke our speediest horses in three smooth-running chariots and bring them fast to the palace gates.'

Eurymedon lowered a helmet on my head. I tied the chin-strap and said, 'You're optimistic, brother! We're going to be killed – but I mean to finish Copreus and every traitor my blade can find before I die. No one shall say a descendant of Pelops fled like a cur from his heritage!'

'A most edifying sentiment.' Menelaus strapped on sword, slipped arms through grips of a waisted shield. 'None the less I intend to survive, after doing what damage I can. Those bastards are due for a nasty surprise – we're armoured, they are not. Ready, Agamemnon?'

I hefted my spear. 'I am ready.'

'Right.' Menelaus glared at the quartet of Companions and squires. 'Don't stand there looking like dejected donkeys! Harness those chariots! Run!'

233

Accoutred for battle, spears in hand, we clanked along the corridors, descended steps, passed through the Hall where a handful of idling gentlemen watched us in surprise, and crossed the Great Court. At the Throne Room's pillared portico a sentry clashed to attention. Voices murmured through open doors. We marched in shoulder to shoulder.

The ringing of mail turned every head, cut talk like a Cretan axe. We thrust roughly through the crowd, shields battering men aside. I stopped at the throne and turned and looked them over. Thirty noble Heroes, supposedly the bravest, most sapient and experienced, king's counsellors and friends, the bedrock of Mycenae. Copreus and his cronies clustered in a group, cloaks wrapped close, hands hidden.

Menelaus bent his head to my ear. 'Spotted the enemy? You take Copreus, I'll have the one on his left. Deal with the rest as they come.'

I said, 'My lords, I am King Atreus' eldest son and acknowledged heir, therefore I proclaim myself successor to his throne. I await your acclamation.'

A taut silence. An old bald-headed Councillor quavered, 'Of course, of course. Always been understood. Atreus told us years ago. No question —'

A Hero at the back lifted a hand and shouted, 'I salute you, Agamemnon!'

'And I!'

'And I!'

All younger Heroes, I noted. Copreus shuffled closer. He said, 'You must know, my lord, another kinsman of Atreus opposes your entitlement. We have a right to hear the merits of his claim.'

'Name him.'

Copreus pretended surprise. 'Why, Thyestes, the dead king's brother, who travels from Elis to state his rights in Council.' He took a pace nearer the throne, his friends stepped forward behind him. Menelaus whispered, 'Strike when he comes within spear-reach.'

'Why,' I blared, 'does Thyestes bring Elis' Host to back his claim? Is he afraid his infamy has already reached your ears?' I slammed spear butt hard on the floor. 'Listen well, my lords. This is the manner of man whom some of you want as king.'

In short, searing sentences I repeated Pelopia's dying confession: Thyestes' murder of Atreus, his daughter's rape, his fathering of Aegisthus. Horrified murmurings rustled the audience. Even Copreus looked taken aback, possibly aware how Atreus died but ignorant of the incest.

'Does such unspeakable vileness,' I shouted, 'commend in your eyes the monster who seeks Mycenae's crown?'

'No!' bellowed the three young men who previously acclaimed me. 'A disgusting story,' muttered the aged Councillor.

Voices babbled discordantly. I yelled above the turmoil.

'Who pronounces Agamemnon king?'

Six or seven bawled assent. 'Not enough,' Menelaus murmured. 'Brother, you've lost the toss. Keep your eyes on the sods – they're getting close.'

Copreus spoke sharply over his shoulder. Cloaks parted and the swords came out.

I lunged on the instant. The point tore Copreus' throat; Menelaus' spear spitted another between the eyes, blood gouted from his nostrils. Baying like wolves the pack surged round. Too close for our ten-foot chariot spears. I dropped the shaft, banged shield in a bellowing face and whipped out sword. Those Councillors not of the faction retreated against the walls and watched the fight in horrified dismay. One of my young supporters bravely drew his dagger and leaped on our assailants: a backward swipe cut him down. The blow laid open his killer's guard. I sliced his neck where it joined the shoulder, the sword edge grated on bone. The clashing and the shouting hammered the painted ceiling.

Back to back we hewed to the entrance and slew two more as we went. A sentry barred the doorway, I severed his arm at the elbow. We trotted across the Court – you can't run fast in battle armour – charged a spearman guarding the palace portal and slithered down the steps. Chariots stood on the road.

'You've stirred a hornets' nest by the sound of it, my lord,' Talthybius said. 'Mount quick – we must pass the gates before somebody gives the alarm.'

I loosened my helmet's cheekguards and wiped a sweaty face. Mycenae's towering citadel receded in the distance; a shaft of wintry sunlight washed the walls pale gold.

'Golden Mycenae,' I muttered, 'my city, my kingdom, my

inheritance by right. I swear I shall return – on The Lady's Womb I swear it.'

Talthybius whipped his horses. The chariot rocked at a gallop on the road to Sparta and safety.

Chapter 9

IN Argos Diomedes informed me that King Adrastus, bedridden and ailing, had appointed him Regent. Although he had been told Atreus was dead he knew nothing of the way he died or the palace intrigues and revolution which made me run for my life. I explained our predicament and surmised that Thyestes already possessed Mycenae, while an Elian Host was encamped around the citadel. Moreover Thyestes would probably send armed parties to pursue and capture Atreus' surviving relations.

'You're my guests,' said Diomedes shortly. 'I'll let nobody intrude on Argive hospitality.'

The years and hard experience had toughened Diomedes, seasoned blunt-jawed, snub-nosed features to the texture of supple leather, broadened the thickset frame and stamped on his bearing a brusque authority. He was very much in command of affairs in Argos. I noticed unfamiliar faces among the palace Heroes: youths newly awarded greaves and estates, replacements for nobles slain in the Theban War, all fanatically loyal to the son of dead Tydeus. Adrastus almost alone remained from the old regime: a sick old man incapable of ruling.

Argos was not completely recovered from the appalling casualties inflicted in the war. Dorians and Goatmen, detecting the kingdom's weakness and confusion, harried across the Arcadian border in growing strength. They had recently burned a settlement, massacred the inhabitants and carried off stock. (The first instance, but not the last, of the Goatmen's attacks on fortified towns. Five years later they descended on Mycenae.) What with these misfortunes and internal preoccupations I thought Diomedes would find difficulty in refusing Thyestes' demand to surrender Menelaus and myself. If it came

237

to the crunch Argos could not oppose a Mycenaean Host supported by Phyleus' Elians. I refrained from mentioning to Diomedes this cogent reason for cutting short our stay: it would offend his pride, stiffen his obduracy and bring disaster on his head.

Therefore I thanked my friend for his invitation but insisted we press on to Sparta where Tyndareus had promised a haven in time of trouble. The advent of two travel-worn Heroes accompanied by no more than a Companion and squire apiece and an exiguous train provided an unhappy contrast to my previous arrival in ambassadorial splendour. A rumour, but no details, of Mycenae's dynastic upheaval had filtered to King Tyndareus' ears. He gave us a hearty welcome and, after we had bathed, changed clothes and eaten, listened interestedly to my description of the events which had sent us helter-skelter into Laconia. I told him the whole tale, concealing nothing however discreditable to the House whose name I bore.

Tyndareus clicked his tongue. 'What a revolting story! I must say,' he murmured reflectively, 'Atreus and Thyestes between them have committed almost every crime under the sky. Atreus killed his son and wife, married his niece, fed a nephew to the father. Thyestes seduced his brother's wife, raped his own daughter and sired on her a child. The sons of Pelops certainly know how to sin!'

I said stiffly, 'I can't deny our blood seems tainted; but the blight has not afflicted – yet – the second generation. However, if you feel our kinsmen's wickedness contaminates Menelaus and me, we shall instantly remove ourselves.'

Tyndareus laughed. 'Don't be pompous, Agamemnon. I was merely expressing a wondering admiration. Few of our pedigrees bear close inspection: our ancestors by all accounts lived abominable lives. Oedipus, for instance, married his mother – and he's distantly related to my wife. So who am I to shoot an arrow? No, you're very welcome here – stay as long as you like. I'll tell you this: I consider Thyestes a usurper and will help you all I can to throw him out.'

The king allotted us spacious quarters in the palace and added to our inadequate retinue, providing squires, slaves and concubines, horses, chariots, clothing and other accoutrements befitting Heroes. For Menelaus and I were destitute, owning nothing but the armour we wore when fleeing Mycenae: a condition we remained in throughout our exile, entirely dependent on Tyndareus' generosity. Our demesnes were lost to Thyestes; without land to support his station a Hero is nothing, has nothing, can exist on nothing save charity.

Which, in the days that followed, made all the more remarkable the trickle of Heroes and Companions who followed us to Sparta from Mycenae, sacrificing everything in constancy to Atreus' banished heir. Thyestes also exiled certain lords suspected of disloyalty; these embittered men became the most devoted to my cause. From Mycenae and her tributary cities thirty-three arrived eventually in Sparta to live on the king's munificence, and formed in time the core of the force that won me back my throne.

I own to missing various humbler members of my household abandoned in Mycenae: a squire or two who had learned my ways, some faithful slaves. I did not regret the concubines – the sword is what's important, not the scabbard. Most of all I regretted Gelon's absence – a friend I had come to depend on for more than his clerkly abilities. He would willingly have followed me to Sparta; but Scribes are bound by the tenets of their sect to be strictly apolitical: they are fettered to their work, and not their lords. In Mycenae he continued to account and administer the lands I had lately held, demesnes now passed to Thyestes' greedy hands, and served him dutifully as he had served me.

Unbothered by a Marshal's constant duties, by palace plots and traitors, I settled into the routine of a gentleman of leisure. With Menelaus I hunted, contested in games, drove in chariot races, watched sporadic Spartan inter-city battles, feasted in the Hall and enjoyed the willing concubines Tyndareus bestowed, particularly an intricately expert courtesan from Samos. (I discovered very early she was planted in my household by Tyndareus as a spy, an ordinary precaution any wary ruler takes. Once that was understood we did famously together.) But, while the moons passed by, I found time hanging heavy on my hands. It was years since responsibility of one kind or another had not crammed work in my days from dawn till dusk.

Idleness bred mischief. Clytemnaistra still awaited her in-

239

tended bridegroom Broteas of Pisa. Possibly because she was confident her betrothal guaranteed security she treated less aloofly my circumspect advances. Frequently I joined her when she walked abroad, taking the air on the city's outskirts or examining the wares in craftsmen's workshops. With her ladies always in attendance any advances I made were necessarily restrained; ribaldries had to be stealthy and insinuations veiled. These canopied conversations secretly amused her, as I could tell from the glint in slanting eyes, red lips parting on teeth like small white pearls. She was fully aware her body excited my lust, enjoyed my frustration and cunningly tantalized my ardour. When a nip in the air caused her ladies to shawl their bosoms she deliberately left her magnificent breasts uncovered. I was accustomed since babyhood to women's naked breasts; and it was a measure of Clytemnaistra's potent sexuality that hers could stir my loins.

Because I had nothing much to do she gradually became an obsession, the pursuit excelling hunting and every other amusement. I ascertained her daily routine, accompanied her when walking, sat beside her at races and games and drove her chariot to hunts. (Spartan ladies attended meets but, unlike some athletic Mycenaean females, never followed hounds.) Only in a chariot could we speak unheard by others; and at last, when driving to a lion hunt, desire overcame me and I declared my passion.

Clytemnaistra said coolly, 'I don't understand your proposals, my lord. You cannot offer wedlock, because I'm promised to Broteas. Am I to believe you wish to bed me?'

'If I could marry you I would,' I declared fervently. 'Allow me at least the touch of your lips. I beg you, Clytemnaistra!'

'And the touch of other things besides, no doubt. Such as ...' Wilfully she cradled her breasts, a finger stroked a nipple.

I almost fell from the chariot. 'You goad me beyond endurance! I want you, my lady, more than anything on earth! Revoke this unworthy marriage. I can give you —'

'Give me what? Attend to your horses, my lord; they're on the point of bolting. You have nothing to give – a landless Hero banished from his city. Why should I not prefer a man who is lord of his realm?'

'Lord of Pisa,' I snapped. 'No better than a village, and tributary to Elis. You cast yourself on a dunghill.'

'Indeed? Can you promise me anything better?'

'One day,' I said earnestly, 'I shall recover Mycenae, kill Thyestes, rule Achaea's wealthiest kingdom, extend her power and dominance. I promise you that, and ask you to share my throne.'

'An empty pledge, my lord. Your hands hold nothing but air. And you've forgotten something.'

'What?'

'I love Broteas, and shall be happy to share his midden.'

In a fury I whipped up the horses, and arrived at the meet at a breakneck gallop. After consigning my voluptuous companion to a squire's care I climbed a steep and rugged hillside behind hounds, outstripped Castor and Polydeuces and killed alone a snarling lion held at bay.

Every thrust of the spear was aimed at a sultry, sensuous face.

＊　　　＊　　　＊

Travellers from Mycenae told that Phyleus and his warriors, having seen the usurper crowned, had returned long since to Elis. Thyestes had taken control. All tributary Wardens accepted him without demur except Bunus Lord of Corinth, who closed the gates and declared the city independent. Thyestes mustered a Host; after a perfunctory siege the garrison rebelled against the Warden and surrendered. Thyestes castrated Bunus, plunged red-hot rods in his eyes and roasted him slowly to death on a spit.

While such episodes made me angry they were of no consequence to Tyndareus, until a result of the change in Mycenae's rule transformed indifference into fury. A cursory message announced abrogation of the compact for shipping wheat. Tyndareus was so furious he almost went to war; only further information carried by mariners making harbour in Spartan ports restrained him from assembling the Host. Thyestes, it appeared, acted under duress; the Hellespont was firmly barred to Mycenaean ships; corn from Krymeia ceased to flow.

Barely a year had elapsed since the earthquake levelled Troy. The people worked like slaves to rebuild the fallen stones, a new city rose on the ruins: a smaller, shrunken city, houses built with hastily gathered materials and crowded in dense rows where once broad streets had run. Yet Priam felt strong or spiteful enough to proclaim the Hellespont closed: a decree the Trojan fleet enforced. Mycenaean master mariners, still bound by Atreus' edict, made no attempt to fight through the straits and slunk tail between legs to Nauplia. Priam likewise expelled our ships from the inner harbour.

Thyestes despatched an embassy, which returned with a sharp rebuff. He then ordered Periphetes to sail his squadron to the Hellespont, force a passage and sink any Trojan galleys which opposed him. Periphetes took all twelve triaconters and fought an encounter battle in narrow, reef-fanged waters. Outnumbered three to one he escaped by the skin of his teeth with half his warships sunk. Thyestes in retaliation imposed a loose blockade on Trojan seaborne trade. The effort absorbed a large part of Mycenae's mercantile marine; most Trojan ships escaped the net; and Priam's merchantmen voyaged unhindered to Colchis and Krymeia and harvested the wealth they denied Mycenae.

This was the start of the Trojan War: nine years' intermittent tussles at sea, ship-borne raids on the Trojan seaboard, and a year's campaign on the wind-raked plain of Troy.

Tyndareus ordained a rationing scheme for Spartan corn supplies: an example soon to be followed by Thyestes in Mycenae, Argive Diomedes and Nestor in Pylos. While the shortage was not yet acute an adverse season, flooding or drought, could engender serious famine; wise rulers accumulated reserves in city granaries. Meanwhile Tyndareus, assuming the Krymeian supplies permanently lost, debated means of persuading Thebes to relax her grip on Orchemenos' cornlands. He asked me whether Creon might be persuaded to negotiate a trade agreement like to the one Thyestes had revoked. I replied it was unlikely.

'Thebes sells the corn she controls to her neighbouring realms and makes a healthy profit. She has no economic necessity to trade elsewhere – and is inveterately hostile to all Achaean kingdoms south of the Isthmus. Only force will compel a change in policy.'

'So. We therefore return to the question of war against Thebes. You saw the campaign of the Seven. Assuming we don't repeat Adrastus' tactical mistakes, what in your view are the chances?'

I said carefully, 'No single power can conquer Thebes. The city is impregnable, she can call on allies close at hand, on abundant supplies, and on a formidable Host equal in fighting quality to any in Achaea. You'd need an expedition embodied from several kingdoms.'

Tyndareus pensively pulled his ear, dislodged an earring and swore. 'Damn these trinkets! I've been feeling my way towards precisely such an alliance – not very successfully so far. Of the cities at enmity with Thebes only Pylos and Argos have shown any interest.'

'Neither at the moment will support a Theban campaign. Pylos and Elis conduct a running border war, raid and counter-raid. Argos isn't ready for hostilities; though Diomedes' energies may change the situation there in a year or two.'

'Which, if you're right – and I think you are – leaves Sparta and Mycenae. Will Thyestes be persuaded to march on Thebes?'

'Who can plumb his murky mind? I shall be sorry, sire, to see you allied to my most malignant enemy.'

Tyndareus merely grunted. With that realism transcending sentiment which marks all successful rulers he sent an embassy led by Castor and Polydeuces to Mycenae, carrying his proposals for a joint campaign in Boeotia. The Twins brought back a brusque refusal. Thyestes considered Thebes too strong, and maintained that a sea war aimed at re-opening the Hellespont afforded better chances of restoring corn supplies.

'Not his real reasons,' said Castor.

'A shifty rascal,' Polydeuces said.

'He's heading for trouble.'

'Setting his Heroes against him.'

From a staccato duet some basic facts emerged. Not content with the wealth accruing from royal demesnes, Thyestes began appropriating Heroes' estates both near Mycenae and in her tributary cities. The exactions bred a sense of insecurity among the nobility at large. Aware of a growing resentment Thyestes banished a few refractory Heroes – some fled to Sparta – packed Mycenae's citadel with men he could depend on and, as it were, drew a protective mantle about himself. Consequently he was in no position to engage in foreign campaigns; and had even cancelled Atreus' plans for conquest along the Corinthian Gulf.

'Calls it a policy of benevolent neutrality,' Castor said.

'The fellow's frightened,' declared Polydeuces.

King Tyndareus scowled. For days he brooded the problem, snapped bad-temperedly at all and sundry and ordered the execution of Leda's swan when it pecked his leg. Only the queen's tearful pleadings saved the bird from a well-merited death. While we observed from the top of a mound a ritual battle between two little towns whose names I have forgotten – one of those minor campaigns the Spartans conduct among themselves to keep their warriors trained and fit – he broached the subject again.

'I told you, Agamemnon, I'd help you eject Thyestes, though at the time I hadn't the faintest notion how it could be done. Economic necessity welds the claims of friendship, and I'm considering waging war against Mycenae.'

By this time I had nearly resigned myself to lasting exile in Sparta, a forgotten pretender existing on Tyndareus' charity, a cynosure of pity among my peers. Hope flooded my heart like a rising tide. But an inbred caution whispered doubt: could Sparta's Host prevail over one I had trained myself, whose qualities in battle almost certainly surpassed all rivals? I swallowed the thought: fatal to plant uncertainty in a potential saviour's mind.

I said simply, 'My gratitude, sire, is beyond expression.'

'You haven't heard it all.' Chariots wheeled and clashed and lifted whorls of dust. A collision snapped poles and splintered wheels, a Hero threshed in agony till a spearman's point impaled him. 'Clumsy lout deserved to die,' Tyndareus remarked. 'Thoroughly bad driving. About this proposition. There's a condition.'

Royal concessions always demanded conditions, I reflected mournfully. 'Yes, sire?'

'When you've recovered the throne you'll join me immediately in a war on Thebes, together with any other allies we can find.'

To haver would be disastrous. When the sceptre nestled firmly in my grasp I could consider the factors at leisure and, if prudence dictated, postpone the operation or withdraw. After all, you cannot hazard kingdoms to repay a debt of gratitude.

I said, 'For that you have my oath.'

'Good. Recovering Mycenae is a project requiring careful planning and preparation, in which I'll need your help. We've heard about your expertise as Marshal of the Host.' A whirling cut-and-thrust encounter caught his eye. 'Did you notice that? As neat a bit of spearplay as I've seen – a low thrust glancing upwards to the throat. Ends the battle, I think: a leader's killed.' Approvingly Tyndareus watched the contenders draw apart, start counting bodies, totting up the score.

Meanwhile I thought furiously, trying to screw up my courage.

For days I had been remembering the king's unspoken preference for me as Clytemnaistra's spouse in the days when Atreus lived and I was undisputed heir to Mycenae's crown. My circumstances since were greatly changed – royal successor become landless Hero – but Tyndareus seemed determined to recover my throne. Therefore he had every reason to feel as he had before. Should I nudge his memory? Or, with my future still uncertain, had he resolved to give Broteas his daughter?

I licked dry lips, and ventured all on a gambler's throw.

'Sire,' I began uncertainly, 'you've promised me your aid to attain my greatest ambition. I hesitate to ask another favour, but ... You have it in your power to realize my dearest wish, a boon to place me always in your debt – and none the less redound to your advantage.'

Tyndareus said coldly, 'I can't conceive what else you want. Nothing is more valuable than a throne.'

'For me, sire, there is. Your daughter Clytemnaistra's hand in marriage.'

Which clearly demonstrated the abysmal infatuation that ensnared me. I will not labour my folly: a madness bitterly punished in years to come. I had tried over the moons to exorcise obsession by strenuous physical exercise, hunting, racing, wrestling, by rampantly bedding concubines until they cried for mercy, by feasting and in wine – in everything but work: there was none for me in Sparta. All to no effect. Clytemnaistra's beauty bound me in chains of desire; only within her body could I quench the fires of lust.

You may believe this or not as you will: on looking back I find it scarcely credible myself.

Tyndareus' expression showed less surprise than I expected. My pursuit of Clytemnaistra could not have passed unnoticed in a society so closed as Sparta's.

'We mentioned this on your previous visit. Broteas is due any day. He'll wed my daughter and take her to Pisa. My word is pledged.'

'Consider, sire,' I prompted, 'the advantages to be gained by marriage between your House and mine. With Sparta and Mycenae inalienably related they can together dominate the whole Achaean world!'

'Provided you regain the throne, which is by no means sure. Nor does it always work,' Tyndareus grumbled. 'Leda is the king of Aitolia's daughter, yet Sparta and Aitolia remain opposed as fire and water.'

'Besides being rulers,' I reminded him, 'we would also be friends.'

'Don't talk bull's-milk!' Tyndareus snapped. 'Friendship has nothing to do with politics. Besides, Broteas has paid me a hefty bride price: a hundred cattle and a thousand sheep and goats. I've no intention of returning the herds. The wedding, damn and blast it, must go through.'

At that point I deemed it best to cease persuasion. The king obviously preferred a dynastic union with the House of Pelops and Mycenae to a profitless connection with petty Pisa, and cursed himself for yielding to Clytemnaistra's will. I had made my offer and planted the seed; best to let it germinate undisturbed. Tyndareus was not the man to allow his daughter's whim to defy high policy's prescriptions.

We descended from the mound; Tyndareus bestowed a garland of bay and laurel upon the victorious city – three dead against the loser's five; maimed warriors did not count – and we drove at a leisurely pace to Sparta.

Maira, my concubine from Samos, revealed the results of the king's meditations. When I lay pleasantly satiated beside her after an exhausting tumble she gently tickled the instrument of her pleasure, and murmured, 'They say Lord Broteas arrives within the moon to wed my lady Clytemnaistra.'

'Everybody knows that,' I answered irritably, my desires

instantly aroused, not by Maira's manipulations, but in longing for the woman I had lost.

'And everyone in Sparta knows you are mad for the lady. You can't prevent the marriage, my lord.'

I slapped her hand away. 'Let me alone, you bitch. I have never thought of interfering. And what's it to do with you?'

Maira propped chin on hand, and touched her lips to mine. Her nipples brushed my chest. 'When the couple are wed the king has kept his word. If anything happens afterwards how should he be blamed?'

I seized her by the shoulders and rammed her hard on the bed. Glowering into her eyes I said, 'What are you implying? Out with it – or I'll call a slave to flog you!'

Maira smiled. (Have I mentioned her entrancing mouth, small tip-tilted nose and a body like golden fire?) 'If some misfortune befalls Lord Broteas on the journey back to Pisa – why then, my lord, the lady Clytemnaistra is free to marry again!'

I released her and rolled on my back. 'Has the king suggested this?'

Maira's amber eyes rounded in surprise, twin circles of shocked astonishment. 'How can you say such a thing? What have I to do with the king?'

'Don't be stupid. We both know you're one of his spies.' I rested forearm on brow and thought. 'Utterly impracticable. Broteas travels guarded by a retinue of warriors.'

'A small retinue, perhaps a score all told. I saw it myself when last he visited Sparta.'

I hardly heard her. I would need help, I mused, and who would dare to concern himself in so treacherous a venture? Not the Mycenaean Heroes, and certainly not Spartans. I said aloud, 'The idea's impossible.'

Maira snuggled closer. 'A man named Dracios holds Aigion on the Arcadian border. Aigion is naught but a robber stronghold, Dracios a freebooter, his followers unprincipled ruffians. They'll do anything you ask if paid enough.'

I stared at the ceiling. Tyndareus' hand in the business loomed abundantly clear. Maira – an exciting wench, but brainless as a sparrow – simply repeated instructions learned by rote. Useless to probe to the roots: for fear of a tortured death she would never implicate the king. I said caustically,

'How very interesting. Am I expected to seek Dracios in his fastness?'

'By a strange coincidence,' said Maira guilelessly, 'he is now in Sparta, residing at a house in the silversmiths' quarter. I can show you the place, my lord, if so you wish.'

No harm in meeting the fellow. 'Very well. Now, you horrible little spy, let's see what else you can do.'

I grabbed her hips and swung her astride my crotch.

*   *   *

I pondered deeply before interviewing Dracios. The risks of the enterprise sparkled like menacing spears; the reward – Clytemnaistra. Provided the plot succeeded I could expect the king's implicit support. Failure, and exposure, must drive me from my Spartan haven to sanctuary in Pylos or even farther afield.

A stimulating conversation with Clytemnaistra finally pricked me to action. We were watching herdsmen corralling bulls – dangerous work : two men were fatally gored – and she responded to my raillery more freely than ever before, displaying a talkative vivacity instead of her proud reserve. I could not beguile myself that she was yielding to my charms : allusions in her chatter made it plain her defences were lowered solely because her marriage was drawing near. She felt happy and safe in the thought of her betrothed's embraces.

I decided to liquidate Broteas.

I saw Dracios in a squalid house shouldered by silversmiths' workshops. A blackbearded, dark-skinned, shock-haired villain, short broad body a mesh of muscles striped by ancient wound scars. He spoke an outlandish brogue, an amalgam of Arcadian and Spartan dialects. I introduced my object cautiously, fencing with words. Dracios brusquely interrupted and came straight to the point.

'You want me to waylay Broteas on the road to Pisa and kill him? Consider it done, my lord.'

I blinked. 'How did you know?'

Dracios hawked and spat, ground his foot on the gob. 'Why d'you think I'm in Sparta? Not for fun, I promise you – hate the infernal place. Give me Aigion any day. Let's arrange the details and I'll be on my way.'

Cautiously I mentioned payment – an obstacle barring the

road to attainment like a landslip crashed from a mountain. The services of Dracios and his gang must come exceedingly expensive; and I owned no cattle or sheep, only a meagre hoard of bronze from King Tyndareus' bounty.

The chieftain checked my stumbling inquiry.

'All fixed.' He saw the question shuddering on my lips, and held up a horny, filthy hand. 'No names, no punishment drill. Now, I'll see Broteas pass on his way to Sparta, and will watch for his return.' Dracios cackled coarsely. 'With a blushing bride in tow. When do you intend to appear, my lord?'

'We'll plan particulars later. Foolish to mount an operation without reconnoitring the scene. I'll come with you to Aigion.'

I left Sparta unadvertised and travelled to Dracios' stronghold a long day's journey distant, Talthybius driving the chariot. I told my Companion we went to examine a possible hunting ground : how much he swallowed, then or later, I do not know. (I had debated bringing Menelaus into the plot, and decided against. My brother had old-fashioned notions about gentlemanly behaviour and what a Hero could honourably do and couldn't. I am constantly surprised that, holding these ideas, he rules Sparta so efficiently today.)

Aigion materialized as a small rock-ramparted eyrie perched on a hilltop, the inhabitants impoverished and brutish. Dracios did not improve on acquaintance; his attitude was disrespectful, his manners abominable. I suppose he must have been a Hero of sorts descended from a family tucked away for generations in this remote mountain fastness, living by cattle raiding and inexorably reverting to the barbaric existence of Achaea's population before Zeus descended from Crete. His followers were the roughest, toughest scoundrels I have seen.

Some way short of Aigion the trackway narrowed to a defile piercing wooded, precipitous hills. I picked this as the likeliest place for an ambush : Dracios' bandits could hide in the trees and fall unannounced on the Pisans. The chieftain concurred; and after making detailed plans I returned to Sparta where I learned Broteas was setting out from Pisa to claim his bride.

King Tyndareus off-handedly passed me the information while inspecting an annexe he was building to the palace. (In Sparta, unconfined by walls, expansion offers no problems; all you do is knock down humbler dwellings.) He added, 'I'll have to entertain the fellow, lay on junketings and banquets. I hope they won't interfere with any arrangements you've made. I hear you're going to hunt in a new and promising area.'

Subduing a qualm – although aware I possessed the king's tacit approval it was slightly alarming to find his spies reported every step – I kept my face expressionless and said, 'Very promising, sire. With your permission I'll organize a meet there directly after the wedding.'

'Certainly.' Tyndareus nonchalantly examined the plastering on a wall. 'I hope you have bloody good sport.'

Despite my self-control I winced. In Laconian rustic idiom the name Broteas *means* 'bloody'.

The bridegroom duly arrived; apprehensively I scrutinized his retinue. Pisa could not afford a magnificent cavalcade. He brought half a dozen Heroes, their squires and Companions, thirty-odd spearmen and the usual train of servants: a troop considerably inferior in numbers to Dracios' savage ruffians. Broteas himself belied his gory name: a pale, slim, good-looking man with finely chiselled features, long blond hair and a suggestion of effeminacy in the slack-lipped, petulant mouth. I could understand his appeal for Clytemnaistra: a comely weakling attracting a strong-willed woman who would mother and direct him.

The festivities were splendid and prolonged: banquets, boar and lion hunts, gorgeous reviews on the Field of War, chariot races, games. Contrariwise the wedding in the Hall was a short and simple ceremony. Witnessed by Spartan and Pisan nobles a Daughter cut a lock of Clytemnaistra's hair and dedicated it to The Lady, Broteas took her wrist and declared her his fond and willing wife. The bride, to my vexation, looked radiantly happy and hung on her willowy husband's arm like an oak entwining a sapling.

I departed immediately for Aigion, taking again Talthybius, two chariots and a dozen spearmen who, accoutred in marching order, mysteriously appeared as I was setting out. (Tyndareus obviously considered that realism demanded more than a couple of men to 'rescue' his daughter.) After passing Dracios' scouts lurking near the defile to give warning of Broteas' approach we encamped under cover in a thicket near by. On the third noonday a ragged ruffian skipped into the thicket, said the column had been sighted and ran to tell Dracios' band hidden on the slopes above the pass. I told my party to stay concealed – they had no active part in the ploy, and the fewer witnesses the better – and hid under tamarisk bushes beside the track.

The column trundled into view, Broteas and Clytemnaistra riding the leading chariot, Heroes and spearmen following, baggage wagons clattering in the rear. They marched without scouts or guards, confident of safety inside friendly Laconia's borders, and entered the defile's mouth and vanished round a bend. As the last ox-cart disappeared a resounding clamour echoed among the rocks, shouts and screams and clashing weapons, the scrape of hooves and stamping feet.

I trotted along the track.

A brutal little battle was coming to an end. The men from Aigion quickly overwhelmed a retinue trapped in a narrow ravine and unprepared for attack. A Pisan Hero or two continued to fight it out, desperately trying to ward with shields a forest of lunging spears. Avoiding the scrimmage I thrust to the column's head. Broteas' chariot lay tilted on its side, frightened horses plunged in the yokes. He sprawled face down in the dust, a spear-shaft slanted crookedly between his shoulder blades. Clytemnaistra crouched above the body, face hidden in hands and crying aloud. I gripped her beneath the armpits and unceremoniously hauled her up.

'Hurry, my lady! Escape while you can!'

I hustled her, terrified and dazed beyond resistance, through confused and noisy wreckage of the ambush. The fight was over, the last Pisan warrior killed. Dracios' men prodded followers into a bunch and plundered the carts. (Slaves and booty were promised as part of his reward.) Nobody hindered our going; Aigion's lord drilled his scoundrels well. He waited at the throat of the pass, leaning against a boulder above the road. A cynical smile split the swarthy face and he lifted spear in salute. I hurried on, supporting a near-swooning Clytemnaistra.

On reaching the thicket I bundled her into a chariot and took the reins, told Talthybius to mount the second car and the spearmen to make all speed for Sparta. Flogging the horses hard I galloped my prize to safety.

*   *   *

Naturally the affair raised a rumpus in the city: royal bride-grooms are rarely slain so quickly after the wedding. Tyndareus, professing astonishment and anger, vowed he would send a warband to annihilate Dracios' gang. (Later on he did so, and massacred every living being in Aigion. 'All the evidence gone,' he confided to me contentedly.) I won unmerited renown as the paladin who single-handed rescued Clytemnaistra from rape and death or slavery: the kind of Heroic feat the bards rejoice in telling. Only Talthybius doubted: I saw questions in his eyes that wisely never passed his lips. Menelaus had his suspicions. 'I can't twig what you've been up to, brother,' he snorted, 'but it's unlike you to plunge your hand in a hornets' nest unless you've made sure you won't get stung. Death or glory escapades are not in your line at all.'

I laughed, and swore he was jealous.

Clytemnaistra, meanwhile, retired into the ladies' quarters and nursed her grief. We had exchanged hardly a word during the rapid ride from the ambush; after delivering her at the palace I saw her only at a distance and made no attempt to accost her. 'Leave her alone,' the king recommended. 'She'll recover soon enough. The girl's tough as thrice-boiled oxhide.'

The summer days rolled past, sharpening to winter and mellowing into spring. Clytemnaistra emerged from her seclusion, discarded her mourning veil and shared in the palace's pastimes. I met her on social occasions, exchanged civilities and received belated thanks for saving her from Dracios. (By that time he was dead.) I was careful to alter my approach, eschewing the banter and bawdy hints which formerly marked my wooing. Instead I endeavoured to impress myself upon her as a serious, respectable and eminently eligible suitor.

Which turned out damnably difficult. While engaging her in edifying and horribly boring prattle I craved to fondle those arrogant breasts, to stroke her belly and loins, probe the secret mysteries hidden between her thighs. I felt so madly lustful whenever I was near her I even forgot the benefits – political and pecuniary – that marriage to King Tyndareus' daughter would scatter in my lap.

My restrained and sympathetic demeanour gradually thawed Clytemnaistra's icy reserve; slowly she recovered her acid sense of humour. We conversed easily, without constraint; and she accepted me as her regular escort when walking abroad or driving: a habit Tyndareus subtly encouraged. So, on a sunny springtime afternoon we strolled a path that led to the Field of War where the Twins had arranged an archery competition. At the drystone parapet of a roadside well I stopped, took courage in both hands and said, 'My lady, I have something important to ask you.'

'Here and now?' Clytemnaistra looked at the cheerful throng that surrounded the Field an arrow-shot from where we stood. 'Already we're late for the contest – and Castor has wagered a two-year-old bull on his winning.'

'I beseech you to listen.'

Thoughtfully she scanned my face, recognized the urgency and fervour. 'Leave us, Melite,' she told the lady-in-waiting hovering at her elbow. 'Now, my lord, what is it so crucial that archery must wait?'

'With the king's approval, Clytemnaistra, I offer you my hand in marriage.' I embarked on the ritual pedigree chant accompanying formal proposals. 'I, Agamemnon son of Plisthenes son of Atreus son of Pelops son of Tantalus sprung from the blood of Zeus declare I shall endow —'

'That's enough.' She perched on the well-head's coping, smoothed the pearl-trimmed frill that aproned a billowing skirt. I know your ancestry, my lord, and a good deal more about you than you think. My father has already pressed me to accept you, declaring that in becoming your wife I shall also become in time Mycenae's queen. How can I be queen of a city your foremost enemy holds? I'm no believer in dreams, my lord.'

'Nor I. I shall regain my throne.'

Clytemnaistra plucked off a loosely sewn pearl, dropped it into the well, lifted her head and stared me in the eyes. 'Will you swear on The Lady's Womb?'

I blenched. No one can accuse me of being over-superstitious, but there are certain vows too terrible to be lightly undertaken. Then I looked at the thrusting breasts, swallowed and said, 'On The Lady's Womb I swear it.'

Triumph glinted briefly in hard green eyes. 'Unendurable torments rack those who break that oath, agonies such as mortals cannot imagine; death, when it comes, is greeted as happy deliverance. I will be your wife, Agamemnon.'

A shout of applause thrummed the air from the Field of War. I said uncomfortably, 'You take me in the hope of winning a crown : ambition compels consent. Have you no liking for me as a man, Clytemnaistra, or even love?'

'Love? Liking? Can emotions so fragile endure in a union such as ours – a marriage based for your part on carnality and policy? Don't look so surprised : I read your motives plainly from the start. As for me, my lord, love died in the pass near Aigion. I am a widow, no longer virgin, and desire simply to retrieve what I can from the wreckage of my life. Do you blame me, drowning in a quagmire of despair, for seizing a rescuing rope?'

I can see now, in the face of so blatant a declaration, I should there and then have abandoned my intentions, ought to have run from Clytemnaistra as from a deadly disease. Instead, recalling the labours involved in building a bridge of deceit and dishonour to span the void that yawned before my goal, I said weakly, 'Time heals wounds. I shall cherish you, my dear, and help you forget the miseries you have suffered.'

I took her hand and helped her from the wall. She said lightly, 'If you plight your troth on a well-head are the omens fair or foul? I must ask the Daughters. And now, my lord, let's go to the Field and discover whether Castor has won his wager.'

*   *   *

Our wedding celebrations coincided with the arrival in Sparta of Theseus King of Athens. Tyndareus, an economical man, organized joint festivities. Ostensibly Theseus had come in response to feelers the king had put out for an alliance against Thebes; an excuse which gratified the Athenian's restless itch for adventure and exploration. I had not set eyes on the man since he deserted Ariadne in Naxos. The years had changed his appearance, tinging grey the sun-bleached hair and beetling bushy brows, sinking deep in the sockets his flint-grey eyes. That his perfidy stayed constant was soon apparent.

Theseus' wife had recently hanged herself after unsuccessfully attempting to rape her husband's stepson. Her death removed the last restraint on Theseus' fornications. Gentlemen in general keep concubines to slake desire; but the King of Athens preferred to sink his shaft in ladies of noble birth: a dangerous quirk invariably leading to trouble. Resounding scandals erupted from frequent rapes and seductions; no good-looking woman, young or old, was safe from his depredations. Certain Athenian Heroes, discerning Theseus' lineaments reflected in their children, were growing a little tired of their ruler, particularly as with increasing age he neglected governmental duties and wandered far and wide in search of fresh adulteries. Nor did he confine himself to the opposite sex. A Thessalian called Peirithoös accompanied him everywhere; seldom were the couple seen apart. I have not the slightest doubt that Theseus practised sodomy among his other vices – a disease, perhaps, that Athens caught from Thebes.

Tyndareus, content that his diplomacy seemed to be bearing fruit, feasted the visitor liberally and entertained him royally. Theseus happily accepted everything he was offered; when, between the revels, Tyndareus in Council tried to pin him down to business the Athenian proved considerably less forthcoming. Like every creature bred in that nasty city he was devious and evasive and obviously dishonest. Tyndareus tried bribery – he didn't call it bribery, of course – and Theseus received golden dishes, cauldrons, bronze and thoroughbred horses and tendered airy promises in return. Tyndareus never managed to bind him by an oath, nor would Theseus instruct his Scribes to draw a written compact. The Spartan sadly recognized he had landed in his net a fish too slippery to hold.

Theseus, in short, had no interest in alliances; though he certainly showed eagerness in other directions. His evil reputation caused sensible husbands and fathers to keep a vigilant watch on any female relatives who attracted his attention. I regret to state that a number of ladies shamelessly encouraged his advances; how far the liaisons went I wouldn't care to guess. (The hussies still live in Sparta, still united to their men: what point in dredging up old gossip?) Nobody – except the husbands concerned – minded Theseus' intrigues overmuch; but when he started ogling Tyndareus' younger daughter the most phlegmatic Heroes began to simmer.

Helen was rising fourteen, a lovely, vivacious child. Even at that early age she allured men like bees aswarm on heather. Whether she was conscious of her prowess is hard to say; I suspect she had a fairly good idea. I hasten to add I ascribe to the gentlemen forming her little court the most irreproachable motives: her gaiety and beauty aroused in their hearts – I think – nothing but innocent pleasure. Prominent among her devotees was my brother Menelaus. Continually you saw them hand in hand about the palace, a beautiful gold-haired girl and strong-limbed red-headed Hero. He took her in his chariot and pretended to let her drive, small fingers on the reins guided and protected by sinewy brown hands; he gave her a miniature bow and taught her to shoot. Under his tuition Helen was developing into something of a tomboy; her ladies in waiting clicked disapproving tongues.

Surveying these diversions I once jokingly twitted Menelaus on the subject of dirty old men. (Unjustly; he was barely thirty-two.) My brother was not amused. 'Keep your filth behind your teeth,' he snapped, 'or you and I will find ourselves at odds.'

Into this charming idyll Theseus swooped like a vulture hunting carrion. He flattered Helen, showered her with gifts – gold bracelets, necklaces and earrings – and ousted from her company and favour a coterie of Heroes and Companions. Inhibited by the knowledge the Athenian was a guest from whom Tyndareus wanted favours, they could not snub the intruder as he deserved. Menelaus, likewise a guest relying entirely on the king's benevolence, raged impotently and was rude as he dared be. Helen, the fickle hussy, cold-shouldered her fuming followers and wantonly encouraged her admirer who, I must admit, had thoroughly mastered the methods of winning a woman's heart. What motivated the man is hard to say. I can only conclude he was so frenetically over-sexed that anything in skirts became a goal to be attained whatever the cost.

The price, in the event, soared high for all concerned.

In the midst of these commotions I married Clytemnaistra. After the celebratory banquet I led her to a bridal suite the king had bestowed, allowed my squires to undress me and impatiently awaited my bride's arrival in bed. When at last her ladies were gone I entered the bedroom stark, and hot as a stag in rut. Clytemnaistra lay naked, coverlet cast aside, her magnificent ivory body a vision to animate stones.

I curbed my ardour, stretched beside her, kissed her lips and caressed her breasts. Thence, gently and excitingly, to belly and loins. She stayed still as a marble image. I used every art to arouse her, every provocation my concubines had taught. I might as well have tickled a corpse. Unable any longer to control my frenzy I straddled the inert form and forced her thighs apart. She shifted her buttocks and made herself comfortable, sighed a little and inspected the ceiling. Vigorously plunging and heaving, I won not the slightest response. Nettled by her lethargy I braided my energies and, before dawnlight paled the windows, pierced her four times more. Clytemnaistra passively submitted.

Bewildered and exhausted, I summoned slaves and squires and went to have a bath.

It was all most disappointing.

* * *

Events a few days later swamped marital frustrations. Theseus and his Heroes failed to appear in the Hall for noonday dinner. Somebody suggested they might have gone hunting independently: a breach of manners unsurprising in Athenians. A search of the palace environs disclosed followers and spearmen still in quarters, but not a Hero or Companion anywhere in the city. Nobody could say where they had gone. The king testily opined, since their retinues remained in Sparta, his errant visitors would reappear next day.

Then a frantic lady in waiting, weeping and wringing her hands, announced Helen was nowhere to be found. Apparently the child had gone with Theseus in his chariot: a not unusual occurrence, for he had displaced Menelaus in the little hoyden's favour. Although the sun was sinking the king instantly ordered charioteers to hunt his missing guests. Nightfall ended the quest; the search parties returned home. Tyndareus confidently asserted that Helen's disappearance was simply a thoughtless escapade. At dawn the seekers went out again.

Castor and Polydeuces, quartering the countryside, uncovered the quarry's tracks. The lord of a small citadel a day's foot-journey north from Sparta told them Theseus and a retinue, driving fast, had passed his gates the previous day on a road that led to Tegea. He had noticed in their company a young and pretty girl.

The Twins returned to Sparta at a gallop.

'Theseus will have passed Tegea by now, heading for Mantinea,' Castor told his father.

'Then he'll strike to Argos across the mountains,' Polydeuces surmised.

'Kidnapped Helen.'

'Taking her to Athens.'

'Can't catch him before he's bolted into his burrow.'

'Got too long a start.'

Tyndareus, in a flaring temper, mustered an armoured warband from every Hero present in the palace, put the Twins in command and ordered a chase. 'This is war,' he said. 'If necessary you'll pursue to the walls of Athens. I'll mobilize and send the Host in support, but while it's on the march your chariots must fight alone. Whatever happens,' he ended grimly, 'don't show me your faces again until you've recovered Helen.'

Menelaus insisted on accompanying the Twins; afterwards he described to me the Spartan war in Attica. Fifty chariots headed north on Theseus' trail and halted the first sundown in a coppice near Tegea. A shepherd who bartered mutton for their supper related an infuriating tale. A band of Heroes stopping to water horses in his pasture had drawn straws for possession of a girl-child in the party. The leader, whom he accurately described, had won.

'Sodding bastard Theseus,' Menelaus gritted.

Before sun-up they yoked horses, galloped through Mantinea, traversed laboriously the winding mountain passes and descended into the Argive Plain. At Argos they again nighthalted; Diomedes gave the travel-worn Heroes shelter and food in the palace and seven Venetic horses in exchange for animals lamed by the hectic pace. On the third day, by-passing Mycenae, the warband reached Corinth. The Twins passionately urged they press on across the Isthmus; Menelaus, more provident, refused to attempt the fearsome road past Sciron's Rocks in darkness. The Warden (Bunus' replacement) said Theseus was a full day's march ahead and going like a hunted hare. A laughing girl in his chariot seemed to be relishing the headlong ride.

Menelaus tore his hair. The Twins muttered joint obscenities.

After crossing the Isthmus they journeyed till dark and camped near Eleusis. The band was now in Attica, a land assumed to be hostile. They leaguered chariots, mounted guards and counted the cost of a whirlwind drive over bonebreaking roads and rugged mountains. Forty-two chariots remained in harness; the rest had been left at the wayside with broken axles, wheels and poles. Limping horses disposed of a couple more.

The Twins debated plans.

'Failed to catch the turd,' Castor said despondently. 'Holed up now in Athens.'

'Can't take the place with forty chariots,' Polydeuces complained.

'Have to wait for the Host.'

'Won't arrive for days.'

'We can't sit here doing nothing,' Menelaus declared savagely. 'We've numbers enough to ravage the land, burn villages and crops, kill cattle. By harassing his property we may tempt Theseus out.'

The Twins cheered up; Menelaus' advice accorded with their own impetuous natures. For the next three days the Spartans wreaked an orgy of destruction, moving fast from village to village and setting the fields alight. They avoided fortified citadels, but audaciously raided a harbour right under Athens' nose and burned fishing boats and galleys. Daily they expected warbands hurtling from the citadel seeking vengeance, daily they were disappointed. Theseus stayed firmly behind his walls.

Commanded by Tyndareus' warlord Marathus, the Spartan Host, chariots, spears and baggage, reached Eleusis. The operations thenceforth assumed the character of a war of extermination. Smoke clouds smeared the heavens above Attica, a stench of death and burning soured the air. Marathus attacked citadels the Twins perforce had spared, razed walls and massacred garrisons. A tardy Athenian warband was driven helter-skelter from the field. When little was left to destroy the Host surrounded Athens, blenched at the daunting citadel towering on its rock, and sent heralds to demand Helen's surrender.

'Don't know what the blazes we can do if Theseus refuses,' Castor said.

'Tricky,' Polydeuces agreed. 'Athens is quite impregnable.'

The heralds brought back the surprising announcement that Theseus, days before, had taken ship and sailed for an unknown port. A certain Menestheus, a sprig of the royal House, now ruled Athens as Regent. Menestheus swore ignorance of Helen's whereabouts; Theseus before he fled had despatched her secretly to some hiding place in Attica. Would the Spartans please find her quickly, the Regent implored, leave Athens' territory and allow her population to repair the havoc wrought.

'I'd like to try an escalade and teach the swine a lesson,' Polydeuces said, eyeing the precipitous mount.

'Not a hope,' said Castor. 'Let's start a thorough search.'

The hunt concentrated on the few settlements still intact. Menelaus, roaming with a warband in the neighbourhood of Aphidna, rounded up some peasants and put them to the question. (A routine practice involving gouged-out eyeballs.) A screaming victim revealed that a recently arrived young lady lived in Aphidna in charge of an elderly matron: he knew not who they were or whence they came. Menelaus cut the goatherd's throat, ransacked the village and found his quarry in one of the better houses. He levelled Aphidna, and took her away.

My brother told me that Helen, though unharmed, was serious and subdued, her merriment missing. A short captivity had transformed her from girl to woman. She was reticent about her experiences and refused to speak of Theseus. The matron who looked after her turned out to be Aithra, Theseus' mother. She had clearly become devoted to her charge; Helen tearfully pleaded she remain as her serving woman. Menelaus saw no harm; and the mother of an Athenian king quitted her native land as a Spartan slave.

Castor and Polydeuces persuaded the bellicose Marathus to rally his widely dispersed Host and march to Sparta. (Marathus, deceived by easy victories over cowardly Athenians, boasted he would demolish Thebes before returning home. Luckily for Sparta's fortunes the Twins – not normally famous for prudence – declined to step beyond Tyndareus' orders.) Within two moons of Helen's abduction she returned to her father's embraces; her scatty mother was scarcely aware she had been away. I thought the girl looked pale and unhappy, inclined to fall into brooding silences. Menelaus devoted himself to restoring her spirits.

The episode lost Theseus his throne. I learned later that his Heroes, led by Menestheus, blamed their ruler's licentiousness for the calamities Athens suffered and forced him to fly for his life. He intended to find sanctuary in Crete; a storm blew the ship off course and swept him ashore at Scyros. He died there a year or two later, murdered, according to rumour, by the lord of the island. Theseus was an unsavoury character, but I have no doubt the Athenians will magnify his deeds and construct around his memory an unmerited reputation. Athens has little to boast about, and dredges credit from dunghills.

So bewitching, beautiful Helen sparked a devastating war from which Athens had not recovered by the time of the Trojan campaign. She is also given the doubtful credit of launching the fleets against Priam. Already the bards are romancing that Paris' later abduction drew vengeful Achaeans to Troy; but that was merely the pretext, and never the genuine cause.

*   *   *

King Tyndareus granted his son-in-law an extensive estate at Therapne, a pleasant little settlement a morning's stroll from Sparta. I removed with Clytemnaistra to a spacious manor surrounded by vineyards, fields and pastures whence, by careful husbandry, I garnered ample revenues. My precarious life as a landless Hero came to an end.

Clytemnaistra outwardly was all that a wife should be: dutiful, obedient, a model mistress of the household. We established a companionable relationship which made slight demands on affection, let alone love. In bed she remained compliant and torpidly unresponsive despite my strenuous efforts to fire her passions. At last I acknowledged defeat, abandoned a pointless battle and paid periodical homage to a body which failure and frustration made all the more desirable. Perhaps if I got her with child she might become less frigid; but she showed no signs of pregnancy. I began to wonder whether I bedded a barren sow: misfortune for any husband, calamity for kings who must breed sons to preserve the royal succession.

To cool my blood and preserve my health I brought Maira to

Therapne: she compensated – almost – for the raptures I'd expected from my wife. While perfectly aware I bedded other women Clytemnaistra never reproached me or betrayed any signs of jealousy, reserving her vindictiveness for the unfortunate concubines themselves. Pretending Maira had neglected some petty household chore she had her whipped. When Maira, sobbing, showed me the weals I quietly informed Clytemnaistra that the woman, my personal property, was beyond her jurisdiction.

She said, 'The slut was insolent. Am I to accept impertinence from slaves?'

'If she gives you cause for complaint tell me. I'll ensure she doesn't transgress in future.'

I sternly reprimanded my bedmate, who denied she had ever offended Clytemnaistra. 'I keep well out of her way because I know she wants to hurt me,' she said tearfully. 'I hate the bitch – a dangerous, vicious harridan!'

I slapped her across the face. 'Hold your tongue. If you speak of my lady like that again I'll have you beaten to death!'

Such domestic frictions were transitory irritants in an otherwise tranquil existence. I busied myself with ploughing, sowing and harvesting, pruning vines and breeding cattle and sheep; and tried to forget Mycenae and the throne that I had lost. I once gingerly reminded the king of his promise; he recommended patience, declared the time unripe. Thyestes, said Tyndareus, was like an apple rotting on the tree; when a harsh wind shook the branches the fruit would fall of its own accord. A fire smouldered in Mycenae; when it began to glow Sparta would fan the flames.

Prohibited from detailed information which his spies supplied to Tyndareus I collected what news I could of the world outside. King Adrastus on his sickbed abdicated in favour of Diomedes, who now ruled Argos in name as well as fact. Mycenae's naval war dragged on in desultory fashion: the Hellespont remained closed. A scandalized public opinion had compelled Thyestes to send his incestuously begotten son Aegisthus to Elis where he lived as Phyleus' ward. Nestor ruled peacefully in Pylos, Creon tyrannically in Thebes; Athens proclaimed Menestheus king. And a half-forgotten pretender mouldered away in Sparta.

262

Tragedy in Arcadia led indirectly to the ending of my exile. Castor, Polydeuces and Lynceus of Messene joined forces in a cattle raid across the Arcadian border. After a successful foray the trio and their followers drove the plundered herds away. Evading pursuit they settled around camp fires and amicably discussed division of the spoils. An argument arose, words and insults flew, the hasty-tempered Twins laid hands on spears. Within moments Spartans and Messenians were fighting like wolves. Lynceus died; a spear in the bowels killed Castor; his surviving followers carried Polydeuces, mortally wounded, to Sparta where he lingered for days before dying.

King Tyndareus, subduing a bitter grief, faced the realization he had no heir to his throne – always a dangerous factor in any Achaean kingdom. A glittering prize is dangled within reach of ambitious Heroes, intrigues begin to fester, factions form and plots, perhaps, to hasten the king's demise. Tyndareus gave his sons a splendid funeral and afterwards, ever a realist, started to mend his fences.

The king called Menelaus and me to a private consultation in a vestibule of the royal apartments and, after seeing us comfortably installed in chairs, goblets in hand, bewailed the political void the Twins' extinction had opened. 'I'm the last of the Spartan royal House. If I nominate as my heir a Spartan Hero I'll be swamped by rival claims, and jealousy will breed disaffection. Directly I'm dead – if not before – there'll be civil strife in Laconia and the kingdom will disintegrate into separate warring cities.'

'Have you no blood relatives living?' I inquired.

'Twenty-one bastards. None legitimate. I'll have to find a suitable successor from an alien city, a man from a ruling House connected by marriage to mine.' He took a gulp from his cup and deposited it on a three-legged greenstone table. 'You, Agamemnon.'

I felt dumbfounded and dismayed. Mycenae was my heritage, and I wanted nothing else. Moreover Tyndareus, though old, was tough as rawhide and might live for years. Could I rusticate indefinitely in Sparta in hopes of a foreign crown? An admirable city – but not to be compared with magnificent Mycenae. The prospect he unveiled appalled me.

'You do me honour, sire.' I trod cautiously; Tyndareus held

263

my future in the hollow of his hand. 'However, I foresee a serious drawback. We discussed, if you remember, an alliance against Thebes – which will never be accomplished so long as Thyestes rules. An alliance,' I said pointedly, 'directed to freeing Orchomenos. I believe corn in Laconia is running short.'

'True. We've had to introduce strict rationing.' Tyndareus retrieved his goblet, frowned blackly into the bowl. 'I promised my help in regaining Mycenae, and I hate going back on my word. But with Castor and Polydeuces gone ... damned difficult predicament...'

Menelaus coughed. 'Sire, Atreus appointed Agamemnon his successor, Mycenae remains his heritage by right. He *must* be restored, for in setting him on Mycenae's throne you'll gain enormous advantages which by keeping him in Sparta you will lose. Meanwhile you need a successor. My blood is Agamemnon's, my ancestors were kings. Why not designate *me* as Sparta's heir?'

I choked on a swallow of wine. Never had it occurred to me that my stolid brother cherished high ambitions.

'Bless my soul!' exclaimed Tyndareus, equally surprised. 'What a curious idea! Admittedly your lineage makes you eminently fitting, but —'

'With Agamemnon ruling Mycenae,' said Menelaus earnestly, 'and myself acknowledged heir to Sparta's crown the kingdoms are joined by blood relationship, an inseparable union which will dominate Achaea. Militarily, politically and economically we shall be invincible.'

'You have a point.' Tyndareus found his goblet empty, bellowed for a squire. 'But there's a snag. I have a sound excuse to nominate Agamemnon because he's already my son by marriage and hence will be acceptable to my Heroes. Whereas you —'

'I want to marry Helen,' said Menelaus firmly.

Tyndareus spluttered. 'She's just fourteen – a child. You can't —'

'She'll be of marriageable age within a year. We can be officially betrothed whenever you grant permission.'

By heartily rating his squire the king found time to recover his balance. 'Steady – don't overfill the cup! Dammit, boy, you've slopped wine all over the floor. Clumsy idiot! Get a cloth and mop it up.' He took a satisfying swig, leaned back in his chair and said, 'I'll think it over. Are you' – cocking a grizzled eyebrow at my brother – 'fond of the girl? I thought you were just a playmate.'

'I love her.'

'Hr'm. She's a minx – you'll find her a handful. Hr'm. Certainly a solution, if Agamemnon's determined to kick Thyestes out. Well, I can't answer on the flick of a whip. I'll talk to Helen and let you know my decision. Your cup's empty, Agamemnon. Where's that blasted squire gone?'

Crossing the Great Court afterwards I complimented my brother on his statecraft. 'A master stroke, by The Lady – a royal daughter employed as a lever to wedge you into the Spartan royal line. You're deeper than I realized, Menelaus.'

'You judge me by your precepts,' he said soberly. 'The opposite is true. I'm passionately in love with Helen, and use Tyndareus' quandary as an instrument to win her.'

*   *   *

Tyndareus' spies in Mycenae reported increasing tension. The Trojan War brought a steady attrition of ships and crews, while Thyestes refused to admit his naval strategy could never re-open the Hellespont. A land campaign being out of the question the war arrived at a deadlock. Mycenae, like Sparta, had rationed grain; a disease attacking corn in ear caused harvests to fail and accentuated shortages. Goatmen and Dorians, becoming ever bolder, irrupted frequently from Arcadia and savaged isolated settlements.

Thyestes seemed incapable of decision. He roistered in the palace, granted his cronies estates sequestrated from nobles he disliked, and neglected the kingdom's routine administration. He fought no campaigns, and seldom sent his warbands to chastise rustlers or Goatmen. Young, aggressive Heroes have to hone their energies in wars and so, deprived of outside enemies, they fought among themselves.

The kingdom stagnated.

So far so good, Tyndareus observed. The soil of insurrection was ripe for cultivation; fertile patches had to be found for sowing the seed. On the pretext of negotiating trade in oil and pottery he sent a deputation to Mycenae whose real purpose was to encourage dissident Heroes in raising a palace rebellion when the Spartan Host drew near. 'If intrigue can topple Thyestes we might be spared a battle,' the king said thinly. 'To fight warriors whom you once trained, Agamemnon, could prove expensive.'

The remark revealed Tyndareus' private doubt that Sparta unassisted could, in fact, defeat Mycenae in open battle. (I had no doubts at all: if Mycenae's Host took the field in strength they'd give Tyndareus a tremendous beating.) Therefore I gladly accepted his decision to send me on a mission to Diomedes. 'He's been your friend and comrade on campaign,' said the king. 'Ask him to prove friendship by lending his support. A token force will do at a pinch: it will at least impress on Thyestes he faces Sparta and Argos combined. You'll have to bribe Diomedes: kings don't help for nothing.'

'What can I offer? I own neither land nor gold.'

'You'll soon possess both in plenty. Meanwhile, sell what you haven't got. Argos has always hankered after Troezen; fear of Mycenae prevents her taking the city. Promise Diomedes a free hand in subjugating Troezen. I believe he'll swallow the bait.'

I persuaded an unwilling Menelaus to accompany me to Argos. His reluctance sprang from a conviction that Helen was unwell; since her return from Athens eight moons before she had certainly looked off colour, her sunny vitality quenched. The woman Aithra, Theseus' mother, guarded her like a watchdog and generally kept her confined in the women's quarters; you seldom saw her running about the palace. Menelaus swore her abduction had gravely affected Helen's physical and mental health. I was not so sure. She seemed a resilient creature, and by all accounts had enjoyed her alarming adventure. Probably, I guessed, at over fourteen she suffered puberty's onset.

I overcame Menelaus' misgivings, and together we journeyed to Argos.

Though handicapped by a scarcity of corn – as was every kingdom south of the Isthmus – Diomedes had almost restored Argos' former strength. He received us amiably and lent a ready ear to my proposals. I emphasized the Theban stranglehold on food supplies, promised faithfully that, as king, I would bend Mycenae's resources in a bid to shatter Thebes, seize the Orchomenos granaries and institute free trade in corn.

266

Diomedes' experience in the War of the Seven had left him no illusions about the force required to overcome Thebes; he doubted we could muster sufficient strength. I told him Sparta promised a Host, I bespoke Mycenae's, we could prevail on Pylos and Elis to mobilize strong warbands.

'All this,' said Diomedes, abstractedly studying a frieze of hounds and huntsmen adorning the Throne Room's seagreen walls where he heard our plans in Council, 'depends on deposing Thyestes. A fornicating scoundrel – he treats Mycenae's throne as a fountain of debauchery. Extraordinary to think he's Atreus' brother.' Diomedes ruffled his wheat-gold hair, fixed hard brown eyes on mine. 'First we've got to win you a crown. If I agree to reinforce Tyndareus what advantage may Argos expect – apart from the ominous prospect of a hard-fought Theban war?'

Diomedes had rapidly acquired a ruler's avariciousness. I said, 'Mycenae won't hinder you from taking Troezen's tribute.'

'Very sensible.' Thoughtfully he stroked the carved cedar-wood arms of his throne. 'I have lately been considering a rational partition of the Argolid between Argos and Mycenae. We hold Epidauros, you give us Troezen. Should not Hermione, a sheltered harbour, also logically submit to Argive rule?'

The suggestion kindled a fiery argument, Diomedes and his Council contesting Menelaus and me on a noisy verbal battle-ground. Hermione, like Troezen, was a city which owed continuing independence to rivalry between more powerful neighbouring kingdoms, each unwilling to see the other acquire additional wealth and strength. Diomedes, regrettably, had sound basis for his reasoning: both cities geographically fell within Argos' ambit.

I proposed a compromise.

'If Mycenae grants you Troezen and Hermione, will Argos in return restore the tributes of Midea and Asine?'

The Council vehemently dissented. Diomedes propped chin on knuckles and watched the heated faces. I had turned a facet of his arguments against him; for if the disputed cities could be claimed as lying in Argive territory then Midea and Asine were certainly appendages to Mycenae. At last he clapped his hands together and said, 'Enough, my lords. I decree the exchange is justified.' He smiled genially. 'When you hold Mycenae's sceptre, Agamemnon, you shall have the tributes of Midea and Asine. You may also assure Tyndareus that when his warriors march Argos' Host will support him.'

Diomedes grinned widely when he saw the gladness in my face. He knew as well as I that rather than forgo the backing of his troops I'd have yielded more than Hermione – perhaps Nauplia, even Tiryns. (Afterwards, assuredly, I'd have mounted a brisk campaign to wrest them back.)

Though Diomedes feasted and entertained us admirably we did not linger for long in Argos: I was keen to goad Tyndareus to action. On return to Sparta I sought an audience and assured him the Argives would reinforce his Host. He demanded details, congratulated me on recovering Midea and Asine and continued, 'I'm in touch with Mycenaean dissidents – more than you'd have guessed. Revolution seethes in Thyestes' palace. They yearn for Atreus' golden days, and are happy to crown his son.' Irony edged his tone. 'Or so they believe – your unfortunate sire Plisthenes seems totally forgotten. No matter. We'll strike while the bronze is molten – I've ordered the Host to be mustered.'

I dropped on my knees and grasped his hands. Tyndareus patted my shoulder. 'No call for thanks. I gain nearly as much as you: a king for your son by marriage is always politically useful. Which reminds me. You'll find a pleasant surprise awaiting you in Therapne.'

He would divulge no more, and I was far too happy to bother – the granting of my supreme desire transcended all else in the world. Talthybius drove me, singing joyfully, the short distance to my home – my home for not much longer, I mused contentedly. I bathed and scrubbed away travel dust, donned a deerskin kilt and clean linen tunic and sauntered to Clytemnaistra's rooms. A slave girl opened the bedroom door. Covered by fleeces and blankets my lady reposed on the bed.

An infant wrapped in swaddling clothes mewed on the sheets beside her.

Stunned into speechlessness I faltered on the threshold. Clytemnaistra said languidly, 'You have a daughter, my lord.'

'Why,' I stammered, 'didn't you tell me you were ... I had no idea ...'

'A pregnant woman grows rather rotund. I assumed you used your eyes.' (An unjustified remark. Loose flounced skirts, frills and aprons easily conceal the signs.)

'When was she born?'

'The child is three days old.'

Cautiously I touched the babe's red wrinkled face. It cried and waggled tiny fists. A girl – and I needed sons. Too late to have the infant exposed; all Sparta must know it was born; you rid yourself of a girl-child directly after the birth. I stooped to kiss Clytemnaistra's lips. She turned her head away.

I said, 'You are well, my lady? The delivery was not difficult?'

'I am well, but I have no milk. A wet-nurse suckles the child.'

'What name will you give her?'

'With your consent I shall call her Iphigeneia.'

'Iphigeneia,' I pondered. ' "Mother of a stalwart race." Very fitting. You must cherish her carefully, so that she may fulfil the promise of her name.'

'I shall indeed, my lord.'

I left the bedchamber, and in the portico met Menelaus, come to pay his respects to mother and infant. After he had complimented Clytemnaistra, and recoiled from the whimpering brat with unconcealed revulsion, I called for wine and honeyed figs and we took our ease in the vestibule, enjoying the summer sunlight splashing between the pillars. We discussed the imminent campaign; and Menelaus declared he intended remaining in Sparta.

'Henceforth my destiny lies here; there's nothing for me in Mycenae. And I want to look after Helen.'

'You are besotted, brother.'

'Helen,' he continued, ignoring my jibe, 'was seriously ill while we were away in Argos. She is now recovered, though still delicate and weak. I saw her this morning very briefly – we had hardly exchanged greetings before that beldam Aithra sent me about my business.'

'What ailed her?'

'A stomach sickness, I understand. Aithra was taciturn and vague. Helen,' my brother said dreamily, 'is more beautiful than ever. The disease has thinned her, wasted girlhood's puppy-fat, planed the angles of her face to absolute perfection. Never have I seen so lovely a woman – for woman she has become, no longer a child.'

'A paragon,' I said dryly. 'Is she more cheerful than when I saw her last?'

'Still somewhat melancholy and serious, her laughter lost. But,' said Menelaus earnestly, 'I shall attend her every day and strive to restore her spirits.'

'Yes – you don't want a moping wife. Nor,' I added bitterly, 'one who hides her feelings under a cold, indifferent husk.' Irritated by the recollection I finished my wine and stood. 'Come with me to the pastures, brother. The mare I bought from Castor foaled while we were gone – a likely-looking colt, my steward says.'

We strolled the fields, talked horses and disremembered women.

* * *

The Host that King Tyndareus led met little opposition. At Argos we were joined by Diomedes; two hundred chariots and three thousand spears tramped the stony road to Mycenae, dispersed an irresolute warband waiting in ambush and came within sight of the citadel's huge rock walls. The gates yawned wide; warriors on the ramparts flourished spears and shouted welcome. Elders of the Council, unarmoured and unarmed, filed from the gate and offered submission. Escorted by my exiled Heroes, helmeted, shielded and mailed, I trudged up the winding pathway and entered Mycenae's palace.

Bloodstains and crumpled corpses blemished Great Court, porch and vestibule – evidence of recent sharp contention. When Thyestes' scouts reported the Spartan-Argive Host he sounded Alarm and ordered the citadel's garrison to battle stations on the walls. The summons fired revolt; dissentient Heroes Tyndareus had encouraged refused to take up arms; a party loyal to Thyestes attempted to force the issue. A short and bloody conflict erupted in the palace; the loyalists were killed or driven out.

They left Thyestes behind.

He was captured in the fighting and imprisoned in an oil-store in the basement. I descended to gloomy warrens, a riddle of rooms and passages, and found him crouching on the floor amid tall earthenware jars. His captors had stripped his mail; he wore kilt and woollen tunic. I stopped at the door, dismissed the men who guided me there – except a brace of spearmen; you never knew with Thyestes – leaned against the jamb and said, 'The end of your road, my lord. How would you like to die?'

He lifted a snarling face, and spat at my feet. 'Why pretend a choice, Agamemnon? The death you inflict will be hard and tormented. What does it matter? At the finish, however painfully you kill me, I shall be dead.'

'Indeed. Do you remember a day long ago in Aerope's room, when I promised to kill you slowly?' Meditatively I considered the savage deep-socketed eyes, the bull-necked head and bulky shoulders. His hair was dappled white: I realized with sudden surprise this malignant son of Pelops was now an aged man. 'You've many crimes to appease, Thyestes: my mother's death, Atreus' murder, Bunus of Corinth's tortured end. A woman called Clymene, whom you probably don't remember. And all the fools who've died on your behalf.'

Thyestes sneered. 'Am I supposed to weep for those who have gone? You mistake me, Agamemnon. You may kill me slow, and listen to my squeals – and never will you hear me cry remorse!'

True enough, I thought. I had seen men die in terrible ways: cradling tumbled entrails spilled from bellies slashed in battle, writhing impaled on sharpened stakes, roasted alive above slow-burning fires – and knew that agony obliterated all vestige of sensate thought. Suffering swamped remembrance of *why* they died.

I determined that Thyestes should be conscious to the last.

A childhood memory came to my aid from days when Menelaus and I had played at hide-and-hunt among these underground chambers. I recalled a tiny room, an alcove adjoining a wine cellar that was used for keeping tablets listing quantities and vintages. I left the spearmen to guard Thyestes, found my way to the place and peered inside. A dark windowless stone-walled cell, the roof so low a man bent double, the floor so narrow he must lie curled up. Satisfied, I ordered slaves to deposit within the room a pitcher of water and platters of bread and meat – the more he had to eat the longer he would live – and afterwards fetch plasterers and masons. When that was done I returned to the oil-store. The spearmen at my bidding stripped Thyestes naked, prodded him to the cell and thrust him in.

I stooped at the entrance hole and said, 'I have provided food and drink, and time for reflection. Strong and brawny men like you don't die very quickly. You may, in the end, feel remorse after all. Farewell, my lord.'

The workmen walled him in, and there I left Thyestes.

*　　*　　*

I called to audience in the Hall every Hero and Companion in the citadel and with Diomedes and Tyndareus at my shoulders proclaimed myself Mycenae's king. The shout of acclamation shivered rafters in the roof. I postponed for seven days a formal coronation – the whole place was in ferment, servants had fled to hiding, nobody knew where Thyestes had hidden the regalia. A chariot galloped to Sparta to summon Clytemnaistra: a visible reminder that I could call on Sparta's aid, a discouragement for wavering Heroes.

Tyndareus and Diomedes sent the bulk of their warriors home, keeping as a precaution a warband each in Mycenae. They remained as my guests in the palace and passed the days in hunting. I found myself too occupied for such frivolities: after sliding into ruin in Thyestes' dissolute hands the realm's administration required overhauling. I restored demesnes to Heroes Thyestes had robbed, and inspected the state of treasuries, stores and granaries. I revelled in the work – lacking so long in Sparta – for to governance I was born. My friend Gelon reappeared from gloomy basement cubicles where Scribes conducted business, and shyly offered his help in checking accounts. I immediately appointed him Curator of Mycenae, an office he holds today.

A panoplied escort, spears and chariots, befitting a daughter and consort of kings guarded Clytemnaistra when she entered the citadel gates. She brought Iphigeneia in Aithra's charge, her Spartan ladies in waiting and, because I had so directed, my body-slaves and concubines. Spectators packed the roadsides, crowded rooftops and ramparts and exclaimed in wonder at Clytemnaistra's beauty, her proud and regal bearing. I could not help admiring her myself: she rode a crimson gold-encrusted chariot like an Amazon from one of those ancient fables. After greeting my queen respectfully I conducted her to luxuriously furnished quarters on the palace's second floor.

I was crowned next day in the Hall. A multitude of torches bathed in golden radiance the gaudily patterned ceiling, blazoned in resplendent hues the lions, stags and charioteers rampaging on the walls. Torchlight spattered darting flecks from Heroes' brazen armour, transmuted into gold the cuirasses and greaves, danced on cascading helmet plumes dyed scarlet, yellow and blue, shot sparkling gems from points of ten-foot spears. Ladies in brilliant dresses clustered in the gallery, leaned perilously on the railing and gazed round-eyed at the pageantry below.

Robed in gold-embroidered purple I sat on a marble throne, Clytemnaistra beside me on a chair of inlaid ivory. The kings of Sparta and Argos stood on either hand, each wearing splendid armour, gilded graven breastplates embossed in rich designs. Solemnly a Daughter tendered Mycenae's jewelled diadem. I placed the crown on my head, and lifted high a gold and ivory sceptre.

'I, Agamemnon son of Atreus son of Pelops descended from King Zeus through thirty generations hold the kingdom and the glory of Mycenae. May The Lady in Her mercy grant me wisdom and prosperity.'

I advanced to the blazing hearth fire where a milk-white bull calf kicked against the tethers. A Daughter proffered a sharp stone axe. I judged the blow with care – a bungled stroke presaged the direst fortunes – and smote cleanly behind the poll. The beast grunted, collapsed and died. A collective sigh of relief swelled to a rapturous roar. I sprinkled blood on the flames, returned to the throne and faced my applauding nobles.

A tempestuous voyage had ended, my ship was safe in port.

*   *   *

The coronation banquet rollicked far into the night. I left the Heroes carousing and, escorted by chattering squires, unsteadily wended my way to the royal apartments. The Hero on guard smiled sympathetically and assisted me through the door. Clytemnaistra drowsed on the bed, Iphigeneia slept in a cot, a slave woman snored on a pallet. A single oil lamp lighted the room. I kicked the slave awake, recognized Aithra's wizened features and bade her depart. I tottered to the bedside, unfastened cloak and dropped it on the floor, fumbled my kilt belt's buckle.

'Make room.'

Clytemnaistra drew the coverlet to her neck. 'I cannot receive you, my lord. Childbearing, you should know, leaves a mother torn and tender.'

'Rubbish!' I swallowed a hiccup. 'The birth was a moon ago. Women can take their lovers within a dawn and a dusk. Move over!'

Eyes sharp as twin green stones glittered in the lamplight. 'If you force me I shall call for help. The guard will irrupt on King Agamemnon striving to rape his queen. A fine salacious titbit for the populace to savour!'

My temper flared, I called her scabrous names. She answered never a word, a look of cold contempt on her face. The infant woke and cried. I flung from the room, ignored the startled Hero leaning on his spear, lurched along the corridor to a bedroom reserved for guests. I told the slave who kept the chamber to bring Maira from the women's quarters, stripped my kilt and stretched on the bed.

I was dozing when she sidled in, desire drowning in dreams. Maira's titillating fingers swiftly rekindled the fires: I mounted like a stallion and plunged my weapon deep. Then, lulled by her whispered endearments I dropped asleep, woke sandy-mouthed and thirsty. Maira slipped from the bed, held a pitcher to my lips. I drank avidly, water dribbling chin and chest. Refreshed and fully awake, I kneaded my concubine's buttocks and proved my manhood again.

Afterwards she snuggled close, her legs entwined in mine, whispered a ribald anecdote which made me shake with laughter, and murmured, 'I had not expected your favours tonight, my lord, for I thought you would celebrate so momentous an occasion in the queen's embraces.'

'Not possible,' I grunted. 'She has lately given birth, and protested ... frailty.'

Maira's amorous undulations stilled; she lay so quiet I thought she slept. Soft fingers stroked my brow. 'A specious pretence, my lord, as any mother can affirm.'

'So I thought. What matter? You've taken her place – one sheath is good as another.'

Her lips caressed my ear. 'The queen lies to you. Her womb has never carried a child.'

The words hardly penetrated the skin of my wine-fuddled wits. I scrubbed hand on aching temples and said, 'What are you babbling about? She's just had Iphigeneia.'

'Iphigeneia is not Queen Clytemnaistra's child.'

'You're mad. The brat's my daughter and hers.'

'Neither.' Maira unclasped her arms from round my shoulders, sat up and hugged her knees. A false dawn's leaden light bleached the sky beyond the windows. 'The baby was borne by Helen, the father Theseus of Athens.'

Staring wide-eyed into the shadows she spoke hardly above a whisper in a low, monotonous voice. 'Theseus raped Helen when he held her fast in Athens. Her time drew near, and Aithra in desperation blurted the truth to your wife. Together they hatched a scheme to shield from disgrace and dishonour the purity of Sparta's royal line. Directly the babe was born Aithra carried her secretly to Clytemnaistra who, already feigning labour, pretended the child was hers. That, my lord, is the parentage of the girl you believe your daughter.'

I swallowed an arid lump that blocked my throat. 'You weave fantasies, you bitch! How could Helen's travail be concealed? Her nursemaids, household servants, midwife —'

'One midwife, and Aithra, delivered her, my lord. They tied a cloth round Helen's mouth to stifle her shrieks.'

I writhed on the bed, beat fists on thighs. 'How can I believe this? If they took such pains to keep the birth secret why is it that only you should know?'

'The midwife was my mother. She told me that very day, and swore me to silence.'

I gripped Maira by the hair, tugged her flat on the bed. Leaning close I glared into her eyes. 'So. A brittle vow, it seems. And this clucking midwife still roams free to tattle far and wide.'

Maira breathed in shallow gasps. 'You are hurting me, my lord. No. Her tongue is stilled for ever. My mother died an agonized death after drinking from a bowl of milk that Aithra gave her. Which is why to you alone I have broken my oath.'

'You have told no one else?'

'Never a soul, my lord.'

I lay back and knuckled my eyes. Sweat started from my pores and runnelled chest and belly. Questions whirled through my brain like flotsam borne on a torrent. I could not doubt the story's truth: Maira risked her life in the telling. Always she had hated Clytemnaistra and was certain she, through Aithra, contrived the midwife's murder.

What induced Clytemnaistra – passionless, cold and calculating – to pretend the child was hers: a masquerade fraught with danger and disgrace? Love for Helen, perhaps, a selfless, devoted deed to hide her sister's shame. Difficult to credit; I had found no whit of tenderness in Clytemnaistra's character. Perhaps malevolence drove her to foist the bastard on me and gloat secretly on my cuckolded ignorance. Did the woman hate me so intensely? Why? She could surely know nothing of her husband Broteas' killing. Could she? No – impossible.

Suffocated by nightmare thoughts I clambered from the bed and paced the floor. The window framed a pallid sheen that painted grey the chequered tiles I trod. Tables, chairs and coffers crouched in the shadows like beasts of prey. Maira watched me mutely, dark eyes wide and fearful.

Fury choked my breath. I stopped in my stride, stared sightlessly into the gloom. Go now to Clytemnaistra, throw the accusation in her teeth! Seize the brat by the heels and spatter its brains on the wall!

I clenched my fists and won control, forced myself to examine the problem coolly.

High policies were involved. Were Helen's rape exposed, should anyone be told she had borne a child by Theseus the disgrace would blast in fragments her marriage to Menelaus, shatter his hope of one day ruling Sparta and mine of seeing the kingdoms joined in brotherly alliance. More. Should the infamous scandal be blazoned abroad Clytemnaistra must also be shamed; then I could do no less than put her away. However valid the reasons Tyndareus would be angered; the revelation would smash our friendship, finish the Spartan alliance, end my hopes of breaking Theban power and bring to crisis point the scarcity of corn. Within a year of winning the crown I'd be ruling a starving realm.

A hint of the truth would destroy the ends I had swindled and murdered to gain.

It must never come out. How many people shared my knowledge? Helen, Clytemnaistra, Aithra – none, for her own security, would betray so dangerous a secret.

One remained.

I looked at the bed. Maira lay unmoving, her naked body a still bronze statue carved on the bedsheet's white. Scourged by blazing hatred and yearning for revenge she had blabbed the tale to me. Could she be depended on to curb her tongue in future?

While the sweat dried harsh on my skin I considered the question coldly; and decided not.

I went to the bedside and knelt beside her. Maira lifted her arms and stroked my face and whispered words of love. I grappled her throat in both my hands, thumbs on windpipe, pressed with all my strength. She gurgled, flailed her limbs and writhed, her fingers clawed my chest. I held her fast, the soft brown neck like a flower-stalk in my grip, lifted her head and forced it back, and heard the backbone snap.

I lowered the limp form, wiped palms on a rumpled coverlet, stumbled to the window.

Above the palace rooftops dawn's rose-red fingers brushed Saminthos' peaks, the mountain leaned like purple ramparts against a honey-pale sky. I sucked great draughts of cool clean air, and stretched out arms to a wakening world, a world that sprouted dangers and adversities. Like phantoms fleeing at cockcrow a vision of the burdens capered before my eyes: Thebes, the Goatmen, Troy, the Corinthian shore – obstacles towering higher than Saminthos' distant pinnacles. To cleanse the honour of my House I must hunt down and exterminate Aegisthus, that misbegotten child Thyestes spawned upon his daughter.

And somehow I must pluck from my nest the cuckoo fledgling Iphigeneia.

Much remained to be done.

A rising sun drenched gold the mountain crests. Nothing was unattainable. Nothing lay beyond my grasp, beyond the reach of Agamemnon, king of men.

If you have enjoyed this book and would like to receive details of other Walker Adventure fiction titles, please write to:

Adventure Fiction Editor
Walker and Company
720 Fifth Avenue
New York, NY 10019